THE TWO HEARTS
OF KWASI BOACHI

THE
TWO HEARTS
OF KWASI BOACHI

Arthur Japin

Translated from the Dutch by Ina Rilke

ALFRED A. KNOPF
New York
2000

THIS IS A BORZOI BOOK
PUBLISHED BY ALFRED A. KNOPF

Translation copyright © 2000 by Ina Rilke

www.aaknopf.com

Originally published in the Netherlands as *De zwarte met het witte
hart* by Uitgeverij De Arbeiderspers, Amsterdam, 1997.
Copyright © 1997 by Arthur Japin

This translation first published in Great Britain by Chatto &
Windus, London.

Library of Congress Cataloging-in-Publication Data
Japin, Arthur, [date]
[Zwarte met het witte hart. English]
The two hearts of Kwasi Boachi / Arthur Japin ; translated from
the Dutch by Ina Rilke.—1st American ed.
p.   cm.
"This is a Borzoi book"—T.p. verso.
ISBN 0-375-40675-1
I. Rilke, Ina.
PT5881.2.A59 Z9313 2000
839.3'1364   00-034907

Manufactured in the United States of America
First American Edition

Kwasi Boachi as a young man

Willem I (1772–1843)
m.
Wilhelmina (1774–1837),
daughter of Friedrich Wilhelm II, King of Prussia

Frederik (1797–1881)
m.
Louise (1808–1870),
daughter of Friedrich Wilhelm III,
King of Prussia

Marianne (1810–1883)
m.
Prince Albert of Prussia (1809–1872)

Willem II (1792–1849)
m.
Anna Pavlovna (1795–1865),
daughter of Paul I, Tsar of Russia

Louise (1828–1871)
m.
Karl XV (1826–1872),
King of Sweden

Maria (1841–1910)
m.
Wilhelm Adolf (1845–1907)
Prince zu Wied

Sophie
(1824–1897)
m.
Carl Alexander, Grand Duke of
Saxony-Weimar-Eisenach
(1818–1901)

Karl Alexander
Grand Duke
(1818–1848)

Hendrik (1820–1879)
m.
a) Amalia Maria (1830–1872),
daughter of Duke Bernhard of
Saxony-Weimar
b) Maria Elise of Prussia
(1855–1888)

Willem III (1817–1890)
m.
a) Sophia (1818–1877), daughter of
King Wilhelm I of Württemberg
and Katerina Pavlovna
b) Adelheid Emma (1858–1934),
daughter of Georg Victor,
Prince of Waldeck-Pyrmont

Wilhelmina (b. 1880)

PART ONE

Java 1900

19 February

The first ten years of my life I was not black. I was in many ways different from those around me, but not darker. That much I know. Then came the day when I became aware that my colour had deepened. Later, once I was black, I paled again.

On every tea field I had, I always planted some poinsettias, also called flame-leaf or euphorbia. A touch of scarlet amid the green every hundred yards or so prevents blindness among the pickers. Seeing the same colour for hours on end causes the vision to blur, like staring into the sun. A single flash of a different hue restores the contrast.

Such a lone red plant has a remarkable effect on its surroundings. Everything that is green draws together. Before the eye, all the variegated shades of green in the tea bushes, which were clearly distinguishable at first, blend into one sea of colour. Differences disappear. The decor becomes monotonous. What else is there to say other than—yes, how green it all is. A very green sort of green. Or rather: it is offensively un-red!

Conversely, the red plant itself burns a brighter red when set off by the green than when it grows among its peers. In the bed I always reserved for poinsettia seedlings, there was little to distinguish one plant from its neighbours. My poinsettia did not turn scarlet until I planted it out in new surroundings. Colour is not something one has, colour is bestowed on one by others.

It is 1900. Anniversary celebrations are popular this year in Buitenzorg society. Wedding anniversaries, the anniversary of Grandmother's demise, Madame's umpteenth change of hair colour. Anything for a celebration. Indeed the new century is being fêted week in week out, and only so that ghosts may be laid. Everyone wishes to convince themselves and each other that all is well and that bygones should be bygones. A great show is made of having no fears about the future.

And so word has been put about that it is half a century since I arrived in the Indies. Congratulations for nothing! Notwithstanding my profound reluctance, Adeline Renselaar, Mrs. van Zadelhof's cousin, has set her mind on having a celebration. She has already involved three families in her machinations, and was even seen in the Deer Park last week, chattering to the governor about this very matter.

A small committee of organizers sprang a visit on me this morning to discuss the timing and location of my jubilee. They enquired after the sensitivities of my elderly stomach, so that they might take them into account when planning the menu for the banquet. The style of 1850, which is the date of my arrival in Java, is to prevail in every detail. It is no concern of mine. The expense appears to be immaterial.

"We do not see much of you at our social gatherings," said Mrs. Renselaar, that stout harpy with her eagle beak. "Of course that is your business entirely, but you cannot deny us the right to celebrate on your behalf. That would be unfair. One cannot grudge other people their pleasures. Besides, I wish to deepen our acquaintance. To think that we have been exchanging greetings all these years without the faintest idea of what was going on in each other's lives. But now, now that my husband has told me about your, well, about the *affair* . . . What I mean is, the least we can do now is pay tribute!"

I only heard half of what she said, because the whole time our farcical exchange lasted I could smell my coffee fields burning. I saw Willem Gongrijp give a little shudder of glee at each gust that came our way. He is the self-appointed master of ceremonies, while everyone knows he cannot wait for me to croak so that he can get his hands on my land. With him on the committee there is no need for a wicked fairy. I answered their questions with due civility, but when I finally got rid of them, the sense of time running out weighed heavily in my room. I crossed the river

4

and sought eternity in Wayeng's lap—twice in fact—but there is no love strong enough to deflect me from my thoughts.

I left her embrace in the night. I needed fresh air. Aquasi junior, who lay beside us, woke up and wheedled for attention. So as not to disturb Wayeng I took my son outside. We sat together for a while, until he fell asleep with his head on my knees. Not being used to this, at first I hardly dared move. Now and then, however, I had to shift my position because my muscles had become stiff. He did not seem to notice. He turned over and lay sprawled on his back, utterly serene. I brought my hand to his face and traced the contours without touching him. After a while I became bolder and stroked his hair. It is soft and loosely curled, quite unlike mine. I stroked it again and could not stop. I was brimming with love. The sky was overcast, but now and then the moon emerged to show me a glimpse of his face.

My son is nine years old. I am in my seventy-third year. By the time he leaves school I will be seventy-six. By the time he falls in love . . . I will not live to see him a grown man. (I would wish him to study at Delft in Holland, but funds are low. I think I shall write another letter to our young queen, informing her of my plans.)

I am too old. I do not even know whether my children see in me a father or merely a kindly old man who visits their mothers from time to time. That is the price one pays for having postponed happiness for so long.

There I sat with my child. I was seized by the notion that one day he will want to know what sort of man his father was. I cursed Adeline Renselaar. It is because of her poking about in my past that I am beset by such thoughts.

20 February

It was still night when I returned to my house. I sought out the boxes that I had secluded in a safe place. Not safe enough. I have often considered burning all these letters and notebooks, but could never bring myself to part with them. They are all I have left to remind me of the other men I have been.

Just before daybreak I felt the need to relieve myself. I was already holding the chamber pot when something in me rebelled. I stared at the hairline cracks in the Delftware and felt utterly out of place in the darkly panelled room with its velveteen curtains. I set off for our small outdoor washroom, but halfway there I changed my mind and made for one of the trees, opened my clothing in the open air, which gave me a childish thrill, and let my water splash against the trunk. For the first time in years I noticed the impudent croaking of the frogs, although it is never absent. I stooped to see the foam blister and sink among the roots, first dark, then silvery white in the gloaming. It was a signal for butterflies, and a few minutes later the place was teeming with them.

It is of course improper to relieve oneself against trees, at any rate once one's student days are over. In fact I never do so in the open. Never. I leave that to the natives. But this morning I was overcome by an indomitable urge. Oddly enough I felt no shame.

The sapling that served as my urinal is not a native species. It came from a consignment of seeds, fruits, plant cuttings and rootstocks I ordered from the Gold Coast. The greater part of the consignment was lost to the rains. But this shoot was willing. The tree it came from is not overly delicate, and will adapt to any environment. It is the tree that was called *kuma* by us, in the kingdom of Ashanti. There, I believe, it was common practice to relieve oneself against trees. I have no recollection of any embarrassment.

The story of the tree is, in brief, as follows: One day Osei Tutu cut two branches off the kuma tree. He planted them in the earth, at some distance from each other. One cutting adjusted well to its surroundings, sending down roots in the soil—*asi* in the Twi language. It sprouted buds and bore fruit. The other cutting shrivelled and died. Osei Tutu founded his capital of Kumasi, seat of the mighty Asantehene of Ashanti, at the foot of the thriving kuma tree. *Kuma-asi*, the soil under the kuma, is my native soil.

It was this story that I wished to tell my servant this afternoon. I was in my study hunched over my papers when the old rogue stole over the veranda. He let down the blinds against the sun, which at five o'clock sinks beneath the palm fronds and glares into the house. Feeling mellow towards him, I beckoned him to my side and thought to divert us both with some musings on the kuma tree.

"Osei Tutu cut off two branches," I began. "He planted them in the earth, at some distance apart. One of them adjusted well and rooted. The other withered and snapped. Our capital city marks the spot where the tree thrived. Kuma-asi, seat of the mighty Asantehene of Ashanti." I noticed his eyes wandering, so I leaned over to set him at ease and, speaking to him, man to man, I took him into my confidence.

"Osei Tutu was my great-grandfather. Did I ever tell you that, Ahim?"

"Only three times since this morning, tuan."

"You are a liar," I said. "I just happen to have these old letters in front of me. Pure coincidence. Memories. I have not given that old tale a thought in years."

Ahim said nothing and made to dust off the portrait of the young Queen Wilhelmina, which I keep on the ornamental easel by my desk. But his smile stung me like a nettle. So I barked: "Have you been to the post?"

"Of course."

"Well?"

"Nothing."

"You are lying!" I roared.

I am not in the habit of raising my voice against servants. Not that I have any others besides Ahim.

"You have been stealing my letters, to sell at the thieves' market behind the madhouse. Don't think I don't know. Or flogging them to that man on Gunung Batu. You think my letters contain state secrets in code and that the assistant resident's spies will pay good money for them. I know what you're up to. I'll have you arrested and whipped this very afternoon."

I am well aware that it is at least six months since I received any letters, and even then there was no message from our young queen, although I have written to The Hague three times already

7

and maybe even four. Not a word from Weimar, either, although I send a lengthy missive there each week. The grand duchess is dead. She died years ago. I learned this from the Saxon envoy, whom I meet regularly in the Botanical Gardens, where we sit on a bench under the casuarina tree and converse in what little German I can still remember. But he assures me that her poor Carl Alexander still thinks of me and even asks after me now and then. Sasha is a man of honour who would not forget an old friend, so where have his letters got to?

Of course I know that Ahim is not embezzling anything—he is too dense to be wicked—but his insolent grin riled me, and I was only paying him back for going out of his way to torment me, a defenceless old man.

"So what did you pilfer this time? Post from The Hague, I shouldn't wonder. Disappointing, was it? Those royal dispatches contain nothing but kind words," I sneered. "They are tokens of respect. From your queen to your master!"

"The letters have stopped," he had the effrontery to say. He was right, of course, but there was no need to rub it in. I lowered my voice ominously so as to intimidate him.

"Do you know what we Ashanti used to do with liars?"

"Indeed I do, tuan. Cut out the tongue and impale the body by the palace gate so that it may be pissed on by the people," the villain replied, as if I was beginning to bore him.

"Quite right," I said, as coolly as I could. "Those were the days."

"And yet I go all the way to the post office every week. Even though I know there will be nothing."

"You're lying. From now on I will go myself."

"You are too old, tuan."

"And you can call me by my rightful name, you cur."

"As you wish: you are too old, Prince Aquasi." Ahim bowed his head, but not low enough to my taste. I am amazed at how little it takes for me to lose my temper nowadays.

"You can stuff your Judas ways you know where. Ahim, pay attention! The letters. I have written three to the young queen and two to the grand duke, all of them unanswered."

"They have forgotten you."

"If you have already been to the post, then it must have been too early. What do you care whether you do a decent day's work? Go back there, I tell you."

"The courier from Batavia had already been and gone by the time I arrived. Your wife was there. Ask her."

"Wayeng?"

"No, Lasmi. She was on her way to see the doctor with little Quamina. There was a package for him, which the clerk asked her to deliver."

I have never heard of the post from Batavia arriving at Buitenzorg later than two o'clock, not even in the rainy season, but I was beyond reasoning.

"I want you to go anyway."

"I am not getting any younger," Ahim protested. "It takes me an hour on foot. Do you expect me to make the return journey in the dark?"

"That is immaterial to me. It will teach you not to tell a pack of lies and leave me empty-handed." A pity that a man seems the weaker for his show of strength. Ahim was unimpressed.

"I'll go for the next delivery, as I always do, Raden."

"Are you saying you won't do as I say?"

"There is no point."

"I shall have you beaten."

Ahim sighed and retorted wearily, as if to a slow-learning child: "In that case I will lodge a complaint with the resident. There will be a court case. Nothing but trouble. And who will go to the post office for you next week? Times have changed, Raden Aquasi, Prince. Not for me, though. I am the last slave in Java. Just my luck."

"What do you know about slavery, you simpleton? When I was a boy I had slaves of my own. Not just one, over a hundred. They were men, tall and broad-shouldered. Not soft-bellied like you, with your womanly wrists. They had big teeth, not filed into little points like yours. A hundred strong men, just for me. Do you know what I would have done with you then?"

"Yes, their heads rolled every day."

9

"And do you suppose they cared?"

His indifference enraged me, and I started shouting. "That they cared, is that what you think? Not on your life. They were proud to be dispatched to their ancestors at my hands. They stood in line with patient faces. Strong features, sincere smiles— wide, not like those girlish half-smiles of yours, which do not even hide your contempt. No, they were glad to die for me. They were men. You wouldn't understand. You were born to be a hindrance."

And as if to substantiate my accusation he had the impertinence to answer back. "If I were merely your servant, Prince, you know I would have left long ago. If I were looking for a well-paid position, or had to support a family, I would have packed up and left when we were still at Suka Radya. I would have stopped working when my wages stopped. Just like the others. And if I had borne a grudge against you . . . No, whether you like it or not, we are doomed to stay together. I saw you when you first came. I saw how you struggled. And I will see you go, too." With these words the old fool shambled off, as if I had signalled the end of the conversation. He let down the remaining blinds, muttering: "I will stay. And tomorrow, tomorrow I suppose I shall go to the post office again."

I pretended to be touched by his sentimental ramblings, and continued in a convivial tone.

"Do you think it possible that my letters never reached Holland?"

"First you accuse me of lying and then you ask my opinion. You were feverish again this afternoon, when you were resting. I heard you cry out. The watchman heard you too. You were babbling in your sleep. What are you afraid of?"

Am I bound to answer my servant's questions? I remained silent, but the shameless brute was undaunted.

"Shall I look into the future?" he asked. "Or into the past?"

"Those are heathen practices."

"And making heads roll isn't?"

I shrugged. "It is you and your constant harassment that make me think of such things in the first place."

Ahim responds to criticism like another man to a pat on the back. He just smiles and tilts his head like an old spinster. It gives him an infuriatingly condescending air.

"Well, what shall it be, cards or tea leaves?"

I was not in the mood for either.

"I've had enough of the past," I said. "More of it keeps coming."

"We are old," said Ahim. "That's what happens with age."

"My head has been pounding all day with the sound of the knives chopping down the coffee plants. Each blow triggers a memory."

"The plantation. Yes, it is sad. Now all we have left are paddy fields."

"Because you are too damn idle to work, that's the trouble. Am I to be pestered with your visions of the future on top of everything else? Bring me some writing paper. And tell them to stop chopping for the day. I cannot abide it any longer."

Ahim shuffled to the writing desk, brought me a sheet of paper and demanded to know who was to be the happy recipient this time.

I said nothing, and to mislead him I scrawled on the paper, muttering under my breath, "My very dear old friend . . ." But he interrupted me.

"The grand duke of Saxe received a letter not long ago."

"How would you know? It is quite possible, probable even, that you mislaid it somewhere. Deliberately. Get out of my sight or I'll have you flogged."

"And who do you suppose would cook for you tonight, tuan?"

It was not, as it happens, my intention to write a letter. Since yesterday's visit I have been tormented by the notion that, when the worthies of Buitenzorg dance the polonaise at my jubilee or on my grave, they will think of me as an endearing little old man with tightly curled grey hair they cannot resist tweaking. I am filled with the desire to confront Willem Gongrijp and his cronies with the man I once was. But I lack the strength. Realizing how feeble I have become made me wish to put some order into the thoughts that are still harboured in my soul. I set about arranging them into a speech, which I hoped would make my jubilee audience sit up and listen. So as soon as Ahim left I started off with the facts, as follows:

I am Aquasi Boachi, born prince of the kingdom of Ashanti on the Gold Coast of Africa. I was educated at Delft, but have lived in Java for the past fifty years and at Suka Sari since 1888. The said estate, which I run, having an extent of 89 bahu or 630 hectares, is located in the residency of Batavia, section and district of Buitenzorg, east of the main road to Gadok, two and a-half posts southeast of Buitenzorg station at an altitude of 959 Rhineland feet. The owner is Mrs. M.C. van Zadelhof, née Tietz. She leases me her land for an annual sum of 21,800 guilders. The population living on the estate, which counted 804 souls upon my arrival, has more than doubled in the past twelve years: there are now 1963. They are content, which is no mean achievement considering that the profits have not increased during that time, indeed in some years they have decreased. I have had to desist from the cultivation of tea. My production nowadays consists of rice and, until recently, also coffee. Whereas in 1889 my coffee yield still amounted to 51 picul, two years later it was only 30 and, because of unseasonable rains and the poor quality of the soil, that figure has dropped to 1½ picul, being a mere 63 kilograms, for the whole of last year. Consequently I have been obliged to discontinue coffee planting altogether and consider expanding the area under paddy, which crop seems indestructible. It is not a rosy picture I paint, but I am proud to say that not a soul on my estate has suffered from these setbacks. Not a soul, I say, except myself. I find consolation in the love of my children. Of the five I have fathered, three survive. My son Quamin works on a tea estate in the Preanger. The two little ones, Aquasi junior and my daughter Quamina Aquasina, were born of women that live and work on my land.

I had to stop there, for into my mind's eye surged a bevy of ladies wearing party hats, smiling and hiding behind their fans. It cannot be helped; their celebrating my arrival in their midst half a century ago amounts to the same thing as celebrating the fact that, thanks to me, they have had something to gossip about all these years. I am not married. My children were born of gentle native women with whom I live in free love. They are much talked about in the parlours of Buitenzorg. Suddenly the prospect of addressing an audience made up of tattletales and vultures repelled me. I reflected that they might be less amused if I ventured to tell them how I once attempted to court a white woman in the theatre at Batavia, in the manner of their own Dutch men. After all, that manner permits young ladies first to pick their husbands and then their lovers, so they have nothing to complain about.

It goes like this: a gentleman with a mind to love does not leave his hat in the cloakroom, but takes it inside and places it on the rim of the balcony in front of him. This is a signal to the ladies, whom he fixes with his opera glasses. He gestures how much he is prepared to disburse. If she raises her left hand to fan some air at her cheeks she is favourably inclined; waving the right hand means the bidding is too low or that a renewed advance should be made elsewhere.

I made no headway myself. It cannot have been my hat that you found unappealing, Ladies, for you did not object to being seen next to less stylish models than mine. Thank God for the native women hovering around the *tempeh* stall by the stage door, where luckless men such as I could buy their favours for a cup of rice. But the love of Adi, Lasmi and Wayeng, the mothers of my heirs, has delivered me from seeking love among the rejects. I love them as they love me. I will leave to them all I possess, and I find more fulfilment in our children than I can ever explain to a Batavian audience in a few factual statements.

So I tore up my first draft. It was correctly phrased, but how can a life be summed up in dates and figures? The crucial events do not follow one another in orderly fashion, like the staging posts along the Great Post Road to Surabaya. The tracks have been effaced. Why is it, when one shuts one's eyes, that some people come to mind and not others?

13

Ahim is right—quite contrary to his custom—when he says that I am plagued by dreams during my afternoon rest. Even if I do not sleep, as soon as I close my eyes the memories come thick and fast. But I rarely picture Java. The images that flood my memory are never of the people I encounter daily, nor of animals, nor even of the dense greenery that has been the setting of so much of my life. Judging by my memory, fifty years in the Indies have gone by in a flash, whereas a falcon hunt at Het Loo palace back in Holland has lasted forever. The archives of the mind are wanting in indexes—save for a few catchwords maybe. But perhaps these are all that is needed.

Sometimes I imagine that God is interested only in the broad sweep. We leave our marks on the white canvas and we cannot make head or tail of the result. But He, a creative artist if ever there was one, takes a few steps back and sees what the smudges represent. If He manages to recognize me in the cautious daubings I have left behind, that is the best possible proof of His existence. I have always held that, for people like me, it is best to make one's mark in the margins of existence, inconspicuously. But in retrospect I am struck by how much of the last fifty years is a blank. Is that cause for celebration?

21 February

All this talk of anniversaries reminds me that it will be fifty years tomorrow since my cousin died. I think it was then that I lost the ability to be at one with my actions. If it is true to say, as I believe it is, that the merit of love is that it lends distinction to whosoever is loved—the one serving as a foil to the other—then we loved one another. I became distinct by virtue of the contrast between us.

I know it is late. A man does not reach the stage of full recollection until his dying days. The year of my birth is supposedly 1827. I still live well, although my health is failing rapidly. The first debility is insomnia, which is hardly surprising as I have never been a sound sleeper. The nocturnal hour, when a man must part with consciousness, has always filled me with anguish. Simply closing my eyes gives free access to the demons and the dead, which clash with my strong desire to comprehend and control all that surrounds me.

Nowadays the shades of the past have access day and night. A good night's sleep might give me some temporary relief. But I have turned necessity into virtue, and have learned to love all my visitors. I catch myself looking forward to this or that person returning to me in my reveries. The pleasure it gives me to dwell on the past is nothing but a symptom of my old age. Daring to admit that you long to return—there is no more to dying than that.

Taking leave of this life is one thing, taking leave of this century quite another. Little cause for celebration there. All the commotion makes me nervous.

In September 1847 Kwame and I spent two days together, secluded in my student digs at Delft. It was fine weather on that Saturday and Sunday before Kwame's embarkation and before I too made up my mind to leave Holland. We wanted to be alone with our thoughts. On the evening of the Friday I decided to absent myself from Professor Oudshoorn's lecture the next Monday, as this would give me two full days in which to devote myself with all my heart to Kwame, my beloved cousin, my blood brother, the man once designated to be my king. Having the extra day meant that we could postpone our grief at parting until after the weekend.

I am facing another departure. And there is to be a feast in my honour. The date is drawing near, and there are no more extra days to be won by playing truant. That is what the next century means for me.

22 February

Something irks me. In her torrent of words last week Adeline Renselaar said something that keeps nagging at the back of my mind. It took a while to sink in, but now I can think of nothing else. She had a conspiratorial air. Her husband had spoken to her of my *affair*. My affair? Which affair? What kind of gossip is this?

At daybreak this morning I called at Wayeng's house. She was surprised to see me. I asked her if I might spend the morning with Aquasi. And so it happened that I took a walk with my son. He was very talkative, and all I did was listen. I realized how absurd my intention had been. How could a nine-year-old child be expected to listen to the misadventure of an African boy a lifetime ago? He grew tired and I carried him home in my arms with difficulty. My heart is not up to the strain. I was drenched in perspiration.

No sooner was I back in my house than I opened my boxes again and spread out the contents on my desk: diplomas, certificates, van Drunen's report on the Dutch expedition to Kumasi, his notes on our education, letters from all and sundry, paper cutout silhouettes, my scrapbook with friends' dedications. And although my physician tells me I should not drink, I resolved to get excessively drunk just one last time.

23 February, 4 a.m.

The best plant cuttings grow in dung—even a child knows that. I have just, in a moment of mischief, done the rest of my business in the garden as well. When I finished I broke off two branches from the kuma tree. That was not difficult to do, because, although the tree can withstand the most violent storms and changes colour with the seasons, it does not thrive on alien shores the way it thrives in Africa. I planted the branches in the earth, at some distance from each other. I shall instruct Ahim that, should one of them strike root, my grave is to be dug beside it. Give him a little diversion.

WEST AFRICA 1836–37

I

I could not sleep. The air was filled with noise and the glow of countless fires tinged the sky. Kwame lay beside me, thrashing about. We were tired from our recent visit to the sanctuary of Twi. I ordered the doors and shutters to be closed. My bedroom, which I had shared with my cousin since the death of his father, was situated in the middle of the palace, far from the street, but there was so much commotion that the noise reached us in our private quarters. Although I tried to silence them the servants chattered in the forecourt.

For weeks we had heard the drumbeats from Abonu announcing the slow approach of an immense trade delegation from the Castle of Elmina on the coast. The court was making ready to receive them. That was all we knew. I nudged Kwame again and again until at last he sat up, for at night and unable to sleep I always felt more lonely than during the day. We asked each other riddles and played word games, in which I lost the gilded collars of my guard dogs to Kwame, for he was always more adroit with words than I.

When we had returned from the sanctuary of Twi, the roads to Kumasi were already thronged with people, and the capital itself was full of the splendour of Ashanti. The parasols of tribal chiefs were to be seen everywhere, rising high above the crowd. Commanders wearing silver breast-plates played dice with warriors in exotic costumes. They sat in the shade of gilded canopies erected by our goldsmiths around our royal mausoleum on the hill of Bantama. Packhorses and donkeys, as well as some camels and sacrificial goats, were tethered to the plane trees, which had grown from seeds donated by Portuguese pioneers. The animals produced a stream of excrement which trickled from the palace grounds towards the valley, where the food stalls were doing excellent business. Cooks with sweat pouring down their faces rushed about with *fufu* dumplings in hot sauce, which they distributed to weary mothers and whimpering children. Men sat on bales of straw treating their blisters with spittle and asses' milk. The merchants who had joined the surge to the capital now flooded the market with goods from their homelands: scented oils, dates, figs, and viscous oriental confectionery of many colours. The usual trade in yam and manioc, banana, peanut and citrus was suspended to make room for local artists with their golden ornaments, insignia, drinking vessels and sceptres, their gilded headdresses and furniture plated with precious metals, for which Kumasi was renowned all over the world. Banks of saffron and red pepper lay spread out on palm leaves whose edges were trampled by the crowd. Broad fish from the River Volta with gaping jaws lay side by side with emery-skinned eels from the Tano and slippery giant snails; purple devils from the Pra estuary jostled with the muscular tails of the catfish that swim upstream, against the strong current of the Ofin and the Birim. Old women stooped to inspect varieties of gum and medicinal roots, amulets, little bundles of magical leather-craft, tanned red and patterned with black. Cloths were shaken out while weavers explained the meaning of the local symbols to those who were strangers to these parts. There were lengths of glossy black for funerals, but also the finest *kente* cloth made of a thousand bands of red and yellow, and, for the exclusive use of tribal chiefs, there were sandals with golden toe-studs.

The crowd thickened as the day wore on. Men accompanied by veiled wives treated themselves to morsels of roast beef, monkey, wild boar or antelope at the meat stalls, gave a pittance to a band of street singers or mocked them and told them to make way for the people parading past: tall, shuffling men from the east, shaven-headed girls from across the river, slave traders' wives from Mali who even veiled their eyes, naked huntsmen from the savannahs around Damongo.

The Twi language was suddenly alive with accents from every corner of Ashanti: the sharp consonants from the north, which must make themselves heard over sandstorms, the lisp of the Volta fishermen, the nasal singsong of the forest-dwellers in the south. And there was the Twi that provoked laughter among the pure Ashanti, spoken by the conquered tribes across the river who had been taken by their masters to be sold as slaves in Kumasi. One could hear the drawl of the Ga, the effeminate cheep of the Ewe, and the voices of the dwarfs from Talenso, defeated weaklings from Dagoma, Dagaba, Fra Fra and Kusasi, who were unable to pronounce the sound *ouè*.

It was this cacophony that kept us awake all night. When Kwame and I grew tired of our games I drifted off, only to be rudely awakened by the bickering of a couple of drunk priests. My head ached and I cursed the language of my birth. Little did I know that I would have lost the ability to speak it a few years later. I put my fingers in my ears and buried my face between Kwame's shoulders.

Before dawn our servants came to clothe us, and in the gloom we were led outside to the city gates of Kumasi, where the forest path to Accra begins. We saw a great mass of people advancing over the hills. The moisture exuded by the tightly packed bodies hung like a mist around the city.

My father, the Asantehene Kwaku Dua I, sat on his throne before the great crowd, shaded by parasols of gold brocade. Wearing a red cloak edged with silver, his arms and legs weighed down by ornaments, he stared into the distance. Next to my father, on an ivory seat encrusted with diamonds, sat Kwame's mother, my aunt. She was the sister of the Asantehene and consequently the paramount woman.

To her left sat the bejewelled members of her lineage: the *oyoko*, family members connected by the red female bloodline, which governs succession. Each mother and grandmother had gathered her *yafunu* around her, the "children from one belly." To her right, sitting in a wide circle on gilded stools and richly worked carpets, were those who were related to our royal family by way of the *ntoro*, the male kinship, which was the white lineage of the seed whereby the soul is transmitted.

Close to my father sat Badu Bonsu II, king of Ahanta, who was one of his closest friends. Around him were gathered the council of wise men: astrologers, judiciaries, fetish priests, diplomats, keepers of customs, symbols and traditional music, magicians, architects and physicians. A place of honour was reserved for the geomancers, who knew where to look for the gold and precious stones embedded in our soil. Before them kneeled young slaves. their heads bowed and their hands brimming with white-gold pendants and fetishes of amethyst and emerald. Flag-bearers formed a guard of honour for the late arrival of dignitaries. There were skirmishes between the bands of musicians, buffoons and dancers, each claiming what they considered their rightful places. In the thick of it all, four black-suited Europeans with heat-stricken, drawn faces were working their way towards the front: they were the Reverend Brooking, an English missionary, and envoys from Britain, Portugal and the Netherlands. The latter was Jacob Huydecoper, a stout, red-faced fellow, who had served as assistant in the city since 1836. Bowing deeply, he greeted Kwame and me with the title of "Prince," although it was obvious that there was some confusion in his mind about our identity and the precise nature of our link to the throne. We did not return his greeting. These men were underlings, condemned to spend their lives in a place forsaken by their own god. When they were not felled by the climate, they were drunk on palm wine.

On either side of our family, as a sign of honour to Ashanti unity, stood battle formations drawn from all the states of the Union of Ashanti: Kumasi, Juaben, Bekwai, Nsuta, Mampong and Kokofu. Each *asafohene*, wearing the commander's fighting tunic decked with gold-inlaid amulets and *grigris* to ward off evil, headed a squad of 200 *akwanrafo* with cocked rifles. In addition, each was flanked by a close array of 150 fighters attended by dozens of *asansafo*, the "empty-handed," whose task was not to carry provisions but to see to the swift removal of booty. The *kyidom* bringing up the rear were recognizable by the plumes tied to their spear-points. Altogether there were six full armies: thirty-seven regiments in seventy-seven subdivisions. On platforms strung across the hillsides a dense multitude had assembled, in which 120 golden parasols betokened the presence of the same number of village chiefs. Each of these had brought, in addition to the village elders and their women in all their finery, 400 armed troops, 200 slaves and 100 gifts. A vast assembly of functionaries, a full *oman* of each state headed by its *omanhenes*, accompanied by all those who had earned the honour of joining the excursion to the capital, occupied the outermost reaches of the city. There they mingled with the wholesalers and heads of village clans who had gathered together. The Asantehene himself was too far away for those at the back of the crowd to even catch a glimpse of him, which gave rise to widespread grumbling. There was some scuffling and molesting of beer girls. They had no idea of the ceremonies taking place on the other side of the sea of people.

On this day Kwame and I, both of us named, in keeping with tradition, after the Saturday and Sunday of our respective births, were in the tenth year of our lives. We were positioned among our families: I to the left of my father, while Kwame, being the eldest son of the queen mother and heir apparent to the Asantehene's throne, was directed to the right. Our shoulders were elaborately draped with the colourful *adinkra* cloths, after which we were told to sit still. Both of us failed to do so, which earned us each a box on the ears from my father. We had to be patient. To while away the time storytellers were summoned to do their work in the oppressive heat.

"Osei Tutu broke two branches off the kuma tree . . ." one of them began. I shot a look at Kwame, who collapsed into nervous giggles when our eyes met.

We had heard the story of the founding of our native city too often: the battle Osei Tutu had fought to throw off the yoke of the Denkyira, his shrewdness in allying himself to five other rebel tribes so that he might later subdue them and thus forge the different domains into a single nation with a common language and common religion—it had all been subsumed into the legend of the archetypal founding father and his kuma tree. Every child in Kumasi imbibes the story of the fruitful branch and the withered branch with its mother's milk.

Kwame Poku was the only son born to the Asantehene's eldest sister. His father was the famous Adusei Kra, the *atene akotenhene*, commander of all the warriors of Ashanti. Adusei Kra was seen in public only at official events. Severe and menacing in full regalia.

Seven years before Kwame's birth, Adusei Kra had led the Ten Thousand southwards on a legendary campaign. Upon his arrival at the coast he had defeated the English, one of those European peoples who had given the Ashanti kingdom and the outlying West African states the name *Gold Coast*. Adusei Kra sent the white men scurrying back to their fortresses, after which they only ventured outside to bring gifts and to grovel.

In his forty-second year the great warrior fell ill. He called for the fetish priest to conduct the ceremony whereby his strength and bravery would be passed on to his son, my cousin Kwame, who was designated to be the future king of our people. When he had done this Adusei Kra drifted into a sleep resembling death.

In those days the palace children avoided Kwame. They were alarmed by the severity of his expression, which his father seemed to have vested in him along with his other qualities. Kwame spent much of his time in our wing of the palace in order to prepare himself for the throne that he would occupy once my father had died. I ran into him from time to time, but he always kept his eyes fixed on the floor and I did not venture to speak to him. Besides, I had my own reasons for sadness.

I missed my brothers Kwadwo and Kwabena, the only two who had the same mother as I. She was my father's first wife. My brothers were a little older than me and they were dearer to me than anyone else in the world. They were the only children who had free access to my room. One day I could not find them anywhere. I had three sleepless nights before someone dared reveal the truth to me. My father had handed over his own sons to the British envoy, who was to conduct them to Fort Cape Coast.

I was inconsolable. Never before had an Ashanti prince left our territory. How could my brothers be obliged to travel the same jungle paths that the slaves conquered by my father had been forced to tread before? Were Kwadwo and Kwabena to be given to white men in exchange for Dutch gin and muskets? I had horrible visions of their plight. Eventually I was issued an official statement to the effect that the two princes would return within a few years as grown men; they would have amassed large fortunes and would come with beautiful wives, but I felt they were lost to me. Less than a month later news came that they had been ambushed on the way by Abyssinian caravan drivers and killed for their golden ornaments.

I could not comprehend why my father had sent his sons to their deaths in this way and wished to hear some explanation, some remorse—just a cry of grief, if nothing else—from his own lips. But he did not show his face in the family circle for weeks, probably out of shame, and whenever I did set eyes on him the circumstances were too formal for me to approach him. My mind reeled with questions, but an Asantehene does not speak for himself. From the time a new king has been pressed three times on the Golden Stool—the repository of the spirit of Ashanti which was made to appear out of the sky by Osei Tutu's priest—he employs the services of a speaker, who never leaves his side. The speaker is deputed to communicate the Asantehene's opinions, thoughts and feelings. And although it still happened, albeit rarely and only in the most private quarters of the palace, that Kwaku Dua became once more the father he had been before his accession to the throne—when he was called simply Fredua Agyeman and would draw me on to his lap or take a stroll in the street holding my hand in his without this attracting any attention—I could never trust him again. I became apprehensive. My love was numbed by doubts. From then on, if my father happened to see me red-eyed, and sank down on his haunches to comfort me, I would brace myself and say it was nothing, just some grains of sand that had blown into my eyes. An Ashanti knows the salutary power of taboo: grief that is unspoken does not exist.

In the old days I used always to be bathed together with my brothers. It was great sport. We wrestled with each other, splashed and drove our servants to despair. From now on I was bathed alone. I tried to put a brave face on it, but one morning a sudden douse of cold water unleashed my grief. The sense of loss was like a blow to the stomach. I fled to the dressing room, sobbing, and sent everyone away.

There I was, huddled in a corner, when Kwame came in. He had seen my servants leave and thought the place was unoccupied. I raised my head and our eyes met. I saw at once that his reticence was not inspired by arrogance. He immediately dismissed all his attendants and sat down by my side, consoling me by breaking into sobs himself. I told him about my own sadness and asked him to tell me about his.

"You know," he said, "the family of a brave man always has some reason to weep."

From that day on we bathed together.

Not long afterwards Kwame visited me in my apartments. He had never done so before. The tuition he was receiving brought him into contact with many of those who were close to the throne. He had plied them with questions as to the motives underlying my brothers' departure, and had come up with the following explanation.

Kwaku Dua, my father, had developed a keen interest in all things European. He was the seventh Asantehene of the Union of Ashanti, but he was the first to view the old contacts as more than a means of acquiring alcohol and arms. He was seized by the notion that the science and knowledge of white men might well be of service to our people, especially now that the European nations had, for reasons incomprehensible to us, abolished slavery. The trade in slaves had not been wholly wiped out by the abolition, but it had declined so dramatically that the prosperity of our outlying regions was at risk.

The Reverend Brooking, who strutted around Kumasi wearing the regulation high black collar of the Wesleyan Missionary Society even in the midday heat, encouraged my father's interest. He proposed sending my brothers to London for a spell, no doubt with the aim of converting them, and eventually, through them, our people as well. My father liked the idea of an English education for his sons, even though the religions of Europe struck him as absurd. He did not tolerate Christian worship in his realm. Indeed, some years later he even had Brooking's head, complete with collar, impaled on a stake in front of his palace. Religious teaching of any kind was the least of his concerns. The Asantehene's interest in this venture focused on science and progress, on his relations with the British government and on the expansion of trade. However, the murder of my brothers had nipped all these ambitions in the bud.

Kwame could tell that I was not cheered by his information. Soon afterwards he came to see me again, and we took to playing together for a while each afternoon after his lessons.

Gradually, as we listened to each other's hopes and fears, I felt my loneliness ebb away. Kwame, burdened by the high expectations the court had of him, found consolation and sustenance in our friendship. He developed into a promising heir apparent, and in due course our people were convinced that the future Asantehene would know no fear.

We became so inseparable that people said we were beginning to resemble one another. "As the dog-tamer resembles his dog," Kwame said. When we finally asked if we might share the same room and the same bed, no one was surprised. My father was pleased with the positive turn our association was taking. So Kwame moved out of his room in the eastern wing and into mine, which was located outside the main building next to a spring where, by dint of an ingenious system of conical vessels, the water burbled into a small basin, even in the driest months of the year.

Soon afterwards Kwame assumed his manly duties to general approval. Although his mother continued to be the head of the family, it was Kwame who led the elaborate farewell ceremonies when his father, Adusei Kra, was on his deathbed. He behaved in the most dignified manner and did not flinch once while the Asantehene's eyes were upon him. Now and then I gave him reassuring signals that only we understood. Under the scrutiny of the other children and wives of the dying man, Kwame and the fetish priest conducted the rites at his dying father's bedside: a burning oil lamp passed three times around the face about to lose its expression, water sprinkled on the hands about to abdicate their power and on the feet that need travel no more, and three final splashes of water on the tongue.

An Ashanti does not fear his dying day. His death is merely the ultimate fulfilment of a promise made at birth. But the time of death is never without meaning. He who dies young is a curse to his nearest kin. A dead infant will be spat upon and mutilated by its parents, and must be buried in the place where the women relieve themselves in order that the child's soul may be dissuaded from returning. An advanced age attests to good behaviour. Old men with white hair and manifold children are cosseted and covered in gold. But Adusei Kra's death was untimely, and dying at his age was suspicious to say the least. The ancestors might be summoning him so soon because he had committed serious misdemeanours. It was left to Kwame to produce an explanation for the premature departure of his father's soul. The two of us fancied that Adusei Kra had lost his life to a host of vengeful spirits. For such is the fate of the warrior from the very first day he begins to kill: the more bodies he claims from the enemy, the more numerous the spirits massing against him. It was just as well, I reassured Kwame, that Adusei Kra had been able to avert the worst misfortune that can befall an Ashanti: dying childless. No one could accuse him of being *kote krawa*. He was no "waxen prick."

"The tree has fallen," Kwame announced to the people. He assisted his mother in laying out the corpse; she used a large sponge to sprinkle water on Adusei Kra's loins and cleanse them, just as she had done in the night when he had begotten his son. The slaves and private servants of the deceased were rounded up and sent to accompany their master with a single blow of the sword. In the meantime the ancestors had to be informed of the coming of the fresh soul. The heavy rhythm of sticks beating against the skin of elephants' ears stretched taut over talking drums, the male and female *atumpan*, led the women and girls to begin a chant: they were glad the dead man had lived so well, glad the dead man had shared his life with them, glad he was setting out on his last journey, glad he was awaited, glad he would be there later to await them when their time came. Glad, glad, glad.

That night I lay against Kwame and held him tight until the sobbing stopped. He told me the last words spoken by his father, with which he had revealed the secret of victory: each attacking phalanx of Ashanti warriors is tailed by a horde of sword-wielding *afonasoato*, ready to kill their own fighters at the slightest hesitation or attempt to flee.

Kwame's father had saved his final breath not to tell him he loved him, but to impress upon his son the Ashanti battle cry: "To advance is to die. To retreat is to die. Better then to advance and die in the jaws of battle."

In keeping with tradition, the body of Adusei Kra was laid to rest in a room, where it stayed until the flesh dropped from the bones. Only then would he be buried—in silence—beside the ancestors. It was in this period of waiting that Kwame and I paid a final visit to the deceased. This was no mean feat. Upon opening the door we found the corpse covered in flies. We flailed our arms to drive them away. When we set eyes on the body we saw that it had lost its pigment. It had turned white. To us, white was the colour of death, of the spirit world, the colour of all that is drained of life.

In these hallowed months of mourning Kwame showed a growing interest in the rituals of maturity. Besides, there were new customs to be learned by us both, now that our budding manhood was visible when we were bathed. We were instructed by the fetish priest in the knowledge that is kept from boys until the pubic hair begins to grow. The gods, he assured us, looked kindly upon the promise of our bodies. Fertility prayers were to be recited in order to placate the spirits attending to adult functions of the flesh, which, far from being familiar, had seldom even entered our minds.

But all this did shed new light on the nights we spent together, in which we found a certain consolation, and a closeness that was addictive and deeply reassuring. I sensed that it would be prudent to keep silent about the intimacy between us, preferring to remain a child. I noticed that Kwame was equally reticent once the innocence, and with it the lightheartedness, of our games vanished. We felt that our intimacy arose more easily from a wrestling match than from an embrace, but never found the words to express it.

We enjoyed going to the sanctuary of Twi, not out of piety but because it was one of the few chances we had of getting away from our peers, who teased us for our taciturn ways and quiet friendship. Even when I publicly renounced my old beliefs, many years later, I still thought wistfully of the animistic pantheon at the lake of Twi. The story that goes with it is this.

When Osei Tutu drove the spirit named Twi off his land to make way for the city of Kumasi, Twi sought refuge in the lake nearby, where he leads a reclusive life in water that abounds in fish and has turned the colour of his blood. The spirit named Twi, who is said by some who have met him to resemble a human being, does not wish to be disturbed anew. This is why the local fishermen avoid rippling the surface, and move their craft carefully over his resting place using their hands as paddles. To make sure that Twi lacks nothing and has no reason to leave his refuge to seek what he needs in Kumasi, plentiful offerings must be made under the canopy of the rainforest, where all the gods are venerated with like devotion.

Our pilgrimages to Twi familiarized us with the cruelty and mercy of nature. These expeditions lasted three days, in the course of which we encountered strangling orchids, death trees, parasitic fungi, spitting cobras, acid-spraying insects and the poisonous milk secreted by the teated shrub. In the heart of the forest, where each living creature leeches on another, smothering and destroying in the constant battle for the scarce rays of sunlight, there are also mutually sustaining bonds. Looking closely one finds that, in the midst of all the violence, extraordinary alliances are sometimes formed, the better to survive the struggle for life. Never was I in closer contact with the divine than at those moments when nature revealed to me the root of friendship.

Under the guidance of the priest we learned that the natural world around us is no different from the nature within ourselves. Mutual dependence is the basis of alliance. This was instilled in our minds by means of a game, during which each of us was blindfolded in turn. The one who could see had to guide the other through the forest, stepping cautiously at first and then faster and faster, until both were running fast. Thus the seeing guide learnt responsibility, and the blindfolded follower learnt to rely on his comrade. Eventually we were both able to run at full tilt, blind and elated, without even holding out our hands protectively. Trust is one of the senses.

The morning after our final visit to Twi we waited outside the city gate for six hours until the trade delegation from Elmina arrived. Although there were occasional scuffles, the mood was on the whole dignified and proud. The storytellers were replaced by the troubadours, who whiled away the lazy midday hours with recitations as old as our people. Each rhyme corresponds to a particular *adinkra*, a traditional pattern that symbolizes an adage that is sung to the child from the moment it can recognize the lines in its mother's carrying cloth. I remember this one:

> *The nkónsónkónsón says: there is a chain*
> *In life*
> *In death*
> *A chain of one people*

One blood
We form new links
At birth
At death
Whosoever we are

The *nkónsónkónsón* is a symbol made up of kidney-shaped links, like two slightly dented eggs joined together, two bodies rolled into one. There is a chain.

Looking back I fancy that it was the *nkónsónkónsón* that graced my ceremonial dress that day, and that I traced its golden lines with my finger as I listened to the song. But I have no memory of this.

What I do remember is that the sun was well past its zenith when an earsplitting, alien salvo in the forest made the birds take flight in terror and signalled that our patience was to be rewarded at last.

2

Amongst my most private documents, I treasure the report written by Deputy Commissioner van Drunen, officer of the Dutch expedition to the king of Ashanti.

They knew the negroes would not carry more than sixty or at the most eighty pounds, yet orders were given for large palanquins to be constructed. And also the cases and chests, with a very few exceptions, were far too heavy. Some weighed more than four hundred pounds, so that the contents had to be repacked. Still the slaves can only be compelled to carry them by violent means and threats of harsh punishment. Not only that: the palanquins are too unwieldy to be conveyed across the dense jungle. The refusal of certain officers to accommodate themselves to the manner of travel most suited to the ter-

rain has therefore necessitated clearing a path five foot wide from Elmina all the way to Kumasi. Add to this the lack of knowledge of the negro languages, and the immensity of the difficulties faced by such an expedition to the heartlands of Africa can easily be imagined.

On 13 September 1836 we embarked on the merchant ship Princess Marianne. The soldiers received instructions for the voyage, but questions as to the task awaiting us in Africa were left unanswered. Our mission remained strictly secret. After two days Captain A. Plug weighed anchor and set sail for the Dutch possessions on the West Coast of Africa. After calling at Santa Cruz on the island of Tenerife we proceeded without impediment on our voyage until the 26th of the following month, when we dropped anchor upon reaching the Fort of St. Antonio at Axim on the coast of Guinea. Five days later we sailed some little way eastward to the Fort of St. George d'Elmina, which has been in Dutch hands since 1637. There we disembarked and set foot on the Gold Coast.

Our embassy, headed by Royal Commissioner Major-General Jan Verveer, was too numerous to be lodged in the fort. We officers alone found accommodation in the Engineering Corps' quarters. The privates were directed to the vast storage cellars, which have fallen into disuse since we are no longer licensed to send slaves to our South American colony of Suriname. The men complained about the lack of air, the stench and the chill in the clammy windowless dungeons, and were issued with two barrels of rum.

Fort Elmina has become run down since the ban on trade in West Africans. The financial loss incurred by the ban remains enormous. Although the minister of Colonies is at pains to recoup the loss by recruiting West Africans to serve in the East Indian army, in the first year no more than forty-four slaves were pressed into service. The task of our embassy is to establish a permanent recruitment depot for the provision of at least one thousand men annually.

. . .

A few days after disembarking, one of the native assistants was dispatched to the king of Ashanti to advise the sovereign of the embassy's arrival and to request permission to enter his realm. By mid December both men had returned, accompanied by a caboceer, a sort of mayor, four ensigns and a band of armed men and slaves sent by the sovereign to serve as our escort. They brought the most satisfactory tidings and reported that His Highness hoped to see us in the following month.

On 7 January 1837, at eight o'clock in the morning, we departed from Fort Elmina. Major-General Verveer and myself were conveyed in palanquins each carried by four negroes. The secretary, a physician, the resident of Fort Axim, an official of the coastal administration and Welzing, a mulatto serving as interpreter for the native tongues, were conveyed in hammocks borne by two negroes. Thirty-six negroes were engaged for this purpose, while another 192 served for the conveyance of the goods, rations and other travelling necessities. A band of 380 slaves from the interior bearing gifts for the king of Ashanti had already been sent ahead. They would wait for us to join them in the vicinity of Kumasi.

Verveer's palanquin was preceded by a petty officer with the banner at the head of our military brass band which numbered thirteen musicians attended by two negro servants. In his wake came the halberdier of Elmina, a brigade of sappers, the engineering corps, the laundry boys and lesser servants with a number of women, followed by the caboceer, four captains and a troupe of seventeen armed men who had been sent by the king of Ashanti to escort us. Our party thus numbered more than one thousand men.

Our journey started in a north-easterly direction across the salt plain, past the plantation of one master Simons, where we made a brief halt. The emissaries of the chiefs of Elmina, who had accompanied us thus far, took their leave here, wishing us success with our embassy in a land no regiment had ventured to enter until now.

From there we proceeded on our journey through bush territory, where we observed scattered fields planted with sugar cane and pineapple, and soon came upon the first settlement or crom, named Ameeäno. The population numbered about one hundred and twenty, mostly living in wretched huts made of straw smeared with clay and roofed with leaves of palm or banana. The band struck up as we approached, as they would do upon arrival at every settlement. They usually played our national anthem or some other patriotic tune.

We continued in a north-westerly direction to the settlement of Simmiën in the fertile valley where General Daendels used to own an estate. We were welcomed by the firing of guns. We made a halt to drink the pitchers of palm wine that were offered to us, in return for which we gave some bottles of rum. Finding a large number of fallen trees on our path we were obliged to cover the distance to the settlement of Afatau on foot. Arriving there around one o'clock in the afternoon, we decided to set up camp for the night. Our three tents were pitched. Two of them served as accommodation for the officers, the third as a kitchen. As a rule we consumed our main meal, prepared by a skilled negro cook, at four or five o'clock. The evenings were spent listening to our musicians, who would play for a few hours in the open air. Sometimes, when it was worth our while, we visited private dwellings.

Reveille was sounded each day at dawn, at which time the bearers and servants were ready for departure. However, the slowness of certain officers in preparing themselves often prevented us from setting off at an early hour, which is imperative in these regions if the oppressive midday heat is to be avoided. Sometimes we did not depart until ten o'clock.

On the second day we traversed a forest with tall trees. After two hours we arrived in the settlement of Sodoffer, where the local caboceer, surrounded by grandees and fetish priestesses, came forward to welcome us. They offered us palm wine, and we gave them rum and Dutch pipes in return.

A long winding path led to the large settlement of Abakrampa, the seat of the Fanti kingdom. Our ceremonial entry, which took place at half past two, was unfortunately ruined by a heavy downpour. A band of armed men rushed forward to greet us, firing their muskets and singing war songs. The king of Fanti, a tall, handsome man aged about forty, awaited us at the far end of a clearing within the settlement. He was surrounded by dignitaries, all crowded together in the shade of enormous umbrellas held over their heads by slaves. We passed them one by one, starting with the lowest ranks. We greeted them all, but shook hands only with the king. To do so we had to side-step a huge fellow reeling off the titles, deeds and battle exploits of his master while brandishing a silver-hilted sword in front of our eyes. As it was still pouring with rain, the king invited us into his home. We were led down a narrow passage into a court-yard with four open rooms facing the centre, three feet above the ground. They were all clean and spacious. The earthen walls were whitewashed, the floor was sprinkled with red earth. A few negro stools and a leather armchair constituted the furniture. While we sat there the buffoon continued to leap about and shout at the top of his voice. His master seemed to find this amusing. Meanwhile our tents were pitched. There we received the king's gift of two sheep, a pig, fifty yams and three pots of palm wine. After a series of tedious expressions of gratitude we sent the king two jerkins of silken chintz, bolts of brightly coloured cotton cloth, each 14 or 16 ell in length, some strings of coral, a few crocks of rum, tobacco and Dutch pipes.

The following day we left Abakrampa, which compared so favourably with other settlements by virtue of the neatness of the dwellings and the cleanliness of the eight hundred inhabitants. We passed the settlement of Akroofoo, where our arrival was once more celebrated with gunfire and where the women were especially welcoming. From there to Tuacua and Ed Jerri our route traversed several hills and the path had not been widened to make room for our palanquins, so that we did not reach the settlement of Paintry until four o'clock, after a most uncomfort-

able journey. We took to our cots early, but the rain persisted all through the night and the roar of lions, leopards and other wild animals in the vicinity of our tents alarmed us greatly.

The following day, 10 January, we reached Jan Comadie, residence of the king of Assim. Three hundred clamouring negroes milled around, firing their guns dangerously, while the population danced and sang to the beat of our brass band. His Highness was flanked by a fetish priest and priestess with painted torsos and surrounded by a troupe of slaves wearing multicoloured tunics covered in bells. He was presented with an East Indian silken chintz tunic, strings of beads, rum, tobacco and pipes, whereas all we received in return was one cabree or African goat, and eleven bunches of bananas. The aim of our visit was to dispel a rumour that a Dutch general had disembarked at Elmina with a large party of officers to eradicate the Assimers. It transpired that some of our own slaves, young Ashantis, had been spreading the rumour. This palaver lasted for some time and yet we returned to our tents without having resolved the situation. But hardly had we arrived there than the king came with the offer of a recruit, whom we engaged in the service of King Willem against payment of two ounces of gold (eighty guilders). Here we had our first experience of the great difficulty in reaching agreement with these people on the value of our gold, because of their endless queries about the weight and quality.

That evening we invited His Highness for a glass of punch, in the hope of gaining his favour. He arrived with eight musicians playing drums, hollow elephants' tusks or buffalo horns, and gourds filled with gravel. They wished to enter into a competition with our band! When it was over His Highness was moved to observe that, however pleasing his music had sounded to him previously, it no longer did so. He ordered his men to desist from playing.

The caboceer had a curious way of sharing the drink with his slave boys. They opened their mouths wide as if to shout, whereupon he took a sip of the punch and squirted it straight into their mouths from a considerable distance. His adroitness was such that it was clearly a common practice.

After the departure of the guests we missed a fine goblet from one of the travel cases. News of this was conveyed to the king. An hour later the glass was returned with the message that the miscreant had already received his punishment, consisting of cutting off both his ears.

The next morning found us on a rough track that had not been previously widened. Our progress was slow. The following day the route up to the river Curacio was fair, but when we had crossed to the other side we had to force our way through dense undergrowth. Before we could enter the settlement of Koochua we had to traverse a vast marshland and after fording yet another river we came upon the settlements of Abandu and Fusu. It was in this manner that our journey proceeded for days on end: through rivers teeming with highly dangerous creatures and across hills covered in tall guinea grass, which hampers passage and stifles the breath. At the settlement of Prasso we crossed the river of the same name in a canoe. Having arrived at the other side we entered Ashanti territory at last!

Our journey during the following days took us through a rolling landscape dotted with pools and a small, steep mountain, the only one we saw on our entire journey. The vegetation became progressively less pleasing.

In the settlement of Eduabin our sojourn was unfortunately protracted. First of all we received a messenger from the king of Ashanti, who welcomed us heartily into his territory and also brought instructions for the caboceer. The nature of those instructions soon became horribly clear. Not long after our arrival we saw a multitude of men and several women emerging from their dwellings. We then heard that the king of Kokofu, chief ruler in the realm of the Ashanti king, had died. "His tree has fallen," is the local expression. The fleeing women were his blood relatives. Within a few minutes two negroes appeared; they had leafy branches around their necks and carried large knives. They searched all the dwellings for slaves that had

36

belonged to the deceased ruler, in order to slaughter them. We were informed that in Bipolsa, a previous settlement where our music had made a very good impression, some sixty men had already had their throats cut.

That same evening we observed how forty men were taken prisoner in order to be sacrificed in Kokofu during the funeral ceremony. At one o'clock in the night several Ashanti officials and courtiers came to tell us on behalf of His Highness that the demise of his highest-ranking subject necessitated his absenting himself from the capital Kumasi; he was due to attend the funeral ceremonies in Kokofu with his entire retinue as well as the full party of dignitaries who had travelled to the capital from all regions to witness the arrival of our embassy. His Highness requested us to remain where we were until further notice.

Messengers from the king came daily, bringing us palm wine and a sheep, and inquiring after our well-being. On 24 January, in the hope of persuading the king not to keep us waiting too long, we sent the halberdier of Elmina and our interpreter to Kokofu with gifts of one chest of loaf-sugar, one chest of wax candles, several pounds of tea and a small porcelain tea service. They returned with disheartening tidings: we were to remain in this wretched place for at least another ten days. On the 26th a hurricane known as Travados struck, with heavy thunderstorms, and we were obliged to abandon our tents and seek refuge in a house. To distract us from the violence of the elements, our palanquin bearers and porters from Elmina offered us two serenades with dance, which lasted until late at night and attracted the participation of the local population.

On the 29th we were very pleasantly surprised. The king sent us a gift of six young women, all blood relatives of the king, with the notice that His Highness wished them to provide entertainment and consolation for us officers, and thus to dispel the tedium of our stay in this place. Escorting the women was a great band of torchbearers, followed by one hundred and twenty slaves with bananas, twelve with yams and one with a pot of palm wine. The following day Verveer ordered our thanks to be conveyed to the king. On the 31st we *again received six slaves laden with bananas, two ditto with palm nuts, five with beans, three with vegetables, as well as sheep and a pitcher of palm wine. On 1 February the king, believing his gift of women to have been prized by the officers, regaled us with three more of his blood relatives.*

This was all very well, but on the 4th we sent an interpreter with the halberdier of Elmina to the king once more, with the urgent request to let us know once and for all on which day we might expect to make our entry in the capital.

That very afternoon we were visited by a cousin of the king, who was a grandee at court, with a large retinue. Their message was the following: that the king, his master, and the Ashantis in general, had the deepest respect for the king of Holland and His Majesty's subjects; that they all, without exception, considered themselves his servants; that none of them had ever had occasion to meet a man of such distinction and high rank as the Royal Commissioner Major-General Jan Verveer with such a large party of ranking officers and men; that the king was doubly saddened by the loss of his blood relative because of the delay this caused to the embassy's entry into Kumasi, which was all the more regrettable for the advent of the "evil days." It seems that a superstition of the negroes forbids all work and consultation during these evil days in the firm belief that everything undertaken on those days will come to nothing. As a consequence, His Highness was prevented from receiving the foreign visitors.

The king, he continued, had sent him to request humbly that the embassy be patient until 10 February. He assured us that His Highness would have received the emissaries of any other nation, thereby exposing them to evil influences, but not their beloved Hollanders.

Since the market for the multitude of persons in our company was very poorly supplied with provisions, the royal broadcaster known as Thjoucho arrived the following day to announce to all the inhabitants of this and all other settlements in the area that they had a duty, so long as the embassy sojourned in these parts, to bring all victuals and other stocks to the market daily. The prices had been fixed and it was decreed that anyone avoiding these duties would be punished in keeping with certain laws. The usual punishment consists of cutting off one or both ears for a first offence and the loss of nose or lips for recidivist behaviour. From then on the market was amply supplied daily with all provisions, for the duration of our sojourn.

We departed at last on the 10th and arrived in Kasi at two o'clock. The following day we received a visit from the king of the lands of Becquin, the second in the Ashanti Empire. He was clothed in his warrior's dress, made up of a colourful jerkin, ditto hose, sandals with heavy gold rims and a cap made of tiger skin with attached tail. On the 12th we proceeded to Faverhan, where we received notice that we could enter Kumasi the following day.

The next morning, 13 February, we set out for the capital at seven o'clock in full regalia, followed by the men bearing our gifts for His Highness. The capital is surrounded by marshland, which was flooded at the time with 10 to 15 inches of water. This caused further delay. We officers were conveyed over the water one by one, which took fifteen minutes each. At last we arrived at the outpost of Kumasi, where we were joined by the slaves bearing gifts for H.H., who had travelled ahead of us. We wished to proceed on our journey as soon as possible, but were obliged to halt for a large band of guardsmen. Verveer declared that it was not fitting to keep us waiting any longer, after so many disappointments. Messengers kept coming with requests to wait a little longer, and eventually we sent notice that if we were not permitted to proceed at once, we would return to Faverhan and indeed would return home without concluding our mission. The reply to this was that H.H. was seated, and that the procession might advance within a short time.

We retorted that the meaning of their "short time" was most unclear and that we did not comprehend why, if all was in readi-

ness, we were still obliged to wait. We decided to continue our advance without their permission. We arrayed the slaves in such a manner that the numerous gifts appeared to best advantage. Major-General Verveer instructed the brass band to play the national anthem and we made our way through the crowd of armed men with considerable effort. The guards however did not obstruct us. We proceeded from the outpost and completed the last leg of our journey in one-quarter-hour. To everyone's displeasure our previous delay turned out to have been unnecessary. Both the king and his grandees had been seated in readiness all morning, and their boredom had reached such proportions that foolish children's rhymes were being chanted to while away the long hours of waiting.

3

Thirteen pale-faced musicians emerged from the trees. They generated such a pandemonium as Kwame and I had only ever heard from the coppersmiths on a busy workday. Birds flew up in fright. Yet the pounding rhythm sent a ripple through the crowd: all around us muscles were flexed and bodies started swaying to the blasts of noise.

The musicians were followed by a standard-bearer, a party of white servants in hunting gear and one hundred black slaves in pairs. Each pair carried a litter laden with gifts: Chinese fans and vials of scent, Brussels lace and soap from Cologne, champagne, ginger, jams and preserved fruit. There were also costly textiles, gold fringes, gold braid and silver thread. A length of poppy-red serge was draped around a marble statue of Psyche: this creature, half bird and half man, was so white as to seem luminous. Three litters were laden with Dutch gin in stoneware crocks. There was Malaga wine in abundance and liqueur in mahogany casks. A handsome pair of handguns with attributes was presented to my father, as well as a silver-inlaid walnut case containing a hunting rifle with decorative facings, and lastly an open-work cuirass overlaid with silver and gold.

The band struck up again when the gifts were put on display. A lavish palanquin borne by six slaves appeared at the bend in the road. On it sat a man in full regalia, shaded by a dazzling orange awning. An interpreter announced him as His Majesty's highest servant, Major-General Verveer, Governor-General of the Dutch East-Indian Army, envoy of King Willem I of the Netherlands. Two red, white and blue Dutch flags fluttered behind him, partly screening the next palanquins from view. One of these was occupied by a man who seemed less intent on making an impression of grandeur. He even looked somewhat embarrassed, and in this he was distinct from the others. His name was announced as Deputy Commissioner van Drunen.

Then came a straggling party of several hundred porters and men with chopping knives, which were by now blunted from cutting a path in the forest. Bringing up the rear were a number of slaves bearing what appeared to be large chunks of stone and columns of marble which they carried over their shoulders with incomprehensible ease, as if they possessed the strength of gods.

Until then all the *uburuni* we had known had been harmless and laughable: white men with ever-sweaty faces which they kept mopping to no avail. The shade of their skin was that of a corpse. Word had it that the smell they gave off was the same. These envoys would set about mastering some ingratiating words of Twi in the hope of gaining a residue of gold dust or—until this was prohibited by their government—a small consignment of superannuated slaves. And once they had paid for their acquisitions with far too many rifles, they would stagger away, blissfully drunk on palm wine. Their constitutions were frail, and in the place behind the palace gardens where men go to relieve themselves they were more likely to be seen vomiting than passing water. But on the whole they were not troublesome.

This time, however, a white man was being carried aloft. Until then this had been my father's privilege, the only exception having been made for Kwame's father when he returned victorious and his warriors vied for the honour of bending their backs to bear Adusei Kra. And here was a white man borne by six black backs. This had never been seen in Kumasi. I stole a glance at the Asantehene, expecting him to take punitive measures. He did not bat an eyelid.

When the whole delegation was in formation, my father accepted his gifts and gave the signal for leave-taking, without granting Verveer so much as a glance. This gave rise to some consternation among the Hollanders. In order to attract attention to themselves they ordered the band to strike up yet again. That helped. Kwaku Dua halted and listened. Verveer declared through his interpreter that this piece of music had been composed for the occasion and that it was entitled "March for the King of Ashanti." But I looked in the eyes of his officers and knew this was a lie. Years later I recognized the tune as part of *Der Freischütz*, a rousing piece of music by von Weber, which was played to general acclaim at parades in Vienna and Paris.

My father was won over. The guests were directed to a stone building with a Dutch tricolour flying from the roof. It had been erected, the Asantehene informed them through his speaker, especially for the Hollanders. Another lie.

When the Dutch officials presented themselves that afternoon we made them wait for a suitable length of time. They carried their own chairs, which they put down in the forecourt, and there was a moment of alarm when they almost turned back because they deemed the place unfitting for their station and because they were not received forthwith. My father sent some dignitaries to explain that the European measurement of hours was unknown to us. Consequently they were invited to come back the next morning.

The following day Verveer again presented my father with a cuirass. The resident of Fort Axim put it on and strutted about to display the beautiful workmanship. My father put his thumb in his mouth and gave several shouts of admiration, but stayed on guard nonetheless. He asked if the cuirass did not warrant the use of epaulettes, whereupon Verveer removed his and handed them to my father, which was precisely what he had in mind. The Hollander was over-confident. He let it be known that it was customary in his homeland to find the doors of friends open to them, while the doors of enemies would be opened by force of arms. Needless to say, the next morning, 15 February, the palace gates remained closed to him.

From van Drunen's report:

By the 16th the Asantehene showed himself to be more accommodating, and sent us eight persons from his court accompanied by four speakers. They came bringing gold dust: 6 ounces 8 English pounds for the governor; 2 ounces 8 Eng. for his second in command; the secretary, resident and physician together received 4 ounces 8 Eng.; the assistant and interpreter together 1 ounce 2 Eng.; the white servants 9 Eng.; the black servants 9 Eng. Altogether 16 ounces 9 Eng. gold dust, all wrapped in fine silken cloths. This did not add up to a one hundredth fraction of the expenses of our expedition! Also an ox, a pig, six sheep, ten guinea fowl, and two hundred chicken eggs were brought. In addition ten slaves arrived with a supply of pineapples, eight with sugar cane, forty-six with yams, fourteen with African nuts, fourteen others with sundry vegetables. One thousand and twenty-five slaves were laden with bananas, twenty-one with firewood and two with palm wine, making up a total of eleven hundred and forty bearers. In the meantime jesters arrived, mainly repulsive dwarfs and hunchbacks, who lurched about for the purpose of amusing Verveer. To no avail.

But on the 17th the governor-general made a cunning move to speed up the ceremonials. Having presented the Asantehene with champagne, confectioneries, toilet water, two pier glasses, two flower vases and a mantel clock, the governor-general requested permission to present the king's son with a gift, too. A timid youth, not fully grown, stepped forward.

Verveer handed this child, Kwasi Boachi, a dagger, declaring that he should use it in defence of his Fatherland and the Ashanti people. In jest he conferred the rank of general upon the boy. The king was visibly moved. Before we departed, the king ordered an organ, of which the pipes were broken, to be brought to us with the request to repair it, which demand we were of course unable to satisfy. Then H.H. requested us to dance for him; however, we replied that white men are not accustomed to leap about on an earthen floor.

On 19 February at two o'clock Verveer received word that Kwaku Dua I was on his way. The members of the band arranged themselves in a semicircle and launched into the so-called "March for the King of Ashanti." The retainers of H.H. were so numerous that most of them were obliged to remain outside. Only Kwame Poku, the king's nephew and heir to the throne, and his son Kwasi Boachi, were admitted, along with nine young girls belonging to the royal family. The king and his courtiers were heavily laden with gold; the former was literally bowed down by the weight. A porcelain jug of palm wine was brought and two golden-eared calabashes. When H.H. took a draught of wine, his trusted slaves held a bowl under his chin into which he deliberately spilled some liquid from his mouth: this spillage was eagerly drunk by them. When H.H. spat on the ground, we saw his bodyguards take up the royal fluid and rub it into their skins. We presented H.H. with portraits of our own royal family and a camera obscura.

The negotiations were now underway and proceeded during the following days with varying degrees of success, but at this time Verveer fell ill. His condition declined by the day. He suffered greatly and we began to understand why these regions are known as "the white man's grave."

On 26 February we took a stroll in the night and I tripped over some obstacle in my path. The orderlies escorting us lowered their lanterns and to our horror we saw three freshly sev-

ered heads of young negroes lying before me. It was the great feast day of the fetish named Ady, on which occasion it is customary for all to shake hands with the king and his grandees. Preceded by our musicians we made haste to join the ceremony, but could barely reach H.H. through the dense crowd. A large number of people were sacrificed on the graves of the royal family that day. This ceremony was performed once each month. *

Although Kwame and I were informed of the progress of the negotiations, we were indifferent to their nature. We amused ourselves with the gifts and enjoyed the attention that was lavished on us. The Dutch dagger, given to me by Verveer, was my very first weapon. Kwame and I took turns to wear it. Our delight pleased my father. This gift in particular softened him towards the Hollanders, who understood that they had succeeded in influencing the Asantehene's mood through his son. From then on there was an unspoken connection between me and the negotiations.

The governor-general's illness lasted for two weeks. This was taken to be a sign that our gods were not in favour of his mission. Nevertheless van Drunen and the other officers succeeded in

---

*It is true that slaves, condemned men and defeated warriors were executed in Kumasi. But I must add that it was not known to us in those days that the northern tribes also belonged to the race of men. The notion of a single human race, comprising a diversity of coexisting peoples who were in essence equal, was foreign to us. In Europe, too, that notion had only recently arisen, and the practical implications were still inconsistent. We knew only one people—ours—and the dangers to which our kin were exposed. As a boy, the routine executions were little different to me from the slaughter of goats. Later in life this boyhood insensibility filled me with shame, until I discovered that a man's life counted for just as little in Europe at the time. The wars fought between 1792 and 1815 alone caused the sacrifice of one million five hundred and thirty thousand lives, not counting the loss of life in epidemics spread in the course of the conflicts. Another two hundred thousand souls died in the war between Russia and Turkey, and an equal number in the Polish uprising. At the very time that van Drunen was startled by a few heads lying on his path, tens of thousands of heads were rolling in the Caucasus.

bringing the affair to a satisfactory conclusion. A contract was drawn up: in exchange for firearms the Asantehene promised to supply the Dutch agent Huydecoper with one thousand male slaves/recruits annually. (Slaves *slash* recruits, a script notation that would earn the Dutch much international notoriety and an official complaint, served against them by England, for infracting the law against slave trading.)

As a token of goodwill, Kwaku Dua was promptly issued with 2000 rifles, valued at 32,500 guilders, and 812½ ounces of gold. He was left in no doubt as to the expectation that, prior to the delegation's departure, a similar token of goodwill would come from him. My father acceded to this and promised to reflect on a suitable collateral for his side of the contract.

Not until 13 March was Verveer's health sufficiently restored for him to sign his name to the terms of agreement. My father put a cross on the document. Now that their mission had been accomplished, the Hollanders were anxious to return as soon as possible. My father invited them to stay another forty days. Verveer declined the offer with as much civility as he could muster, and the date of their return was set for seven days later.

During that final week Kwame and I spent most of our time with the delegation. Each day we presented ourselves at the guests' quarters, where we were entertained with games. We were, for instance, given brightly coloured playing cards with pictures of Holland and taught to play Snap. In the darkened officers' tent we were regaled with magic-lantern shows. Wolves and giants loomed inexplicably on the canvas. The moving figures and their adventures became just as dear to us as our own tales of Spider Anansi.

Another favourite haunt of ours was the building site by the palace gate, where the Hollanders had made a clearing in a forest in readiness for the construction of a vast Greek temple. Eight Corinthian columns were erected on five tall steps. The richly ornamented altar, four giant urns, and capitals adorned with open-work acanthus leaves all gave the impression of weight and solidity. We offered our help and surprised the other children in the family by lifting great chunks of marble above our heads. In reality the entire structure was made of wood, painted to resemble marble, and had been transported all the way from Holland in sections ready for assembly. The wood, which had got wet during the passage across the marshland, was becoming warped in the dry air of Kumasi, and the Hollanders had great difficulty fitting the sections together.

Among our new toys there was one that held a particular fascination for me: a shiny board with carved figurines of ivory and ebony. Van Drunen took it upon himself to teach us the game, which I found more appealing than our *wari*, at which I nearly always lost to Kwame. As we did not yet speak a common language and the interpreter was needed elsewhere, this good man sat himself down on the ground with us and explained the rules and skills of the game by means of hand-signals. While we were thus engaged he acquired his first knowledge of Twi by imitating the words we spoke, and we in turn learnt our first halting words of Dutch. The guttural pronunciation of the Dutch terms for the chess game sounded especially hilarious to our ears.

Kwame was drawn primarily to the carved figurines themselves. He gave names to them and, in contravention of all the rules, pretended that they kissed each other and gave birth to infant pawns. As for me, I was filled with a passionate desire to comprehend van Drunen's moves, to learn how to predict them and surpass him in mental prowess.

Van Drunen also devoted an entire afternoon to exciting our interest in another use of the chessboard. With a few words and many gestures he demonstrated to us the wondrous multiplication of a grain of wheat. On the first black square he laid a single grain, on the white square next to it two grains, on the following squares four and sixteen grains respectively. While he was counting out the two hundred and fifty-six for the fifth square, Kwame's interest flagged and he wandered off in search of someone to tell him a story with the magic lantern. But I wanted van Drunen to go on. When he saw that the principle was dawning on me, he traced what were to me then incomprehensible ciphers in the sand, and enthusiastically poured two handfuls of grain on the board, thereby flooding all the squares. Then he brushed off all the grains, pointed to the heap of wheat and the ciphers in the sand by turns, and then stabbed his finger meaningfully at the sixth square. I jumped up, took the sack of wheat from him and emptied the contents over the chessboard. Van Drunen slapped his thighs and roared with laughter, shook my hand and called some sergeants to tell them what I had done. Then I brushed the grains away again and stared at the many squares which still needed filling, racking my brains to understand the mystery I had just been demonstrated. Although I could not find an explanation nor the words to express what I had observed, I had been stirred by intimations of a world existing outside the one I knew. I felt the same excitement as during our initiation rites with the fetish priests. When I raised my eyes I saw the soldiers grinning at my emotion. Their amusement embarrassed me deeply. I realized that this was familiar ground to them, and that I was looking in from the outside. This was not the only secret knowledge they shared, and they were tickled as much by my exclusion as by their power either to reveal or withhold a subsequent secret.

I gave up on the chessboard and grains and ran away to find Kwame by the magic lantern. My mind was reeling with my discovery, but I kept it to myself. I snuggled up to my friend and watched the story in pictures of one Struwelpeter, who was only a child but whose fingers and nose were snipped off as punishment for no other crime than failing to keep spotlessly clean.

One morning in that last week van Drunen instructed a few soldiers to entertain us with hand puppets. Half hidden behind a cloth, arms aloft, they played a wooden husband and wife who kept beating each other about the head with sticks. Kwame and I were rolling over the ground laughing, when I suddenly noticed my father's presence. His arrival had not been announced, and he was without his retinue. The look in his eyes was vacant. He stood there for some time, watching us. Finally he gave a nod of assent and left, as if the sight of Kwame and me enjoying ourselves had reassured him.

On the evening before the Hollanders' departure, Kwame and I were summoned by my father. The Asantehene received us in the throne room, but the council of dignitaries was absent. There were some tribal headmen in attendance, including Badu Bonsu, the king of Ahanta, but after a few kind words they withdrew. My father addressed us through his speaker, as was his custom. They had discussed the matter beforehand. The speaker adopted a formal tone, almost a drone.

"Kwasi, Nana has taken an important decision, a most fortunate one for you," the speaker intoned, eyeing me. *Nana* means papa. It was the customary term of address for the sovereign, but coming from the lips of the speaker it always made me feel slightly cheated.

". . . important for your future. Nana has decided on a great mission. He has heard numerous encouraging accounts of the riches of Europe, of the knowledge of the white men. You shall go to gather them on our behalf."

"Just as they have come to us, so we shall go to them." It was my father himself who was speaking now. He did not look at me, but kept his eyes fixed ahead as if he were addressing a crowd.

His speaker added: "Nana has organized it thus. The Hollanders will feed you and teach you all they know. Nana will miss you, but finds comfort in knowing that you understand what this means to our people."

I understood nothing. I glanced at Kwame, and when he did not react, at my father.

"Tell him about the son of Adusei Kra," he told the speaker.

"Nana, in his great wisdom, has understood that you, Kwame Poku, are still in need of solace after the loss of your father. So he does not wish to separate you from your friend."

My father lost his patience. "That is not the only reason," he broke in. "Kwame is the son of my sister."

"Nana lets it be known that you are his special concern, since you are the son of his beloved sister. If the gods are willing, you will one day succeed Nana. So in your case a knowledge of Europe may be of even greater consequence."

"But Nana," I asked, "where are we to go?"

"Overseas," the speaker replied.

"Far away?"

"Yes, far," concluded my father. He dismissed the speaker, telling him to take Kwame with him. Once my father and I were alone his attitude changed. He rose, held me tight and kissed me, but I did not have the strength to hug him in return. I was like the dead at the hour of their own funeral, astounded by the truth, but no longer capable of taking any action.

"Kwasi, Kwasi . . ." he murmured again and again, rocking me in his arms, ". . . we will love you when you return. As we do now. More even. You will be an important man. More important than I. Kwasi . . ." At this point he was called away to attend to the Dutch envoys.

From van Drunen's report:

When the palace gates were opened, the men who had escorted us into the inner courtyard fled: they are forbidden to see the king's women, on pain of death. The Asantehene, thronged by hundreds of his women, came to us, not walking, but dancing! He shook hands with each of us, whereupon we occupied the seats that were assigned to us. Before us sat a score of eunuchs. H.H. took a seat among his most prized wives. Most of them wore white paint on their torsos and faces, and had shaven heads. But others had let their hair grow in certain places to form a pattern of crescent moons, snakes, rosettes, and so on. They took turns to perform a dance, and sang fitting songs. When H.H. himself began to dance once more, all his women showed their approval: they ran towards him, whirled around him and tried to mop the perspiration on his head with their cloths. Subsequently they sang some songs of their own composition. The king's sister arrived a little later; she was dressed in an embroidered yellow silken shift and lace veil. She was accompanied by fifty female slaves, all of whom filed past us, dancing and strik-

ing all manner of contorted poses. The proceedings as a whole were impressive in their exotic splendour, and the grandeur of the occasion was the more marked for never having been witnessed previously by either Europeans or natives.

After the meal the king went to the palisade of his palace, where he was completely taken by surprise in the gloom of the night by the spectacle which we had mounted for him with considerable effort and expenditure. Suddenly, the white frontage of our temple, topped by the Dutch flag, was flooded with light as if by magic. The illumination was achieved employing the most modern techniques. Within the Greek façade stood a statue, which was lit up from behind by means of mirrors. The columns were lit from below with focused light beams. With the aid of lenses from the magic lantern, moving images of rippling water, a burst of flames and passing clouds were projected. Beyond the façade stood urns with Bengal fire. Above them hung a blazing sun with rotating rays. On either side of the temple preparations had been made for an elaborate display of fireworks by way of a grand finale.

No less than three times did the king let it be known that he had enjoyed the spectacle. Each time he asked whether the edifice was now really his. The governor-general assured him that this was so, but unfortunately, a few minutes after the show had ended, a fearful storm arose, which blew the temple to pieces and scattered the wooden wreckage all over Kumasi.

The evening was concluded with the presentation, by the treasurer, of the gifts the Asantehene wished the Dutch embassy to convey to King Willem I: a golden pipe-bowl, a golden rudder, another silken shift, with the request that His Majesty wear it as a sash, six tiger skins, two live panthers, two macaws and a hawk.

The Asantehene then contributed two private gifts by way of assurance to the Hollanders of his devotion and of his intention to live up to the negotiated agreement: the gifts were his son Kwasi and his nephew Kwame. He declared that the young princes were to depart with us to Holland. He was sending his nephew, the heir to the throne, to accompany his son, in order

that the two might find solace in each other during their stay in
that distant land. He requested us to take the best care of both
boys, with which entreaty we readily promised to comply.

When he sent for the boys to be presented to us they were not
to be found, which angered H.H. so greatly that he uttered some
apologies and terminated the festivities there and then.

Kwame and I had run off into the forest, to get as far away as possible from all the fuss and commotion. We whiled away the evening without finding the words to express our bewilderment at the unthinkable morrow that awaited us. We ran about, making a lot of noise with our laughter. We shouted louder and louder, until we found ourselves in the clearing with the newly erected temple. The place was deserted. We sank down among the wooden struts and fell asleep side by side.

We were woken up by a blast that seemed to signal the end of the world. The fireworks the Hollanders had placed all around seemed to have made an inferno of the temple along with the surrounding vegetation. The earth trembled. We were at the very centre of an explosion such as we had never seen before. There was nowhere to turn. We felt certain that we were about to die, and huddled close together under a sky ablaze with hellish red and lurid yellow. After a while some Dutch soldiers approached the temple to extinguish the smouldering fires with water. We had a few moments in which to compose ourselves, but another shock was upon us: hardly had we crawled out from behind the columns than the noise of the jungle, which had made itself heard again once the pandemonium had ceased, suddenly fell silent. The soldiers noticed this, too, but did not know what it signified. We did. We ran away as fast as we could. A moment later the air was filled with the roar of a tornado tearing through the forest. Branches snapped and were blown away. Trees were uprooted. The temple was blown apart by the storm, and with the flying debris at our heels we fled into the palace.

That night Kwame and I slept apart. Each of us spent the night in the arms of our inconsolable mothers. Clearer than my memory of my mother's face is my memory of the cloth she was wearing, of my head buried in the patterned fabric covering her heaving bosom. I do not recall any words of farewell either, only the rhythm of a song, sung in a halting voice. This is how I picture the two of us: she is sitting cross-legged on the floor, I am resting drowsily in her arms, and all the while she singsongs the adinkra symbol of Anansi, the five-rayed sun:

> *Children of the spider Anansi are we*
> *And the wide world is our web:*
> *Love, lust or fate*
> *Bring us to the furthest reaches.*
> *Whichever way we turn in that world-web*
> *There are threads to grasp*
> *And threads to let go.*

On the day of our departure we sat tall in the saddles of our Arabian stallions, apparently unmoved. While the Dutch officers received yet more gold and slaves, Kwame and I were ready, our faces inscrutable.

Close to van Drunen and the musicians, who struck up their "March for the King of Ashanti" as a last salute, we headed the long procession. As we filed past the palace my father stood outside in the gallery. He waved his hand.

We came across scattered debris from the temple. Where the path disappeared into the forest, we passed two pillars and fragments of the collapsed frieze. The relief had been painted in grisaille, portraying a scene of strong white warriors with curved breast-plates and banners clustered around a triumphant woman on a throne guarded by a lion rampant. She wore a helmet, and although she held a spear in one hand and a shield in the other, two infants suckled at her large white breasts.

4

We had left everything: parents, kinsmen, toys, beds and clothing, servants, beliefs and native soil, our past and our future. For two boys who had been severed from their roots so abruptly, Kwame and I were remarkably composed on our journey to the Dutch fort of Elmina. The past was still too close and the future unconscionable. I do not believe either of us shed a tear. We made up for that later.

Despite all the romantic notions about travelling, the truth is that it dulls the senses. The traveller is always one step ahead of his feelings. New impressions eclipse concern for what is left behind. While amassing experiences of the world outside, his inner being goes to waste. Such is his state of mind until the next destination.

On 1 April 1837, around noon, Kwame and I set eyes on the sea. We dismounted quickly and raced across the palm-studded beach. Then we stopped in our tracks, awed by the pounding surf. Never had we seen the waters of the lake of Twi as enraged as this. But when the soldiers and porters, tired of the long hot journey, tore off their clothes and plunged into the waves we overcame our fear and followed their example, albeit gingerly. We took a gulp of water to quench our thirst, but had to spit out the brine at once, much to the amusement of the Dutch soldiers. They cleaved the water like fish. Great white bodies circled around us. Now they were naked we saw their skin was covered in hairs, either fair or dark. We had only seen this on animals.

The Dutch red, white and blue could be seen flying from the fort that loomed in the hazy distance: Fort Elmina. A salty fog hung low in the sky, with swirls of black smoke. The latter disquieted Verveer. He wished to proceed at once to the fort, without observing the official ceremonies of arrival. There was not even time for the band to play the patriotic tune they had struck up at each village we encountered on our way to the coast. The drums were silent as, at a brisk pace, we made for the Fanti settlement at Elmina.

There was a smell of burning. Two whole neighbourhoods had burnt to the ground only recently. People fled when they saw us coming; even an old woman lying on the ground, badly burnt, was abandoned by her relatives. The Dutch soldiers laid her on a stretcher, after which we hurried through deserted streets to the harbour. We rode over two drawbridges into the fort. Verveer withdrew at once, followed by his adjutants Tonneboeijer and van Drunen, in order to be briefed by the commander.

Meanwhile the palanquins were unloaded. The fresh recruits were herded into the slave cellars. There was some confusion as to where to house the panthers. Kwame and I were at a loss in the midst of the commotion. Although the unfamiliar glare of the whitewashed walls made us uneasy, we hardly dared to move. So we just stood there waiting for someone to find us. The salty air deposited crystals on our cheeks. We ran our tongues over our upper lips and it tasted as if we had been crying.

Van Drunen reappeared at long last; he directed us to a small cubicle with one bed. It was situated in the officers' quarters, high above the courtyard. That evening we were both assigned to sit at table with the major-general, who—it must be said—treated us properly as princes. He instructed his adjutant Tonneboeijer to satisfy all our wishes, while Peter Welzing, the mulatto interpreter, was charged with keeping us company so that we might learn about the situation in Elmina.

After supper van Drunen drew our attention to an elegant, sinuous pattern that had been worked into the railing of the balcony. It was the letter W, he explained, and it stood for the initial sound of the name of the king of Holland. He made us say the name again and again until we could pronounce it exactly as he did. After this he took a torch and guided us on our first tour down the dark passages of the fort.

The old castle dates from 1482. It was built by the Portuguese on a cliff sacred to the inhabitants of Elmina. To appease them, a small sanctuary for the heathen godhead was created in an alcove. Van Drunen showed us the altar and laid an offering there of coconut and yam. He did so without ceremony or untoward display, indeed as if he were accustomed to doing so.

When the Dutch seized the fortress from the Portuguese a hundred and fifty years later, they laboured diligently to turn Elmina into the most important slaving post on the west coast of Africa. They reinforced the walls and expanded the storage spaces. They constructed a landing-pier and invented more efficient means of regulating the traffic of goods to and from Elmina. The walls of the dark cellars were fitted with iron rings, to which the merchandise was tethered. Here the odds were stacked against the men and women whom my father and his father before him had procured against payment. Many of them died an early death from exhaustion, starvation or injuries; others took their own lives in the putrid, writhing mass.

Van Drunen pointed out a narrow slit in the wall, through which a man could only just wring his body. One by one the slaves wrenched themselves through the opening and stepped on to the landing-stage, where they were assessed and sorted, counted, branded and herded into the hold. In this way the whole of the Dutch colony of Guyana was supplied with slaves.

The gallery over the women's depot offered escape to a select few. The officers would gather there, accompanied on feast days by men of lesser rank, who had been away from home for so long that they could no longer control their lust. From the gallery they looked down on the female slaves, who did not cower and hide, but rather drew attention to themselves. In their despair they even jostled for prominence. The Dutchmen would make their choice from among these women, whereupon a rope ladder was lowered from the gallery. There was a scuffle to climb the ropes, but those who succeeded were thrown back into the crowd. Only the women who had been singled out were taken up on to the gallery. Such a woman would be taken to bed by the soldier, and as soon as he was done she would be lowered back into that sea of misery.

Yet she was better off than the others. She had a glimmer of hope while she waited anxiously for the signs of pregnancy, for if she was with child her departure would be delayed until after the birth. If she was lucky enough to give birth to a half-caste, she would be freed and granted the use of a hut in the village and a little land. There she would live, among the Fante, together with her bastard child who was both her shame and her redemption. The child was baptized with the name of its father. This is why there are Africans in Elmina who go by Dutch names such as Bartels, Vanderpuye, Hensen, Bosman or Vroom.

Van Drunen led us to our cubicle. We took our clothes off. They were our only possessions. He draped the robes carefully over the back of a chair. After he left we tried to sleep the way we used to sleep in Kumasi, but were kept awake for a long time by the pounding of the surf against the battlements and the memory of our elongated shadows against the subterranean vaults. We thought we heard echoes from the depths of that labyrinth, footfalls on the steps, which led from nowhere to nothing.

That same night, 1 April, Major-General Jan Verveer wrote the following letter to the minister of Colonies:

It is with the greatest satisfaction that I give Your Excellency the assurance that the reception accorded to me in Kumasi surpassed the most lofty expectations and notably that the entire attitude of the king of the Ashanti has been profoundly gratifying. The Dutch flag has become that of the Ashanti, and will fly from the king's palace henceforth. It pleases the king to call himself the subject of our honoured Sovereign. And the unconditional manner in which he has committed his beloved son and his nephew to the care of Your Majesty's Government with a view to their acquiring a Dutch education speaks volumes, in my humble opinion. Enclosed please find the contract signed by myself and by His Highness the Asantehene of Ashanti with a cross in lieu of a signature. However, to ensure a sound understanding of the situation and to eliminate all grounds for potential criticism I wish to reiterate, in the present missive, the distinction between the recruitment of these thousand men and the acquisition of slaves in the past.

These recruits are to be issued an advance payment of their wages in Kumasi, which they may use to buy their liberty from their former masters. They leave the capital as free men on their way to Elmina. Upon arrival there however they are <u>charged for the sum of their advance payment</u> minus twenty guilders, which are permitted to them as ready money. The remaining sum, which they owe us, will be subtracted from their wages in the East Indies. They are unfamiliar with our money and raise no objections.

The Ashanti troops are engaged, in keeping with <u>my stipulations</u>, for at least <u>fifteen years of service</u>, and the vast majority for an <u>indefinite period</u>, which they believe to signify <u>the rest of their lives</u>. I have deemed it judicious to abstain from entering a note to this effect in the agreement for reasons Your Excellency will have no difficulty surmising.

The men recruited in Kumasi in my presence meet all your requirements. More than half the men are of the stature of our grenadiers, the majority being northern negroes, known as Donko, well built, strong, good-natured, passionately loyal to their leaders and utterly content—in the full sense of the word—with their lot. Moreover there is no injustice in the enlistments, for it is not possible, even if we would so wish, to restore these people, some of whom come from so far afield as the banks of the Niger, to their native lands; while the men themselves firmly believe that if they were to return to their homeland it would only be to have the worst form of slavery thrust upon them once more.

Verveer's shrewdness in adopting the term "advance payment" becomes painfully clear upon closer scrutiny of the contract, signed at the bottom with a blotchy cross by my father. The contract, like Verveer's letter, is full of underlined words and phrases. Take the fourth clause, stating:

before such a slave or serf can be definitively enlisted into Dutch service, he is issued by the Dutch Government the necessary *funds to purchase his liberty from his master or owner, and to obtain it, such that he can and must be regarded, prior to his enlistment, as <u>a man in full possession of his liberty and thus entitled to make his own decisions, in all things alike, such as a free-born man might make</u>.*

Let me be quite clear on this point, for it is of the greatest importance to me that there be no doubt as to the nature of the transaction for which Kwame and I served as security. Since the recruits had bought their freedom from their former masters, they were, legally speaking, not slaves at the time of their enlistment. (The impositions on slavery at the Congress of Vienna in 1815 meant that recruitment of enslaved men was forbidden.) But to obtain the funds for the purchase of their freedom these unfortunate men had to sign a contract binding them to the Dutch Army, whereupon they were dispatched at once to Elmina. Their sole deed as free men consisted in surrendering their liberty to another master. Once they arrived in Elmina the "advance payment" was converted into a debt, which would take them very many years to repay given their meagre East Indies wages, the more so since the Dutch government even deducted expenses for the effort and investments involved in their "liberation."

Many men lived their lives in a slavery that differed from the old slavery only in that it had no name and consequently escaped scrutiny. So it is hardly surprising to encounter certain telling slips of the pen in the commander of Elmina's register of "Dutch soldiers" from Kumasi: when the word "slaves" crops up, it is crossed out in favour of "recruits."

When we awoke Kwame and I missed our robes, which van Drunen had draped over the chair the evening before. They had been replaced by trousers, shirts and also a pair of jackets with tails, which the quartermaster had fashioned out of old uniforms. We had never worn trousers, let alone long underwear. We sent each other into spasms of laughter exploring all the ways of poking our heads out of the various openings. We were still stark naked when van Drunen came in, demanding to know what the noise was about. He was most indignant at the disappearance of our robes. It transpired that they had been thrown on the fire with the kitchen waste before dawn, which left us without a single memento of home.

It was a Sunday, and the date was 2 April. Sweltering and uncomfortable in our new clothes, we were taken into a brick building in the middle of the courtyard where we were put in the front row of benches, with our interpreter beside us. Behind us sat the officers and men. The whitewashed walls were bare, except for the numbers of the psalms. Van Drunen made us clasp our hands, pretending it was a game. This was our first church service, which the interpreter translated for us. This Sunday the minister chose psalm two to be sung, in honour of our presence on their hallowed ground:

> *Why do the heathen rage so furiously together,*
> *And why do the people imagine a vain thing?*
> *The kings of the earth stand up and take council together,*
> *Against the Lord and against his Anointed, saying*
> *Let us break their bonds asunder, and cast away their cords from us.*

It didn't sound half as jolly as our own songs.

That afternoon the sun above the fort was blotted out by plumes of smoke from the settlement. Once again Elmina was ablaze, and when the fire was finally put out towards nightfall, no fewer than sixty homes were in smouldering ruins.

Trouble had been brewing in Elmina for some time. The commander of the Dutch fort had apprehended a caboceer for sacrificing a slave girl in memory of his deceased sister. The man was given a life sentence of forced labour, whereupon his fetish priests threatened to kill all the slaves unless the caboceer were restored to liberty. Thereupon the commander, not eschewing violent means, freed the slaves and had the priests put behind bars. But the grudges continued to fester.

Over dinner that night the commander discussed the situation with Verveer. The latter proposed to make a virtue of the devastation. Why not take it a step further and demolish the remaining maze of alleys to allow for the construction of wide streets? Had not Napoleon done the same during his great campaigns? Verveer was in excellent spirits. Not only would the boulevards be easily patrolled by his troops, but also the local population would be grateful to him for embellishing their town.

The next day, Monday 3 April, we were taken to the great hall and placed on either side of the major-general, who was to receive a delegation from the town. To be aligned with white men put Kwame and myself in an awkward position. The protesters were advised to cooperate with the efforts being undertaken to improve their town. They refused. Kwame and I could not help noticing the dark looks the men of Elmina cast in our direction.

On Tuesday 4 April we were taken by the governor of Elmina and Major-General Verveer on our first stroll through the devastated compound, while the others, led by van Drunen and Tonneboeijer, looked for a suitable site for the construction of dwellings in orderly rows, street by street. The people were hostile.

On Wednesday 5 April, early in the morning, we returned to the clearing. Kwame and I helped to mark off the streets with bamboo stakes, which we found entertaining enough. But when the people comprehended the extent of the plans, they gathered together in a crowd and, headed by the women, gave vent to their anger. The assurances they were given of grand avenues running across their town did not appease them, and we were obliged to return to our quarters post-haste. We thought it was all part of an exciting game, until Kwame was badly hit by a flying stone. The governor would not allow us to go out again that day.

At night we heard an angry roar in the distance. Quite quickly, it grew louder. The drawbridges were raised, and from the tower we saw a mass of people advancing on the fort, throwing stones and waving branches they had set alight. They tore out the stakes we had driven into the ground that morning, and deposited them in a heap by the gate.

At midnight, forty men marched from the fort accompanied by two pieces of ordnance, with a view to forcing the native king and his rule into submission. General Verveer himself was at the ready on the parapet with several officers manning the cannons in case of trouble. We watched the troop movements from the battlements. At one point we actually helped when the battle array in which van Drunen was riding was targeted by a group of spearmen. We flailed our arms and jumped up and down and shouted so loudly that van Drunen's attackers took to their heels.

By dawn the Hollanders returned to the fort without having fired a single shot. They brought with them eight dignitaries and the king. After that things quietened down and the marking stakes were replaced by the people themselves. The prisoners, however, were not set free.

The king of Elmina was by no means the first black sovereign that we had seen in captivity, but he was the first we saw being held in a dungeon by white men. This was unthinkable to us. That night we collected some fruits so that we might offer them to the Fanti king. Van Drunen, touched by our gesture, escorted us with the interpreter to the prison complex.

The stench inside was appalling, emanating for the most part from the pair of panthers that were being kept in the death cell. They sharpened their claws on the doorpost, which was carved with a skull and cross-bones. Next door, through the bars, we saw the king. He was sitting on a wooden block, and was shackled to the wall. Van Drunen opened the door of the cell and gave us a little push to go inside. The king looked at me steadily. I greeted him with the proper respect and tried to say with my eyes how deeply I regretted his treatment. Kwame took the dish of fruit from my hands and stepped forward. The king rose slowly, seemingly indifferent to his approach. When Kwame was standing right before him, he summoned up his last ounce of strength and gave the dish such a violent kick that the fruit was splattered against the vaulted ceiling. Kwame recoiled, and so did I, as the prisoner lunged at us as far as his shackles permitted. For an instant our eyes met. Then he spat in my face and launched into a tirade in Fanti, although he could see there were tears in my eyes. Van Drunen tried to pull us away from the enraged man, but we were transfixed.

"What is he saying?" I screamed at the interpreter. I was beside myself. "Tell me what he's saying!" At that point a gob of spit landed in Kwame's eye, whereupon van Drunen picked us up, one under each arm, and swooped us out of the king's reach. "What is he saying?" I clamoured.

"A black king," replied the interpreter with downcast eyes, "does not eat from white hands." Meanwhile the king raved on. Kwame, horrified, held out his arms to him.

During the last three weeks of our stay in Elmina we did not venture out of the fort again. Our wish to eat in our room was granted. Van Drunen visited us there daily, and tried to cheer us up. He gave us lessons in the Dutch language and told us endless anecdotes about the Dutch people. The only times we left our room were to take a stroll up and down the pier jutting out from the fort into the sea, or when enjoined to do so for the religious services and, on one occasion, for the public flogging of a Dutch soldier.

The young soldier had absented himself from roll call for four days running. He had been found in a neighbouring village with his native sweetheart. During a public atonement he was shackled to the church wall, stripped and given twenty well-aimed strokes with a stick, causing deep wounds in his flesh. But his will seemed unbroken. Kwame was deeply impressed; that white men should treat each other so harshly took away his last vestiges of trust. "So no one," he said, "is safe with them."

That afternoon, we were lounging on the pier listening to the sea when Kwame shot to his feet. I followed his gaze. Up on the parapet, in an embrasure, stood the young soldier who had been beaten so viciously. His wounds were exposed, his face was swollen and streaked with tears. He staggered to the tower that rose out of the sea, clambered on to the crenellations and hoisted himself further up. When he reached the top he sat for a while with his head on his breast, getting his breath back. I do not know how long we stood there watching, but I remember that we did not speak. Not even when the lad scrambled to his feet, stepped to the edge and jumped.

He fell forty metres, landing on the sharp rocks flanking the pier. I was about to scramble down to him, when I noticed that Kwame was still staring up at the battlements, open-mouthed, as if he had seen a miracle. For the first time since we had left Kumasi there was a spark of vitality in his look. Then he turned to me and smiled, noted that his change of heart was pleasing to me, took a deep breath and mouthed the first words of Dutch that he had memorized during van Drunen's lessons: *"Ja, Mevrouw!"**

We ran along the pier to inspect the broken body. This was our first intimation of the power of love. The young soldier died of his injuries three days later.

On 26 April, a few hours before our embarkation, Kwame thought he saw his mother by the gate. He had never doubted she would come to his rescue. He ran out to meet her but soon saw she was a Fanti. She had come to sell snails. My friend was inconsolable, and I could do nothing to distract him. In the afternoon, accompanied by Verveer, van Drunen and the officers, we boarded the *Governor MacLean,* with Captain Freebody at the helm. The anchor was weighed and the sails hoisted. I was never to see Africa again.

*"Yes, madam!"

JAVA 1900

Buitenzorg, 12 March

Ahim has been impossible for days, while I need all the concentration I can muster in order to reconstitute the events of my
youth. I would do well to discharge him. He has taken it into his
head that it is too tiring for me to spend all my time writing. He
says I do not look well, which is a bit rich coming from a man
with a hangdog look like his. If I do indeed have a tormented air
at times it is only because he inspires it. He keeps disturbing me
throughout the day—and now that I have been working late also
during the night—with petty excuses.

"Does the Prince wish for this, shall I bring the Prince that?"

If I say no he persists. If I say yes he rebukes me for not having
made my request earlier. I send him away. I threaten him with
punishment if he dares to show his face once more, but within
the next hour there he is, padding around me again.

"Not too hot? Not too cold? Have some more soda water!"

Sometimes he spends hours in the kitchen in the middle of
the night making snacks and squeezing the juice out of fruits,
only to have a pretext to intrude yet again. I'll be damned if he
isn't jealous of my dedication to my pen.

17 March

I concluded the description of my origins this morning before
sunrise. I must have nodded off over my writing, for I awoke
lying on the sofa amid a cascade of cushions. Ahim had carried
me there, undressed me and covered me with a blue sarong,
knowing that blue has a calming effect on my nerves. Thanks to

his fuss I slept without interruption until he came in with my evening meal. I ate like a young man. And then—and this was highly unusual—I longed for company. But it was dark by then and the sudden gusts of wind presaged rain. I told Ahim to fetch me a bottle of Chateauneuf from the stock I keep in my blanket chest for special occasions. I drank several glasses. I had seen no one but Ahim for almost a month. I had spent all my days working on the African part of my memoir. It is quicker to live than to recollect, it seems.

It is curious how, once you have hit upon something you thought you had forgotten, you want to shout it from the rooftops. Now that I had done what I set out to do I did not feel at rest, but was filled with nervous elation. After my third glass of wine I called Ahim, telling him to pour me another. I then emptied the bottle into the glass and motioned him to drink. He was flustered. I raised the glass to his lips. He looked as if I were offering him a lemon. It seems he cannot tolerate wine, so after a few sips I sent him away to fetch a lantern. He returned with the light, but when he saw me making ready to go outside he did his utmost to restrain me. He even grasped at my arms, as if in fright. When I wrenched myself free a button flew off my shirt. With a shock I recalled an article in the last *Aurora Yearbook*, stating that "alcohol is the most hazardous among East Indians of a bilious temperament; a sip can be enough to unleash a fatal rage in the soul."

Quite possible. Ahim was the most bilious man I knew.

So I proceeded on my way to Wayeng's house in the rain. She had a visitor: Lasmi. Quamina Aquasina lay asleep under the mosquito net with Aquasi junior. They had flung their arms and legs around the rattan bolster lying between them, and suddenly, old fool that I am, I was moved by the utter abandon with which those babes embraced their Dutch wife and each other. I was proud of my family and heartened by the warm welcome the women accorded me. Wayeng prepared a dish of fruit and roused the children to greet their father. I exulted in their fondness and reproached myself for having neglected them of late, setting greater store by my memories than by those dearest to me. I began to tell my children what had been occupying my thoughts, but soon saw their eyelids droop. No, worse still, I saw them trying hard to keep them open, whereupon I hugged my darlings and patted them and said they could go back to their dreamland. After all, I have now put the whole story down on paper. If they have questions about their roots they can always consult my memoir. Too tired to be a virile consort to Wayeng that night, I fell asleep in her arms.

18 March

Had another visit from Adeline Renselaar this morning, without her usual entourage this time. She thought I might be a little more forthcoming during a tête-à-tête. She was still counting on me to collaborate with her plans for my jubilee celebration. Today she tried the charming-female tack. Well, it's a bit late for that. Twenty years too late. Adeline's charms have to be seen to be believed. They come out of a jar. She is twice the size of other women and wears a bustle so large that she cannot sit down in company. For the duration of every social encounter, like ours this morning, she strikes attitudes. She assumes a pose, holds it until her muscles begin to twitch, and then strolls about airily, swinging her improbably long arms, until she has her back to the window where she strikes the next pose in dramatic lighting— hey presto: a tableau vivant! It is a miracle she has never knocked something over.

But then Adeline is the prima donna of our amateur dramatics society here at Buitenzorg. Indeed she insisted on reciting her latest role for my benefit: Desdemona! For a moment I was afraid she would press me to play the part of Othello, but she was only interested in her solo performance. I groaned and pretended to be suffering from sickness, St. Vitus fits, beriberi and an ague all at once, but she ignored my grimaces. After her finale, during which she was to be throttled by the Moor—which deed made him my favourite stage hero—she came to the point.

"My dear Prince, or what am I saying? Isn't it time we were on more familiar terms? What do you think?"

"I would rather not."

"Mister Boachi, Aquasi, dear old man, I wish you could bring yourself to see me for what I am—your family. All that grouchiness is nothing but a mask. Do take it off."

"Madam, since you seem to think that all the world's a stage, may I remind you that my life is not another of your sketches. There is no role in it for you. My stage make-up has taken many years to apply. If it is not to your liking, please proceed to the variety theatre!"

"Delightful! How amusing, a little play—how very clever!" she exclaimed, clapping her hands. The sound was muffled by her kid gloves. I gave up and let her have her say.

"Your fête. We have had consultations with the manager of the Society, and also with the owner of Tjiwaringi. The latter has a good, high-ceilinged hall, which can be rented for receptions quite inexpensively, and there is a charming podium. Do you have a preference for either one?"

"No podium at all sounds ideal to me."

"You are not taking this seriously. Never mind, I suppose it is not fair to presume on the honoured person himself for organizational support. I would hate to impose on you. You have no idea how much I am enjoying the preparations. And everything seems to be going according to plan. Everyone is enthusiastic. It looks as if you have become one of the most beloved members of our community. Why the dark look, *mon Prince*? You are cynical. You do not believe me. I tell you that half the town is already wreathing laurels, in a manner of speaking. That look! All right then, shall I tell you . . . there is a slight possibility—do not get me wrong, only a slight possibility—that the governor himself will engage in the event. A great marquee by the Deer Park, the same as on New Year's Day!" She clapped her hand over her mouth and stared at a corner of the room as if the entire circus were parading past already.

"Mrs. Renselaar," I interrupted, "I do not doubt the goodness of your intentions, but the general euphoria concerning my person, such as you describe it—even if it were sincere—cannot but pain me. You are right, I am a bad-tempered old man. That is what fifty years of Java have done to me. And you wish to celebrate that fact? *How*, may I ask, do you intend to do that? By rousing the enthusiasm of the same people who have ignored me for half a century?"

"That is not true."

"Well, not the same people, perhaps, although the distinction is hard to draw. If I have won their sympathy by approaching the end of my life, then that is a bitter thought. Where were they when I embarked on my career? When I had problems with my workforce? When I needed a mortgage? Why were the doors of their balls closed to a dark-skinned young man, and why would they wish to dance at his fête now that he is old and faded?"

"If you mean, if you are insinuating that . . . I always say, the prince, our prince, is a true Hollander. Truer than most, I should say. After all, you could have been a prince of Orange yourself, if, that is, if you were, if you were not . . ."

She had forgotten her lines. I decided to prolong the moment by keeping silent.

". . . what I mean is this. We regard you as one of us. Do you hear? And this is something I feel very strongly about. We have taken you to our hearts!"

"Hurrah!" I said meanly, "and that makes my life a success, I suppose."

"Your tone! So dreadful. I honestly believe that you despise me. Me! While I am the one, I . . . from the very first mention of your misfortune . . ."

"Misfortune?"

"That life of yours!"

"Which misfortune?"

"Well, I'll be honest with you . . . I wept! I resolved to improve our acquaintance and if possible to offer some amicable companionship by way of retribution."

"Retribution?"

"But no, you would rather hang back with a disgruntled look on your face. You choose to exclude me. Me! who have come to you to deepen our acquaintance, really to get to know you."

"Dear lady, what on earth have you done that might warrant retribution," I cried, "except wasting my time with your histrionics!" I had to raise my voice to get a word in edgeways.

"I feel responsible," she said solemnly, laying her hand on her bosom, "for your fate."

I aped her grand gesture, adding a scornful shrug of the shoulders for good measure. She was beside herself.

"I of all people . . . and I had so looked forward to our meeting. From the moment my husband told me . . . But I was mistaken. I should not have come. I should not have cared a whit for your affair. But that's just my way you know, I can't abide injustice. And now . . . now . . . You are taking advantage of my feelings. You are wicked. A monster, a devil, Mephistopheles in person!" She had worked herself into such a state that she burst into tears. Not like the Desdemona of the Indies this time, with great sobs racking her heaving bosom, but like a disconsolate little girl, quietly, almost inaudibly. And for all my resentment I felt pity for the poor woman. I sent Ahim to make her some lemonade and moved her to the porch, where I sat her down, bustle and all, in the rocking chair. I drew up my own cane chair and sat next to her. We said nothing, but I held one hand on the back of her rocking chair, moving it gently. The soothing rhythm calmed her, just as I had hoped. After a few minutes she took my other hand in hers, and we sat like that for some time, gazing into the garden.

"Of course I had heard rumours," she recommenced quietly.

"Of course," I said. A young capuchin monkey landed in the flame tree. We watched it hunting for food among the flakes of bark.

"Most remarkable rumours," she continued in a low voice, "quite disparate. Some I never credited, but nearly all were respectful."

The monkey in the tree, having sated its appetite, leaped away and vanished into the thick foliage. Adeline took out a handkerchief and blew her nose daintily.

"My husband and I are childless. God wished it so. I spend my days alone, at home. Now that Richard has been promoted I even spend the entire week alone. All alone. You know what that means." She sipped her lemonade and composed herself. "Richard works in Batavia nowadays. Since his advancement six months ago he leaves the house on Monday morning and I don't see him again until Friday evening. You have children. You are fortunate."

She wanted to rise, but could not bring herself to let go of my hand. "I have become accustomed to solitude. Believe it or not. Appearances are against me, I know, but I assure you that it is with the greatest difficulty that I engage in social relationships. Each time I must overcome my own sensitivities. Our dramatics society is my only distraction. Acting allows me to forget myself. And when I go out I brace myself, ruffle up my feathers like a fighting cock. I see the ladies and gentlemen aglow with complacency and I know: I am not one of them! But I shall not give up. I shall outdo myself. Transcend the misery of my situation. I am acting my part, which is that of a foolish old crone. It is a balloon that you have punctured with your sharp intellect. But I have no choice, don't you see, not when I am among the others. In our Dutch colony it is either sink or swim." She started crying again. This time I was not to be shaken.

"Why are you telling me these things?" I said in my coolest voice. I dreaded being subjected to a melodramatic soliloquy.

"God did not bless me with motherhood, but He gave me something in its stead. Something extra, a special sensitivity. You could say it was something beyond the normal, although I myself have no truck with all that nonsense about magic and *guna-guna* one keeps hearing. No, let's just call it my sixth sense."

"Your sixth sense," I echoed, just to please her. "What is it?"

"It is love!"

"Since when was that a sense?"

"It is the love that has accumulated in me . . . like, like the deposit of hairs on the drain in the washroom! There is nowhere for it to go! I know I sound absurd, you must think I'm out of my mind, but what can I do—this is how I feel. My sorrow has made me hypersensitive. I can tell the emotional state of people from afar. Once they come near I can read them, the way one reads the *Illustrated Review*. Like an open book. I can sense disturbances with a precision that would make the meteorological office in Batavia green with envy."

I was suddenly worried by the possibility that Ahim had fortified her lemonade with rum. To make matters worse she fell silent at this point and gazed at me, as if she had just revealed a state secret and expected a medal for her service.

"But if the human mind is so transparent to you," I asked, "why is it hard for you to deal with the members of the Dutch community?"

"Precisely because I can read their minds. I can tell when the ladies and the gentlemen say one thing and think another. About each other. About me. Nothing escapes my notice. I hear a conversation and at the same time I catch the asides, the cries for help from the psyche, and all the underlying signals as well. During the most inconsequential tea party I perceive more agitation and clamour than anyone else would notice at the evening bazaar. It is both a blessing and a cross I must bear. I will say no more." She rose to her feet. Hearing herself pour her heart out had done her so much good that she was wholly recovered.

"I am only telling you . . ." she said, "and only you, you should be the first to know, because . . ."

"Because?"

". . . because I recognized something in you."

"Recognized something?"

"Yes, I recognized myself in you."

She raised her arm, stabbing the air with her index finger. I was reluctant to let her proceed, because with her sort you find yourself in the middle of a seance before you know it, listening for spirits to knock on the table.

"The love has accumulated. We are incapable of admitting so much emotion, and think we are guarding ourselves against life."

To stop her from pursuing this train of thought I slipped my arm through hers while we took a turn on the grass. Now and then she stooped to pick a flower, which she tucked into her hair.

"It was my idea to have a celebration. I thought you could do with some distraction. I was mistaken. If you oppose my plans for a fête we will put the whole thing off."

I was about to say "Please do," when it struck me that I ought not to begrudge her this pleasure. I mumbled my assent, reluctantly.

"What did you say?"

I mumbled again.

"This won't do," she cried. "What did you say? Louder please. I am sensitive, not clairvoyant!"

"I said, madam, that if you are of a mind to mount a feast in honour of an old man, the least he can do is stay alive until the event comes to pass. Be warned, though: I am old. Too old for frivolity. And I shall come wearing the mask I am wearing now."

She leaned forward and kissed my cheek. She stood still to insert a final flower in her straggling coiffure, which by now resembled the kind of apparition natives dread on a moonless night.

"But I will make no plans without your approval. I shall discuss each and every detail with you."

"That is not necessary, I assure you."

"But it is. And all I ask is this: please tell me a little about yourself from time to time."

"No," I said firmly.

"Naughty! Naughty!" She gave a little laugh and wagged her finger at me. She took a few steps towards the garden gate, then turned around. "Goodbye, *mon Prince*, dear Aquasi Boachi, and I beg you—do not take a simple woman's emotions amiss. Dear Lord, I have really let myself go again this time, ranting like the madwoman of the Moluccas!"

She flounced her skirts and ran off as if I were about to give chase.

19 March

When I opened my shutters this morning, young Aquasi was sitting on his haunches under a tree in the yard. I beckoned him. He saw me, but did not dare come near. This angered me. It was ten in the morning, and it took me considerable effort to secure a place for him at the Reformed School. I wish him to be educated at a respectable institution. He is the only pupil who lives among the natives. And he is the brightest of the lot.

I called his name. I tried telling him to go to school, but he did not budge. Ahim said the boy had been sitting there for hours. I got dressed and ordered breakfast to be served on the veranda for two. But my son refused to come near. At long last I took a plate and brought it to him. He had been crying. I asked him why he was not at school. He said nothing, but the way his eyes avoided mine gave me the answer. I felt a stab of anger and grief and bit my lips.

"Are they giving you a hard time?" I asked, and immediately regretted my question, for he started sobbing. I hugged him tight, telling him that these things happen to us all and that he had to be strong. Then he explained that his classmates had taunted him with the name "Snow White."

This is a Dutch joke. The Javanese name for the African recruits in the Dutch East Indies Army was *blanda hitam,* or black Hollanders. After a long life of service, these old recruits, procured by my own father, had retreated into small villages in Semarang and Purworedje. Their half-caste descendants display the same features as my beloved children. The Hollanders, with typical humour, called them by the deprecatory nickname of Snow White.

"Does your teacher know about this?" I asked. Aquasi nodded. "And has he punished the wrongdoers?" He shook his head.

My first impulse was to go to the school, give the teacher a hiding and explain to the class about the high birth of my son. Ahim opposed the idea. Aquasi's anxious looks told me he was right. I calmed down. I went to sit under the tree again, beside my son and told him he was the descendant of a great king. It was my intention to restore his self-confidence. But he stared at the ground as if to say: So much the worse! I sent Ahim to fetch him some goodies from the kitchen. When he returned he offered them to the child with a sweeping bow, in a way he has refused to do for me for years.

"For Aquasi and Aquasi," he said, beaming, "the two princes of Ashanti . . ." I do not believe he was mocking us. I was relieved to see my son's face brighten. I told him he ought to be proud, and went on to mention various details of his ancestry.

20 March

Today I had a disconcerting encounter with Mrs. Renselaar. I was taking a stroll to the Botanical Gardens, where I had not been for several weeks. Happening to pass her house I felt obliged to make a brief social call. After the customary civilities she pressed me yet again to speak of my history. I must admit that her plea was not entirely unwelcome this time. The past haunts me. I happened to be carrying my manuscript under my arm. It was time to let someone else read my words, and in order to silence Adeline I entrusted the papers to her. She reacted like Salome to the head of John the Baptist.

Since her last visit I have had some difficulty in deciding what my attitude to her should be. The irritation she arouses in me has abated somewhat. The interest she shows in my person seems—certainly compared to her customary histrionics—almost sincere.

Late in the afternoon her husband came home: a formal man. He was most surprised to find me there. Indeed, one might even say he was shocked.

"Well now," he said nervously. "Well now, what a coincidence!"

When he heard that I had written an account of my early years for his wife to read and that I had come to deliver the manuscript to her (that was her version of events) he drew her sternly into the other room. What passed between them I do not know, but she was as white as a sheet when she returned. Soon afterwards her husband excused himself and left the house, in what struck me as unseemly haste.

I asked Adeline whether they had had words about me. At first she denied this, but after some persuasion she was more forthcoming. She explained that her husband, who is a ranking civil servant, had been appointed to some confidential post, second only to the governor. His first assignment had been to put into order the affairs left behind by his predecessor. Over the past few weeks he had covered so much ground that he was ready to dispose of the superannuated dossiers. He went through all the files, sifted out the informal chits from among the documents of consequence, after which everything that was no longer relevant to the day-to-day administration in Batavia was dispatched to the Ministry of Colonies in The Hague.

On a Friday evening some time ago he mentioned having come across a dossier that had greatly surprised him: mine. It is to be sent to Holland soon. Adeline enquired after it again a few days ago in the hope of gleaning a few anecdotes for her speech at my anniversary celebration. But he refused to discuss the subject this time. He said he had since come across material that was classified as secret. He asked her to put all thoughts of my case out of her mind.

I was perplexed, and eager to know more, but Adeline already regretted having confided in me. She said it was pointless to ask her husband for further details and made me promise not to approach him about this matter. She seemed so distressed that I gave her my word. All she knew was what her husband had told her: that the odds had been wilfully stacked against me and that I had received unjust treatment from the State of the Netherlands.

"Not much news there," I said, realizing that she was making a mountain out of a molehill again. "You can read the whole story in my papers which are now at your disposal."

"Your words are safe with me," she declared.

"I hope you will not be disappointed. It is a sad tale, but you will not find any secrets."

When I rose she apologized once more for her husband's behaviour. It seems that he too is opposed to her absurd plans for a grand celebration of my jubilee, but that has only hardened her resolve.

Aquasi went to school today as usual. He came to see me later. We did not mention what had been troubling him, but he was lively and I was reassured by his laughter. After he left I asked Ahim to order some more writing paper and a set of new pens.

22 March

I have received a message from Mrs. Renselaar. To my surprise it was brief. She was moved by my story. However, she cannot see any connection with the material that has come to light in her husband's archives, as they contain only matters pertaining to the Dutch Indies. She has been pestering Richard to say more and, in a moment of weakness (anything to keep her quiet), he has now revealed that the secret concerns the progress, or rather the lack thereof, of my career in the Indies.

If it was not the injustice done in Africa, then which injustice could it be? I force myself to think of other matters. I have enough on my mind as it is. Young Aquasi has put certain questions to me. I am now obliged to formulate the answers correctly and yet in such a way that they will not sadden him unduly. There is so much to say. The memories, once unleashed, are harder to rein in than I thought. Last night, for instance, I had the following recollection:

One day, when I was a young man, I was sitting on my usual bench in the park at Weimar, which was named "Ashanti's Höhe" in my honour. The same children played there every day, and I dandled two of them, a boy and a girl, on my knee. The little girl stroked my cheek and said: "You, black man with your white heart."

I was so moved that I was at a loss for words. Then she inspected the palm of her hand to see if some of the black had rubbed off.

Part Two

DELFT 1837–39

I

"But has the ship of state struck her last sail of decorum, sir, or is it only in my dreams that princes merit conveyance in a carriage?" The lady in the bonnet filled the front door of number 161 Oude Delft with her indignation. She did not deign to look at van Drunen during her tirade. Instead, she placed her plump hands on her knees and stooped to smile at Kwame and me.

"On foot! All the way from the barracks! Is that a token of respect for young personages of royal blood?" She hesitated whether to curtsey or to bow. Being too stout to do either, she took a step forward, bent her knee, jutted out her posterior, bowed her head and waved one arm grandly as if she were wielding an épée.

"They'll clip the Angel Gabriel's wings next and tell him to come down by ladder! Princes, I'll have you know, travel in a carriage, or they do not travel at all. And at this late hour! This cannot be a suitable time to venture outdoors, can it, my dears? But do turn them around for me, sir, so that I may see the little princes. Come on now, show them to me." Without taking her eyes off us she cried: "The princes have arrived! Mr. van Moock! Mr. van Moock! Where has he got to?"

At that moment I coughed. My throat never did get used to the Dutch climate. The lady recoiled as if stung by a wasp.

"Goodness gracious me, what do I think I'm doing? The evening air! Full of germs, diseases and unwholesomeness. Do come inside at once, please do step inside! Dear me what a darling little thing! And you there, negro princeling, what's the matter with you, are your eyes crossed?" She grasped my face and shook it

81

from side to side. "Ah no, it was just the fright of it all, you're looking much better already. Never mind, you dear little thing, I'm no
oil painting either, am I? Am I? Don't anyone contradict me!" She
spun round with a swish of her skirts and walked off, clapping her
hands to say we should follow.

"The drawing-room. Into the drawing-room with you. And
some hot chocolate at once, of course." She turned impatiently.
"But sir, why are they just standing there? Are they afraid of me or
do African princes expect to be carried on a litter? No, how silly of
me, they don't understand a word of what I'm saying!" She was
close to reaching out to touch us again, so I decided it was time to
put our lessons into practice.

"*Ja Mevrouw,*" I ventured.

"He can talk! He can talk, Mr. van Moock! Come here at once!
Princes, my good man, talking princes!"

Compared to Fort Elmina and the barracks of Hellevoetsluis,
where we disembarked in the late June of 1837 and stayed during
the summer months, the van Moock boarding school and everything in it seemed overstuffed and smothered. The air was heavy
with the smell of furniture wax, copper polish and blacking.
Every inch of wood, metal and stone was hidden under a layer
of textile: there were cloths covering the table, the settee and the
birdcage, curtains in front of doors and bookcases. Drapes smothered the windows, cushions the windowsills. The walls were lined
with orange baize. The profusion of fabrics made me long to
crawl under a comforter, but van Drunen sat us down on soft
poufs while Mrs. van Moock pattered down the corridor, letting
out cries of excitement.

"To the drawing-room, Mr. van Moock! Annie, some chocolate! And wake up the boys, all of them! We are receiving high
company in the drawing-room." She rang a bell in the hall, at
which the house came alive. Footsteps drummed on the floorboards overhead, voices rang out on the stairs and in the basement. Windows and doors flew open. A young lad popped up
from behind the fender, others came running in their nightshirts,
and very soon we were at the hub of a circle of boys. They had

been told of our arrival, yet shrank from the sight of us. Then a remarkably smart looking youth appeared on the scene: not a stain on his shirt, not a wrinkle in his jacket, shoes polished to a bright sheen. He was dark-haired and muscular, his chin already shadowed. The other boys waited in suspense for his reaction. After a brief moment he extended his hand.

"Cornelius de Groot is the name!"

We looked at his outstretched arm, not knowing quite what to do. There was some sniggering. Although we had made the acquaintance of officers, seamen and diplomats representing the Ministry of Colonies, no one had actually shaken hands with us before. Cornelius gave me an encouraging look, and signalled with his eyes that I was to take his hand. I glanced at van Drunen. Then, to end our embarrassment, Cornelius grasped our hands in turn and shook them warmly.

"On behalf of the pupils," he said pompously, "it is my privilege to welcome the princes of Ashanti to van Moock's establishment."

"I think you mean Mister van Moock!" a stern voice intoned. A gaunt figure stood in the doorway. Two boys who had been sitting down jumped to their feet. The headmaster had a long, bony face and large eyes, half hidden under enormous eyebrows, rather like the furniture under all that padding. Van Drunen made the introductions.

"Good heavens, Kwasi and Kwame . . ." said van Moock. "What extraordinary names. We ought to have been informed of this at the time of enrolment."

His wife came in with a biscuit tin, followed by a servant girl hunched over a tray laden with beakers of milk. When the girl set eyes on us she could barely stifle a cry of alarm.

"Kwasi and Kwame . . ." said van Moock, shaking his head. "No, that won't do, it won't do at all." He took two slates from the cupboard. On one he wrote, pronouncing each letter carefully in turn: A-Q-U-A-S-I, and handed it to me. On the other he wrote A-Q-U-A-M-E, slowly re-pronounced what he had written, erased the initial A and handed the slate to Kwame. Then he took a step back and savoured our new names from a distance.

His wife broke off a piece of gingerbread for us. The taste was appalling, but I smiled at her. She took our slates from us with a pleased look and returned them to her husband.

"Nobility resides in the heart, sir, not in spelling."

That night we were taken to a room on the second floor, where van Drunen bade us farewell. Over our heads were slipped long nightshirts with ties at the neck and wrists. We had separate cots on which the bedclothes were stretched taut and securely tucked in at the corners. This was to prevent rumpling. The starched sheet pressed on my throat. I was afraid I would suffocate, but told myself that everyone in this house would be sleeping thus, presumably without coming to any harm. I would not let them get the better of me. My mind was made up. I resolved to keep my body still and imagined how pleased Mrs. van Moock would be when she came to liberate us at daybreak.

"Dratted cloth all over the place!" grumbled Kwame after a while. I could hear him wrestling with his covers. He wormed himself out of his cot, came over to mine, tugged at the bedclothes and freed me. I moved over to make room for him. He lay down next to me and folded his arms under his head. As he did not speak, I thought he had fallen asleep.

Nagging doubts about Kwame's welfare had, lately, mingled with my private grief. It was hard to say where these doubts came from. He had not done anything out of the ordinary. We had both concealed our emotion for the duration of our voyage to Europe, each of us cheering the other up when we were close to tears. We never mentioned the cause of our unhappiness. But Kwame was always braver than I, which gave me a feeling of inadequacy, of giving him less support than he gave me.

I thanked the gods that we had each other. Lying in bed together I felt safe. I waited for Kwame's breathing to fall together with mine, which normally happened of its own accord. But that night his chest shuddered as it rose and fell. To find out whether he was still awake I whispered: "Cho-co-late."

"What?"

"It's just as if everything sounds better. Grander: Bonbon."

"The taste is the same, though," he replied crossly. "A-quasi, Q-uame, Chu-cu-laht . . ." He was wide awake now, and in belligerent mood.

"Bonbon," I said, tasting the sound. "Bon-bon."

"*Fufu*," he said. "That's what I'd like—*fufu*. *Fu-fu!*" This was the first time either of us had referred so directly to something from home since we left, although I myself had been thinking for weeks about the taste of roast boar in hot sauce, which our slave Kofi used to cook for us during our wakes at the sanctuary.

The mattress was so soft that we kept rolling to the middle. To overcome this I turned on my right side and lay with my knees drawn up. I made Kwame take the same position. His nightshirt got twisted around his body, and he tugged at the ties to loosen them, ripped the shirt off and flung it into a corner. I did not follow suit.

"You're keeping yours on?"

"Yes."

He shrugged. After a moment's silence he blurted: "The whole night?"

"Yes."

"And what if you have to pee?"

"No idea."

He made a show of getting out of bed.

"Since you have no idea how to pee I'm going back to my own bed."

"But I don't have to pee," I said.

"Don't you? We'll see about that." He lunged at me and started to tickle me, knowing that I could not stand it. I struggled to free myself. The bed creaked as though on the brink of collapse. He did not stop. To muffle my shrieks I pressed my mouth into the pillow.

The next morning we explored the boarding school. It looked smaller, less awesome, in the stark light of day. Our room overlooked a canal. Through the narrow window we observed the busy scene across the water, with market folk and worshippers streaming into the Old Church. Carts laden with goods were being pushed over the cobbles. Barges jostled on the canal, the skippers praising their wares at the tops of their voices.

Our room was by far the best on our floor. It was also the only room with just two cots, the others being filled with six or seven each. The maids, Bertha and Annie, slept in the garret. Bertha, who was thin and too old for heavy chores, did the dusting and helped in the kitchen. Annie was not yet eighteen, and seemed slightly retarded. She was constantly ordered about by Bertha, who kept a sharp eye on her as if she were prey for a hungry pack of boyish wolves. The first floor was out of bounds. It smelled of almonds and benzine. The private quarters of the headmaster and his wife were located there, as well as a storeroom and the room of young Master van Moock, who was away at college studying for the ministry. Down in the entrance hall were four doors. One led to the drawing-room at the front of the house, where the boys received visits from their families, although such occasions were rare. Another, likewise at the front, led to the classroom, where the lower halves of the large windows overlooking the canal were screened. The other two doors gave on to the dining room and a small library cum study. Silence had to be observed there at all times, although the floorboards creaked every bit as loudly as our bed, which made such a racket that it felt as if the slightest movement would alarm everyone in the house.

Fifteen steps led down to the basement kitchen, from which rose the smell of cloves, coffee and candy sugar. Halfway down the steps was a small door to the courtyard, which was where the boys were drilled by the headmaster. It was a very draughty place.

"This country is so windy," Kwame remarked, "that you wonder why they build all those windmills to make even more wind."

There was a washroom with two privies, only one of which was for the pupils. This gave rise to considerable irritation every morning. The other privy was less cramped, and was reserved for the van Moocks and their private visitors. Sometimes, when the door was ajar, you could see that there were actually two holes in the wooden seat, one for number twos and the other for number ones. Next to each hole was a pail of water, ready-filled. Compared with our privy, which you had to flush with a bucket that

86

you had to fill first at the pump—an arduous job in summer as in winter, and frequently skipped—the van Moock's closet was palatial, and the boys would throw envious glances inside. But however long the queue in the courtyard, no one dared use it. Neither Mr. nor Mrs. van Moock ever mentioned the penalty, but it was obvious that anyone caught trespassing would be beaten.

We entered the classroom the first morning eager to hear what we were to learn in our lessons. Van Moock greeted us civilly enough, but he wore a stern expression. He had evidently decided that it would be beneficial to our education for us to be treated in exactly the same way as the other boys. But it was too late for that. Our classmates stared at us, open-mouthed. I was accustomed to standing before a crowd at home, but this was different. Just as the previous evening, there was some sniggering. We did not know what was expected of us, and when we were motioned to our desks, we hesitated. It was only a brief moment, but I felt that the boys had closed ranks, thereby claiming respect for their superior numbers. I thought I had better acknowledge their claim and lowered my eyes, the way I was accustomed to do in the past before the council of elders and the priest at the sanctuary. From the corner of my eye I could see Kwame holding his head up defiantly.

There was an atmosphere of intimidation in the room, the kind of menace you cannot see or hear, which has no name, and which I had only experienced in nature until then. When a group of animals masses together, be it in defence or in readiness for attack, a certain equanimity comes over it, a stolidness that I desperately wished for at that moment.

Let me put it this way: the atmosphere in the classroom made me feel the way I used to as I stood on the shore of the lake of Twi. I knew about the terrors under that quiet, mirror-like surface, and yet I craved to break the tension. To jump in. I stood there, imagining what it would be like to abandon myself to the forbidden watery deep, to look up and see the ripples fanning out overhead until the surface was a mirror once more. I never dared. My fear was always greater than my craving.

I kept my eyes fixed on the floor. Van Moock, although aware of the tension in the room, did not comprehend it, and said, somewhat irritably: "Come on then, hurry up. Or are you waiting for your shadow?"

Peals of laughter. "So may I request that you open your copies of Xenophon forthwith . . ."

We slid into the twin desk that had been assigned to us and aped the other boys. We raised the lid, took out one of the books, and opened it. We had no idea.

"Well now," muttered van Moock, "never mind about the *stades* and *parasangs* covered by the army, can you tell me what happened next?" He waved his index finger in the air until he decided which boy to single out: a tow-haired lad on the other side of the aisle, who squirmed under his gaze. "Master Verheeck."

"Sir?"

"I should like to hear from you how the Persians fared."

The boy turned to the next page, then back a few pages, then forward again. He cleared his throat, hooked a finger under his collar, leaned towards his neighbour for moral support and shot us a quick glance.

"Is there something amiss or are you so moved by the words as to be unable to speak?"

Verheeck raised his eyes from the textbook in front of him and looked at us again. A grin spread across his face.

"Well sir, er, the thing is, the princes . . ."

"You mean Masters Boachi and Poku."

"They're holding their book upside-down." There was more sniggering. Van Moock rapped on his desk with a ruler.

"In that case they may not have mastered the Greek language as yet. A good opportunity," he said, "for you to be of assistance."

"But sir," said Verheeck, almost shouting to make himself heard over the buzz in the classroom, "they haven't even got out their Xenophon—they're looking at their Psalter!" Van Moock's eyebrows shot up.

"Aquasi Boachi, take your pen and write your name in your copy-book. Come along now."

I glanced around the room. The looks I was being given, scornful, triumphant, did not make me any the wiser. I flipped the pages the way I had seen Verheeck do, and heard him chuckle.

"Yes sir," I said, groaning with mortification, "yes sir, yes sir."

At that point the huge fellow sitting in front of me turned round. The class fell silent. It was the oldest boy, Cornelius de Groot. He gave me a little wink without the others noticing, took my pen from the desk, dipped it in the inkwell, wrapped my fingers around it, taking care to position my index finger properly, and opened my copy-book. I stared at him. Unseen by the others, he wrote in the air with his hand. I rested the nib of my pen on the paper and imitated his movements. For a moment it was quiet in the classroom, but then Verheeck guffawed so loudly I thought he would explode. Cornelius's reaction was swift and violent. I was startled. Reaching out from his seat he grabbed Verheeck by the scruff of the neck and twisted his collar until the little pest was red in the face.

"D'you know *their* language, then?" he hissed, and did not let go until the tow-haired lad shook his head. Van Moock gave Cornelius a token reprimand, but was unable to hide his approval. All around us the boys reluctantly bowed their heads over their books again. Cornelius's action had altered our status. We were still outsiders, but no longer unprotected. I gulped a few times from sheer relief and glanced at Kwame, shocked to see the rage in his eyes. He was gripping our seat so hard that a tremor passed through it, as though he might break it in two.

"Right, your turn Master de Groot," van Moock resumed in a sarcastic tone. "I am most eager to hear your rendering of Artaxerxes' reply."

I laid my hand on Kwame's arm so as to make him relax his grip of the bench. Years later I could still identify the marks he had scratched in the wood with his nails.

Only gradually did van Moock realize the extent of our ignorance regarding school subjects. After lessons on that first day, he summoned us to dine with him in his private quarters, forgetting that our absence at the boys' table would give rise to ill feeling. Mrs. van Moock had dressed for the occasion, and did not conceal her delight at the company of princes. Bertha, not knowing our taste in food, had prepared a meal without spices, although she had placed some savouries along the edge of our plates. She could not resist coming to the door and looking in from time to time, while Annie served the meal from the sideboard. She peered round the corner, and stood there open-mouthed until she was dismissed. Kwame tasted every dish, but in the end all he ate was mashed potato sprinkled with pepper, which reminded him of the yams we ate at home. I ate everything I was served.

Van Moock asked us to tell him about Africa, which we were not eager to do. Fortunately he interrupted us every few minutes with queries ranging from topography, history and science to chemical compounds and political, social and legal matters. I had never imagined that there could be so many questions Kwame and I would be unable to answer. The flush of excitement on van Moock's face reminded his wife of what she had found so attractive about him long ago.

"Goodness me, my dear Simon," she said warmly, "what a great and responsible task lies ahead of you! Well I never! So challenging, too!" Mr. van Moock reached out for her hand and agreed. Instead of being daunted by his great responsibility, he seemed elated. He sent for a bottle of port and raised his glass to the two rough diamonds that had come his way.

After dinner he led us to the library, where he pulled out one book after another, indicating the treasures he would soon bestow on us. His pleasure at this prospect was contagious. I was grateful for his enthusiasm, and resolved not to disappoint him. He gave us our first extra lesson that evening. With gusto.

2

Words

We had already set about learning a little Dutch before we arrived in Holland. As soon as we left the shores of Africa we had to forgo the services of an interpreter to express our wishes. Being young, we were quick to adapt to new sounds, and it was not long before we had mastered the pronunciation of the more guttural consonants of the Dutch language. It was like the twittering of birds: you don't understand what they're saying but go on talking to them regardless, and after a while you think you can make some sense of their song. In bed at night we would try imitating the sounds we had heard during the day, we practised them together and had a good laugh while we were at it, and before we knew it we could get our tongues round them quite easily.

The limited range of Dutch words and phrases we had picked up by the time we disembarked at Hellevoetsluis expanded rapidly during our stay at the barracks. We were soon able to make ourselves understood, not that our meaning always came across as intended. There are attractions to being a stranger in a new country. The newcomer can fend for himself after a fashion, but is still deaf to all the nuances, hints, inside jokes and asides. He finds himself in a sort of limbo, which makes him oblivious to verbal offence, allowing him to savour each word before he has become attuned to taste and aftertaste. The newcomer is given the benefit of the doubt, he is indulged and little is expected of him in return.

Simon van Moock did not follow a preconceived plan in the lessons he gave us. It was simply his task to pass on knowledge, of which he took a broad view. Sometimes he would stop in the middle of a mathematics lesson to discuss an item in the newspaper and place it in a wider, historical perspective. On occasion he would put off an oral test for which we had been studying hard merely because the weather was exceptionally good, and collecting sea shells on the beach was no less salutary than comprehending the use of the Aorist in Homer.

"My knowledge is like that of Montaigne," he said, sounding rather pleased with himself. "In the French manner I know a little about a lot, and a lot about little. 'The seeker of true scholarship should go out into the world and find it.'"

One of his many fields of interest was nourished by his correspondence with one Dr. Wallace Evelyn, fellow member of the Wesleyan Society in London. Dr. Evelyn had been on friendly terms with Jean-François Champollion until the latter's death in 1832, and had over the years kept van Moock abreast of the French scholar's progress in the decipherment of hieroglyphics. As the Rosetta Stone gradually disclosed its secrets, thereby rendering an ancient tongue accessible, van Moock experienced a vicarious thrill at witnessing the birth of language itself. In later years, he assiduously collected transcriptions of all subsequently discovered tablets, on which subject he went on to philosophize with Baron van Westreenen and other amateurs. He welcomed the unique opportunity to indulge his hobby by instructing Kwame and myself in the basics of grammar and script. Although our classmates showed little enthusiasm for the history of writing and the origins of the alphabet, van Moock devoted many days if not weeks to this subject in class. His efforts had little effect initially, apart from the fact that we learned to draw cranes and scarab beetles and exchanged greetings morning and night with "Hail Ptolemy, Saviour of Egypt!"

Until then our lives had been shaped by the art of memory. In the Ashanti perception, all knowledge of the arts and of the world itself is stored in the memory of each individual and in the collective memory of the people. There can be no communication among men, no interaction and no shared belief without this pool of inherited knowledge, nor indeed can there be any poem, craftsmanship, healing, or understanding of the self. The memory is exercised continually, and those blessed with a talent for cultural expression are cherished and honoured. Europeans have a different way of storing knowledge. Van Moock's explanation was that the list of great deeds and achievements had grown so long over the centuries that people had taken to writing them down many ages ago.

He gave a resounding exposé of how the twenty-six letters of the alphabet, already in use for over two and a half thousand years, enabled every word or conceit, regardless of the language it arose from, to be recorded and reproduced. He claimed that man owed his rise from savagery into a civilized state exclusively to the invention of writing. However, when Kwame asked how all this reflected on us, his tone became less strident.

Van Moock never wavered in his conviction that the ability to write was infinitely more valuable than the ability to remember. He set great store by the possibility of putting one's thoughts on paper so that the sheet might be folded and sent by post to be read on the other side of the world. But Kwame insisted that knowledge can only be kept alive inside the man, the particular form in which it is preserved varying from one man to the next. Keeping words on paper holds them captive, separate from the man so that they become distanced from the lifeblood of the people. Once a story has been written down it is lifeless. Besides, said Kwame, it is easier for a man than for a piece of paper to travel the world. In the end the only advantage of the written message over the human messenger is that the former allows itself to be folded in two or four.

Kwame's protestations were short-lived. We practised writing our names.

"But my name doesn't look like me at all," Kwame said, much to everyone's amusement. "Where are my arms and legs?"

Kwame and I were taken aback by the speed with which an abstract concept could be translated into words. The shock of putting down our thoughts and dreams on paper gave rise to a certain unease, as if our most private feelings were suddenly exposed for all the world to see.

I remember a distinct turning-point. I was strolling down an alley in the town—I can still picture it clearly—when a pigeon landed at my feet. I have always felt a special bond with that species, for we had pigeons in Kumasi, too, although they were of a less grey variety. I had some lumps of candy-sugar in my pocket, so I crouched down and offered them to the bird. Suddenly I was bowled over by the realization that this bird had a totally different name in the Twi language, and yet both words denoted the *same creature*. I was dumbfounded. It sounds absurd, I know, but I actually had to steady myself against the wall before I was composed enough to take in what this signified. The pigeon was so alarmed that it refused to be fed any more tidbits.

It was not that I had believed, previously, that each particular sound represented a particular object—of course not—it was just that I had never thought about these things. But the sudden understanding that this bird could be named and identified no less satisfactorily in my new language filled me with a double-edged emotion. On the one hand it signified the loss of yet another bond with Kumasi, on the other I was thrilled by my growing vocabulary. I decided to apply myself to learning all I could of my new language.

In the same period of transition Kwame experienced a different, albeit related moment of discovery. Although this event, too, may seem inconsequential to an outsider, his shock was greater and more harrowing than mine. This is what happened. In due course Kwame had to acknowledge that, while the singers of Kumasi memorized their heroic epics in verse form so that they might summon them at will, a valuable alternative would be to record the events in writing for posterity, given that the history had grown too lengthy to be entrusted to the memory of a few men. One afternoon, when van Moock with his usual enthusiasm instructed us to take out our copies of the Anabasis, he waxed quite lyrical on the subject of Artaxerxes' written exhortation to his mercenaries to launch an attack on his brother's army. Van Moock gave an impassioned account of the ensuing battle during which countless lives were lost, illustrating his words by groaning dramatically and clasping his chest as he received a deadly thrust from an imaginary javelin. Kwame's agitation at this passage was hard to comprehend. He felt ill, left the classroom and, although he was told to stay in bed for the rest of the day, he apparently ran all the way out of town and spent the next few hours rushing around the meadows, to the stupefaction of the farmers. It was not the command to kill that distressed him, for such orders can be given by word of mouth equally well—it was that such a decision could be put in writing, thereby making it immutable, incontrovertible. Once dispatched, the command distances itself from the commander, who in turn distances himself from the dire consequences of his words. His victims do not die by his hand, nor by his direct will, but by means of lifeless signs on a piece of paper. To Kwame, this simple fact gave a haunting sense of cruelty to the words he was learning to write. He realized that it was not only possible to record the past and the present, but also to anticipate such deeds as would be done in the future. So the letters of the alphabet were fraught with danger. However, it was not long before we were so proficient at writing that we took it entirely for granted and Kwame forgot his misgivings.

Kwame's revelation, which might strike some as negligible, risible even, was a flash of insight that lasted no longer than my own experience with the pigeon in the alley, and the effect was the same for both of us: we resolved to master our new language as perfectly as possible. What I enjoyed most was being able to read about things the others knew already. As for Kwame, he was driven by the desire to make the words bend to his will.

After a while, all the attention that was lavished on us started to irritate the other boys. It was not long before Karel Verheeck declared quite openly that the reason we were behind in our lessons was that we were savages. He even read out an essay he had written on the theme: "In the beginning was the Word, and the word was God." He launched into a hardly inspiring enumeration of all the peoples, even the most backward ones, as he put it, that had devised ways of writing that word. Cadmus taught the alphabet to the Phoenicians, the Ten Commandments were penned by Jehovah himself, and Brahma copied the holy Vedas on to a leaf of gold for the benefit of the Hindus. Ogmios, the Gallic Hermes, gave the Irish the skill of writing, as Odin had given the runes to the northern tribes. Nebo passed his inscriptions on to the Assyrians, and Thoth to the Egyptians (at this point in his discourse the boy threw van Moock a solemn look). But also the amulets of Abyssinia and the prayer wheels of Nepal, he went on, and even the carved skirts of the priestesses of the Little Death expressed the secret sign for God, while unlettered mountain folk wore little leather pouches round their necks containing scraps from the Koran inscribed with that name. The illiterate men of Palermo wore the name of the Madonna carved on their chests, and even in the backwaters of Holland there were those who sought to cure the sick by fanning them with the pages of the Book of Psalms. That we, princes of Ashanti, had been deprived of the ability to write the name of God spoke volumes about the backwardness of our people.

Of course this was not true. We had our symbols just the same, but the dreadful thing was—and my anguish was too great for me ever to admit this to Kwame or anyone else—that I believed Verheeck.

Much later, when we were in our last year with the van Moocks, by which time Kwame had learned to study independently, it was his turn to read out his essay in class. He gave a brilliant exposé of the use of signs among primitive peoples, and set out to show that they were not inferior to the letters of the alphabet. His final proof, he read triumphantly, lay "in the practice of the West African Ardah to tie knots in thin cords: a skill of such sophistication as to make each knotted strand tell a story. As with the common alphabet, the message is in a code that is understood in the same way by sender and receiver."

He also reminded us of the power of memory, which he still held in higher esteem than the written word. (Here he was making a mistake, of course, for he owed his entire argument to his ability to consult books in his search for evidence!) He quoted Thomas Aquinas, who apparently took memory to be one of the four most important virtues. The churches of Europe, Kwame concluded, were covered in ideographs (not in words, like mosques): "The invention of the alphabet did not deter painters and sculptors in their quest for a means of depiction that would evoke the universe in a single image. The written word was evidently not considered adequate to express the might of God and nature. Even in God's own house His word calls forth enhancement in painted allegories, images that appeal to a shared knowledge. For the path of virtue is not determined exclusively by the Holy Scriptures, but also by past misdeeds, both individual and collective, whose memory is transmitted from one generation to the next in the form of an innate sense of good and evil."

Verheeck had already left school by this time, more's the pity. By this time, too, Kwame and I were drifting apart, and I was too alienated from his way of thinking to hear the anger in his heartfelt discourse. What I remember most clearly is his relief at having successfully risen to this challenge: he was as cheerful and lively as he had been in the old days at Kumasi. A few weeks later, though, his moodiness returned. It was around the same time that we realized our African heritage was steadily being eroded by our new language. We found we had forgotten most of our Twi.

goat, soap, dog, wood, rose,
wheel, cock, beech, dove, shed

We were quick to learn. We snapped up everything that came our way, indiscriminately, but to exemplary effect. To van Moock's profound satisfaction, we caught up with the others in a few months. He boasted about our progress to his friends at the Wesleyan Society. It happened sometimes that after he had dispatched a letter to London in the morning he was so impressed by our afternoon's achievements that he would dash off a second epistle after class—sometimes followed by a postscript—and send the maid with it to the postmaster so that it might catch the same mail coach. His pride gratified me immensely, but Kwame found it annoying. While I rejoiced in showing off how much I had learned, Kwame would answer questions briefly, woodenly, almost reluctantly. He did not enjoy being praised for his effort. He never volunteered to reveal all he knew about a subject, whereas when we tested each other in our room he was at least as quick and clever as I. He actually seemed to take offence at van Moock's amazement and admiration. I, on the other hand, was eager for compliments, and made sure always to have a little surprise in store for my master. It was better to be commended for each nugget of acquired knowledge, I thought, than for the whole treasure at once.

It was not that I was vain—quite to the contrary. I needed acknowledgment as I needed my daily bread. I was obsessed with the idea that the other boys knew things I knew nothing about, and my fear of exposure gave me nightmares. Each night I would be alone and blindfolded, on enemy ground. I knew I would have to arm myself as sturdily as possible before the inevitable battle would begin. Each snippet of knowledge from which I was excluded turned into a faceless evil spirit. Tens of thousands of these spirits rose up before me, and I struggled hard to get rid of as many as I could, only to find their ranks replenished with new ones from day to day. The need to conquer these enemies was all-consuming, and I had to summon all my strength to unmask them, after which I gave them names and places, and befriended them.

Van Moock made it quite clear that we were doing very well in all subjects. As he kept repeating this I was inclined to believe him. Still, I was constantly aware of the danger of a sudden hiatus that could strike at any time during a conversation; there would be a faltering of the voice followed by a complete blank, and all eyes would be fixed on me. For a long time I was plagued by this fear, and it made me shy. Later on in life I overcame my timidity, but the fear of exposure never went away. It is still with me. Day in day out.

We did not get on quite as well outside the classroom. The boys seldom addressed us in a casual, friendly manner. They tended to club together, forming a silent, forbidding front. Time and again we had no choice but to stand up for ourselves. During dinner, for instance. Each day we would find our plates laid a little further down the long wooden table, until one afternoon we were obliged to sit at the very end, where there was a permanent draught. We took our plates, squared our shoulders, and made for the head of the table where we squeezed in among the other boys. They made room for us grudgingly and pretended not to notice our presence. The next day we arrived in the dining room to find our pewter plates arranged on an old chest by the door. Everyone stared at us. I sat down, but Kwame pulled me to my feet again. He swept his plate from the chest. I did not dare follow suit, and motioned for him to put it back. There was some stifled giggling. I prayed desperately for them all to start eating, but no one did. I did not dare look, but in the end I heard someone getting to his feet. It was Cornelius. He took up his plate from the table, strode to the chest and sank down on the floor beside it. Two other boys followed his example, and then a third, until the six of us were sitting in a small circle by the door. From that day on we were at liberty to sit wherever we liked.

One hundred B.C.: arrival of the Batavian tribe.

Each day started with drill in the courtyard at six-thirty, unless van Moock took us for a walk or swim. Now and then, when he was angling for a financial grant or other privilege from the local council, he would order us to sweep the market square, or else the street in front of some dignitary's house. There was a strict pecking order among the band of pupils during these exertions. The older, bigger boys, Cornelius, Verheeck, van Woensel and Termeeren, shirked their duties whenever they could. They had no qualms about letting the others do their work for them, and would even make the youngest boys like Mus, van Wersch and Tonnie Voorst take their places three times out of four. Sometimes, when we were exercising in the open air, the older boys would vanish altogether, without van Moock flying into a rage. I used to think he did not notice. Now I can see that their absence came as a relief to him after the constant exertion of discipline.

To be honest, the unfairness did not bother me at first as much as Kwame. We were both afraid of the leaders, but I could not help admiring their boldness, in which I was sorely lacking. And though I would have died rather than disobey van Moock, I fantasized secretly that I was one of them, that they would suffer me to swim in the lake in their company, after which we would all clamber, dripping, on to the bank together, and that we would run off into the fields with our bare bottoms, scaring the daylights out of the farm girls.

Of course the leader is just as separate from the group as the outcast, each being on the fringe, albeit at opposite ends. They are two sides of the same coin, and this lonely recognition draws them to each other as much as it keeps them apart. It enables them to see the masses for what they are, to put a face to the crowd. In that respect I have always recognized a hint of myself in Cornelius.

> *Even though I am only a boy,*
> *Holland is my greatest joy,*
> *My kind masters give me food and drink*
> *They teach me to cipher and to think.*
> *I vow that once I am a man,*
> *I will serve my land as best I can.*

The other boys were allowed to leave the premises every Wednesday and Saturday afternoon, and sometimes also on Sunday morning after church and Bible reading. We were allowed to accompany them on these unsupervised outings, but we had no wish to. The first months we watched the others go, but the idea of following them did not occur to us. We had begun to feel at home in the school building, and the world we saw from the windows looked bleak, angular and stony. We simply did not see the town with its streets and squares as a place where games could be played the way we used to play in the forest at home. So we saw no reason to venture outside the grounds, until Mrs. van Moock turned up in the classroom one day when Kwame and I were having an extra lesson while the other boys had the afternoon off. She addressed her husband sternly, saying: "Simon, here is some money and I declare there is more to learning than books, and so, and so"—she rushed forward and pressed some coins into our palms—"and so, what I mean is I want you boys to buy me two loaves, and a bag of sweets as well—and don't you try to stop them, sir, for my mind is made up."

Van Moock slammed shut his copy of the *Metamorphoses*, from which he had been reading to us. "Now boys, you heard Mrs. van Moock: two loaves and a bag of sweets. Off you go." Mrs. van Moock held the door open for us. As we went past she handed us our caps and scarves, then lingered on the doorstep until her husband bundled her inside. "My dear Mrs. van Moock, that was a very good deed you just did," he said, whereupon he shut the front door.

The autumn of 1837 had given way, without any warning, to a cold spell such as we had never experienced before. You would have thought the Dutch were weaklings the way everyone complained bitterly about the sudden change in the weather. I myself quite liked the cold. It made the skin on my face tingle and feel taut. In Holland even the wind reminds you of the nature of your skin.

People preferred to stay indoors during winter. They peered out from behind their curtains. An inquisitive face appeared at the window of a house across the canal. Further down, a sweeper brushed some rubbish into the water to join the rest of the market debris on its way to the sluice. We were standing by the front door, and would have been quite happy to stay there for some time had not a carriage come thundering past, making us jump out of the way. The coachman swore at us. This did not upset me, because he would have sworn at anyone under the circumstances. I took Kwame's hand.

It made no difference whether people pointed and stared or made an effort to dissemble their surprise—the one reaction was no less noticeable than the other. A lady and a gentleman whose path we crossed stopped in their tracks, nudged each other and stared at us open-mouthed until we had passed by. Then they turned round and followed us, at a little distance so as not to attract attention. If we took five steps they took five steps too, if we paused, so did they. Kwame and I exchanged a look of complicity: we would lead the couple a dance. We crossed the street quickly and recrossed it several times, dawdled a little way, then raced ahead again, until we ducked into an alley to spy on our shadows as they came hurrying past, pretending they were taking a perfectly normal everyday stroll.

At the other end of the alley we found ourselves in a neighbourhood with dwellings made of wattle and daub and with straw roofs. There were children running about on the unpaved sandy ground, and they were barefoot in spite of the cold. A knot of women huddled around a fire, on which they were boiling a pot of cabbage leaves. They offered us a taste. Kwame declined, but I took a sip from the ladle and when I raised my eyes I saw that Kwame had taken off his shoes and stockings and was racing around in the sand. I tried to calm him down, but he was so excited he did not even hear me.

I walked away, leaving him behind. He soon caught up with me, but when we turned into a street paved with cobbles his shoes were still dangling from his hand, and I hissed that he should put them on at once. It was not the cold that I was worried about.

We went into a small bakery. Our presence was attracting rather a lot of attention from passers-by, who followed us inside and made a purchase simply to get a closer look. The baker was pleased with the extra custom, and gave us each some goodies with the request to stay around for a while. Kwame was unwilling, but I was glad to do the man a favour . . . Well, at any rate I did not want to offend him. I sent Kwame home with the loaves for Mrs. van Moock.

When I finally went out into the street again with a gift of two steaming apple fritters, I was loath to surrender my new-found freedom, and instead of going straight home I clambered up the old rampart behind the bakery and decided to take a stroll around the town. From my elevated position I had a view of the layout of the streets and also of the countryside on the other side.

The first thing people tend to do when they claim a piece of land is mark it off with straight lines, as if to cross out the work of nature itself. The flat grassland of Holland offers no such solace.

I recognized the road our carriage must have taken when we arrived in Delft. I could see several roads converging on the town from different directions, and I wondered which one we would take when we left again. All those roads, where did they go? I shut my eyes and spun round a few times until I felt dizzy. Then I opened them wide, taking my time to let the entire panorama sink in. I spotted a windmill, which I knew from an engraving in the school corridor. There was a scattering of farms, with workers in the fields and low dunes in the distance. Close by I could see the rectangular meadows and the little boathouse in the bend of the River Schie, where van Moock had taken us swimming in the summer . . .

A violent thud on my back left me gasping for breath. When I came to, the first thing I noticed was the freezing cold air pouring into my lungs. It smelled of grass. I prolonged this moment, as if I knew that from now on nothing would ever be the same. I stared ahead, insensible to the danger threatening from behind. Verheeck jumped on to my back and held me fast. He had two accomplices, Gerrit Toorenaar and Kobus Mus, the smallest and dullest boys in the school. They twisted my arms on to my back. Verheeck stood in front of me, legs apart and hands clasped behind him, a pose no doubt inspired by the framed print in our classroom showing the defeat of Vercingetorix. He was playing Julius Caesar, rising on his toes and throwing his head back so as to observe the loser from a suitable height.

"From now on," growled Verheeck, "from now on, every time I ask: What are you? you must say: I'm a dirty nigger! Got it?" He gave me a taste of what would happen if I disobeyed by kicking me in the groin before I had a chance to say a word.

"So tell me now, what are you?" His tone was icy and unhurried. He waited patiently for me to get my breath back.

"A nig-ger," I said, bewildered. Next I was punched on the chin.

"Wrong!" Verheeck said. "So you're dumb too. All right then: a dumb dirty nigger. Tell me: what are you?"

"A dirty nigger."

He struck me.

"And dumb too, dumb too!"

"I am a dumb dirty nigger."

"Sir!"

"Sir," I echoed, whereupon Verheeck's minions let me go at last. I expected them to fall about laughing after my humiliation, the way they did when someone made a fool of himself in class, but they were silent. They wore stern, adult expressions. This was not a game. The incident was just as momentous to them as it was to me. They had accomplished their mission and were satisfied that everyone had acted according to plan. I, too, felt strangely calm as I walked home. I went up the stairs to my room and sat down on my bed. Only then did I feel the leaden weight of what had happened. I trembled with exhaustion. I felt more tired than ever before, and could not bring myself even to lie down. I sat like that, transfixed, for an hour, perhaps longer. I said the words over and over again under my breath, so that Verheeck would never have cause to attack me again: "I'm a dumb dirty nigger. I'm a dumb dirty nigger."

Mon chou, mon bijou, mettez vos joujoux sur mes genoux
et prenez des cailloux pour chasser les hiboux.

I awoke to find that the spirit of rebellion within me had collapsed under its own weight. Taming an animal means that it learns to hide its anger. It slows down, its step becomes heavier. I could feel my resistance trickling down through my pores into my inner being, where I could keep it and nourish it without running undue risks. I got out of bed and went down to breakfast as I did every day, conscious of a new threat to be dealt with. The rest of the day I did my best to look unmoved. Still, there must have been something unusual about my expression, for van Moock forgave me a stupid mistake in a division sum, and afterwards his wife insisted on reciting a little poem to me. Even Bertha the maid slipped me two toffees after supper, so I feared they all knew how I had been humiliated, although that was not likely.

That evening I went straight upstairs after supper. When Kwame came up a little later I pretended to be asleep. He was not taken in and demanded to know why I was acting so strangely. At first I refused to talk, and when he pressed me I told him I was missing my mother. He believed me. He sat on the bed and put his arm around me. We listened to the noises of the school as it settled down for the night, the church clock striking the hours and the dying sounds of drunken revellers crossing the bridge. It was quiet for a while. Then Kwame began to sing, and I do not know whether he was doing it for my benefit or whether he thought I was already asleep. Perhaps he was singing just for the sake of memory. In a low hoarse voice he sang of Spider Anansi's web, but lost track of the words in the second verse. It was some time before he got under the covers and curled himself around me.

I was wearing one of the nightshirts that had lain unused in the wardrobe since our first night in Delft. Kwame held his breath. He ran his fingertips over the fabric briefly, then rolled over on to his back with an angry sigh. I had fastened the drawstrings tightly around my neck and my wrists, in a desperate attempt to cover up my shame and so keep it to myself.

The next time Verheeck set eyes on me he knew he had been successful in asserting his superiority. It only made him more cruel. I recited the magic words dutifully, after which he left me alone, and I even felt grateful for having been told the words that would set me free. I thought long and hard about what they meant. Having been surrounded by white faces for the past year, I was well aware that I was different and a Negro. But why dumb? and why dirty? I was neither. I knew that for a fact. And yet I repeated the words in my head all day long, over and over until I was sure I had them on the tip of my tongue in case of an emergency. And there were emergencies three or four times a week. You would think the boys would grow bored soon enough, but the taunts became such a routine occurrence that they must have been addictive. Saying the magic words was usually enough, but not always. Sometimes my tormentors decided I had not been quick enough to respond, or that I did not look solemn enough, or spoke too softly, or showed too little respect. As they were not sure whether bruises showed up on my skin, they would aim their blows on the small of my back and thighs to be on the safe side, for they could rely on my keeping that part of my body clothed in front of van Moock.

People adapt themselves to circumstances. That is the trump card prized by despots and oppressors. Their victims bend so as not to break. Adjustment is a matter of survival. The minority toes the line drawn by the majority. And while your view of the world hardens, you discover that your pride is soft and malleable, like the skull of a newborn baby. You can actually divide yourself up into separate beings: one part of you lives in fear and shame, while the other half functions as if nothing is the matter. As simple as that.

In spite of everything I was determined to continue my exploration of the town. At first I tried to persuade Kwame to come with me, but he was not interested. So I set out on my long walks alone, along the canals and past all the workshops and stores. People were friendly. They shook hands with me and asked me to step into their shops. They offered me sweetmeats so as to prolong my stay until word got about and customers poured in. I knew their motives were mercenary, but I did not mind for it gave me the opportunity to talk with all sorts of people. I learned a lot of new words, found out about prices and profit-making, how to keep accounts in a ledger, and observed the craftsmen and their tools. I watched the people at work and seized every opportunity to discover more details of the Dutch way of life and the character of the Hollanders. My curiosity knew no bounds. I was obsessed by the desire to understand exactly what it was that made us so different from the townspeople of Delft that there was always someone staring at us in wonder. I wanted to remove the sense of wonder, and for that I would have to become a familiar face in every street in the town. Verheeck could not stop me. The ever-present fear of meeting him made my excursions all the more adventurous, I thought, and the fact that I could always say the magic words if the need arose gave me a feeling, however misplaced, of power. I imagined that this strange land offered a range of different magic formulas, which enabled me both to extricate myself from awkward situations and to win affection. I was interested in the whole range.

can, will, may, must, shall, might

Such was the mood of the autumn and early winter months. Whenever I crossed Verheeck and his cronies I did what was demanded of me and left it at that.

I became resigned to the boys' behaviour and would not have thought of making a fuss if Bertha had not taken it into her head one day that the boys could do with an extra strong broth in winter. She went to market and bought a sackful of fish heads, for which she drove a hard bargain, as well as a pound of sole for the van Moocks, who refused to eat all but the very best quality fish. Thanks to a generous sprinkling of bread crusts, condiments and parsley the brew did not taste bad at all. That same night, however, the school was in an uproar. I stumbled down the stairs pressing my fists against my belly only to find that there was already a queue of boys in the courtyard waiting to use the privy. Panic-stricken, I tried to control my bowels by sitting down on the frozen ground, but this did not help at all. I cringed and squirmed and was about to sink to my haunches there and then to alleviate myself in full view of everyone—which would not have embarrassed me in the least in the old days—but my dread of being tormented for my lack of control stopped me. A stab of pain made me do the thing that was as obvious as it was unthinkable: I made for the van Moock's private closet, slammed the door behind me and sank down in relief. But that was not the end of it. My bowels were in a dreadful turmoil, and I could not run out again as quickly as I had anticipated, so I sat there doubled up with pain, giddily picturing Mrs. van Moock in nightcap and curlers and how she would shriek when she discovered my lifeless body in the morning. Then the door flew open and I found myself staring at a face so horribly contorted that the end of the world seemed nigh. Then I saw that it was Cornelius.

"Dammit Boachi, hurry up man—come off it this instant!" he groaned, but I could not possibly do as he said.

"Come and sit here," I said, pointing to the second hole in the mahogany seat, intended for passing water.

"Next to you?" he spluttered, and for a moment his astonishment seemed to make him forget his anguish. "How do you mean?"

"You know, here, next to me," I said, at which point I was convulsed by a fresh cramp. Although I felt quite faint, I could still make out the rasp in de Groot's breathing. He slipped inside, bolted the door, sat down next to me and did his business. We stayed there for a long time, perhaps half an hour or more, without speaking. I could hardly believe my ears when I caught the sound of quiet sobbing. I glanced sideways and in the weak lamplight coming in over the door I saw Cornelius wiping his cheeks with his sleeve. He was crying.

Until now Cornelius had been the only boy I dared to address. He had stood up for me on two occasions, so it was natural for me to feel drawn to him. However, he always seemed surprised when someone talked to him, whether it was me or anyone else. He did not seem to like being spoken to, and always reacted gruffly. I rather looked up to him, but Kwame accused me of grovelling, although he could not help feeling some sympathy for him too. Besides, he was the only boy in whose presence Kwame and I felt free to exchange some words in Twi. I would greet Cornelius whenever I crossed him in the corridor, and if he dropped his pen I would pick it up for him. He would grunt in response. That was as close as we got. It was close enough.

So there I was, sitting in his stench, and he in mine. Good spirits, my mother used to say, smell of dung, not flowers, the better to draw attention.

"Are you crying?" I asked, whereupon Cornelius let out a yelp of outrage.

"Are you mad?" he said, sniffing loudly. There was a moment's silence.

"Well, you could be, couldn't you?" I burst out. I was as piqued as he was.

"Never!" He swore as his body was racked by a spasm, but although his intestines rumbled so alarmingly that the boys waiting outside made rude remarks, I don't think it had the desired effect. He wiped the sweat off his forehead.

"Haven't done for years," he said in a confidential tone. The intimacy of the moment left us both paralysed, and neither of us dared to break the silence.

Finally he got up, as suddenly as he had sat down. "Take my advice," he said, cleaning himself with a dash of ice-cold water from the pitcher. "Once an outsider always an outsider. Hard luck. You'll never be one of the boys. But once people are scared they're all the same. You must fight. You must be stronger than they are. That's the only hope we have of gaining respect." He shut the door behind him and reopened it two seconds later. "If you like, I'll teach you about that some time. I'm good at it."

The next morning we all had to stand to attention and were not allowed to have breakfast until the boys responsible for the filth in the private closet owned up. I was reluctant to step forward, and could feel Cornelius's eyes burning on me. Since he was one of the culprits, no one dared to point in our direction, not even when a number of boys, including Verheeck, were singled out to clean up the mess.

When things were back to normal Cornelius took me aside. "You were a damned good sport," he spluttered, and his voice turned gruff as he added, "you know, about last night." He seemed to regret having raised the subject.

"Well, who'd have done the same for me, eh? Kept me company like that." He plunged his hands in his pockets and walked off. After a few steps he turned round and said, without meeting my eyes, "If they bully you, let me know." It sounded more like an order than an offer of help.

I did not doubt that he would take my side against Verheeck any time I wanted. I could have told him everything right there, and the taunting would be over. I said nothing, and was persuaded that my position had improved considerably. I gauged my chances and took careful stock of the situation.

The very next time Verheeck and his cronies bore down on me, which happened two days later, I braced myself. I took too long to utter the required words, and Mus starting cracking his knuckles and clenching the fist of one hand in the palm of the other.

"I'm a dumb dirty nigger," I blurted, and my tormentors let me go with a look of regret. "But . . ." I said. I was so anxious that my voice would falter that I ended up almost shouting: ". . . but this has got to stop."

"Really?" Verheeck said coolly. Toorenaar chuckled.

"Yes," I went on, lowering my voice. "Because if Cornelius hears of this you'll be the ones getting a beating."

"And who do you suppose would tell him?"

"Not you by any chance?" scoffed Mus, and he rose on tiptoe so his face would be level with mine.

"I'm not saying anything yet," I said, tipping my head back slightly like Caesar. "Not yet."

Mus looked at Toorenaar, who in turn was staring at Verheeck. Their silence gave me the courage to go on.

"It should never have happened," I said. "It is wrong. But now things have changed. First it was my shame, now it is yours. If you ever do it again I shall tell him everything."

"You do that," grinned Verheeck. "You do that, then he'll know what a tell-tale you are." And he punched me harder than he had ever done before.

Now I had evidence. Torn clothes. Cuts and grazes. Injuries I could show. There was even some blood in my urine. I staggered home and heaved myself upstairs. Boys on their way to a ball game in the courtyard stormed down the stairs as I went up. Upon reaching the landing on the first floor I bumped into Cornelius. He was in a hurry to catch up with the other boys, and I was in his way.

"What's the matter?" he asked. I opened my mouth to tell him but my words were stifled by sobs.

"Now now, my friend. Tell me what is the matter," he said sternly, putting his hand on my shoulder. He was not given to smiling on the best of days, but this time his lips curled encouragingly at the corners. His hand on my shoulder! Cornelius was treating me as no other white man had ever treated me before. He had called me his friend. He considered me his equal. At least that was how it seemed to me—he deemed me worthy of his friendship!

Suddenly it was unthinkable that I should tell Cornelius the truth about my humiliation. He would be so disappointed in me! *I am a dumb dirty nigger!* The words meant nothing when I was taunted with them, but had I not spoken them myself? I had learnt them by heart; they were on the tip of my tongue. Now that I was fluent in Dutch and had learnt a little French, German and English, I began to comprehend the potency of language. My mindless repetition of those lies had made them true, and they had made me feel ashamed of myself. How could I ever say those words again without forfeiting the last grains of respect? Of course they were just words, but I was terrified that Cornelius, too, would believe them, just as I had myself. That he and everyone else would see me for what I evidently was. That would mean Verheeck had got the better of me. The words would have won.

I stepped aside, shook my head and started climbing the next flight as steadily as I could. He merely shrugged his shoulders. Behind me I could hear the clatter of his footsteps as he plunged down the wooden staircase on his way to the courtyard to join the other boys.

Batavia, Buitenzorg, Sukabumi, Bandung, Garut, Semarang, Surabaja, Madiun

I did not come to my senses until spring. I must have been blind. One morning when I got up Kwame stayed in bed, which was unusual. Most days he was awake before I was; he would jump out of bed and wake me up. This time I washed and put on my clothes alone. Then I opened the shutters, but he was still lying there motionless. I asked him how he felt, but there was no reply. I pounced on his legs and tickled the soles of his feet, the way we did for fun sometimes. He drew them up. I bounced on the bed, trying to reach the beams in the ceiling. He did not react. I dropped down beside him, flung open the covers and was about to grab his shoulders to give him a good shake when I recoiled in shock. There were blisters on his arms—burns! Two of them were moist and ragged, a third one was still inflated. The surrounding skin was puckered, black and scabby. I had seen this before. I had the scars of the same kind of burns on my ankle, and some more on my right arm. I curled up in grief and rolled off the bed. I cursed myself and sobbed, banging my head against the bedposts. Kwame's eyes were wide open the whole time. Unable to bring himself to look at me, he stared blankly at the wall.

What fired my spirit at last was his look of utter defeat. I was flooded with a great rage. I stormed down the corridor to the boys' dormitory, where Cornelius was just getting out of bed.

"This afternoon," I said, turning on my heel, and although it was a long time since he had made his offer he knew at once what I meant. I went down to Bertha in the kitchen to fetch some warm water, clean cloths and a spoonful of butter to clean and treat Kwame's wounds. I knew from personal experience that this would make him feel better. I applied a poultice with cold water from the pitcher but he still refused to meet my eyes. When I was done I hugged him, but could not help feeling that something was wrong. Never had we needed words, but now that they could have helped we could not find them. It was as though the shameful silence we had both observed far too long had wedged itself between us, keeping us apart. I drew up the covers and left Kwame in bed. I ran down to tell van Moock he was ill, came back upstairs again and flung open the door to the second dormitory. I was after Verheeck, but he was already downstairs, so I opened the locker by his bed and turned it upside down. I did not find what I was looking for. Then I ripped open the ticking of his mattress and plunged my hands into the straw. In the stuffing I found the remainder of a cigar, short and thick, just like the one he had used to brand Kwame and me. I took it with me to the dining room and deposited it in Verheeck's bowl of porridge. His companions held their breath. He kept his head down over his breakfast and fished out the soggy brown mess with great concentration. Then he paused, as if unable to make up his mind whether to take another spoonful or not. He took his time considering the options, while his shoulders twitched as if with stifled laughter. Finally he leaped to his feet and lunged at my throat. Chairs were knocked over as we wrestled and rolled over the floor. That morning he was stronger than I. I was obliged to give up because my eye was flooded with blood, but the tide had turned and his defeat had set in.

Later in the day, Cornelius gave me my first boxing lesson, and it was clear to everyone what this was for. I practised day in day out: punching sandbags, tree trunks and even Mrs. van Moock's petticoat, which Cornelius had stolen off the washing line and stuffed with a cushion, and which he aimed at my head at the oddest moments to keep me alert. Once I had had enough practice, I stood my ground during the six assaults by my tormentors that followed, and when I braced myself for the seventh encounter Verheeck spat on the ground at my feet and all three of them turned away, as if they had lost interest.

Tell me, Muse, of a man weary of his lengthy travels and far from home . . .

I kept up my sparring sessions with Cornelius all through the summer. My body grew stronger. It was fun developing my muscles for such an obvious purpose. I tried persuading Kwame to join in, but to no avail. I kept a wary eye on Verheeck at all times, but from then on neither Kwame nor I suffered harassment.

Six months later we had still not breathed a word to each other about the humiliations we had endured, nor indeed about my antidote. Then one night when Kwame was tossing and turning, unable to sleep, I asked him what was the matter.

"It's the boxing," he said, as if that were an answer.

"What about it?"

"It's stupid."

That was all. I said nothing, but was filled with childish rage at my cousin's obstinate refusal to acknowledge my effort, let alone to show any gratitude. He dropped off to sleep eventually, but I was so infuriated by his indifference that I had to shake him awake to make him listen.

"At least it has helped us!"

"Don't be silly, Kwasi," he said wearily.

"At least we belong now, sort of." I punched him, but he did not seem to mind. He clasped my wrists, tightly at first so that I could not wrench myself free, then gently and warmly so that I did not want him to release his hold.

"They put up with us, and that is not the same."

3

"I come from a large family, and we were by no means wealthy— and there is nothing wrong with that, I'd have you know—but when we had visitors, they would be offered some refreshment!"

Mrs. van Moock wore a frock of green silk which crackled like a bunch of dry twigs. She swept to and fro through the salon. Her nerves were playing up after spending the entire morning fussing over our outfits. The announcement that the carriage from the Ministry of Colonies had come for us had sent her upstairs in a panic. She had come down wearing this frock, which was too tight for travelling. Twice during the ride she ordered the coachman to stop, and then again when we passed a sluice-keeper's dwelling, because she needed to relieve herself.

"Having to wait all this time, how distressing. After all we have not come on our own behalf, we are merely complying with a royal summons. Surely a small tray of *petits fours* would have been appropriate under the circumstances." Taking each of my hands in turn, she smoothed down my splayed fingers one after another to make the gloves fit snugly. Then she did the same for Kwame, straightened our caps and instructed us to hold our little silk parasols loosely in our hands. She had spent our entire clothing allowance, which the Dutch government provided twice yearly, on fitting us out for the occasion.

"So that your father, Aquasi, when he receives your portrait, will say: Look how well the headmaster's wife has taken care of my beloved sons!"

The artist lived in a canalside mansion in The Hague. The room in which we were kept waiting for more than an hour was his studio. There were wax models and two plaster torsos. To Mrs. van Moock's horror there was also a human skeleton, which was wired up to allow it to strike a variety of poses. The walls were lined with glass cabinets containing sea shells and geological specimens. There were also natural history exhibits, and several glass jars containing fleshy insects and small rodents floating in preserving fluid, including some exotic ones which we recognized from home. Kwame stared at the small creatures, awed by their nakedness: the fur was bleached, the skin pulpy and flaked. I was especially fascinated by the fact that they had been sliced open, so you could see their insides. Mrs. van Moock shuddered. When I came upon a pair of babies' heads with lace collars in formalin, she flounced off to the far end of the room and ordered us to stop looking in the cabinets.

We sat on a bench facing three paintings of volcanoes, one of which was smoking. Their slopes were fronted by a patchwork of small, wet fields and clusters of huts on piles. Dutch ladies holding parasols strolled amid the greenery, which reminded us of home. We stared at the scenes from Java for such a long time that we got tired of them, and were relieved when notice was finally taken of our presence.

"Now remember," Mrs. van Moock whispered urgently as she rose to her feet and tugged at her bodice, "you are his equal in rank, since he is a prince himself, but you had better make a little bow all the same. He is a famous artist! All the royals of Europe have had their portraits painted by him."

"And so now it's our turn!" I said proudly, nudging Kwame.

All he said was: "Who's paying for this?"

Silhouetted against the sun that poured in through the conservatory windows we saw a small figure sitting quite still on a low couch, with one leg folded beneath him and the other knee drawn up. His elbow rested on his raised knee, so that his hand hung down loosely. Mrs. van Moock gave him her version of a curtsey.

"Come now, boys, greet Raden Saleh!"

We came closer and bowed. He inclined his head and motioned us to approach. His look was gentle and his round-cheeked face seemed longer than it was due to the receding hairline. His hair was as black as ours, but not curly. It had been brushed to stand out on both sides of his face. Most arresting of all were his eyes: narrow and with a downward slant at the corners, like the tail of an ornamental fish. The pupils were the colour of his skin, which was darker than that of any white man, but still considerably paler than ours. He ran his eyes over our foreheads, cheekbones, chins and mouths, and then up again, without meeting our eyes.

Then he sighed and exclaimed in a high-pitched, soft voice, "So very dark!" He sounded dispirited. He looked past us at Mrs. van Moock, as though she were to blame.

"Black skins have so little definition," he sighed.

"The boys know some poems by heart," she ventured, in the hope of mollifying him. "Perhaps it would be interesting if they . . ."

"A white skin, at least, glows with life. It can be given depth, and also transparency." Clearly the prospect of painting our portraits inspired little enthusiasm in him. "A white skin can be painted—provided the artist is skilful enough—to look as though one can see through it."

Mrs. van Moock took a step back and laid her hands on our shoulders. She gave us a little squeeze of complicity, and spoke in a cool voice.

"I have had the honour of viewing your self-portrait with my own eyes, at the exhibition in The Hague two years ago. Now I see you in the flesh, I must say it was an exceptionally good likeness. Quite remarkable."

"Thank you, madam."

"The colour of the boys' skin," she continued sternly, "is a shade darker than yours, but that is all. So I am confident you shall succeed." At this, she turned and left the room.

Raden Saleh stirred at last. His slender fingers swung gently, as though his long nails were tracing circles in an imaginary pool. After a while he rose to his feet in a single flowing movement.

A white canvas of vast dimensions had been erected in the glassed-in bay. It was four yards high and at least as wide. The artist signalled to his servant to lower the blinds, and directed us to two chairs.

Then he took his sketch pad and began to draw. Every half hour or so he told us to change position, so that he might see us in a different light. Eventually he ordered the room to be darkened completely, and placed an oil lamp before a convex mirror in such a way that a bright shaft of light illuminated us from one side. He selected a variety of colours and spent a long time mixing shades with which to render the tones of our skin. Then he made some more sketches on paper. Finally he put away his sketch pad, slid his drawing utensils into their case, wiped the traces of lead from his hands, bowed his head and sent us away.

It was less than a week since Cornelius de Groot had given me my last boxing lesson. I had made good progress during the year, and by now I was in the habit of exercising my muscles, whether I had a sparring partner or not, by lifting weights, doing press-ups, and arm-wrestling with anyone who cared to take up the challenge. The pains in my chest, which had plagued me all winter, disappeared in the spring, and I attributed my cure to physical exercise. I often stood in front of the mirror in my shirtsleeves, staring at my reflection, and I kept track of the circumference of my chest, arms and thighs by tying knots in strands of wool. I was proud when the seams of my shirts needed letting out, and was often to be found, that summer, at the constabulary, where I was allowed to use the men's gymnastic equipment. I compared the bare torsos of the men to my own. The difference in size between me and them fuelled my resolve.

The disparity between Kwame's body and mine increased. I pointed this out to him and tried to persuade him to follow my example, but never succeeded in arousing his enthusiasm. He seemed utterly unimpressed by my physique. I could not imagine that he was content with the childlike, undeveloped contours of his body, the sight of which, when he undressed for bed, was beginning to irk me.

Cornelius commenced each boxing lesson in a gentlemanly fashion, with due ceremony and observance of the rules and rituals of the noble sport, but at the first blow to his body he would go wild, throwing all caution to the winds. He soon regained his self-control, but was inclined to take certain liberties with his own instructions. Afterwards we would change our clothes in silence. I began to imitate his fastidious habits of dress. He taught me how to press my trousers, and I took it upon myself to polish his boots and mine daily. He revealed to me the secret of his dazzling toe-caps: fresh sheep's fat. It had a penetrating smell which I soon associated with my new friend. Kwame found it repellent.

Until then the only body I knew as well as my own was that of my cousin, for I went to sleep each night at his side, but soon I became equally familiar with Cornelius's. The differences I noticed between us were just as confusing as the similarities. Of course the bond of friendship between him and me, like that between myself and my cousin, was based on trust, but while the intimacy with my old friend had a soothing and relaxing effect on me, with my new friend it made me eager and alert. I discovered that friendship does not necessarily offer comfort and complacency, but that it can be challenging to the point of pain. Some friendships can be strained to their very limits, until it hurts, only to grow stronger as a result, the way muscles develop by exertion. But I did not have a preference for the one type of intimacy over the other; I valued both in equal measure.

On the Sunday before our visit to Raden Saleh I had stripped to the waist for a sparring session with Cornelius. Our sparring had soon lapsed into wrestling. Grains of sand clung to our sweaty shoulders. We were rolling over the ground like savages, when a carriage drew up. A gentleman alighted hurriedly, and separated us by force. Hearing my name I looked up, and found myself face to face with Commissioner van Drunen. I threw my arms around his neck, and he did not shrink from my embrace despite the stains I left on his clothing.

I reassured him as to the nature of our wrestling match, and he told me he was on his way to headmaster van Moock with a message concerning Kwame and me. He offered to take me with him in his carriage, so I quickly put my shirt on and got in. Cornelius made to follow me, as though it was the most natural thing in the world—after all, there was nothing he and I did not share when we devoted ourselves to our favourite sport. But when he climbed into the carriage van Drunen restrained him, saying that he wished to be alone with me. Cornelius paled, much as if I had delivered him a smart punch in the solar plexus. He stared at me incredulously, waiting to see what I would do.

I said nothing, and did not protest when the carriage doors were closed. Van Drunen called out in parting that he was a sturdy young man and perfectly capable of walking home, but Cornelius stood at the roadside, transfixed.

From Commissioner van Drunen's report on the progress of the princes of Ashanti, 1838:

On 13 July I travelled to Delft to visit the two princes of Ashanti, whose guardianship has been entrusted to me on account of the amicable understanding between the boys and myself dating from our lengthy voyage to the Fatherland. I found them in good health. They appear to be making such rapid progress in diverse fields that Mr. S.J.M. van Moock, the headmaster of the boarding school attended by the princes at a cost of 1000 guilders to the State annually, assures me he has never encountered Dutch chil-

dren with like ability to learn so much in such a short time. Not one of his pupils is progressing more rapidly in any subject than the two Ashanti princes. Indeed the headmaster has requested me urgently to be informed of the intentions of His Royal Highness and the Ministry of Colonies regarding the future education of the boys, so that their current education may be refined in the desired direction. According to the headmaster, the two princes, although equally outstanding in their progress, display disparate temperaments and interests. In general it is fair to say that Prince Aquasi Boachi excels over his cousin in most of the academic subjects, and displays an exceptional talent for science. Quame Poku, heir to the Ashanti throne, excels in the arts; he is a proficient draughtsman, and plays the piano, trumpet, and clarinet with remarkable skill.

Both boys show a keen interest in the Scriptures, and the headmaster has reported several occasions when they interpreted events from daily life in terms of the Holy Bible. He has entrusted the more advanced pupils of his establishment to the cares of the minister of the Reformed Church in Delft, who has intimated that baptism of the two children of nature is by no means ruled out. However, in view of the importance of a true understanding of the Goodness of the Lord our God, the aforementioned minister takes note of the advantages these boys have over their African brothers, who are not fortunate enough to know the Lord. Since the boys have not entirely shaken off their old belief in the powers of nature, Prince Quame Poku being more reluctant to do so than his cousin, there are as yet no grounds for their immediate baptism.

Personally I spent a most agreeable afternoon in the company of the princes, who showed great affection for me. I too have the impression that they are in good health and good spirits, although Prince Quame Poku has a slight tendency towards melancholy. He was eager to hear of the adventures that had befallen us in his former homeland, and was visibly cheered by every detail I touched upon. Such nostalgia does not strike me as abnormal in a child, and as he was on the whole bright and talk-

ative about all manner of discoveries and possessions that have come his way since his arrival in his new fatherland, his occasional tears did not undermine my confidence in his general well-being.

I came upon Aquasi Boachi at play with a schoolmate; he is equal to his peers in every respect, and ever eager for all manner of knowledge. Indeed he enquired after my advancement in rank, after my experiences in the service of the government, and also showed interest in the development of colonial relations in the Gold Coast pertaining to his and his cousin's removal to the Netherlands. For obvious reasons, I informed them of the situation in the most general terms.

In keeping with His Majesty's wishes I advised them of the minister of Colonies' happy decision that their likeness be painted by the celebrated artist Raden Saleh, in order that it may be sent to the father of Aquasi Boachi, the Asantehene at Kumasi, as evidence of their well-being as well as of the good intentions of the Dutch government, and also as a personal reminder to the king of Ashanti of the entente between them, which, notwithstanding the great expense incurred by the government, still remains to be fully honoured.

So we sat for Raden Saleh to paint our portrait—usually once a week, occasionally once a fortnight, but always on a Thursday. These afternoons were somewhat strained. The Javanese prince worked in silence, and although we were not forbidden to speak, we had to sit quite still, especially once he had decided on the pose in which we would be portrayed for posterity.

One day, Mrs. van Moock, who had accompanied us to the sitting, was taking her leave with her usual ado, when Raden Saleh asked: "Have the boys been told about the commander?"

"Which commander, your highness?"

"The canvas is very large indeed. In order to balance the composition I wish to place their benefactor in the centre."

"But my husband has no connections with the army at all!" protested Mrs. van Moock, taken aback.

"Not your husband, my dear lady, but the major-general who escorted them here from Africa. He has acceded to my request and is waiting in the next room."

Major-General Verveer was in full regalia. He had put on weight since our last encounter. It was hard to imagine that this was the same man we had seen in Kumasi, desperately ill and writhing about on the ground. He shook hands with us and inspected the monograms embroidered on our gloves.

"Well well, quite the little gentlemen, aren't we?"

Raden Saleh, who never showed emotion when he was alone with us, joined in with Verveer's laughter. A trifle too loudly.

"They are indeed," he said. "Most convincing, most convincing!"

At first Verveer was only required to sit for his contours to be sketched on the canvas, and once again for the artist's final arrangement of the composition, after which Kwame and I were obliged to do all the posing. It was only when he was working on the faces that Raden Saleh insisted on the presence of all three of his subjects, not least, as he explained, because of the devilishly confounding contrast between the colour of Verveer's skin and ours.

The major-general sat between us on a carved chair with a red silk drapery over the back. I sat to his left on a pouf, my head sightly tilted to face him. My attitude seemed to say that I was struck dumb with wonder and suggested that I was gaping at him like Moses before the burning bush, although my eyes were not fixed on him but on Raden Saleh. It was a most uncomfortable position, which even the son of Amram and Jochebed would not have sustained for very long without getting cramps. Kwame stood at Verveer's other side, with one hand resting on the seated man's epaulettes. The major-general held his hands open-palmed on his lap. Kwame rested his free hand in our supposed benefactor's right palm, and I rested both of mine in his left. The idea was to convey the complete freedom with which we expressed our heartfelt gratitude.

His hands were rough and usually cold. I always tried to delay the moment of touching his fingers. Verveer himself did not enjoy this either. He had received summons from the highest authority to collaborate with the planned portrait for the Asantehene. Not once did he actually grasp our hands. Not once did he give them a little squeeze, or wrap his fingers around ours. To him the hands on his lap were a still life.

Verveer found the sittings increasingly vexing and made disparaging remarks about the art of painting, which Raden Saleh pretended not to hear. It was as though this disdain for his art heightened his sensibility to Kwame and me, and although he never thanked us for our compliance, he did offer us a glass of milk from time to time, with a chocolate pastille or a hot bun. To make the time pass more quickly, Verveer tested us on our knowledge of the Scriptures. Now and then he would ask us to sing a psalm, which he would then interrupt with questions as to the works of charity, the Ten Commandments or the names of Jacob's sons. We reeled them off. Without moving.

"Reuben, Simeon, Levi, Judah, Dan, Naphtali, Gad, Asher, Issachar, Zebulun, Joseph, Benjamin," I droned.

"And his daughter Dina," Kwame added.

Verveer sighed. "I would rather spend a day in the saddle than keep still for half an hour."

"We've only been sitting for fifteen minutes," I said, piqued by his failure to praise me for my good memory.

"And not very still either!" said Kwame.

"*Touché*, Prince Quame!" said Raden Saleh. "The more you protest, Major-General, the longer it will all take."

"But this is the umpteenth time, dammit."

"I have spared you as much as I can until now. If it were just the two boys, I would not have needed you here. But now that I am working on your face . . . After all, it was you who wished to take the central position."

Verveer took his irritation out on us. "Come now, Aquasi, give me the Plagues of Egypt!"

"Frogs, gnats, mosquitoes, cattle murrain, boils, hail, locusts, and thick darkness . . ."

"And?"

"And . . ."

At that moment there was a knock on the door, which was most unusual.

"Not now!" cried Raden Saleh, without looking up from his canvas. We were surprised to see the timid face of his servant peering round the door.

"Raden Saleh, you have a visitor."

"I am busy. You know I am not to be disturbed."

The servant slunk away, but instead of shutting the door behind him he flung it open to admit a formidable lady. A tower of chestnut hair crowned by a small white hat with an upturned brim made her seem even taller than she was. I could feel Verveer stiffen.

"Perhaps you would be so good as to make an exception for me?" The soft line of her Slavonic eyes somehow jarred with the stern, narrow lips. She had a nose like an arrow with nostrils like barbs, was about forty years old and seemed, unlike the other women I knew, entirely at ease in male company. Raden Saleh looked round, flustered, and shot upright, while the major-general shook off our hands and rose to salute. It was our crown princess: the Tsar's daughter Anna Pavlovna.

"Oh dear," she said and motioned for a chair to be brought. "Just look at them!" Her voice was as resonant as a man's. It was also loud and halting. She was not used to speaking Dutch. Some of the consonants made little plosive sounds, as if they couldn't get past her lips.

"We happened to be passing, and remembered the king's recommendation that we make the acquaintance of the Ashanti princes. You are the object of His Majesty's concern, you know," she said, leaning over to inspect us. "Besides, he thought it would please the princess. Sophie? Sophie! Where is that girl? Sophie! She must have gone off exploring again. The young are so forward these days."

The doors to the drawing-room were open, and we could hear the patter of shoes on parquet.

"It is a great honour, madam, to see you here . . ." stammered Raden Saleh when he finally regained his composure, but she took no notice of his civilities.

"Is that enormous canvas for them? But it is twice as large as the portrait you painted of us!" She affected indignation, and her eyes twinkled for the first time since her arrival.

"No canvas is large enough to represent your greatness." Raden Saleh bowed, but Crown Princess Anna Pavlovna was not one to be taken in by flattery.

"I have the likenesses of my father and my two brothers. I wear them next to my heart. No more than an inch high," she said, "but showing each of them just as they are. As they are!"

"Of course. But I did not mean to say . . ."

"Size is not all that matters, sir!"

Kwame could not suppress a smile. We had never seen Raden Saleh flustered. He bowed once more, sent his servant for refreshments and tried to change the subject by pointing out lines of perspective and vanishing points. The crown princess questioned the artist regarding brushwork and the composition of his paints. She seemed to be quite knowledgeable on the subject and suggested an improvement, which was politely acknowledged. Then she turned away from the canvas and approached us.

"Well, Major-General, so these are the jewels you have brought for our crown." She had lowered her voice and I was happy to believe her compliment was sincere.

"At great personal risk," Verveer said, "at the risk of my life."

She looked him up and down with steely eyes and concluded: "A small stake for such gain, sir!"

The major-general gasped for air to protest, then thought better of it. The crown princess ran her finger along Kwame's cheek and pressed our hands.

"Go on, say something, boys!" urged Verveer.

"How do you like it here, *mes petits princes*? Does Holland bear the remotest resemblance to home? My poor dears, have you become at all accustomed to us?"

Kwame and I exchanged looks. No one had ever asked us such

a question before. I smiled faintly, hoping she would change the subject. Verveer slapped his hand on the back of his chair.

"Come now, boys, answer the question!"

I was about to say what I thought she wanted to hear, when Kwame blurted: "No, madam!" He did not even sound timid.

"What sort of answer is that?" snapped Verveer.

"An honest answer, Major-General." Anna Pavlovna straightened her back. "Would you prefer it otherwise?"

"No no, of course not."

"Grey skies and flat polderland, wind, water and aching muscles are not likely to make one forget the pleasures of home, I can assure you!"

At this point Princess Sophie came into the room. She was about fourteen, and carried a glass jar containing a specimen in preserving fluid. She stepped forward quickly, but carefully, to avoid jostling the contents of the jar.

"Come and look, Mamma, he's got a skeleton next door, and things behind a curtain. And look at this, it's got monsters in it, Mamma, look, look! It's ghastly, all hairy and . . ." She held out the jar to her mother, and suddenly noticed our presence. Everything happened so quickly that I cannot say whether she was startled by the sight of us or by the lid slipping off and splintering on the floor. Alcohol splashed over her white frock, whereupon she jumped and dropped everything. Shards of glass flew in every direction.

"Sophie!"

There was a moment of silence, then Raden Saleh got up and said, drily: "A zoological specimen." He wiped some murky liquid from his shoes and rang for a servant.

"I am so sorry," said the girl. She wore her blonde hair brushed back from her forehead and hanging down on either side of her face in fine ringlets. They danced as she shook her head over her own clumsiness.

"It is nothing, Your Highness, nothing. Just some vermin in a formaldehyde solution. My servant will clean up the mess at once." But Kwame had already crouched down to fish the dead insect from the floor, at which Sophie gave a little shriek.

"Mamma, Mamma, he's picking it up with his bare hands!"

"It's a spider," I said.

Sophie took a step closer, shuddering. "A spider? As big as that?" she said, pulling a face.

Kwame held the creature under her nose and stroked the wet hairs with his finger. "It's very soft. Go on, feel it."

Sophie had to fight down her revulsion, she had to force herself to look, but she reached out and touched it. We told her we knew all about spiders, and she regarded us with such interest that we were encouraged to continue.

"Behind the mandible are the glands," said Kwame. "Very useful. Two drops diluted with five gulps of water cures stomach aches."

"How clever!" the girl cried. "Do you hear that, Mamma?"

"And under the legs are some other glands," I added quickly, pointing them out to her. "There. Good for stiff joints."

"Stiff joints?" her mother said, waving her hand to show she wanted a closer look. Kwame pressed one of the little sacs, and a tiny dab of colourless jelly squirted on his finger. Verveer stepped forward to intervene, but Sophie's mother restrained him.

"Who knows," she said. "It can't do any harm." She peeled off her gloves and rubbed a dot of jelly over her knuckles.

4

The summer of 1838 ended abruptly. In the early days of September the temperature dropped fifteen degrees in a single night. That same week it started to rain, and it did not stop until December. This was not the kind of rain we had known at home—a few heavy showers daily—nor the kind of rain that lasted for several days, as we had experienced during our first Dutch autumn. No, from one day to the next the entire country was swaddled in a cold, dripping blanket. The unusual weather conditions gave rise to all sorts of old wives' tales. There had been the same heavy rains in the summer of 1818 and, just as twenty years earlier, prophets of doom arose all over the country, proclaiming that the sixth seal had been opened and the end of the world was upon us. Each Sunday in our room we heard an old man ringing a bell and shouting at the top of his voice about the spire of the great church in The Hague having been struck by lightning on account of the three Willems—king, crown prince and heir apparent—attending a concert of secular music in that sacred place.

Kwame laughed at all the superstition and said we should go to the park. We looked for a place where we would not be seen, took our clothes off and leaped about with our arms outstretched. We used to do this at home. We called such big raindrops "heaven's fingertips." There they were warm and fragrant, but here they ran down our bodies like cold tears. Kwame kept it up for a while, but I put on my wet clothes and ran home as fast as I could.

"The post has arrived!"

It was towards the end of November that Mrs. van Moock burst into the classroom and, in contravention of all the rules, interrupted me in my recital of Paul's epistle to the Colossians.

"The post, sir. An envelope, a card. The finest parchment! Only two weeks from now! Oh my goodness gracious, and what shall they wear?"

I had prepared a little discourse on the subject of "the tolerance of the new life without idols and sins of the flesh," but the headmaster was not listening. He tried to bundle his wife out of the room, but she stood firm. She pushed the embossed card into his hands, which he read while he shouldered her to the door.

"A royal invitation! I knew it. I said so right away. Didn't I say so? Let no one contradict me. My own boys!"

Cornelius turned round slowly to face us. His expression was utterly blank.

Since the day that van Drunen had invited me into his carriage but had refused to take Cornelius, my wrestling partner had been very quiet. I wanted to resume our sparring matches, but he demurred. When we happened to find ourselves alone together he would take off at once, or call out to someone to join us, as though I were an embarrassment.

"He's afraid of you," said Kwame, who didn't think much of the older boy. Nonsense, I thought. Cornelius would always be stronger than me, always the leader. I thought he might be upset because the headmaster made it a little too obvious that Cornelius was a mediocre pupil and I a quick learner. So for a while I tried hard to dissemble my progress. When that did not help to bring us back together, I concluded that our friendship was lost forever. Now there was nothing to stop me from getting the best marks, and I devoted myself to the only sport that contains within it its own reward.

In keeping with the Russian custom, Anna Pavlovna gave her relatives their gifts on the eve of their birthday. And as Sophie's father, Crown Prince Willem Frederik, was born on 6 December, the festivities for his forty-seventh birthday commenced on the eve of St. Nicholas. His wife seized every opportunity for gathering her family around her. While the children were young she would do everything in her power to turn the feast of St. Nicholas into a grand, double celebration.

Mrs. van Moock had provided us with long-tailed morning coats and shirts with scratchy starched fronts. We looked ridiculous, but it was the height of fashion. A small carriage drawn by two horses was hired for us at considerable expense. That afternoon, in blustery weather, we rode to the dunes at Scheveningen, where we alighted in front of a low building. The windows of the two wings, hardly more than large rooms, were brightly lit. Smoke rose from both the chimneys. Music could be heard. The columns at the front were decorated with garlands of dried flowers, twigs of fir tree and small dried oranges. The wind tore at them.

The Queen's Pavilion had been a gift from the king to his wife, Wilhelmina. After her death the year before, it had passed to her son Frederik, who generously allowed his niece, Princess Sophie, to use it whenever she pleased. She loved the seashore.

It was the first time since our arrival in this country that we saw the sea again, but never had we seen it so turbulent. As soon as the door of the pavilion opened we rushed inside, and found ourselves in the middle of a family celebration. The chatter of the company drowned out the pounding surf.

The young princess greeted us like old friends. We were somewhat embarrassed by her effusiveness. She would not let go of our hands and drew us into the drawing-room, made us sit by the fire, called for hot chocolate and pattered to and fro with ladies and their offspring in tow, to whom she introduced us as if we were bestowing a favour on them. No fewer than seven times did she repeat what little she knew about us, our origin and the object of our stay in this country, after which she seemed to tire and simply abbreviated her introduction to "the African princes I told you about." In this way we made the acquaintance of her governess, Mademoiselle Chapuis, and her aunt Marianne, a small thin woman with a flushed round-cheeked face, who had come all the way from Berlin accompanied by her young son Albert for the celebrations. Duke Bernhard of Saxe-Weimar-Eisenach was there with his daughter Amalia and sons Hermann and Gustav. The boys were our age, and they were good sportsmen. After I had wrestled Hermann down in the hall, Gustav invited Kwame to visit him at his home near The Hague for some fencing and riding.

That afternoon the children outnumbered the adults, and besides meeting the sons and daughters of several noble families we were introduced to Prince Alexander, who bore an uncanny resemblance to his mother Anna Pavlovna. He had her Slavonic eyes, her dark hair, and had even adopted some of her gestures. His sister told us we could call him Sasha. He agreed to this graciously, and before the evening was out he reminded us quite plainly that we should address each other informally, as friends.

Gingerbread dolls and marzipan were passed around, but the princess was brimming with excitement. She wanted us to meet her father and her other brothers, but couldn't find them. However, Anna Pavlovna came forward, with a frail white-haired old lady.

"Brrr," Anna Pavlovna shuddered, "the wind never stops blowing in this place!" She looked around the room accusingly. She was followed by Madame Kuchelev, another formidable Russian lady. Kwame asked Sophie if Russian men were even bigger than the women.

The crown princess took the little old lady by the hand—she was Mademoiselle de Sybourg, her former governess, now senile and in the princess's care—and led her to a seat with high arms and back, into which the tiny figure sank. For the rest of the evening all she did was stare into the void and dip ginger biscuits into her cup of tea to make them soggy, after which she licked the sticky mess off her fingers.

At seven it was time for some singing. We were taught several ditties invoking St. Nicholas, which reminded us of the way we chanted for the spirits in our temple by the lake. After half an hour the lights were dimmed and the doors opened. We were showered with confectionery and everyone, the adults in the forefront, raised a great shout of expectation. Kwame gave me a look as if everyone had gone mad. There were more songs, this time not in the drawing-room but in the entrance hall, which was dark. Anna Pavlovna launched into a song, and everyone joined in. A long-robed figure stepped inside. On his head he wore the mitre of a Roman Catholic bishop. It was St. Nicholas. Everyone cheered, whereupon he scratched his white beard and enquired whether we had all been good children. There was a resounding cry—even from the adults—of "Yes!" But the saint was not satisfied with this answer, and asked the question again, adding that anyone not telling the truth would be sent to Spain forthwith.

I began to feel very uneasy. What if St. Nicholas actually put us on a boat all over again—to Spain this time! Imagine being at sea in this weather! I was so confused and frightened that I didn't dare say yes when he asked us again whether we had been good boys in the past year. I was terrified that I had done something wrong, although I always tried to please everyone by being as obedient as I possibly could. This visit from St. Nicholas was turning into an ordeal.

Anna Pavlovna gave a sign for the lamps to be relit. St. Nicholas took a seat and opened the large book bound in red Morocco which lay on his knees. He called for his Black Peters, whereupon two fellows with blackened faces leaped out from behind the cur-

131

tains, waving birch rods. There was a lot of shrieking while the Black Peters lunged at the children in search of those who had been up to mischief. Boys and girls fled in all directions. I stood rooted to the spot, until Kwame nudged me saying that they were all just having fun. I couldn't see the fun of it, but started to calm down.

The next instant, the larger of the two Black Peters, who wore enormous bloomers, pounced on me. He seized me by my shoulders just as he had seized other children before, but when he set eyes on my face his jaw dropped, and he let go of me as if he had burnt his fingers. He bent over with a look of disbelief.

"Well I never!" he blurted. All attention was focused on the pair of us. The Black Peter switched his gaze from me to Kwame and back again, took a few steps back and rubbed his eyes, then looked around the room in wonder, unsure whether he should persist in his role of Black Peter in our presence. No one seemed to know what to do. The lull in the conversation roused Mademoiselle de Sybourg, who raised her hand from her teacup, pointed a soggy finger in our direction, and cried shrilly: "It is Willem! It is plain for all to see. Guillot! Can't you tell? It's our dear, dear little Guillot!"

Now the tension was broken, everyone started laughing and talking at the same time. But that was not the end of it. The Black Peter stood rooted to the same spot. It did not escape him that he had cut a risible figure and that his awkward behaviour was a source of amusement. Suddenly he whipped off his beret and curly wig and flung them to the floor. Under his mop of fair hair, there was a distinct line marking off a band of pink skin from the blackened features of his face. Kwame and I were horrified—it looked as if the man had been flayed alive. He swore under his breath, hitched up his bloomers and stalked off, so incensed that he knocked a side-table over on his way out, sending a crystal bowl crashing to the floor. He slammed the door behind him with such force that one of the panels came loose.

Madame Kuchelev distracted everyone's attention by clamouring for a slice of the cinnamon cake that had been baked specially by the Russian pastry cook, whereupon Anna Pavlovna signalled for it to be cut and shared out. St. Nicholas cleared his throat with much ado, and turned to address us. He told Kwame and me to come and sit on his lap. Some of his front teeth were missing, and he smelled so strongly of tobacco that I had to stifle a cough. The saint said he knew all about us. I found that surprising, as I had never seen him before. I said so, at which he chuckled and claimed to have met my father, too. He knew everyone.

"How is my father?" I asked. St. Nicholas conveyed my father's good wishes to us. Kwame thought he had misheard and asked him to repeat his words, but he had not been mistaken, and the message pierced my soul. This was the first news from Kumasi that had ever reached us, and we were hearing it from a stranger! St. Nicholas mumbled that he could look into people's hearts all over the world, and had seen that my father missed us, thought of us every day and wished us well.

I could see him in my mind's eye, standing on the ramp of our palace in Kumasi, his back to me, staring into the distance. For so many months I had succeeded in banishing him from my mind and now, in front of everyone, he actually turned to look at me. I don't think he knew who I was.

I broke into a coughing fit. Turning the pages of the big red book, the saint had apparently come across mention of improper conduct on my part during school examinations, which was certainly not true, and also of Kwame's reluctance to wash, which accusation was perhaps less far from the truth. However, our crimes were not so serious as to detract from the overall impression of good behaviour, he declared, and he gave us a heavy, colourfully wrapped box and a slice of cinnamon cake, and sent us away.

I could not make up my mind whether to hold on to the image of my father or to let it go, and was so preoccupied by this that much of the further festivities escaped my notice. The other children were given the same treatment we had received. Most of them were reprimanded for disobedience but each of them received a gift, which they unwrapped at once.

We had not dared to open ours. We were new to the custom of concealing gifts in paper wrappings. When the others tore open their parcels I felt embarrassed at not having done so too, but by now I felt it was too late.

Finally the saint himself was given a present by Anna Pavlovna, whereupon a Russian choir sang a mournful song. The chattering resumed, and Princess Sophie came running to show us her gift. It was a mechanical doll, which by pressing a button could be made to sit down at its desk, dip its pen in the inkwell and write "Sophie" on a sheet of paper. Sophie demonstrated her doll twice in succession, and gave each of us a sheet with her name on it. I thanked her, but was dejected and unable to hide my emotion.

"Is it because of my brother's behaviour?" she asked. "You mustn't take any notice. He's just a show-off. He has a temperament. Mamma says there's a lot of my grandpa Paul in him. Temperament, you know. My brother Willem Alexander is a real Romanov . . . Like the Tsar." She eyed me steadily, and added: "Of Russia."

"Yes, yes of course," I mumbled.

"When are your birthdays?"

"Our birthdays?" Kwame asked in surprise. "We don't have any."

"Not right now perhaps, but at some time in the year, surely?"

"No, we don't have birthdays."

"What nonsense, everyone has a birthday!" She waved her hand dismissively. "Everyone except Mademoiselle de Sybourg, that is. Every day's the same to her and she's so very old already, I can't see how she can get any older."

"We've never had a birthday," Kwame insisted.

"No, never," I echoed.

"Why ever not? Or do you celebrate your name-day? That's just as good, I suppose. When are yours?"

"On Saturday," Kwame said. "Yes, my name-day is Saturday."

"And mine is Sunday."

"But that's absurd. Sunday and Saturday, a birthday each week! Whatever next?" She lost her patience, spun round to face Kwame and gave him a commanding look: "Come now, tell me the date of your birth."

"I don't know it," he said.

"He doesn't know!" Sophie turned to me saying, "And are you any better informed, may I ask?"

"Not really," I said. She wrinkled her nose when she laughed, like a puppy about to sneeze. "I only know what I've been told," I went on, "but I have no proof, for I can't remember being born."

"Nor can I!" She thought for a while. "In actual fact . . ." she went on, "in actual fact, my birthday is the only proof I have."

"And when is it?"

"The eighth of April." As an afterthought she said: "So it's not for a long time yet."

"We know that," said Kwame, feeling somewhat left out. "We know the months. We're not stupid." Sophie walked away. I was afraid that we had vexed her, but she soon returned, with the bearded saint trailing after her. St. Nicholas bent over so that he might speak to us face-to-face. The acrid smell of tobacco! I did my best not to start coughing again.

"What's this I hear? Don't you boys have birthdays?"

"No sir," I said.

"But then we must pick a date at once."

Anna Pavlovna abandoned her tête-à-tête with Madame Kuchelev at the other end of the room and sailed over to see what the commotion was about.

"Goodness gracious!" she cried. "What's the matter with them? They haven't even opened their present."

"It's not their birthday," said Sophie.

"Since when does it have to be one's birthday before one can open one's gift from St. Nicholas?"

"You don't understand," the saint said. "They don't have birthdays. They don't celebrate them."

"Never?"

"Never."

"What an odd way of attracting attention," Anna Pavlovna remarked, glancing at us quizzically. The saint hitched up his robe and sat down beside us.

"What was the date of your departure from Africa?" he asked. "You do know that, don't you?"

Kwame remembered exactly. Van Drunen had written it down for us, and as soon as Kwame learned to use a calendar he looked up the day at once, and marked it. It was also etched in my memory because Kwame hadn't spoken a word all day when the date had come round last spring.

"The twenty-fourth of April," he said.

"And the date of your arrival in the Netherlands?"

"The twenty-first of June."

"In that case we shall from now on celebrate your birthday, Prince Aquasi, on the twenty-fourth of April. And yours, Prince Quame, on the twenty-first of June. How does that strike you?"

"Wonderful, Pappa!" exclaimed Sophie. She giggled at her mistake: "I mean St. Nicholas, of course."

Suddenly Willem Alexander, the heir apparent, came in. He had wiped the blacking off his face, but some of it had remained, emphasizing the lines that were already appearing around his eyes, which were small and partially hidden by a fold of eyelid. His cheeks were rosy from scrubbing, and shone with some kind of grease. He had exchanged his bloomers for a suit. He took a glass of port and tried hard to make up for his previous outburst of ill temper. The other Black Peter turned up in his wake. In uniform.

"Hendrik, such fun!" The princess ran towards him. "I was thinking the whole time that you had to be the other silly nigger, but I couldn't possibly see which was which. I was looking for you, as I want to introduce you to two friends of mine, with whom you'll have a lot to talk about, I'm sure. Prince Quame and Prince Aquasi, this is my brother Hendrik."

The young man, with a flushed, plump face, held out his hand and also saluted in acknowledgment of our station, which was superfluous but well intentioned. Sophie put her arm through his.

"He knows the tropics better than anyone. I've had to miss him for so long. I only got him back last summer. And now I shan't let him go again. Go on, Hendrik, tell them. He's seen so much of the world, for someone so young!"

The prince asked for a bite of food, and withdrew with us to the next room. He spoke with ardour of faraway lands. At the age of sixteen he had already rounded the Cape, but the only place in Africa he had visited was Table Mountain. He talked of life at sea and the customs on board, of Rio de Janeiro, Calcutta, Delhi, and the Himalayas. His fondest memories were of the East Indies, which he had visited last year, the first member of the House of Orange to do so. He lowered his voice, twirled his wrists in the air, and from time to time he caught a glimpse, over our heads, of green hillsides, the courtyard of a native temple, a long lost friend. In a few words he brought to life the string of islands on the school atlas: Celebes, Java, Ambon, Ternate.

Sophie was spellbound. She urged him to give more and more details about the wildernesses he had seen and the customs of the peoples he had encountered. She was not moved by a desire for sensational facts, like most people. Her interest in other worlds and peoples was heartfelt and passionate.

Sophie told her brother about the spider in Raden Saleh's studio. To our astonishment he already knew the tales of Anansi. During his stay in the South American colony of Suriname two years earlier, the ambassador had taken the young man, who was bored with official banquets, to a circle of carefully selected slaves. They had fired his imagination with stories of Spider Anansi, his friend Tsetse the fly, his wife Sis Akuba and all their children. To hear those names that we had known as children coming from the mouth of a stranger moved us deeply. Sophie took the coincidence to be an omen. She couldn't get over it. I liked seeing her so intrigued, so I did not explain how the story had got around. Besides, that subject was too unpleasant to be broached on a festive occasion such as this. (When we were in Elmina we discovered that the slaves sold to the Hollanders year-in year-out had been destined for the colony of Suriname. They had been robbed of everything except their minds and their stories.)

We were offered cake with icing, and a glass of punch. Sophie urged Hendrik to tell us some more adventures of Spider Anansi.

137

Now and then I glanced at Kwame. He seemed utterly at ease. Stories you know by heart, like dreams, will never bore you.

Crown Prince Willem Frederik, whose birthday it was, asked his guests to play and sing for him. A young countess with little crooked teeth immediately drew out a score from her bodice and burst into song. She gave a very poor performance, which encouraged the others to do better. After three more songs the crown prince beckoned us to his side. The smell was unmistakable—he was smoking one cigarette after the other—but otherwise all that was left of his bishop's disguise was some flaky dried glue, which Sophie proceeded to pick out of his bushy side-whiskers. He asked us to demonstrate our musical skills. I played an étude on the pianoforte, with moderate success, after which Kwame displayed that his talent in music far surpassed mine. He played some Bach variations on the harpsichord, followed by a solo on the clarinet, which had been hastily procured for him from the Russian musicians.

My own performance was rewarded with polite applause, but Kwame was deluged with praise. He hardly noticed, because whenever he made music he was lost to the world. If I am honest, I think that may have been an impediment to my own artistic development: seeing how effortlessly the muses lured my beloved cousin to other spheres, from which I was barred. Not that I grudged him his escape. I was fascinated by his abandon and tried to imitate his devotion to the arts. My vain efforts only hardened my resolve to understand the mind of the artist. Dreams do not come true by keeping one's eyes shut.

He was playing again when I was beckoned by Anna Pavlovna, who was having a conversation with her eldest son. Willem Alexander, the heir apparent, was quite tipsy by now, and all the more mellow for it.

"*Quelle émotion! Le prince est vraiment talenté!*" Anna Pavlovna remarked, when the last notes had died away. She spoke French so as to keep their exchange private.

"*Ce sont des sauvages bien élevés, maman,*" her son concurred warmly.

He signalled Kwame to come forward. My cousin had some difficulty extricating himself from a throng of admiring young ladies, for which I envied him.

"*Mais venez donc, mon tout petit grand homme, venez ici!*" Anna Pavlovna said, and introduced him to Willem Alexander, on whom it was beginning to dawn that we understood French. He looked at me askance and seemed slightly uneasy again.

"Prince Quame will ascend to the throne one day."

"The throne?"

"Just like you, dear boy."

"Where is this throne to which he will ascend, may I ask?"

"Oh, it is very far away!" said Anna Pavlovna, and she was overcome with emotion. "So very far away, poor dears!" She averted her face. "It is merely the music making me sentimental!" she said primly, without glancing at us. Willem Alexander was perplexed.

Sophie offered further explanation. "Quame is to be the king of Ashanti."

"But," said Willem Alexander, "I was given to understand that the father of the other one . . ."

"They do things differently over there," Sophie began, as if she thought it was rather a good idea. "Dynastic succession passes in the female line."

"Good Lord!" Willem Alexander exclaimed. "Whatever next!" He shook his head and emptied his glass. A hint of mockery had come into his voice.

"Why should Holland provide the yardstick whereby we measure others?" Anna Pavlovna said sternly. "Heaven forbid it should be so."

"Why shouldn't a king use the yardstick of his own kingdom?" answered her son.

Anna Pavlovna rose from her seat and drew herself up, no longer a mother now, but every inch a Romanov, daughter of the tsar.

"For the time being it is your grandfather who is king. And then it will be your dear papa's turn. And after that, who knows . . .?" She sniffed and called for a handkerchief. The message was passed on from one valet to the next until at last her personal page presented the requested article to her on a silver tray, with a deep bow.

In the meantime she had addressed her son with a hard smile on her lips: "Every gardener, dear boy, must know what grows in the forest before he can even mow a lawn." She blew her nose, dropped the handkerchief on the floor as was her custom, and flounced off.

We returned to Delft in the night. Once we were in our room we opened the present St. Nicholas had given us. He had spoken the truth. The package came from my father, but it had been opened, inspected and re-wrapped at the Ministry of Colonies. Among the contents was a notice from Elmina stating that the Asantehene had dispatched six ounces of gold dust in payment for our upkeep, as well as two pairs of necklaces and rings as gifts. The ornaments made us glad that we had not been forgotten, but the gold they were made of was so cold to the touch that we took them off again quickly.

Kwame was very tired, but thoughts of the Black Peters kept him awake. I told him not to take offence at their antics, that it was all part of an old Dutch tradition, that we had curious traditions at home, too. Such folk ways are maintained, but the significance is largely forgotten. Kwame thought that was the worst, the most dangerous sort of tradition. He became quite agitated. Fortunately I drifted off after a while and dreamed I was on a ship scudding across the ocean with a huge pair of bloomers for a sail: I stood at the helm, humming a wordless tune.

"I don't know, sir," we overheard Cornelius de Groot stammering as we entered the classroom the next morning. Our outing had not escaped the notice of our schoolmates: Mrs. van Moock talked of nothing else. Besides, since we had returned so late we were permitted to rise two hours later than normal, and so to miss the first lessons. This was considered most unfair by the other boys, even by those who had befriended us. To make matters worse we came in just in time to witness Cornelius being put in his place.

"Master de Groot, it is not my custom to blame a simpleton for his stupidity, but your case is different. You are shrewd enough outside the classroom. Shrewd enough to take advantage of your peers. So your ignorance must be due to idleness."

"Oh no sir, I have just remembered the answer!"

"Shrewd enough to make notes on your cuff, I see. No, you may not answer the question now. Aquasi, do you know the answer?"

I glanced at the blackboard.

"One-and-a-half-times the quotient of the short sides," I said. I was guessing, and had the audacity to flash Cornelius a quick look of triumph.

"Do you hear, Master de Groot? It is but one year since the princes of Ashanti entered my care, and you have been my pupil for four already. You should take their example."

"I'd sooner take horse-shit for breakfast," Cornelius muttered under his breath, returning my look defiantly. He had never been as crude as this. I remembered how he had said never to lower your guard, especially when you think you have the upper hand.

"What was that?" asked the headmaster, who either had not heard properly or could not believe his ears. "The impudence!" But his exclamation was drowned out by a burst of laughter, which was all the louder for having been suppressed for so long.

Cornelius had imposed certain restrictions on Verheeck and his cronies. The actual bullying was over. I myself had grown too strong. But neither Kwame nor I made any friends at school after that. Conversations would flag when we approached. We withdrew from games and sport of our own accord. We surrounded ourselves with books, and the friends we had made at court were to be our only allies.

That I fell ill was due to the cold, and not, as Kwame would have it, to grief. It started with a stab of pain in my back each time I breathed. Then I started to cough, especially in the morning and at night, and after five weeks I was finding it increasingly hard to breathe during the day too. The squeaking in my lungs grew so loud that I was banned from attending classes until I was cured.

Kwame, always quicker to adapt to the forces of nature than to those of man, did not suffer from the cold, but he refused to pursue his lessons without me. When severe and repeated punishment proved to no avail, the headmaster gave in and permitted Kwame to keep me company in my room, as long as he took his work with him and handed in his copy-books each afternoon.

I was finding it increasingly hard to climb the stairs to the second floor. My listlessness kept me awake, which in turn gave me headaches and pains in the lower back. I lost my appetite and grew thin, until Mrs. van Moock found me in bed one morning drenched in perspiration. She turned back the covers and the look in her eyes told me I was dangerously ill. A doctor was called, who diagnosed bronchitis and prescribed steam baths. Two weeks later the steam baths had not had any noticeable effect, and van Moock decided it was time to notify Commissioner van Drunen.

I received a letter from Princess Sophie:

I am afraid it was I who put your health at risk, by insisting that you both come down to the beach with me that evening at the pavilion in Scheveningen. I hope you will understand that I had grown tired of the company, and even of my mechanical doll. When I had made the doll write my name on enough sheets of paper to give each subject of this kingdom a copy, there was only one thing left to amuse me. To follow the call of raging winter. The sea roared to make me hear. Hendrik's sea. I tried to persuade my brother to take a walk in the storm with me, but he demurred, more convincingly than you and your cousin. Quame seemed quite eager to embrace the elements, the way he used to in the past. I could think of no better company in which to brave the storm than you two, who are familiar with the forces of nature. Had I known of your constitution, I would never have pressed my wishes upon you, but as it is, my memory of the occasion is very dear to me. How wonderful to lean against the wind and be lifted up on its wings, as if one were weightless and airborne. To spread one's arms like a bird, ah, to throw one's cares to the wind! We have so much in common, you and I. I weep for the loneliness both of you must endure. But you do not stand alone. Please believe me. We must trust in God.

And now you are unwell! The respiratory ailment you are reported to be suffering from is not unfamiliar to me. Last summer it kept me in bed for many weeks, and to my great regret I was therefore unable to attend Prince Hendrik's homecoming, because I had been sent away to convalesce. My mother blames everything on the Dutch climate, which she claims is utterly unsuitable for human habitation. "I shall have St. Peter explain it all to me one day," she'll say when she's in one of her moods where you can't tell if she's serious or joking: "and I shall discover why the Lord God created a people so misguided as to choose to live in a bog!" The bad news of your ill health is a cause of great concern to her and to the Crown Prince, who is equally your friend. Steps are being taken to hasten your recovery, which I hope will be speedy. Please be so kind as to convey my respectful greetings to Prince Quame and also to accept them yourself,

Sophie, Princess of the Netherlands.

P.S. Spiritual nourishment can fortify the body, too. Enclosed you will therefore find a play. It is entitled Mahomet, *and was written by Monsieur Voltaire. Mamma is afraid Monsieur Voltaire might have a bad influence on me, but some of his lines have a special resonance for us. I have marked them in the book, and have made them my personal motto: "All mortals are equal; it is not birth that distinguishes them, but virtue."*

Hardly had we received Sophie's missive than Professor Everard, who had treated Sophie during her sickness, arrived at the school. He was also physician to Crown Prince Willem Frederik, whose health had never been good.

The doctor forbade the steam baths at once, wrapped me in mustard poultices and prescribed covering my thorax with strips of cloth soaked in sulphur. Within a few hours the entire floor was filled with the stench of rotten eggs.

The smell in our room was unbearable. I was having difficulty breathing and my heart was beating irregularly, which made me dizzy. I advised Kwame to take refuge from the sulphurous fumes for a while in the next room, but he refused to leave my side. He spent many hours guarding over me at night, making me turn on my side as soon as I rolled over, because that helped me to breathe. By the time he fell asleep it would be morning, and even in his dreams he was alert to every change in the pattern of my breathing, so that the slightest shift would awaken him. Then he would lay his ear on my chest, listening like the doctor. When I asked him what he heard he replied, "A heart like a horse run riot." I scoffed at his comparison, which must have come from one of the modern poems in the anthology Mrs. van Moock had kindly lent us, but later that night I had a feverish dream in which I saw a heart with little legs galloping round as fast as it could.

One night I suffered an especially severe attack, during which I coughed up blood and feared that the congestion in my lungs would stifle my breathing altogether. The doctor who had been summoned in all haste removed some viscous slime from my throat with a spatula. He acknowledged that I had been a hair's breadth away from death by suffocation.

The doctor's treatment left me exhausted, and I soon fell asleep. I was roused some time later by a searing pain in my throat. My sudden awakening took Kwame by surprise. He was sobbing quietly by my side—the first and only time I ever saw him cry. But as soon as he noticed that I was awake he regained his self-control, so as not to worry me unduly. He was quite certain I would get better, he said, and he repeated this assurance so many times that I realized he was in terror of losing me. He rocked me to sleep in his arms, and I do not believe we were ever closer together than we were then. As I drifted off to sleep I realized once and for all that he truly loved me and that he was the only person in the world I need not fear. The next morning I tried to feel the same profound contentment, but did not succeed.

Sourdough paste and Spanish fly were applied. Professor Everard told me that a severe attack always marked a turning-point, either for better or for worse. And thanks to hot compresses, inhalations of herbal vapours, treacly cough-mixtures, and last but not least to Kwame's loving care, I was on the road to recovery. My appetite improved and I regained my strength little by little. By mid-February I was well enough at last to return to the classroom, and also to resume the sittings for Raden Saleh's portrait. There was just enough time to include our new Ashanti ornaments in the painting.

However, my respiratory problem never cleared up completely, and as long as I lived in Holland I was laid low by bronchitis each autumn.

Princess Sophie's fifteenth birthday passed without our receiving the invitation we had hoped for. It turned out that the royal family was in a turmoil. Anna Pavlovna had done everything in her power to prevent Prince Willem Alexander from marrying his beloved, but the fiancés seemed determined to press ahead. She stormed through the corridors of the palace. Her eldest son's bride-to-be was his cousin Sophie von Württemberg, daughter of her least favourite sister Katerina Pavlovna. She was a girl in whom, according to Anna Pavlovna, all the most unstable traits of the Romanovs, which were already troubling her eldest son, had come together.

Worse even than Willem Alexander's imminent marriage was the scandal surrounding King Willem I, Anna Pavlovna's father-in-law. After two years of mourning for his dead wife the old king had had enough of solitude. He had now taken a fancy to countess Henriette d'Oultremont, who was not only Belgian but also Roman Catholic, and a lady-in-waiting to boot!

In the circumstances the palace had thought it wise to reduce the number of social events for a while. Naturally Kwame and I had no idea of all this, and were sad to have been overlooked. As it was we sent Sophie a birthday gift—the collected works of Voltaire specially bound in the finest green leather—with our congratulations and good wishes. In return we received a polite thank-you note, which contained no personal messages or tokens of friendship.

On the afternoon of 24 April, however—the day that had been picked as my birthday—Kwame and I were driven in a carriage to Hellevoetsluis, where the mayor received us at the town hall. He led us into a room where the huge canvas that was to be sent to my father was displayed. Although I thought Kwame's likeness convincing enough, I was at pains to recognize myself in the timid lad averting his eyes from the viewer. It was not so much that my head was raised to our "benefactor" as that I appeared somewhat embarrassed about meeting the gaze of others. On the whole our portraits showed us to be in good health and exemplary of African wholesomeness.

The "March for the King of Ashanti" was played in our honour, and Crown Prince Willem Frederik entered with Sophie at his side, followed by Major-General Verveer, Commissioner van Drunen and Raden Saleh. While we enjoyed an elaborate tea party, the picture was taken to the quay and loaded on to a ship upon which the major-general was set to embark that very afternoon for the voyage to Elmina.

The prospect of returning to Africa was so repellent to him that he could barely keep up a civil conversation. Even while the crown prince was speaking, Verveer's thoughts kept wandering, and he prodded his slice of cake at length, without ever tasting it. His mission this time was to conduct a punitive expedition from Fort Elmina to Badu Bonsu II, king of Ahanta. The latter had ordered a Dutch trade delegation be put to death in retaliation for a crime against local court etiquette: two ignorant soldiers had held their rifles at the ready during a royal audience. Adjutant Tonneboeijer had subsequently set out with forty men to seek retribution from Badu Bonsu, but they had all been killed in an ambush.

After tea we all trooped to the quayside. Major-General Verveer promised to see to the delivery of our portrait in good condition at Kumasi, and went on board. We wished the vessel and her crew a safe voyage.

Two years had gone by since Kwame and I had left the Gold Coast, and now we were returning as a portrait. My heart lurched at the idea that my father and our mothers would soon set eyes on us, but I had the comfort of Sophie standing beside me. Kwame and I waved at the ship carrying our images until it gained the open sea. I gripped my friend's hand. We would have loved nothing better than to change places with the portrait. But we were civilized and held our tongues.

Part Three

DELFT 1839–47

I

*Happy are those who have never set eyes on the feasts
of strangers and have only sat at the tables of their
fathers.*

—François-René de Chateaubriand

"It was she," Kwame said, pointing to the sun. Sophie imitated his gesture. It was Kwame's birthday: 21 June. The three of us were lounging on the curved bench under the almond tree in the park behind Het Loo palace. It was the first occasion, after a cold spring, that the sun's rays were strong enough to warm our cheeks.

"She was the one Spider Anansi fell in love with. He was consumed with desire to be with her. The earth was still bare and infertile in those days. He spun a web between two stones and climbed up to the highest point. But he could not reach her. He spun another web between two boulders, but still he could not reach her. He climbed to the top of a hill and attached his thread to the summit. He had never been as high as this before. What was he to do now? Where could he anchor the far end of his huge web? On the horizon Anansi discovered a mountain range. He set off across the plains until he reached a river bank. He turned to look back. He was far from the land he knew. But his love was greater than his fear. Although he could not swim, he managed to cross the river, and waited on the other side for his body to dry in the sunshine. Beyond the salt flats he travelled onward, all the way to the mountains dividing the plain from the coast. He climbed the highest peak of all, and saw how long his thread had grown. Imagining how vast the dimensions of his web would have to be made him dizzy. The journey had exhausted him, and still he had spun just a single thread. It dawned on Spider Anansi that he had set his sights too high and that his love was impossible, for he would never reach the sun with his web. No, he would never get any closer to his love than he was here, on this mountain top. So he decided to make it his home. Grief-stricken, he watched his beloved sun sinking out of sight in the evening. He wept all night. But in the morning his hopes rose again, because she had not forgotten him. He no longer ate or drank. All he did was dream. A breeze started blowing. Puffs of sand blew across the plains in the distance. The wind gathered strength, became a gale. Anansi dug his heels in. He had no intention of leaving this place, which was the closest he could be to his beloved. He held on for dear life, clinging to the ground beneath him, but his strength failed him. The wind lifted Anansi up and, with only his long thread linking him to the mountaintop, he came closer to the sun than ever. If only he had let go sooner! He soared higher and higher still, while his thread grew longer and longer. Soon he was ablaze, ablaze with love, and overcome with joy. The heat scorched his legs, but he didn't mind. The flames singed the hairs on his belly, his protective shield burst into flames, but he took no notice. He was alight with love and cried out in ecstasy, and at the very moment his beloved engulfed him with her flames, he died of sheer happiness. Like a smoking flamelet on a wick his charred corpse slid down the thread he had spun. His ashes fell to the earth. The wind scattered them across the barren fields and desolate plains. And his ashes made the earth fertile. The sun sank below the horizon and rose again to see tiny blades sprouting from Anansi's remains. She beamed at them to make them grow. She gave them such vigour that they spread all over the earth. And from that green wilderness animals emerged, and the first humans. And from them came you and me and Kwasi and everybody. Born of Anansi's love. That is the origin of all life. Unfulfilled desire."

I screwed up my eyes against the glare, but through my blood-red lids I could see Sophie's shadow. She drew up her knees, wrapped her arms around them and rested her chin on top.

"You can't have made it all up yourself!" she said. I opened my eyes, but had to shut them at once. I tried peering through my eyelashes to make out her face amid the clusters of fiery dots.

"Is that the sort of story your mothers used to tell you?"

"I don't remember anything about my mother," I replied. I preferred discussing things that were new to me. "Well, I know she used to sing."

"Kofi was the one who told us the stories," Kwame said, and he went on to describe our old slave with his watery red-rimmed eyes and ancient wisdom. He gave an imitation of the old slave's spindly-legged gait, and explained what he had taught us.

"Was he blind?" Sophie asked, sounding almost hopeful. A velvet pearl-studded headband held the ringlets away from her oval face. They bounced and caught the light.

"Kofi—blind? What do you mean?"

"I thought he might have been. It's not unusual for a sage to be blind, you know."

"Not unusual, is it?" Kwame said in a mocking tone, which vexed her. She wandered off in search of wild flowers, which she pulled up root and all. When she had gathered an armful she scattered them over our heads, by way of reprisal. Petals and grains got under my shirt, and my skin itched for the rest of the afternoon.

Sophie plied us with questions. About Kwame's mother, and about mine. About when we were little. Kwame did not seem to mind at all. He talked at length of customs, idols and myths that no one in Holland had ever heard of. He glowed, and the princess was enraptured. Her enthusiasm was contagious. So I put aside my dislike of reminiscing, and soon Kwame and I were vying with each other to tell the next anecdote. Sophie was especially interested in hearing confirmation of certain notions she had taken into her girlish head with regard to the circumstances of our birth. She was so excited that I did not have the heart to disappoint her, and eventually I conceded that my cradle had indeed been lined with moss and that it had been suspended from the branches of a blossoming maple tree, where it swayed in a gentle breeze among nests with baby birds. Descriptions of this nature made her cover her face with her hands to hide her emotion. Such scenes, which she herself had prompted me to describe, made her shiver, as though they were familiar to her. I could not help noticing that Kwame did not approve of my white lies. He resumed our true story, but the princess kept interrupting him with the oddest questions. She demanded to know if Kwame had ever seen a white hind in his dreams, and pressed me to say whether the trees in the secret valley gave me advice in matters of love. Kwame began to think she might have been in the sun for too long.

The marriage of the heir apparent Willem Alexander to Sophie Mathilde von Württemberg had taken place three days before Kwame's birthday. King Willem I travelled to Stuttgart to attend his grandson's wedding. He was accompanied by all the princes, including the groom's father, Crown Prince Willem Frederik. Crown Princess Anna Pavlovna, however, was absent. Her refusal to attend her eldest son's wedding was to be the first of many slights to her daughter-in-law. Sophie had to stay behind to keep her mother company and, in the hope of some relief from the grim ambience, she insisted we should celebrate Kwame's very first birthday at Het Loo palace.

After a tiresome journey we alighted from the stagecoach to an atmosphere of despondency. The crown princess had retired to her private quarters on account of swollen eyes from crying. "Well, you might as well go straight back," Sophie lamented, "because Mamma has refused to call the musicians. And what sort of a birthday is that, if there is to be no dancing?"

But there were cakes, and lemonade in three different colours. One of the conservatories was decked with flowers. Sophie's tutor Monsieur Cavin, a Swiss, was the only other guest. He sat in a corner, immersed in *The Genius of Christianity*. Its author, Chateaubriand, was held in high esteem by Sophie's mother, because he had sided against the new regime after the French Revolution.

At long last the crown princess herself descended the staircase. She was very grandly dressed, and her large skirts seethed with exasperation. To everyone's surprise she wore, on top of her plaited hair, a felt circlet sewn with pearls and around her neck some of her famous jewels.

"What are you staring at? The whole country is celebrating the heir apparent's wedding, and you would grudge his own mother a bit of finery?" Aware of the awe her appearance inspired, she took a seat, graciously allowing the folds of her trailing robe to be adjusted by a footman. I was so incautious as to congratulate her.

"Ah well, of course you are right, Master Aquasi, let them be married. Why strive after happiness, anyway?" she said disdainfully. Monsieur Cavin shut his book and withdrew discreetly.

"After all, what could be wrong with a young man taking his cousin from the mad side of the family to be his wife? That is the modern way, it seems. There will be children—but never mind about that. Who knows the lot of them may even render madness fashionable! I for one have no intention of letting it stop me enjoying myself." Having made her point, she ordered her Russian singers to assemble. She was brought a tray laden with sweetmeats, which she pounced on like a vulture on market offal. Sophie took us out into the park.

"What on earth are you doing?" she cried.

In my eagerness to engage her with yet more folklore, I had broken two twigs from the almond tree.

"My mother brought that tree with her from St. Petersburg. Whenever she's sad she has tea served here from a samovar. Then she sits with her eyes shut for hours, pretending she can hear the ripple of the River Neva." We could hear the splash of Neptune's fountain in the *rond-point* where the avenues met. "Have you ever seen it? The Neva?"

"No," replied Kwame.

"No," I said. "I only know my own country."

"What about Holland?" protested Sophie. "You know Holland, too."

"I *meant* Holland," I said.

Kwame stared at me, aghast.

．　．　．

The sun faded early. At dusk we gathered around the stove in the conservatory with the ladies-in-waiting. Several visitors were announced. They had come to congratulate Anna Pavlovna on Willem Alexander's marriage, and she thanked them civilly, raising one eyebrow. Although her low opinion of her son's new consort was widely known, she spoke in company as if the heavens had parted to let Sophie von Württemberg down in our midst.

The ease with which she lied fascinated me. She had the ability to rise above her deepest emotions, to transcend them. I envied her self-discipline. I studied her diplomatic talents, and decided that self-abnegation was something you could learn.

That Anna Pavlovna had deigned to show her true feelings to us earlier struck me as a sign of friendship and trust. But Kwame took it amiss, thinking she didn't care what we thought because we were mere Africans. His dark moods shocked me, but they troubled him even more. At such times he would withdraw into himself, fall silent, and make himself impossible by sulking for hours.

Kwame's glumness did not escape notice. Fortunately Bernhard of Saxe arrived, accompanied by Hermann and Gustav. Not one of the guests neglected to wish my cousin a happy birthday, but they soon gave up trying to engage him in conversation and turned to me instead. I took it upon myself to entertain the company by making sums in my head from numbers called out by those present. Then I quoted Lamartine's poem "Le Lac," and after that I was handed a sketch pad upon which to draw the profile of any guest who cared to be portrayed. Everyone demanded to be sketched by me, and I was showered with praise. Both Kwame and I were commended for our diligence, and I found the applause deeply gratifying, more so indeed than the high marks we earned in class. To me it was the first true acknowledgment of how hard we had studied since arriving in Holland.

But Kwame persisted in his gloom. It was exasperating. Just as I was being vindicated! At the very time when I was demonstrating that our dedication and studiousness had gained us acceptance as equals in the highest society imaginable, he was choosing to behave like a savage. At first I was merely irritated, but soon my gorge rose.

For the first time in my life I was ashamed of him. Of his stubbornness. Indeed, of his presence. How many times hadn't I felt ashamed of myself, but such mortification is not half as painful: yes, you break into a sweat and feel weak at the knees, but you can absorb the pain because it is your own. Feeling shame for someone you love tears you apart like a predator clawing its way out of your breast.

"What's the matter with you!" I hissed. "You're making a fool of us." I took his arm and led him to the group that had gathered around the crown princess. They were playing Snap. Before joining the circle I told him to pull himself together. He muttered something under his breath.

"What did you say?" I growled, and then he repeated, in an angry voice: "If only you wouldn't show off all the time!"

He had the gall to say that! It was outrageous. As if *he* had reason to be ashamed of *me*! I tried to look unconcerned, as Anna Pavlovna would have done, as if the absurd words had never been uttered. The cards had been dealt, but instead of concentrating on his hand, Kwame stared into the void.

So as to avoid further aggravation, I turned away and challenged Sophie to a game at the chess table. I played quite successfully, but she did not notice this for some time.

"I prefer playing with you than with Willem Alexander," she said. "He's such a poor loser."

"I'm not losing."

She seized my bishop with a pawn. I countered her move smoothly, but Sophie was unperturbed. I told her that her confidence reminded me of Napoleon before the Battle of Waterloo.

"Quame isn't playing," she observed. "He's sitting there holding his cards, but he isn't doing anything. Is he scared?"

"Kwame is the worst loser of all," I said. "Let's see . . ." And, with a malicious flick of the wrist I indicated the tour my knight would take to capture her castle.

"But the two of you have suffered so much loss already," she said, giving me a steady look. Unflinching. There was no trace of strategic intention in her eyes. We gazed at each other, and it was as though she was satisfied with my silence. My muscles tensed. I was filled with longing, but did not show it.

"That's true," I said. "But I think I'm a better loser than he is."

"Thank goodness for that," she smiled, "because there goes your knight! I told you there was no advantage to the right of first move!"

We bowed our heads over the board in silence while I pondered my strategy. I was close to calling checkmate, and it was her turn to think hard. "Sometimes I think he blames it on me," I said.

"What?"

"The distance. Between us and other people."

She nodded as if she understood, reached for a chess piece, but wrinkled her nose and changed her mind.

"People are foolish," she said soothingly, "don't let it bother you."

"But it doesn't bother me, I want to be as much like everyone else as I can. I don't want to attract attention."

"Nothing attracts attention like trying to belong." There was a hint of disapproval in her tone, and she slid her bishop forward resolutely. It was my move.

"I know what you mean about distance," she said. "My own family is utterly isolated. People are watching one and judging one all the time, but they don't come close enough for one to get to know anything about them. It's as if my face were disfigured by a scar or birthmark, which sets me apart from other people. Everyone can see it and yet no one dares mention it."

My eyes flitted across the board, unseeing. In the meantime I was groping desperately for words to confirm the perfection of her features, as she no doubt expected me to do.

"Mamma says," she went on, "that loneliness is the privilege of the strong." She surveyed the board and laughed as if she had already won the game. I couldn't make up my mind, and slid my piece this way and that until I gave up concentrating. Which was lucky for Sophie.

The rest of the evening was spent at the card table, where Kwame managed to spread his gloom to everyone else.

"Why don't you play something for us on the piano, Prince Quame," Anna Pavlovna suggested. She enthused at length about his talent and yet he was not easily persuaded. "I beg you, a little musical intermezzo performed by the birthday boy himself would be a suitable finale for this celebration."

"I have nothing to celebrate, madam," he said, averting his eyes. There was a silence. Anna Pavlovna took his hands in hers.

"I know," she said, "I know."

"Oh, Mamma," sighed Sophie, "ça c'est le mal de René." I thought she was referring to young René Labouchère, who sat two rows behind me in class and who suffered from fainting spells, which I attributed to his over-tight trousers. I asked her how she knew him, but she waved dismissively, as if she did not wish to be distracted from emotions she had made such an effort to comprehend.

"When I think about home," said the crown princess, "I always sing one of the songs my mother taught me."

Kwame bit his lip. After a long silence he said: "Out loud?"

"Certainly! Sometimes just the tune will do." She hummed a few bars. Kwame let go of her hands.

"We don't think about home much," I said, for I was finding the situation increasingly embarrassing. "At least that's what I try to do. Not think of home."

Anna Pavlovna shook her head, vigorously but with a look of regret, the way headmaster van Moock did when you gave the wrong answer. She rose up and stepped into her sedan chair.

"People think remembering brings sorrow." Her chair was lifted up by her footmen and she was suspended in midair. "The contrary is true. It is forgetting that brings sorrow."

The summer months at boarding school were quiet. Most of the boys went home for the holidays. Mr. van Moock would try to delay their departure with extra revision and exams up to the last minute. He was sorry to see them go, and urged them to return promptly. "Knowledge," he wrote to the parents and guardians of his boys, "is like the body of an athlete. It thrives on regular exercise. Lack of exercise causes atrophy." Those of us who stayed behind knew that his concern for the boys' pliancy arose from financial straits. Payment of school fees and allowances for board and lodging ground to a halt during the holiday periods—the very time when maintenance to the premises was due. Meals were reduced to twice daily, and the practice of serving roast meat on Sunday was discontinued, because, we were told, it was unwholesome in warm weather. We were not upset by the austerity of the diet, for the van Moocks themselves were clearly short of money. Mrs. van Moock sent her maid away until September, and did all the darning herself, besides polishing the brass and waxing the floors. Mr. van Moock continued to teach us until mid-July. After that we devoted our time to "drawing after the nature of the Lord," which amounted to being sent off into the countryside in the morning with an apple, some coarse paper and watercolours. We were not expected back until supper time.

The first few days saw us flitting about like birds that have just discovered the door of their cage open. We ran this way and that across the fields, carefree and happy. We did not do any painting, but held wrestling matches instead and rolled about in the wheat field. But at the end of the first week van Moock demanded to see some results.

I lay face down in the grass, with a buttercup just under my nose. Clamping the tip of my tongue between my teeth I copied what I saw as accurately as I could, not missing a single vein, petal or carpel. Then I pulled the plant out of the ground and drew the roots in great detail. I poked my fingers into the earth to make sure I hadn't left anything out. Finally I took my penknife and sliced the stalk lengthwise, pulled the skin off the leaves, scraped the pistil clean and drew the whole plant afresh, this time showing the underlying structures. When the object of my scrutiny lay before me in its dry, dissected and wilted state, it occurred to me that my own creation was superior to the original. My pictures were so neatly drawn that they seemed to defy the capricious, unruly diversity of nature itself.

Kwame set to work without any method. Whenever his eye was caught by a likely subject he would hitch up his trousers, lean against a tree, narrow his eyes and stare. He would stay in the same position for as long as an hour sometimes. Then he would take a sheet of paper and start painting—quite at random, it seemed. He would paint energetically for a while, and then stop in midair with the brush poised over his composition, as if he were waiting for it to do the work for him. As he never looked up from his occupation, it was as though his subject came from within rather than from what he saw around him.

I could not bear to watch! Those dreadful smears and stains! Now and then he took a crumpled ball of paper and swabbed his painting with it, the way we had seen Raden Saleh do with a cotton rag. But Raden Saleh had been using oil paints on canvas, and our watercolours were wholly unsuited to such treatment. Dabbing wet paper just makes a mess. Once Kwame had painted his sheet all over, making the composition utterly chaotic, he put his paints aside and set to work with chalk, adding highlights, shadows and little touches to indicate perspective.

Both of us came under the spell of nature. I wanted to know its secrets, I wanted to dig, to determine, to expose its riches. I began to understand the growth patterns of even the most developed species of plants, in which I was especially interested on account of the perseverance and resourcefulness with which they had survived the ages. I learned to distinguish the characteristics of the different families, and made a sport of classifying unusual specimens with great precision. Kwame took a broader view: his eye was drawn to the vanishing point of a country lane, to the swathes of colour in a field of wild flowers. He did not concern himself with stamens or corollas, but would perceive contrasts in a shady distance that to me was simply greyish.

Incomprehensible though it may seem, at the end of the day, despite the chaos of Kwame's brushwork, there would be a picture that somehow captured the essence of the place we had visited. It was infuriating, but true. Kwame's paintings were useless to a biologist, and yet people were moved by them. They inspired in many viewers a sense of nature as God's dearest, most wondrous mystery. My own efforts to sort out the wonders of nature on sheet after sheet of painstaking depiction did not appear to matter to anyone.

We met Sophie only once that summer. It was at a soirée in a private house. We had not been invited as friends of the host, but as curiosities. The hostess kept urging us to play more music, until Kwame asked out loud if she had mistaken him for the young Mozart. But even after that we did not get a chance to talk privately with the princess. She exchanged a few civil words with everyone present. She glanced in my direction from time to time, which I took to mean that she would much rather be running about in the garden with us. I signalled back that I agreed, and to demonstrate the bond between us I behaved exactly as she did, responding to people left and right as if they had said something highly intelligent.

There was no mention that evening of the elderly king's intention to wed his adored but unsuitable lady-in-waiting, although the subject was on the tip of everyone's tongue. The conversation revolved around the festive welcome that had been given throughout the land to heir apparent Willem Alexander and his bride. Sophie mentioned that her brother Prince Alexander was away visiting his relatives in St. Petersburg, and that she herself would pay a second visit to her aunt Maria Pavlovna in Weimar in the autumn. She would be spending the winter in the south of Holland. I could tell she was sorry that we would be separated for so long. Later on, during a quadrille, she whispered to me: "On the last Wednesday of August I shall be in Scheveningen. It will be quiet there. Professor Everard has prescribed seawater baths for Mamma." That was all.

After she left the party a footman brought me a small volume bound in red vellum, containing the stories of *Atala* and *René* by Chateaubriand. It was Sophie's personal copy. She had marked certain passages in pencil. The enigmatic inscription on the fly-leaf, in her own hand, read: "Friends in the Bond of the Creeks."

The next morning Kwame and I went out into the countryside again, but we did not paint or draw. We read each other the stories celebrating the life of nature led by North American Indians.

At daybreak on the last Wednesday of August, a farm cart took us to the royal residence. From there we walked to the Queen's Pavilion in the dunes at Scheveningen. Princess Sophie received us as if she owned the place. Anna Pavlovna stayed in her room, where fresh tubs of sea water were delivered every hour. She suffered from indeterminate ailments, which she blamed on the Dutch climate. She was also absent from the light summer meal that was served on the terrace. Monsieur Cavin read out a few poems by Herr von Goethe, in connection with Sophie's impending visit to Weimar. It was his aim that she should surprise her aunt with her knowledge of the work of the great poet, who had served as tutor to both her uncle Carl Friedrich and her cousin Carl Alexander. We escaped into the dunes with Sophie at the earliest opportunity.

Sophie had everything planned. She and I were Muskogees and Kwame was a Seminole—as the Indian tribes were called in the story of *Atala*. The three of us crouched under a teepee made of leaves. The Seminoles, she declared, had to seal a bond with the Muskogees. She pronounced the names reverently, as if they had magical powers. The Bond of the Creeks! Sophie took all this very seriously and made us swear an assortment of oaths—even that we would live our lives in the wild according to the laws of nature. She pulled out a hairpin, making her curls cascade over her face, and stabbed the pin into her fingertip to draw a drop of blood. But the point was too blunt, and she went off in search of a suitable thorn, leaving Kwame and me on our own.

He was being exceedingly difficult. One minute he was silent, the next he was hurling abuse at me. He didn't want to play Sophie's game at all. But he was too shy to tell her, and demanded that I should convey the message to her. I had no intention of doing so. I thought it was all rather fun. Then he ran off into the dunes, so angry and upset that I ran after him. I think he must have been hiding from me, because I could not find him anywhere. Back in the teepee Sophie and I sealed our bond, but she thought it didn't really count without a Seminole joining in too. I had to urge her to prick my finger, and once I was bleeding we found we didn't know quite what Muskogee did next. She suggested sucking the blood, although it was a disgusting thing to do. In the end we caught a few droplets of each other's blood in the bell of a flower, shook it around and then buried the crushed vial in the sand.

She never mentioned our bond again. But I never forgot what it felt like to belong together, to be alone without Kwame: lonely yet exhilarating.

How long did we lie there in our leafy arbour—a quarter of an hour, an hour, the whole afternoon? In later years I began to doubt whether she really had looked the way I remembered, said what I heard her say, did what I remembered her doing. At the time I believed we were cementing our bond by lying still like that, by keeping silent, close together. Probably we barely touched. Or not at all—but that's the kind of trick an old man's memory plays.

Her white summer frock is sprinkled with traces of brown, dried blood. She blows on them, scratches a persistent crust with her nail and flicks it into the breeze. Takes my finger and studies my sacrificial wound. Wipes it. Squeezes my finger. There is no more blood. She holds on to my fingers with both hands, as if they are big, strange objects. Her eyes scrutinizing my skin. Her fingertips on the back of my hand, rubbing this way and that. Comparing the skin to that of her own hand.

"You can see the pores much better," she says, "a jigsaw puzzle of a hundred thousand tiny black cells." Then she turns my hand over. Like turning a page of a book, to continue reading. The palm is a pool. Cracks in the bleached earth. The dark water has seeped away. The pigment remains along the edge.

"They're pink on the inside, white even."

She turns them over and over.

"Black, white, black, white," she laughs. "The outside is still African, and the inside is steadily turning Dutch. Don't you agree?" She lays my hands in my lap. Sits facing me. Reaches out her arm. Her fingers touch my lips. Pulls down my lower lip: "Pink, too!"

That's how livestock is valued, I reflect, and try to banish the thought at once. She raises my upper lip with her fingers and stares at the gums. That's how slaves are valued.

"Indeed yes! Your tongue, too!"

I clamp my mouth shut, grind my teeth. Then I explode with laughter, she lets go of my face and hangs her head, giggling uncontrollably. She has not replaced her hairpin. Her curls fall loosely forward, hiding her face. I want to see her eyes, and stretch out my hand to draw the curtain aside. The hair slides softly along my throbbing fingertip.

2

On the Noble Savage

Extract from a letter I wrote some years later to Kwame from Weimar:

With each step forward, civilization leaves a footprint behind. We have, unwittingly, come a long way. The distance we have yet to travel is impossible to gauge. So we keep hoping that the goal we can see on the horizon will prove to be the final one and also the highest, and that we will find shelter there before nightfall. If we turn to look back we can distinguish no more than a few footprints. Forty, fifty paces behind us the path we have been at pains to follow loses itself in the ploughed earth. We are glad to have come this far, and wish to pursue our course. Yet our thoughts are drawn to what lies behind us, more than to the uncertainty that lies ahead. There are moments of nostalgia for the valleys that our people claimed long ago. At the same time we are aware that the plains we have cleared and the forests we have burnt offer no challenge. To live is to engage with the impossible.

That is what stimulates us and keeps us going. So we look ahead and persevere. We find consolation in the notion that we carry our past within us. But from time to time we are obliged to shed some of the burden weighing us down—possessions dear to us, now irretrievably lost. Our personal effects consist of memories. And the more we value our memories, the less of a burden they are. So the course of man's development, Kwame, bears a marked resemblance to the course of your life and mine.

You and I are in the unique position of having travelled this enormous distance at an accelerated pace. We ran all the way. There was barely time to catch our breath while we covered the same ground that took Western civilization thousands of years to cover.

Due to the speed of our journey many things eluded us. But if we have learned anything about the soul of European civilization, it is that its bent is nostalgic. No difference there from the sentiment you and I are so familiar with. So when we are confronted with envy of what is taken to be our uncorrupted state, you and I should be the first to understand.

The more man is tamed, the more he longs for the pure state of nature. The new and the old are thus condemned to coexist. Throughout history people have been nostalgic about the past. In art, fashions of dress, furniture and architecture, poetry, indeed in his faith, man always harks back to a previous golden age. Even the ancient Greeks, who were envied by all those who came after them for their natural simplicity and their direct knowledge of the sources of our existence—even they regretted the loss of the true Arcadia of old.

Since civilization does not advance at the same pace all over the world, but flares up at different times and in different places rather like an epidemic, there is throughout history the recurrent shock of discovering a people, a tribe or an individual that has fallen behind the march of progress. Such lone stragglers came to *personify man's estrangement from nature. Such natural beings were envied for what they had retained. Underlying their harsh daily struggle there was believed to be a primeval guiding force. The absence of shame betokened a carefree spirit. Their naive customs touched the European heart, just as the innocence of a stammering child endears it to the listener—reminders of what has been lost for ever. Is not that sentiment, sweet and melancholy, closely linked with love? And can you begrudge others the love they feel for you?*

You can hardly blame Sophie for admiring us for being what she perceived to be "people, just emerged from the hand of God," as she wrote to me once, echoing Seneca—although by then her childish enthusiasm had long been supplanted by mature friendship. She pointed out many other authors, from Virgil and Montaigne to Bernardin de Saint-Pierre and Swift, who celebrated man as formed by nature, far removed from the perverting influence of civilization. As though mankind were a cut of meat and civilization a sign of decay. Their celebration of natural man arises from their ignorance of other cultures. The decay is there, too, but the signs are not the same.

Voltaire's Zaïre was one of many works in the pastoral tradition beloved of philosophers and utopians, in which Christians are bowled over by the innocence of natural man. It made a deep impression on Sophie, for she read it at the very time she discovered feelings of love in her heart. Her elders approved of her fondness for books, and she was promptly given Marmontel's study of the Incas to read, as well as Odérahi *and* Paul et Virginie, *the illustrated works of Marc Casteby and the accounts of explorers such as William Bertram and Jonathan Carver.*

Her interest was further aroused by Rousseau's Discourse on the Origins of Inequality, *in which the Dutch governor of the Cape of Good Hope sequesters a Hottentot child so that it may be educated in the Christian tradition and European customs. Sounds familiar, doesn't it? This boy fulfilled the Dutch missionaries' dream: he became a noble savage. (Incidentally, the boy recants in the end, flings down his clothes at the Governor's feet and runs home naked. But by then the example has been set.)*

Chateaubriand, too, ranks among the authors with such romantic notions. His Atala and René caused a furore throughout Europe. And although "Atala furniture," "Atala clocks" and "Atala coiffures" were already out of fashion by the time we arrived in Holland, it is hard to contemplate the drama of Atala without thinking of that which has befallen ourselves.

It is hardly surprising, then, that a young lady under the spell of these romantic ideas should feel affection for us, two strangers who entered her secluded life like characters in a true story. Is she to be blamed for that? Do you blame me for rising to the challenge of her interest? Then you must blame each youngster who falls in love for the first time.

When Atala, torn between two cultures, ends her own life, the explanation of her misfortune is: "It is your education, savage, that has caused your downfall."
Of course, your personality and mine developed in different directions, and for us to become men it was inevitable that we should outgrow our boyhood friendship. I had noticed this for some time, but did not dare mention it to you. We were together twenty-four hours a day. Our mutual irritation increased, as in a stale marriage. Although the growing rift between our minds saddened me, I told myself it was better that we should form our opinions independently of one another. I thought that sharing our achievements and ideas would be gainful to both of us, that we could support, correct, complement and nurture each other, but instead we became entrenched in our separate views and in the end refused to concede an inch.
What education was it that hardened our hearts? Were we exposed to too little education or too much? Apart from the few occasions when a friendly wrestling match turned mean, we did not fight. Our first quarrel was sparked by reading Atala. You were convinced that the Red Indian girl's misfortune was due to the fact that she, a primitive being, had been forced to adopt the European way of life. This had occurred to me, too, but I tried to banish the thought at once. I made a joke about Atala not taking

her "second" education very seriously, as she had ignored the Christian injunction against suicide. But you were adamant, and obliged me to take a defensive stand. I disparaged her primitive upbringing, and by extension that of all natural peoples. You were enraged and I let you blow off steam, but I did not give in. Giving in would have made matters worse.

You reproached me for being thick-skinned and too forgiving. The opposite is the case. My protective armour is too thin, it does not reduce my sensitivity. It is merely that I have learnt to control my anger, and therefore in the eyes of others I seem invulnerable.

And it was Atala I went on about, so as to steer clear of my own sentiments.

The "Summer of the Bond," as I referred to it to remind Sophie of our secret, was coming to an end when a Hungarian circus visited The Hague. The princess was eager to see the show, but her governess, Madame Chapuis, would not countenance even mentioning her wish to Anna Pavlovna.

One afternoon we heard the clamour of a great procession, complete with musicians and elephants, trooping down the avenue past the palace gardens. We were not even allowed into the front rooms to catch a glimpse of the parade. Kwame and I devised a plan. Sophie provided various articles of clothing which, so she believed, would make us inconspicuous, as well as floppy, wide-brimmed hats to hide our faces. For her own use, she had an apron, stolen from the kitchen. The three of us slunk away behind the rhododendrons, scaled the garden wall and raced down the avenue as if pursued by the devil. Only by yodelling at the tops of our voices or beating a tattoo could we have attracted more attention, but no one stopped us.

The circus tent was orange with blue stripes and had a fringe all the way round. From afar you could already hear applause, shouting and laughter. The smell of damp sawdust and elephant dung made Sophie choke, but when the band struck up she was skipping with excitement. A blonde woman in a glass-fronted booth guarded the entrance. She refused to let us in without tickets, and was unimpressed when Sophie told her who she was.

"Yes," the woman scoffed, "and I am the queen of Cloud Cuckoo Land!" We lingered near the cages of the wild animals and were about to give up when we noticed a loose flap of canvas. Tugging at it until the opening was wide enough for us to slip into the tent, we found ourselves in the space underneath the tiers of planking and peered between the legs of the spectators into the big top, where figures dipped and soared like birds. There were fire-eaters, girls in glittering attire balancing on galloping horses and somersaulting into saddles. Skin-tight costumes, straining muscles in the warm, heavy air, thighs clamped on horses' flanks . . . We were spellbound. Sophie held her hand over her mouth in shock, but nothing escaped her notice. Two elephants, their spirits broken, performed a lumbering act. A man with a white-painted face played the fool, and I was puzzled by how heartily all these white people were laughing at themselves.

At long last the ringmaster stepped forward to announce the grand finale. He warned the people sitting in the front rows of the hazards to come, and ordered all the children to be moved to the back. Four men with whips stood guard over the ring and the drums rolled ominously. The excitement reached fever pitch and the audience stamped their feet on the wooden planks, making a deafening noise in our hideaway.

"Here they come . . ." roared the speaker, recoiling dramatically, "in their most natural state!" The curtains parted. "I must remind you that it is strictly forbidden to feed them, for they come straight from the wild, and eat only human flesh . . ." Another roll of the drums. "Here comes the terrifying Nuba tribe from darkest Africa!"

Years later, when I tried to explain to Sophie why Kwame had distanced himself from her, I reminded her of this incident. She appreciated the degradation we must have felt, she said, indeed her own sense of shame on that occasion had been as profound as ours. She was as shocked as we were, if not more so, by the idea of a defenceless naked tribe being put on display throughout the countries of Europe and forced to perform wild dances, pull faces and prostitute themselves to a jeering public. The idea of the noble savage, which was so close to her heart, had suddenly been reduced to the level of a circus act, a freak show with a bearded woman, Siamese twins or a five-legged foal. She assured me that she would have given anything to spare us this experience. So upset was she by the memory, that I did not have the heart to tell her how she herself had wounded Kwame with her exaggerated reverence for our exotic origins.

To cheer her up I reminded her how I had burst into loud sobs, so loud in fact as to draw attention to our presence under the rows of benches. Suddenly we were staring into the upside-down face of a scullery maid, who had bent double to peer between her legs into the space behind. It took the girl some time to believe her eyes: then she shrieked. She fled, screaming that some of the blacks had escaped and were about to gobble her up. I do not remember who was outside first, the factory girl or us.

In later years I heard tell of many other "noble savages" who found themselves exposed to the oppressive stares of common folk. Naturalism being all the rage, any man of nature could be counted on to draw great crowds. A Mohawk Indian named Sychneta was exhibited in a tavern in Amsterdam; there was Omaï from Tahiti, and the Hottentot Venus whose buttocks could be squeezed for a few pence. Sophie told me about her brother going to see a group of Orange River Bushmen in The Hague, and on one occasion I lost my temper and tore down posters advertising Carl Hagenbeck's Somali show complete with tents, horses, camels, sheep, and, as the newspapers reported, "black children scampering around like young monkeys." I never went to see an exhibition of humans again, although in Kumasi we used to enjoy the spectacle of the conquered tribes from the north, whom we mocked for their deviant speech, their customs, and the characteristic features of their race.

Soon after the incident at the circus we were taken to a different spectacle, in Leiden this time. The minister of Colonies had decided it would be in our interest to study his latest ethnographical acquisitions, which had come from Elmina on the same ship that had set out with Verveer and our portrait some time earlier. No doubt it was intended as a favour to be shown the throne belonging to my father's friend Badu Bonsu II, king of Ahanta. Two skulls dangled from the back like trophies; the one on the left was pointed out as being that of Adjutant Tonneboeijer. We had known him in the old days in Elmina, and Kwame could not resist inspecting the skull at close quarters. The mandible had been reattached with wires and could be raised and lowered. Doing so had a comic effect, which was not appreciated by our elders. We were led into the adjoining room. On a desk stood an object draped in a velvet cloth. When the cloth was removed we saw a glass jar. In it floated the head of Badu Bonsu.

When Mr. van Moock saw the state we were in when we returned, he wrote a missive in no uncertain terms to the Ministry of Colonies. That was the last time we were taken to exhibitions of that nature. I believe both items are still on view in Leiden today.

(As it happened, Verveer's punitive expedition to Ahanta was not an unqualified success. Badu Bonsu was decapitated and his head preserved, but Verveer, ever susceptible to the tropical climate, fell ill and died of a raging fever some days later at Elmina. Instead of burying him then and there, the idea arose to make use of the remaining preserving liquid, which had been prepared in vast quantity. A large sea chest was tarred on the inside and filled with formalin, into which the body of Verveer was carefully lowered. In order to minimize putrefaction, the lid was clamped down and sealed along the edges. The captain set sail, confident that Verveer's remains would return home safely, but on the third day the smell of decay was reported below deck, and in mid-voyage the captain noted in the ship's journal: "The stench from the major-general has become unbearable. Today we held a brief ceremony and put him overboard.")

About a year later, towards the end of 1840, Kwame and I had a violent argument. The king had abdicated in order to marry his beloved lady-in-waiting, and Sophie's father had succeeded him as King Willem II. Anna Pavlovna stood at his side wearing a robe of gold and silver scattered with gems during the coronation in the New Church, which we attended. A fresh wind blew through the kingdom. Festivities were organized in the grand tradition of the tsars, and the richness of the new queen's apparel at these celebrations was a clear signal that the days of austerity were over. The mood of the people was sanguine. The Hague was given a glimpse of future wonders when, on 5 December, dozens of buildings were lit up with gaslight, as if by magic.

We went to the palace in good spirits. Sophie's brother Willem Alexander, now the crown prince, had just become a father, and so it was his turn to lead the traditional St. Nicholas Eve party. As soon as we arrived he drew me aside, grinning roguishly. His boyish enthusiasm was contagious. Besides, Sophie's brother was not someone you could easily refuse. Perhaps I was a little flattered, too, by his confiding in me and needing me as his accomplice. Me! Of course I also hoped to make an impression on Sophie. Willem Alexander painted my lips and put a cap on my head. The bloomers fitted me, but the black stockings were far too wide, and I leaped out from behind the curtain barelegged.

It was not until I was face to face with the assembled guests, who let out startled cries, that I realized what I had let myself in for. There was applause for Willem Alexander's capital idea of engaging a real Moor for the part of Black Peter. Sophie stared at me in disbelief until the musicians struck up again. Just as in other years, the guests fled from Black Peter in all directions. I chased them, brandishing my birch rod and leaping about, until I found Kwame barring my way. He was standing motionless in the midst of the tumult, with clenched fists. There may have been tears in his eyes. At all events, he knocked my cap off my head, tore madly at my jerkin until the seams split, and then bolted. I wanted to go after him, but all eyes were fixed on me. So I put on a funny accent and kept rolling my eyes until everyone was laughing again.

Never had I seen such a miracle as the illuminated streets through which we rode home that night. I tried to enjoy the sight, but Kwame's sullen silence dampened my spirits. When we arrived in Delft I screwed up courage to tell him I would ask Mrs. van Moock to make me a bed in the disused maid's room. I told him we were too old to share the same cot. This feeling had troubled me for some time, but it was only now that I was so angry with him that I dared speak my mind. He looked at me as if he couldn't believe his ears, but when he saw that I was in earnest, he broke his stubborn silence at last.

"I suppose that's her idea, is it?" he fumed, and it was a little while before I realized he was not referring to Mrs. van Moock. "Because you'd rather be in bed with her, wouldn't you? Don't deny it . . . I can tell. All the whispering, the flirting behind my back. You can't fool me. Well, go away then. Go. Now." Ducking to avoid the personal belongings he was hurling at me, I denied his accusation hotly. And yet I was flattered that he should think I was so grown up, that I might be on such familiar terms with Sophie as to warrant behaviour of that kind.

At breakfast the next morning he sulked. Undaunted, I whistled a cheerful tune, as if I was glad to have spent the night on my own. Without looking at me, Kwame replaced his spoon in his bowl of porridge and moved to another table, taking his porridge with him. That evening I found the rest of my belongings in an untidy heap on my bed where Kwame had flung them: books and notebooks, some underwear and the Georgian fan that Sophie had worn at the coronation ball, which was badly creased. My sketch pad lay on top of the pile. Angry words had been scrawled in charcoal across my study of a dragonfly. I had some difficulty reading them, as the stick of charcoal had snapped at least three times, but the message proved to be absurdly formal, and strongly reminiscent of Chateaubriand: "To you I am a wild man in need of civilization; to me you are a civilized man gone wild."

3

*"For several days I have noticed people staring at me
as if I had escaped from the zoo . . . it must be some-
thing very wicked that I am accused of."
"It is not wicked, merely ridiculous."
"That I . . . what? Have robbed the National Bank?
Or that I fell in love with one of the princes of
Ashanti?"*

—Jacob van Lennep
De lotgevallen van Klaasje Sevenster

"Eyes shut!" Herr Professor Deckwitz instructed, as he positioned the points of his callipers on the outer rims of my eye
sockets. He tightened the screw until the legs were clamped on
the bone. "Extraordinary!"

The professor, a short man, wore a white smock buttoned at
the back, like a slaughterer or a surgeon. He held his little fingers
aloft and his arms akimbo, as if he were pouring tea from the
finest eggshell porcelain. He was engaged in determining the conformation of my skull and clicked his tongue as he made a note of
the distance between my cheekbones. Kwame, who was to be
measured next, watched the proceedings along with Sophie.

Herr Professor Deckwitz was famous in Italy for his description of Dante Alighieri's finger bones, which are kept in the
library at Florence. In France he had gained popularity with his
study of Descartes' skull, from which he inferred great intelli-
gence, and with the rediscovery of the penis of Abélard, on
which subject he had little to say because, being a phrenologist,
he drew conclusions exclusively from bone structures. His treatise titled *Tendencies of Physiognomy*, in which the facial features of
humans are correlated with those of animals and their respective
characters, was an international success. Since then Herr Deckwitz had been travelling all over Europe lecturing at universities
and demonstrating his skills for the nobility.

Sophie had attended one of his demonstrations during her last visit to her aunt in Weimar. Ever fascinated by new inventions, she had decided, together with her cousin Carl Alexander, to have her skull measured. She turned out to be "cheerful by nature and blessed with talent, kindhearted and strong-willed, exceptionally intelligent and straightforward." I could have told him that myself.

The princess had returned from Weimar full of enthusiasm. For weeks she regaled us with accounts of the cultural goings-on in the fairy-tale setting of the castle in the mountains. There had been artists and architects, poets and singers. Concerts and plays provided entertainment every evening. She had met Hans Christian Andersen, the Danish writer, with whom she sat in the park designed by Goethe while he tried out new stories on her. She had tramped across mountains and valleys which bore the names of her mother and her aunt. Deep in the forest she had fancied herself to be utterly alone and imagined what it would be like to survive in the wild. Sometimes, when her narrative flagged, I would beg her to go back to the beginning, just for the sake of seeing her eyes sparkle again.

So, when we heard of Deckwitz's arrival in The Hague in January 1842, it was clear what would transpire. One freezing afternoon we presented ourselves at the Queen's Pavilion with a view to enriching the Deckwitz collection with our unique skulls.

After the professor had established the conformation of my cranium he took me aside and pronounced upon the content, although he confessed to some reservations, as the African skull was totally novel to him. The reason for his popularity was obvious: he said only what people most wanted to hear. His manner reminded me of the psychic medium who only recently attended the crown princess after the birth of Willem Alexander's son Wiwill, the fourth Willem in a row. Deckwitz's words were too flattering to be repeated. However, there were two comments that made the blood rush to my head: the first ("You are steadfast in friendship") because I had recently proved him wrong, and the second—he leaned over and whispered man to man—because it struck home: "You are inclined to give in to certain temptations of the flesh." Hardly a far-fetched oracle for a boy of nearly fifteen, but it left me as flustered as if I had been caught red-handed.

In those days I had eyes only for Sophie, and could spare hardly a thought for Kwame. I made myself comfortable in my little room and tried to forget my cousin's lonely nights. It irked me to see Kwame red-eyed at breakfast. I would even go out of my way to rile him on occasion. Since the heir apparent had married Sophie von Württemberg, for instance, I had taken to referring to our own princess as "my Sophie," to distinguish her from the former. Kwame usually pretended not to hear the first time I did so, but at the second mention he would seethe with rage and at the third he would explode. So when he gave me one of his accusing, mournful looks I retaliated by saying "my Sophie" twenty-four times before the end of breakfast. I had surrendered one friendship and embraced another. The new-found privacy of my own bed offered the opportunity of discovering my body, which was reaching maturity at that time. I was possessed of a vivid imagination, which was entirely focused on Sophie. I held on to the images crossing my mind in the daytime, storing them carefully so that I could invoke them at will in the night.

Just as a youth trains the muscles of lower back, shoulders and arms to prepare himself to bear an adult burden, so he stimulates other parts of the body with a view to future service. At the van Moock establishment these practices were common, to the extent that the boys discussed them amongst themselves without shame, indeed with a certain measure of pride. Cornelius de Groot, being the oldest pupil, was considered by most of us to be an example in these matters, and the size of his manhood, which he did not attempt to conceal in the washroom, made us all the readier to believe his monstrous stories. Although we shuddered at the thought of behaving in such a way ourselves, we were all so eager to know more that Cornelius started providing illustrations. That winter I bought several prints for a few cents. In later years I came across my little collection of pictures each time I moved house, but could never bring myself to part with them. They are a reminder of my sweetest discoveries, which were untempered by reality and full of promise. I admit that in my mind's eye the crude figures were overlaid by Sophie's delicate features, but I deny most sincerely that I ever disrespected her. I discovered the highest and lowest of sentiments at the same time. Desire of the body nurtures desire of the mind. Love presents itself in both forms. All the better when they coincide, of course, but each gives satisfaction on its own, too. If the one is lacking, you still have the other.

When he had finished with me, Deckwitz wished to examine my cousin. I sat down next to Sophie. My knee touched hers, but she did not move away. I was very conscious of Kwame watching us. We were sitting directly facing the examining apparatus. The professor adjusted the callipers and noted the width of the boyish jaw with incredulity. Sophie pinched me. She wanted me to whisper the outcome of my cranial proportions to her, but I pretended to be absorbed in the process of measurement.

"Well?" she said impatiently, nudging my leg with her knee.

"It was fine," I said.

She snorted and kicked my shins like a mare held on a too short rein. Laughing. As if I were teasing her.

"I'm intelligent," I whispered in her ear.

"Of course you are."

"More intelligent than some people—he was very clear on that score—more intelligent than some he had measured last year at Weimar . . ."

She provoked me further with a prod of her elbow and if we had been alone we would have been rolling over the floor the next minute. Tickling—that was something she could not abide. I restrained myself, but regretted it at once, for she grabbed me by the scruff of the neck saying: "I'm warning you!"

The professor followed us from the corner of his eye, but did not dare voice his disapproval.

"Ouch!" Kwame cried. The callipers were clamped on too tight. Deckwitz apologized and said he had been distracted by the small scar which was more visible on Kwame's cheek than on mine. We explained about the small cut that is sometimes made in the face of the newborn in Kumasi. Firstly, this makes the infant less appealing to spirits seeking to claim its soul. Secondly, medicinal herbs are smeared into the wound by way of prevention against all sorts of ailments. The professor showed some surprise at the notion of making cuts in a sound body to protect against disease, but Sophie said it was a wonderful idea and well worth trying.

The phrenological examination proceeded. Sophie's gown rustled when she pressed her elbow against mine.

"Seriously, Aquasi, I want to know. Did he say nice things about you? I'm interested. Honestly," she whispered, staring fixedly ahead. I believe I shut my eyes for an instant so as not to contemplate my own impertinence.

"Something very nice," I said, and heard my temples throb as I screwed up courage. "He said I'm in love."

She stared at me open-mouthed. Then she shut her mouth and glanced away, but after a few seconds her eyes were drawn to me again.

"How can he tell?"

"By my ears."

"By your ears?" She inspected the one nearest to her but discovered nothing out of the ordinary.

"That's what he said. Up to my ears in love."

On her guard, she peered through her eyelashes.

"Did he say with whom?"

"No, for that I must consult a specialist in affairs of the heart."

I had thought she would blush or at least burst out laughing, but she slumped back in her chair.

"Oh Aquasi!" After about a minute she repeated my name, sighing this time, from the bottom of her heart. "Oh Aquasi!" She didn't say another word during the whole session. Afterwards she sent us away as soon as courtesy permitted. At the time I didn't mind. I had stopped thinking. Having spoken out made me walk on air.

"If you ask me," Kwame said, "she'll spend the rest of the afternoon inflicting ritual wounds on herself, rubbing medicines into them all and leaping up and down around a bonfire. You have to be so careful with what you say to her." I pushed him into a ditch for punishment.

The time came that there was not very much left that van Moock could teach me. It happened increasingly often that I put him a question he was unable to answer. At one point I even made a pretence of ignorance, merely to boost his morale.

In the meantime preparations were underway for our baptism by Dominee Molenkamp, who was out to impress his superiors. He was sure we would make excellent missionaries to spread the word of God among the Ashanti. However, he had not foreseen Kwame's cool response, by which he was so disappointed that he postponed the baptism for an indefinite period. Mine too, although I had done nothing untoward.

Kwame was not less intelligent than I, he merely seemed to have lost all interest in our school subjects, even Scripture and Morality, which required not only brains but above all the will to reflect. He read the texts dutifully, but was unaffected by them. He also turned against all science subjects, preferring to devote his time to solitary occupations such as drawing and making music. He exchanged his textbooks for novels. I tried, without success, to raise his flagging spirits, and reminded him of my father's wish. "Do you think he sent us to Holland to learn to draw and play music and daydream?" I said gruffly. I thought he had withdrawn into his shell just to punish me. In the end I decided it was time for me to mind my own business.

Now that our education was coming to an end, the correspondence between van Moock, the Wesleyan Missionary Society in London and the Ministry of Colonies grew in length and frequency. The latter intended to send us back to the Gold Coast within the next two years, in order that the Dutch government might recoup some of the monies that had been spent on us. The Reverend Beecham of the Wesleyan Society recommended a period of practical training combining instruction in medicine, architecture and agricultural skills. "Their model," he wrote, "should be Peter the Great of Russia." Even Queen Anna burst out laughing when we told her of his reference to her ancestor.

The Royal Academy of Science had been founded earlier that year, in Delft. Its patron was Crown Prince Willem Alexander, and it was at his instigation that van Moock informed us of the various courses on offer. The dean of the academy considered missionary work a waste of time and was more in favour of converting souls to his own cause. He had even recruited Cornelius de Groot for a general engineering course, although the boy could only pay for his tuition by taking employment as a night watchman. Kwame and I had meetings with several of the professors. With the rich ores on the Gold Coast foremost in their minds, they sought to arouse our interest in regional and practical geology, geophysics and engineering. They seemed to welcome the chance to enhance the prestige of their academy with the attendance of two foreign princes. The fact that we were rather young—sixteen by the time we enrolled—would be overlooked.

For the first time we saw an opportunity to do something for the good of our country. Kwame's enthusiasm was fired at last. He even made an effort to do better in class, but had lagged too far behind to make up for past inattention. I realized that by focusing my studies on the Gold Coast I would be able to fulfil my father's expectations. At the same time, the idea of returning to Africa made me uneasy.

All those years at school I had permitted myself only vague memories of home. It was safer that way: the blur dulled the pain. Whenever I could not avoid picturing my mother in sharp detail, stooping with pursed lips and brushing my nose with hers to press a kiss on my cheek, I would shut my eyes tight and force myself to think of other things—Dutch things. When Sophie caught me doing this once, she thought it very odd indeed. Still, it worked, and I became quite skilled at this trick. After a while it was enough merely to turn away as soon as my mother loomed, and if I still wept it was for the loss of *a* mother, not *my* mother. In due course other memories dimmed, too, and I was left only with shadowy figures in the place of my loved ones.

On the few occasions that I was still visited by dreams of being reunited with my family, the figures running towards me were faceless. I did not understand their words of greeting, nor they mine. We ran dumbly across a landscape in which I had lost my bearings. Unlike Kwame I had never imagined what it would be like to return. Now that I attempted to do so, I found I had no memory of the Asantehene's features. His clothing I could recall, and the Golden Stool, and how his rings were embedded in his plump fingers. Nothing else.

It came as a blow to me to realize that the curtain I had let down between me and my childhood had obscured the faces of my past for ever. That night I visited Kwame's bedroom for the last time. I slipped into bed with him but, as I was drawing up the covers, he turned away from me.

"No, Kwasi," he said, "not any more." And he lay motionless, listening to my stumbling retreat.

After our encounter with the phrenologist I did not see my Sophie again until mid-March, which is not to say that she was absent from my ardent imagination. The vividness of the pictures in my head was sometimes almost as gratifying as if I had seen her in the flesh. The court was in some disarray. The old king who had abdicated was in Berlin, where he had fallen gravely ill in the arms of his lady-love. While the royal family were making up their minds whether the dying man was to be ignored or forgiven, all social engagements were postponed. During those months of separation I wrote Sophie three long letters, to which she replied affectionately but in keeping with court etiquette; she did not refer to what had passed between us during our session with Professor Deckwitz. It was not until Easter that we received an invitation from the crown princess to a *thé dansant*, at which my Sophie was to declaim some verses by German poets. I would have been equally thrilled by the chance to hear her read the weather forecast in Mongolian!

Although anyone who had to put up with Willem Alexander's temperament deserved sympathy, Sophie von Württemberg never inspired affection in me. It was clear that she saw us as belonging to her mother-in-law's camp, along with her two brothers-in-law and her sister-in-law. She thought Prince Alexander weak and spoiled. She detested Prince Hendrik, whom I liked for his probing mind and sincere interest in our well-being. I never knew my Sophie to say a word against her brother's wife, but she too was regarded as an enemy.

Nevertheless, I tried to form an unbiased opinion of Sophie von Württemberg, who would after all be queen one day. Relations between her and her husband were strained. Since I was in the throes of love myself, I felt sympathy for anyone not thus favoured, although I was perturbed by her dislike of Holland, which she found small and unappealing and full of dull folk. In later years people assured me that she was a good soul who suffered an unjust fate and a boorish husband, but in general her melancholy inspired more irritation than sympathy. Indeed, when she had asked Grand Duchess Maria Pavlovna, aunt to both Sophies, for advice concerning her intended marriage to Willem Alexander of Orange, whom she doubted would make her happy, the grand duchess had merely said: "Well my dear, what right would you have to happiness?" This was the sort of reaction she elicited.

However, as a hostess she could not be faulted. With her little son Wiwill on her arm, she personally conducted the search party for Easter eggs. This did not take long, for the gardens of her royal residence, which differed from a gentleman's mansion only in the prevailing atmosphere of gloom, were not large.

My Sophie read aloud from the German poet Schiller. Afterwards she came to my side. She had something to tell me, she said, but was waylaid by Mrs. van Moock, which good lady was delighted to have us under her wing for the afternoon and under considerable pressure from the Prussian ambassador's wife to arrange for Kwame and me to grace one of the embassy soirées with our presence. Under cover of their animated chatter, I reached out for Sophie's hand, but she shrank from my touch. She rose abruptly, and invited Kwame to accompany her on the piano while she sang.

King Willem II arrived at around four wearing his favourite Russian cap, which usually betokened a good humour. He embraced his daughter-in-law warmly, who recoiled from the smell of tobacco. The king had just inspected the new wing that was being built on to the palace. He had drawn up the plans himself, wholly in accordance with the modern Gothic mode. He unrolled his blueprints and sketches of ornamental features. I enquired after the architectural calculations and the amount of tension sustained by the arches, but his evasive answers told me that he was better at sketching than at calculating. The conversation soon turned to the king's collection of paintings, which he wished to open to the public. He even offered us a private viewing in the near future, and Kwame's response was so warm that there was no way we could decline the invitation when it came.

A game of blind man's buff was played in the garden. I did my best to be caught, and soon it was my turn to be blindfolded. I stumbled about with clawed fingers, at which all the children took flight. I sniffed the air like a predator. Sophie's petticoats had been treated with lavender-scented starch. Within a few seconds I caught my prey. I let out a cry of triumph, and made her stand still, demanding a kiss for ransom. Not an unreasonable exchange under the circumstances, I felt, but to my shock her body stiffened. Then she tried to wrench herself free and even dug her nails into my flesh to make me relax my hold. I tore the blindfold off and saw she had turned very pale, that her lip trembled and that there were tears in her eyes. The children watched openmouthed.

"Oh Aquasi!" her lips signalled, but there was no sound this time.

The arrival of Crown Prince Willem Alexander with a party of friends created an awkward interlude. He was accompanied by his drinking partner Jules van der Capellen and the Javanese artist Raden Saleh, and he made his entrance with a young lady on his arm: la Miranda. She was a leading actress with the Italian Commedia, one of the many drama companies that had taken to including The Hague on their tours now that the king provided funding for theatres and concert halls. Raden Saleh was painting la Miranda's portrait, at Willem Alexander's expense. The crown princess reacted with admirable aloofness: she merely offered the actress a little basket of sweetmeats, after which the conversation was gradually resumed.

The artist came to greet us. He was waylaid by the Prussian ambassador's wife: "I hear that your portrait of the Ashanti princes is a masterpiece."

"Too much honour, dear lady," said Raden Saleh, with a slight bow, "for a canvas that has been consigned to the bushmen in Africa."

Mrs. van Moock snatched her hand away from his arm. He listened impassively to the Prussian lady's efforts to persuade him to paint her portrait, then excused himself hastily and made off.

"What an opinionated fellow!" huffed the ambassador's wife. "He seems to think his name is still on everyone's lips."

"That look, so inscrutable!" said Mrs. van Moock, shuddering. It always made her nervous when other people had uncharitable thoughts. "I fear he is all too aware of the waning of his celebrity."

"Tastes change," the other lady declared. "Even the most exotic dish, if served day in day out, loses its appeal after a while. Well, what do you think, would it be convenient for you to visit next Saturday? With the two princes of Ashanti, of course."

Crown Prince Willem Alexander circulated among the guests with Wiwill on his arm. He was tipsy and made a great show of throwing the child up in the air and almost failing to catch him. His wife's cries of alarm made him laugh uproariously. She tried to take the child from him, but was obliged to witness how the proud father sat with all the prettiest ladies in turn, demanding praise for the fruit of his loins. She eventually succeeded in having the child taken to bed, but that did not stop Willem Alexander from showing off his son.

He drew a leather receptacle from his waistcoat pocket. It contained a silver-backed disc framing a portrait of little Wiwill surrounded by his toys. It was a remarkably accurate likeness, but was neither drawn nor painted. The shiny image, which was protected by glass, was handed round for the guests to admire, while the crown prince delighted in the incredulity shown by some. The King merely shrugged: "Queen Anna received one of these from Saint Petersburg recently, a portrait of her brother, and now she wants all our portraits to be fabricated in this manner. It is a new invention."

"The image is obtained by using a method devised by Monsieur Daguerre. I saw this trick being performed in Paris recently," Raden Saleh said disdainfully. "It is a good likeness, yes. That is all it is. But is it art?"

"My good man, what good is art if it is not a good likeness?" Willem Alexander said testily.

"With all due respect, Your Highness," Raden Saleh continued, "there is surely more art in a canvas entailing weeks or months of dedicated labour than in a silver-coated copper plate that has been soaked in dangerous chemicals for a few moments."

"All I want from art," the crown prince rebutted, "is a good picture. You will never achieve such a convincing resemblance, Raden Saleh, not even if you spend the rest of your days perfecting a single face."

The Prussian lady concurred a little too warmly for the crown prince's liking, and he turned away brusquely to show the daguerreotype to us. It was indeed most remarkable. As though you were looking into a mirror that reflected someone else. I was eager to know more about the technique involved, but the crown prince was unable to supply me with details.

"We are to have a portrait of ourselves made soon. Why don't you come along? Then you can fire your questions at the fellow making it."

"A portrait like this?" I asked. "Of us all?"

"Certainly. I insist. Do it for Sophie's sake," Willem Alexander said, "so she can take you with her to Weimar." Out of the corner of my eye I saw his sister nudge him to be silent. But the crown prince was only egged on by her admonition. "I dare say it's still a secret, my dear, but Mamma is set upon having such portraits made of us all. By way of a gift. For you. So now if Quame and Aquasi would be so kind . . ." Kwame certainly did not wish any more portraits to be made of him, he said, but Willem Alexander was unperturbed, for once he was holding forth he became deaf to all others. "The number of portraits is of no consequence. As our artist from Java quite rightly stated, it takes only a few minutes. And so, *ma petite,* you can take all of us with you, and shall have no reason to pine while you are away."

Sophie kept silent, and renewed her attempts to hush her brother. The look in her eyes told me that everything was about to change.

"The cure for heartache!" Willem Alexander exclaimed, whereupon an awkward silence descended. He paused, sensing that he had let the cat out of the bag. I was unable to speak. I had no desire to question him as to his meaning, for I feared that I would see everything in sharp focus at any moment, and tried to prolong the blur as long as possible. It was Kwame who spoke first.

"But Sophie, are you leaving us?" he asked, in a low voice.

Sophie nodded.

"Didn't she tell you?" grinned Willem Alexander. "That is most unusual. She talks of nothing else."

"Guillot, *je vous en prie!*" Her anger had made her break her silence at last.

"All right all right, I won't say another word," he said, and held his tongue for two seconds, until he burst out with: "our little grand duchess!"

"Grand duchess?" asked Kwame. Willem Alexander put his finger to his lips.

The Prussian lady gasped. "Does this mean that we are to believe the rumours from Weimar?"

I had inadvertently lowered my guard, and sustained a shattering blow. For several seconds I was frozen in shock. Mrs. van Moock patted me on the back and then quickly drew her new friend away from me. Kwame took my hand and gave it an affectionate squeeze. He meant well, but his gesture was awkward, not intimate as in the old days, and made me feel even more desolate. The sense of being entirely alone brought me back to my senses. No one would speak on my behalf. I had to speak for myself.

"Carl Alexander is an excellent match." Trying to sound unmoved made my words come out a fraction too loud. *"Mes félicitations!"*

"It's not that simple," said Sophie, but did not meet my eyes.

"The titular grand duke is exceedingly handsome, Sophie tells us. Well read and romantic, too, it seems."

Willem Alexander's jocular tone roused Sophie to defend her fiancé: "Herr von Goethe was his tutor."

He slapped his knee like a street comedian. "So that's why she keeps on quoting Torquato Tasso!"

Sophie stood up and turned her back on him.

"I am sorry, Aquasi," she said, and then spun round to confront her brother, furiously: "I wanted to be the one to tell him!" She rushed out of the room, leaving Willem Alexander behind with us.

He was still chuckling. "That young lady acts as if she had promised her hand to *you!*" This notion, too, seemed to tickle him. "I say, that would be something, just think of it!"

"Indeed," I said, "the very idea!"

If you have never seen the horizon, you do not know there is a limit to your field of vision. In the dense forests surrounding Kumasi you cannot see further than a few yards ahead. Tell this to a Dutchman and he will feel uneasy: he wishes to survey his surroundings and look where he is going. An obstructed view makes him feel shut in.

But this is a mistake. The sight of bushes screening ever denser thickets is not at all oppressive, for it kindles the desire to look farther afield, to set about hacking a path through the forest and exploring what lies beyond. The glint of the chopping knife sharpens the eye, for the more cluttered the view the greater the desire to look beyond.

Indeed, it took Kwame and me a long time to accustom ourselves to the sheer expanse of Dutch views. The skyline in the lowlands held no secrets, and so our interest in venturing farther afield was not aroused. There was nothing to be explored.

At home our eyes were not used to looking into the distance, and in those days we thought we would be able to see everything in the world if it weren't for the trees screening our view. In Holland we discovered the horizon. We walked towards it, but never arrived. It kept retreating as we advanced, shrinking from our chopping knives. From now on our view was no longer limited by greenery, but by the limited power of our own vision.

An obstructed view suggests infinity, whereas a vast panorama is necessarily finite.

Perhaps that is why the Dutch look inwards. Into themselves and others. They do not draw their curtains; they will discuss their ideas, motives and problems in all openness until satisfied that the listener has gained insight into the workings of their mind. The splinters of their hearts, however, are kept in the closet, and they are never to be seen rending their garments in grief.

The life of the Ashanti takes place in the open. His hut is windowless. When his soul is in anguish he storms out into the wild, where he can express his feelings without shame in the shelter of the forest. Europeans take this to mean that Ashanti man is close to nature and driven by simple motives. But the truth is that the Ashanti keeps his thoughts to himself. He would rather plunge into the depths of the unknown than fathom his thoughts. Ultimately, looking inward is as limited as looking outward.

The Dutchman thinks he is showing his feelings, but in reality he is presenting his turn of thought. The Ashanti shows his emotions, but racks his wits in private. Each keeps something hidden: the Dutchman his heart, the Ashanti his mind. This confused me greatly when I first arrived in Holland, and at times prevented me from understanding the motives of those around me. What I took to be disclosures of emotions were merely presentations of facts. The Dutch have even pumped away the sea to uncover what lies underneath.

Standing in the middle of flat polderland I always felt drained of hope, a stranger on alien ground. An unobstructed view on all

sides, but nothing to see. I was painfully aware that in these surroundings there would not be anywhere for me to hide. I was as
lost in the landscape as amid the Hollanders' emotions. Nothing
in my sights but myself.

It was during that same Easter that I told van Moock of my
intention to study mining engineering at the Academy. To his
question as to the motives of my choice, I replied: "The least a
man can do is dig."

A few days later Sophie of Orange and Carl Alexander, the
future duke of Saxe-Weimar, were betrothed. I was not present at
the festivities. A severe bout of bronchitis kept me in bed, but
three days later I was in attendance at a military parade in The
Hague. Princess Sophie and her mother were watching from an
open calèche as the lancers and dragoons presented arms, when
the princess noticed me on the grandstand. She waved cheerfully.
I waved back and both of us broke into a smile when there was a
sudden salute of gunfire. Afterwards there was a reception, during which she introduced me to her cousin. Her feelings of friendship seemed unchanged. She took my arm, giving me assurances
of her pleasure at my presence.

It must be said that her future husband was most charming.
Carl Alexander was tall and had sad eyes, which he fixed on me so
steadily that I felt obliged to say something jolly. Sophie had evidently told him about us, for he was aware of the political situation in the Gold Coast and the reasons for our presence in
Holland. Having travelled widely himself, he was interested to
learn how we had adapted to life in Europe, and invited us to visit
Weimar at the earliest opportunity. Sophie was clearly relieved:
she watched our animated conversation with a beatific smile. I
could not understand how people could have such a high opinion
of love if it did not spare you being deceived by appearances. I
was glad I still had my little pornographic collection, which was
my only solace during those days and nights. The women in the
pictures did not dissemble, they were acting according to their

nature. Sophie's wedding took place on 8 October in the newly built royal gallery of paintings.

The following week we were invited to ride in the royal cortège. Waiving court etiquette, Prince Hendrik insisted Kwame and I share his carriage. He showered us with pleasantries, confectionery and so much solicitude that I could tell Sophie had confided in her favourite brother and had asked him to be kind to me.

The afternoon dragged on. Sophie was finding it hard to bid farewell to her parents. Her father, acting with the clumsiness of a child, pressed upon her a posy of chamomile flowers he had picked in the garden himself. Then the elderly burgomaster of The Hague personally escorted the slow-moving courtly progress up to the city limits. In each subsequent borough there was a pause for a speech and a brass band. Upon arrival at the Navy headquarters in Rotterdam the royal party was given a warm welcome and a speech by the burgomaster. The steamship *Ludwig*, festooned with hundreds of little flags of Holland and Saxe-Weimar, was waiting at the quayside. A canopy had been erected on deck, under which dainty refreshments, prepared by Hendrik's navy chef, were served during a final gathering. It was a lingering farewell. At one point I was overcome with emotion, and withdrew without attracting notice. I went to the bows to look out over the water.

The steam engines burst into a roar. The steel deck reverberated under my feet. The signal for departure had been given, and I was watching Willem Alexander climb into his carriage when the new hereditary grand duchess of Saxe-Weimar came to my side for some last words. She gripped the railing, stretched her arms and took a deep breath of salty air.

"Promise me that you will visit soon. I have also asked Prince Quame. You can come together."

"We have travelled so far already."

The Navy cruiser *Pegasus* came alongside, and Sophie nodded amiably to the crew standing at attention. As she remained silent,

I told her how the vastness of the landscape took away all my desire for travelling. She looked at me in surprise.

"Are you serious? To me each new horizon is an invitation. One you can't refuse. You'll see how different everything looks upriver. Once you are in Germany the Rhine becomes narrower. First it flows between gentle slopes covered in vineyards, then winds its way around rocky cliffs. With each bend the panorama changes. You'll love it, I'm sure. That's where you'll find the unspoiled nature we used to read about in all those wonderful books. I want you to see it for yourself. Oh do say yes, promise me you'll come."

Before I could reply we were deafened by salvos of cannon from the *Pegasus*, which gave us such a fright that Sophie had a tantrum the likes of which I had never seen in a woman. She flung the bouquet she had been given by the Naval commander into the water, stamped her feet on the steel deck and excoriated the crew at the top of her voice. Her words were drowned out by the cannon and the sailors simply smiled, persuaded no doubt that their beloved princess was singing the Dutch national anthem.

4

One evening, in September 1843, I was assaulted. I had been a student at the Royal Academy for several weeks. Kwame was not yet enrolled; he had to spend another year at school to catch up on his lessons. I still had my room at the boarding school, which I had rented for the duration of my studies.

Hardly had I left the building when two fellows pounced on me and put a potato sack over my head. There were about twenty-five of us, all trussed in the same way. We were herded together in the market square, where we were forced to sit on the cold ground. Passers-by stopped to scoff and spit at us while we were loaded on to farm wagons and driven away. We were packed closely together. The lad next to me felt sick and sank on to the evil-smelling planks. The lurching of the wagon did the rest. I could hear him retching. Although my hands were tied, I managed to pull the sack off his head and thus to give him some air. He thanked me and made to do the same for me, which earned him a smart blow from one of our captors. Our journey ended in a large barn, where our hands were untied and the sacks removed from our heads. We were forced to undress, and left naked, with no food or water and only an oil lamp for warmth.

For a while all of us remained quietly where we were. Then someone launched into song, and the rest of us joined in one by one. As my eyes became accustomed to the dark, I recognized some of my fellow students. Alphons Wenckebach was the first to throw me a pained smile, shrugging off the humiliation. Hendrik Linse tried to force one of the small shutters high up on the wall, but they were all securely bolted. Cornelius de Groot sat in a pig's trough. Necessity being the mother of invention, he covered himself with a blanket of straw. A tall, thin lad was the first to take a few steps in the barn, holding his hands fearfully over his groin. He came to thank me for the kindness I had shown him on the way. He introduced himself as Jacobus Lebret, but hesitated before extending his hand to shake mine. We discussed strategies of escape, somewhat sheepishly. Within half an hour we were all huddled together in small groups, in an attempt to keep warm. Evidently the comradeship that would arise from our shared predicament was the object of our abduction. It was a rite of initiation.

The crouching white bodies massed together like a herd of animals. Most of us tried to catch some sleep. I did not succeed, as my lungs were playing up again from the cold. The huddled figures reminded me of Sophie's rag dolls, with which we had enacted the Greek legends. They were Odysseus' men, waiting for the return of the Cyclops. Their coarse stuffed limbs could be folded into any desired position. It was only in the barn that I wondered why I had never minded that none of the white dolls resembled me. I had not even noticed, until Kwame painted one of them black by overturning an inkwell on its head. Sophie had been delighted with the result.

In the middle of the night we were startled by the drunken revelry of our captors, who came staggering out of some local alehouse. They opened the barn doors. Several of them I had seen before, including the ringleaders, who were members of the exclusive Five Columns Club. They made us stand in line and then brought in some rented girls, who proceeded to inspect each of us in turn in a manner which would be impolite to describe and which they soon regretted. I have never spoken of what transpired during that night and I find it difficult even now to mention it. Suffice it to say that we were forced to engage in the grossest behaviour. It was a demeaning experience for everyone concerned.

Towards morning most of our tormentors were exhausted, but the fiercest among them singled Cornelius out for a final drunken diversion. Until then he had resisted them on all fronts but one, and they were determined to break his will. They drove him into the adjoining pigsty and tried to make him get down on his knees among the pigs and root in the filth covering the ground. Cornelius refused, and received a kick on the lower back. He drew himself up. I could see how he was struggling with his pride. At the order "Go on, you filthy swine, root!" a look of such defiance crossed his face that one of his tormentors armed himself with a length of wood. I was tired out. My nerves were shattered. All I wanted was for this to end. I went into the pigsty and knelt down next to Cornelius. Without taking my eyes off him I showed him what to do. I pushed my nose into the dung. He did not follow my example. However, my voluntary debasement made the brutes fall about laughing as they staggered outside.

"It's only a joke," I told Cornelius, trying to sound brave.

"For you it is, I dare say—even at school you were used to bowing and scraping."

"But you helped me then, and now . . ."

"No need," he said, and got up. I stayed behind. The pigs spread a comfortable warmth, and anyway it was all over now. At daybreak our clothes were returned to us and we were taken home. Before going up to my room I scrubbed myself clean in the courtyard. Kwame came down with his wash-cloth. He could not have known how I had demeaned myself, but the contempt in his eyes was more hurtful than the long night of bullying.

I fell into a deep sleep, and had a nightmare in which I was trapped in a burning shed, but I awoke to remember that I was now a full member of the Delft student society Phoenix, and told myself that this made up for a lot.

As soon as I recovered from my attack of bronchitis Kwame and I were baptized in the Old Church at Delft. Headmaster van Moock and his wife sat in the front pew, beaming and catching their breath as if we were their own flesh and blood. Mrs. van Moock pressed a card into my hands:

"Ye were sometimes darkness, but now are ye light in the Lord: walk as children of light." Ephesians 5:8. September 1843, Best wishes, Henriette van Moock.

There were congratulatory messages from Sophie and Carl Alexander in Weimar. Prince Hendrik, acting on behalf of King Willem II, presented us with a Bible. He assured us that his father was most gratified with this milestone. Van Drunen delivered a speech in the name of the minister of Colonies, commending us for setting a good example to the people of our homeland, from which wilderness he had removed us six years earlier in order that we might reap the fruits of Holland.

"Well now," he said, with a hint of regret in his voice, "the seed has sprouted, the weeds have been uprooted, the tree of our knowledge is bearing fruit!" Afterwards there was luncheon with coffee and sultana pancakes.

Kwame behaved tolerably that day, although in the past year he had sorely tried Dominee Molenkamp's patience. I must admit that the dominee's sermons were remarkably tendentious. Kwame was probably right in his belief that the man looked down on our race. To the dominee, the riches of Europe were a sign of God's favour, and the simplicity of Africa, if not a punishment, then at least a judgement. His most important lesson was that we should be grateful for the opportunity of acquainting ourselves with the only true God, a privilege denied to so many of our countrymen.

"Since He sees fit to deny the Ashanti His Word," retorted Kwame, "it must be for their own good."

As for me, I felt quite proud of my baptism, proud that I should have earned a place in such an ancient tradition. And God? I could hardly blame Him for the folly of his servants. They construed His words of grace in their own limited ways. Certainly, He had supplanted the gods of nature that I used to worship in our temples. But those deities had faces, the kind of face you glimpse in a gnarled tree trunk or in a sunbeam glancing off a pool. God has never shown His face to me. That is something I miss. Nor has He ever spoken to me, as a father to His child, although I asked Him every day for many years. I strained my ears in the dark, but all I ever heard was my own voice. Or a reproach from Kwame. I was uplifted by Him, but never consoled.

Some days later we heard, via the Ministry of Colonies, that a messenger had arrived in Elmina from my father Kwaku Dua, requesting tidings of his "European family." Kwame was deeply moved by this news, and pressed me to write to my father at once. I was evasive. A bitter quarrel ensued. Kwame threatened to send a letter himself telling the Asantehene of my refusal to write. I promised to reconsider the matter, but did not put pen to paper. I plunged into student life and surrounded myself with friends until December, when the clubhouse went quiet and Lebret, Linse and Wenckebach, too, left town to spend Christmas with their families. I had not been invited to their homes. On several evenings I tried drinking to forget myself. The boarding school was full of new boys, who left me cold. I was seized by a melancholy that settled into my bones.

Until now my sure method of dispelling downheartedness had been to throw myself into my studies, but this time the gloom persisted. One night when I could not sleep—I was probably a little tipsy, too—I finally made the effort to write. I still have the notebook, containing diagrams of a staircase set at an angle of forty-eight degrees, in which I drafted the following lines to my father:

*Esteemed Asantehene / Father / My Father / Dear Father . . .
etc. Now that we have been notified of your interest in our
well-being, I can inform you that we have made progress
entirely according to your plan and are nearing the completion of our education, thereby . . . / Threads / Broken wings
[illegible] . . . greatly saddened by the dearth of news / Our
departure / our banishment / Father, how is it possible for a
man to part with his son without grief? / Impossible to
describe what that means to a child / not aware? / consequently, Father / the only way I could live with that grief was
to turn away from my past. I embraced what lay ahead, as
Tsetse the fly clings to the sticky threads of Anansi, when life
has broken her wings. The lesser of two evils / to survive /
new life / I disavowed what was dearest to me. Rigorously. To
soften the pain of separation, to reconcile myself to this fate
that has befallen me, I embraced all that is new as being of
more consequence / better / worthier than the old. The only
means of surviving my grief was to lay the blame at your feet,
for the cruel and [crossed out]. The sense of betrayal was
such that I had no choice but to turn a new leaf / failing to
comprehend what your motives might be I aligned myself
with the kingdom of Holland, in the hope of encountering
more fidelity than that shown by my father / fatherland /
Father, Father, help me to keep my faith in you. Save me! All I
ask is but one word to serve me as mainstay, as a sign that I
have not been forgotten / reassurance that my soul may find
consolation in what lies behind me, too / Can the power of
consolation be lost? / Can a soul change colour? Perhaps the
rift is not beyond repair. / Perhaps . . .*

In short: the jottings of a befuddled brain. However, I ended up composing a suitable letter according to the rules of etiquette and good form, in which I provided detailed information con-cerning our progress without withholding my personal sentiments. This letter reached Elmina in April 1844. I did not receive a reply.

By the time Kwame enrolled as a student the following summer, our friendship had matured. That is to say, it was tranquil, heartening, and no longer subject to the vagaries of our emotions. Now and then I invited him to accompany me and my friends on outings. Linse and Lebret grew fond of my cousin. When we went out riding or met for dinner they would ask him to join us. They urged him to become a member of our society. His refusal was without precedent. They protested that he would not make friends among the students of his year if he did not join, and that he would be debarred from attending balls and other social functions.

"I appreciate your friendship," he said. "I am very grateful for it, deep down, but it would be a lie to say I was one of you."

"Doesn't friendship create equality?"

"Take a good look at me, and then tell me you can't see the incontrovertible disparity between us."

I could have kicked him, but Lebret took it all in good spirits. He and Linse devised a plan, which they submitted to the president of the society, who in turn discussed it with the Five Columns Club. The statutes were amended to allow for an "extraordinary membership" giving admittance to parties, lectures and balls, which was duly offered to Kwame. After that we succeeded in luring him into the bar room with us from time to time. Although not gregarious himself, his company was always in demand.

We turned eighteen, and manhood was upon us. Wenckebach had chaffed me ever since my birthday. When Kwame's birthday came near and the heady days of early summer made us all frisky, the time was ripe.

"If you put it off any longer," said Linse, "you'll end up dreading it."

"A year from now it'll be too late. You start feeling intimidated, you see," Wenckebach went on, "and before you know it you won't even dare. You'll end up like the Stockfish." (This was what we called our maths professor, in whom every scrap of life had dried up.)

My friends had, either openly or under some charitable pretext, wheedled their fathers into contributing funds for a "gentlemen's night out." They would pay for Kwame and me, because our allowance from the Dutch State did not extend to visiting brothels.

We took the stagecoach to The Hague, where we dined without paying much attention to the food. We drank a lot of wine and hired a carriage, which took us across the foul-smelling canal that divided the heart of the city from the south-eastern end, where we halted in front of one of the houses of ill repute. On the doorstep our courage sank. We only rang the bell because none of us wanted to lose face with the others. A family of Italians was having supper on the pavement. I thought I recognized the father as the organ grinder Sophie and I used to listen to when he played his hurdy-gurdy by the palace gates. I shielded my face with my collar, but no one took any notice of us.

We were received in the proper fashion, although I noticed that the proprietress took Wenckebach aside to enquire about Kwame and me. She looked doubtful and called for her friend, who eyed us from head to toe. Kwame said she probably did not have anyone who dared take us on, so the two of us might as well leave directly. I restrained him—the milk-sop!—and the next moment our coats were taken from us. A girl led us into a dimly lit, red drawing-room. She lifted the hem of her skirt and tucked it under her belt, revealing a dainty black boot with laces. Turkish cushions were scattered on the settees and on the floor. The walls were hung with paintings of odalisques and oriental baths. Champagne was brought by a prim-looking maid, who averted her eyes and left the room without saying a word. She was quite unlike what I had seen in pictures. I asked Wenckebach, who was less nervous than the rest of us, whether they would all be so shy. His chuckle was drowned out by the stroke of a gong. The double-leaved doors swung open. Twelve girls trooped in. They were scantily clad. Bodice and petticoat, that was all. It was clear that they had been advised of our presence, for all eyes turned immediately to Kwame and me. There was some giggling. Each of us became the centre of a cluster of girls. I was astonished to see how a band of youths, united until a moment ago by their trepidation, can waive all solidarity as soon as a woman makes her appearance. Worse than that: other men cease to exist, it seems, when a man is in courting mood. Kwame and I were entertained by two young girls, who seemed to be less robust and less practised than the others. I suspected they were new, and had been assigned to us by the older girls. They were timid, as we were. We drank some wine. They told us their names were Loulou and Naomi, and claimed they had posed for the leading artists of The Hague. Kwame launched into a discourse on the angle between the torso and the pelvis, but they did not seem to follow. Naomi suggested he might like to make a life study of her, but he said he had forgotten his drawing pen. Naomi giggled, and Loulou hooted with laughter as she went on about certain gentlemen having dipped their pens a little too deep in the inkwell.

Linse, Lebret and Wenckebach withdrew in turn, each of them accompanied by one or two girls. Kwame and I had no choice but to climb the stairs to the first floor as a foursome. Out of the corner of my eye I saw Kwame tickling Loulou between her thighs. Although the sight aroused me, I was unpleasantly surprised. She did not protest, and even tilted her hips so as to ease his way. For the duration of this exchange he looked at me fixedly over his shoulder, to see my reaction to his forwardness. As though he were saying: take a good look, I am perfectly capable of this, too. Even on the basest level we are each other's mirror image.

At the top of the stairs we separated and withdrew into rooms on either side of the corridor. I was with Naomi, he with Loulou.

Things did not proceed smoothly. Naomi lay on the bed while I sat hunched on the chair next to it, struggling with a knotted shoelace. The girl plied me with questions entirely unrelated to our purpose in that room. Civilities dampen every passion, I firmly believe. When I told her so, her response was a torrent of improprieties. I was taken aback, for in my dreams the girls from the pictures never spoke when I was with them, or only a few words in greeting. Their eloquence and erudition always echoed that of my beloved in her palace garden. But this trollop's prattle soon dulled my senses. It was not that I was without lust that first time, merely that conversation was not what I had in mind. Who would have thought words came into it at all?

I ordered another bottle to win a stay of further intimacy, but Naomi was tugging at my clothes. She drew me to the washbasin and, to my astonishment, made to wash me. This was too much. I pulled on my trousers and dashed into the corridor under the pretext of going after the champagne. Upon encountering the maid, who was on her way to deliver two bottles, I took one of them from her and lingered in the corridor. From behind one of the doors I heard Lebret groaning with pleasure, and wondered how long I could decently put off returning to Naomi. Then Kwame came out of his room. His excuse was the same as mine, and the maid handed him his bottle of champagne. We waited for her to leave, then sank to the floor and drank the contents of my bottle. Each gulp hardened our resolve to explore the bodies awaiting us, but we kept delaying the moment. We opened Kwame's bottle, too, and laughed away our misgivings. When Naomi and Loulou came looking for us, we were in excellent spirits.

It was four in the morning when our party stumbled down the stairs of the brothel. We clambered wearily into our carriage. I could barely keep my eyes open, but Linse, Lebret and Wencke-bach demanded to know what we had been up to. They had found Kwame and me and the two girls fast asleep in the same bed. Our blissful slumber suggested an abandon that impressed them deeply. However, I had no recollection of what had passed between us, and never dared ask Kwame if his memory served him any better. We left it at that, and boasted of our prowess.

We had not gone far when the carriage was forced to a sudden halt. A drunken lout had been thrown out of some tavern and was assaulting a streetwalker. To silence her screams he threw her on the cobbles in front of our carriage wheels. The coachman slammed on the brakes and the horses reared in fright. Lebret and Linse tumbled on to our laps. Wenckebach swore at the coachman.

"It's nothing," he shouted. "Harbour folk. This is where you find the women of pleasure, you know." And sure enough, I saw a window with a few of those hapless creatures on display. Their clients had the same needs as we, but not the money to visit a private house. So this was where the flighty girls in my secret pictures were to be found!

The fracas had ended without my seeing the assailant's face. The coachman checked the harnesses and pacified his nags. A few minutes later we set off again at a walk. We turned into a side street where the moonlight barely penetrated, and caught sight of the same couple, embroiled in a doorway this time.

"Not the French way, you bastard, I said no!" I heard the woman cry, but the man forced her to kneel.

I ordered the coachman to stop.

"Leave them alone, master."

"But that fellow has a whip," I said, "and the young lady has nothing."

"That's no young lady, sir. That's Turkish Tilly, serving a client. Tuppence for a hand turn." He evidently had no intention of stopping the carriage, so I jumped out. I ran to the drunkard, who was forcing the woman to do his bidding, although she was almost choking. I did not stop to think and leaped on to his back. He reeled. I could hardly have injured him, but he let out a scream of pain. It was not until the woman rose to her feet that I saw she had taken the opportunity to sink her teeth into her assailant.

"There," she spat, wiping her mouth on her sleeve, "that'll teach him!" The coachman came running with a lantern, but even before he reached us I had recognized the villain by his groans.

Cornelius sat on the ground, hunched over his wounded shame. He raised his head, but he did not speak, nor did he try to stand up; he merely glared at me. His look was accusatory, disappointed. I began to feel I had let him down. He still did not move. I am alone, his eyes told me, and that is how I shall always be. He continued to stare. I could not bear it any longer and kicked him smartly, just to make him react. But he neither moved nor spoke. I dropped to my knees and grabbed him by the lapels, but did not have the strength to shake him. Don't despise me, I wanted to say. The words tore at my throat, but no sound came out. Don't despise me. And yet it was he who had acted despicably.

The coachman stood by with the lantern, watching in disbelief. It was absurd. I had grabbed Cornelius's ankles and was pressing my forehead on his boots, overcome by a sense of defeat even greater than his. I detected the old smell of sheep's fat and, for an instant, yearned for the afternoons when we sat side by side polishing our shoes while he told me unlikely stories: I was his slave, and yet by the same token, by pretending to believe him, I was his master.

I came to my senses when I heard Linse, Kwame and Lebret approaching. Not to add to Cornelius's humiliation, I held them back, telling them that all was now in order and that we should continue our journey forthwith.

Three days later, after supper on a Tuesday evening, a young man came to the door with a message from Lebret asking me to meet him at once.

I was composing my fortnightly letter to Weimar. Sophie and I corresponded about certain tenets of philosophy. Her tone was consistently elated, while I aimed at a more balanced tenor. (Even now I can remember the sentence which I broke off to answer my friend's summons. "Do not our tears serve the same purpose as valerian tincture?" I had written. "As long as we are happy we are wide awake, so as not to miss even the most fleeting moment. But weeping makes our eyelids heavy. A great weariness comes over us, dulling the cause of our misery. All we want is to close our eyes, for grief takes a heavier toll than hard labour . . ." Even the flourishes on the final words are etched in my memory.)

I laid down my pen and quickly drew on a greatcoat. Lebret lived with Wenckebach in student lodgings across town. I was almost there when I was accosted by a man in a cape. I was surprised, for at night my dark complexion tended to frighten people off rather than inspire confidence. However, this man said he was a stranger in town and asked me the way. I was giving him the directions he required when he suddenly leaned heavily on my arm, as though he were feeling faint. I steadied him. He took a few staggering steps, moving away from the street lantern. Hardly had I sensed danger when I was set upon by his cronies. Judging by the treatment I received there must have been three or four of them. My arms were pinned to my sides while the ringleader battered me with his fists. My money was taken. Eventually I sank to the ground. The cobbles were damp. I remember the relief of the cool stone against my wounded forehead. I lay quite still. After a few moments the villains left me for dead. I heard their footsteps recede, but one of them hung back. He placed his boot on my temple and brought down his full weight upon it. I had never harmed him and yet, out of sheer cruelty, he had felt the urge to grind me underfoot. I felt something crack. There seemed to be blood running from my nose into my eye socket, and I blinked a few times to clear my vision. All I saw was a blur. At the back of my throat I tasted a briny sweetness, as though I were shedding tears inside my body. For a split second, before my sense of smell was dulled by the taste of salty blood, I caught a whiff of past comradeship. I clamped my hands around the ankle as I had done a few days earlier, but did not have the strength to hold on.

I regained consciousness in a hospital bed in Rotterdam. The first thing I did was sniff my fingers. The smell of sheep's fat had gone. My hands had been disinfected, for fear that I might rub dirt into my bloodshot eye. There was someone sitting to my right: a chief constable. He asked me to describe what had happened. I was unable to make out the man's features, however I twisted my head, but I could see Kwame, who was sitting on my left, massaging my arm consolingly. I told the chief constable that I had not seen my attackers' faces, which was true. I also said I had no idea who they might be, and reported the sum of money that was missing from my pocket. He enquired whether I had any personal enemies. I protested that I did not, whereupon he said, quietly, that a wooden club had been found on the scene of the crime, in which the following words had been carved: "For the Prince of Apes."

I declared that since my arrival in Holland I had not noticed any hostility towards my race, and advised him to ignore this line of investigation. Then I turned to Kwame and snapped that he was rubbing my arm too hard. Shocked, he withdrew his hands at once.

The chief injury proved to be internal, and the physician wished to keep me in hospital for observation. He applied a poultice against further bleeding. Every hour cold compresses were laid on my right eye. That night and the following days passed in darkness. There was nowhere I could turn for distraction from the thoughts tormenting me.

When Kwame left to go home, I begged him not to tell anyone of my misadventure. I sent the chief constable a message to the same effect. But the very next day I received a visit from Linse, Lebret and Wenckebach, who had slipped away from their lectures to see me. I enquired casually about the urgent summons from my friend that had lured me out of the house the previous evening. My suspicions were confirmed: it had not come from Lebret. I made light of the affair to avoid troubling them, and thanked God that they knew nothing of the offensive inscription on the club.

That night I became so agitated by the fever and the loneliness of my situation that I began to imagine what would happen if my humiliation were made public: my father clapping his hands over his eyes, my mother convulsed with grief and falling into Mrs. van Moock's arms; van Drunen saying he had always feared it would come to this; Anna Pavlovna stamping her feet to make the king call for the death sentence; Crown Prince Willem

Alexander shrugging his shoulders while he waltzed with Loulou, and Sophie . . . Sophie discovering deep inside her the same dull ache that paralysed me.

I awoke bathed in perspiration. The idea that *she* should share my pain was unbearable. Pity is more painful than a beating, for it wounds two people. However well-intentioned, a show of compassion can have the effect of patting a bruise. You become aware of injuries you didn't know you had sustained.

From the moment we arrived in Holland, Kwame and I were conscious of people laughing behind our backs. In that sense we were no different from a hunchback or a beggar, an overweight schoolboy or a redhead. Nothing escaped us.

Shopkeepers stared, hesitated, and then pretended to have noticed nothing out of the ordinary. When we entered a room conversations flagged or turned to a childish mode in which long words were avoided. Courtesies were mouthed with a fleeting look of dismay. As soon as I set foot in an eating-house the customers patted their pockets, no doubt unawares, to feel for their purses. When I strolled down the street mothers took their children by the hand, with a nod and a faint smile. Coachmen soothed their horses. Farmers' wives made the sign of the cross. These reactions seemed innocent enough; indeed they were barely noticeable. And look at it this way: even in a packed concert-hall, the seats beside me remained unoccupied, so at least I always had plenty of legroom.

The difference existed, there was no denying it. It was emphasized by the sentiments it aroused, whether they were enthusiastic or hostile. Both responses kept me alert. The greatest danger of all is when people pretend not to notice any difference. Far from mentioning it, they go out of their way to treat you as an equal, to put you at ease. You do not see your own shame until it is reflected in the eyes of others.

What can we do, we who are different from the rest? That was the question drifting across my mind as I lay blindfolded in my hospital bed. During the night I pondered the advantages and disadvantages of the options open to me. When my bandages were finally removed, I could see only two:

1. Stand out. Cultivate that which makes you different from those around you. Understand where the differences lie, for better or worse, but maintain your eccentricity, cherish it as the unique property it is. This struck me as an infinitely lonely road. Each step would require a fresh struggle with fate. Curiously, this was the road favoured by Cornelius: stand up and fight. But to be able to do that you must have faith in yourself. However hard I looked, I could not find it. Besides, the idea of fighting a never-ending battle repelled me.

2. Blend in. Count the differences and ease them out of the way wherever possible. That entails constant adjustment of the personality, disguising it, altering it to fit that of the other. Take note of what you value in your environment and imitate it. Seek attention only for the few attributes you have in common with the other, and try to conceal the rest. In spite of what Cornelius's boxing lessons had taught me, my nature, at that lonely moment, told me to settle for compromise.

Kwame took the first path, I the second. The one seems brave, the other cowardly, but that is nothing but prejudice, the facile judgement of one who has never stood alone. Battling with the self is no easier than battling with the rest—just less noticeable.

Nevertheless, the poinsettia will never blend in with the tea bushes.

Since that time, my eyesight has been impaired. The right-hand corner of my field of vision is missing. The rest too is somewhat hazy, like opening your eyes under water. I was prescribed spectacles, by which my sight was slightly improved. As soon as I had been fitted with lenses of the correct thickness, I was discharged from the eye hospital.

When I returned to my lodgings in the boarding school, I found my room exactly as I had left it. On the table lay the letter I had been writing to Sophie. I sat down and dipped my pen in the inkwell. I re-read my last line: "All we want is to close our eyes . . ." I signed my name with a lopsided flourish, which looked as if I had been drinking.

Shortly after this incident Kwame abandoned his studies at the Royal Academy. He was making little progress, it is true, but I could not see any lack of ability.

In August 1845, much to my amazement, he enrolled in the Military College at The Hague. He had not mentioned his plan to me or any of our friends. Kwame, the gentlest man I knew, wore military dress ever after. He was to be a soldier.

I pursued my studies satisfactorily, and my friends Linse, Lebret, Wenckebach and I seized every opportunity to visit Kwame in The Hague. We were under the impression that he made few friends among the military. From time to time he would accompany his fellow cadets on drinking bouts and other outings, but he always seemed to have reservations. He did not rejoice in such behaviour, like other young men of his age. Indeed, the discipline seemed to agree with him remarkably well.

I wrote him a long letter congratulating him on the way he had adjusted to his new career, to which he replied with a brief note. "The rock lies immutable in the river," he wrote. "It remains constant, whether it is caressed by soft moss or lashed by heavy rains. Thickets of bamboo grow alongside, tall and dense. Rock and bamboo are equally exposed to the violence of nature. The one survives because it is solid and immutable, the other because it is hollow and pliant." I did not know what to make of this and by return post I sent him a silver pencil and a notebook to carry in his kitbag, because the Almanac for that year was running a competition for the best nature studies.

In September 1846 one of the members of the Five Columns Club bade farewell to the academy. We, as members of the Phoenix society, were beholden to elect a new honorary member from our midst to replace him. Someone suggested Crown Prince Willem Alexander, for, besides being the patron of our academy, he also attended lectures once a fortnight. When he declined the honour—"I seek knowledge and social entertainment, not committee stuff and nonsense"—there was much ado, for the privileges attached to membership of the exclusive club, like the social duties, were not inconsiderable. Moreover the Five Columns Club was veiled in secrecy. Some believed it was a masonic lodge. It was rumoured that members were initiated according to ancient rites that dated back to the Dutch revolt against Spanish rule, and which were normally the preserve of the aristocracy. Linse and Lebret showed little interest in competing for the position, but were willing to offer financial support for my candidature. I threw myself into the fray. The privileges meant little to me, but my aim was to be singled out as *primus inter pares*, and I set out to achieve my ambition as if my life depended on it. There was much rivalry among the candidates. Fortunately most of them soon dropped out of the race either from lack of funds and sympathy, or because of vulgar gossip. After a few weeks, which cost me a fair amount of money, there were only four of us left: Alphons Wenckebach and Hendrick van Voorst tot Voorst, who had the advantage of being well-born, and Cornelius de Groot and myself. Speeches and debates were held, during which Hendrick gave a disappointing performance and subsequently withdrew his candidature. Then Alphons came up with a masterstroke: he invited all the students of his year to a hunting party on his parents' estate. Although Cornelius shot a deer and a wild boar, both he and I fell behind in popularity. Neither of us had relatives who could help our cause in comparable style.

I wrote to Sophie explaining the situation. She offered me the use of the Queen's Pavilion, but I could not see what good a beach party would do in the rainy weather we were having that autumn. She also conveyed news of me to her mother. For the first time in a year, I received a missive from the palace. It was an invitation to the unveiling of the equestrian statue of William the Silent. After some gentle persuasion I was granted permission to bring along some of my fellow students. This was a twist in my favour, although the ceremony itself was ruined by a cloudburst. The common folk ran for shelter, but Queen Anna did not wish her husband to interrupt the ceremony and we were all obliged to remain seated on the grandstand during the downpour. Her chamberlain of long standing, Baron Mackay, made frantic attempts to hold an umbrella over Her Majesty's head, which embarrassed him so deeply that he resigned from her service the following day. All in all, the occasion had the desired effect. The weather cleared and the festivities were even grander than at the coronation. The royal city was lit up as never before, thanks to new-fangled gas lighting that cast straight beams along all the facades. Even the orangeries were illuminated, and the streets glowed with thousands of lamps of every size and description.

Not long after that, I received notice of my admittance to the Five Columns. Wenckebach and van Voorst tot Voorst congratulated me. Cornelius de Groot was deeply offended. He gave up his membership of the student society and eventually vanished from our circle.

My investiture was to take place on 1 March, in the presence of Willem Alexander. The expenses were to be paid by me. I appealed to the Duke of Saxe-Weimar, who granted me the necessary funds so wholeheartedly that there was no cause for embarrassment on my part. The final hurdle was a formality: the speech I was to give on the festive occasion itself. It had to be entertaining and also edifying. I was already making mental notes for a discourse on drilling techniques when I received a message from the chairman instructing me as to the subject of my talk: the land I had come from, no less. For the next week I did not sleep a wink.

Meanwhile a suit had to be purchased, my hair modelled, a commemorative coin struck and, in keeping with tradition, a small portrait made for inclusion in the gallery of honour. Willem Alexander was strongly in favour of using the new invention of Daguerre, which he had recommended to us earlier. I offered to pay for a similar portrait to be made of Kwame, but he still found the idea distasteful, believing that the technique divested the image of its soul. I repeated my offer a few days later, telling him how much I missed him now that he was spending such long periods at the barracks. It was the truth. I wrote to him of the date and time of appointment with the portrait studio, and begged him to be there. I wished to carry his likeness with me.

On the appointed day Kwame did not turn up. Fortunately Lebret had come with me, so I had no time for despondency. I was wearing a new silk waistcoat, yellow with red stripes, and around my neck an elaborate red choker checked with yellow. To make sure that I kept quite still during the long exposure time, the artist strapped me to a wooden frame, at the top of which was a clamp for my head. Rods were inserted into my sleeves, one of which was fastened to a high chair-back, and the other to a lectern. To mask the stiffness of my pose in a pretence of reading, I was given a book to hold in my right hand. Only then did the man turn to his camera obscura.

While I stood there unable to move, a message was brought in from Kwame. I was glad, thinking he had merely been delayed. Lebret was so kind as to read the words to me:

I am sorry, Kwasi. Our lives are not meant to be held captive in pictures. If you want to see my face, just look at your memories. There you will find the Kwame you hold dearest.

I did not move a muscle during the entire sitting.

Dear Sirs, dear fellow members! While the office that you have so graciously bestowed on me is most gratifying for the edification and experience it will afford me, it is also a most daunting proposition. When I cast my eye over my lack of familiarity with the tasks so admirably performed in the past by my peers, when I reflect on the extent of my intellectual ability and capacity for work in comparison with theirs, I am filled with trepidation at the honour of membership. Yet the difficulties inherent in the task that lies ahead are as nothing compared to the far greater, nobler pursuit of serving the interests of the Five Columns Club . . .

I think I must have drafted about twenty preambles. Some of them lasted three-quarters of an hour. They were so elegant that

I could have simply appended the concluding remarks without anyone noticing that the entire speech was nothing but flattery. That was the easiest part. Next I had to marshall all my powers to describe my country. The necessary facts and figures I looked up in the library, as everyone could have done.

CLIMATE *The temperature is uncommonly hot and moreover exacerbated by the so-called Harmattan and Sammering, two land winds, which are liable to last several weeks on end, and to be accompanied by a diversity of ailments such as fever, paralysis of the limbs and so on. Moreover, the high temperatures in the interior of the land are further raised by proximity to the sands of the Sahara Desert and to the Equator. The latter, however, causes tempering of atmospheric conditions, for although the land is only six degrees north of the Line . . .*

In the same manner I gave a survey of the rest of the country, in successive sections bearing such titles as: CONDITIONS OF THE SOIL AND VEGETATION, WATERS, MOUNTAINS AND CAPES. When I reread my own treatise I could imagine it arousing the interest of those who had no knowledge of the country. I gave it to Linse and Lebret to read. They reacted with approval, although their hesitation did not escape me. I knew full well what was missing, and forced myself to rise to the challenge: to tell of such things as only I knew, which were not to be found in books: CHARACTER AND CUSTOMS OF THE PEOPLE.

On 1 March 1847 the premises of the society were decked with garlands. The young men presented themselves in full dress. I was exceptionally nervous. Lebret pointed out that my agitation was out of all proportion, but I did not listen. This would be a turning-point in my life. On that day I felt as though a door had opened which had until then been closed to the likes of me. The fact that I would have to leave my hardheaded cousin behind would not stop me from entering. I was about to show where I stood at last. Concerned about causing offence to my beloved Kwame, I made sure he would not be in the audience. His superiors informed me that he had been assigned to guard duty that evening.

Willem Alexander arrived with Jules van der Capellen almost an hour late, and some tact was necessary to lure the two friends away from the buffet and into the auditorium, but at last, after a brief introduction, I was free to speak as I had intended. I struggled through the courtesies and scientific chapters, and was halfway through my enumeration of agricultural products when I was distracted by the creak of a door being pushed ajar. I looked up, disquieted. I could not make out a face, but for an instant before the door closed again I thought I saw a dark hand on the knob. My voice faltered and I lost my place.

"Plants, silk," I rambled on, "honey, rice, maize, diverse grains, and sugar cane, although it is unknown to the natives, who employ it for purposes of . . ."

A little cough from Linse, who was sitting in the front row, signalled that I was repeating myself. I skipped half a page to be on the safe side.

"Sweet and sour banana."

By the time I came to the end of this section there were beads of perspiration on my forehead. I paused and took a sip of water. This was the moment Kwame, not wishing to cause a disturbance, had been waiting for. He gave me a nod and smile of complicity, delighted at having persuaded his commander to grant him leave of absence. Under his arm he carried a gaily wrapped parcel—evidently for me. He slipped into a seat in the fourth row. I mopped my brow and felt my heart sink. But I had to proceed.

"I intend to speak to you about the customs in the land of my birth. First I wish to invoke your forbearance, should you find it tedious to hear the recounting of events and circumstances of a displeasing tenor, in which the deficiencies, way of life, morals, customs etcetera of a rough, uncivilized and little-known people . . ."

I paused again, but did not dare to look up from my notes. For a few moments I thought of stopping there. These thoughts, which I had so painstakingly written down and copied no less than three times over to get them all just right, I had never spoken out loud. At last I summoned the courage to look into the audience. They were spellbound. Kwame, no doubt sensing my disquiet, nodded reassuringly. There was no going back.

"They are heathens! Fetish worshippers. The Ashanti believe in a supreme being, whom they call Jan Kampong, Lord of All That Is. They also believe in good and evil spirits, and in omens. Also objects can have their veneration, such as the magnet or lodestone. Their belief extends, too, to a life after this life, in the sense that he who is king in this life remains king after death, the slave remains a slave, indeed everyone is restored to his own station and occupation in heaven. And it is in this light that one should regard the custom of sacrificing slaves upon the death of a king, priest or other dignitary, in the firm conviction that the deceased will need their services in the afterlife. The same applies to the numerous human sacrifices occasioned by sickness of one or other luminary in the realm, by the afflictions of war, by accession to the throne or anniversaries, by rites for sowing and reaping and other special events. When the chief of a people dies, his throne is dyed black by soaking it in human blood. The death of a lower-ranking headman may require the sacrifice of no more than one or two children. At the time of my father's investiture as Asantehene, however, the entire population of several villages was designated to follow him into death when he passes away . . ."

Gasps of outrage and shock rose from the audience, just as I had expected. The smile on Kwame's face had faded. He glanced around him. I could see him biting his lip. Then he fixed me with a steely look. I was not going to give up now.

"An interesting example is the yam feast of *odwira*. Each year at the beginning of September, when the yams are harvested, all the district chiefs and military leaders are duty-bound to present themselves with their retinues in the capital. While they parade past the king of Ashanti, two groups of one hundred executioners each traverse the city, sowing dread. They advance slowly, beating their chopping knives rhythmically on the skulls of high-placed victims, as a warning of the fate awaiting certain dignitaries before the end of the festival. In order to remove all suspicion of disloyalty to the Asantehene, these dignitaries order slaves to be slaughtered all over the city. This is not to say that any man found lacking in devotion to the powers that be during the past year will escape execution. At the end of the festival, the holes in the fields left by harvesting the yams are filled with the blood of the victims, thus assuring continued fertility."

Heads were shaken in disbelief, and there was some expostulation.

"You may wonder what induces me to recount the barbarism of a brutish, savage and uncivilized race. What can be the purpose of evoking monstrous acts which in the hearing alone fill us with horror?"

Why did I not hold my tongue? Why did I not spare Kwame's feelings? All I can say is this: his pained expression spurred me on. Not out of cruelty—God forbid! I had no wish to hurt him; on the contrary, my aim was to ease his pain. Indeed his tears inflamed my desire to declare to him: see, they are not worth pining for. The anguish and loneliness that has been our lot is the doing of my own father, of our own people. What more can I say? Does not the wound in our hearts that will never heal attest to unspeakable cruelty and barbarism? Can there be any justification for the heartless manner in which we were banished from their midst? Why not join my cause? Take my hand and let us turn our backs on this barbarian heritage. Let us disown it. Once and for all.

I must confess that I had phrased my discourse with deliberate stridency in order to convince my fellow students that I had truly put the life of the wild behind me. That from now on I was one of them. But in the face of Kwame's obvious misery—even if I myself were the instrument of it—my personal objective paled to insignificance. From then on I addressed my words to him alone, and only through him to the others.

I criticized the religion, customs and thinking of my forebears. I censured the state of knowledge, the traditions of kinship and social relations, of love and work, of the divinities both living and dead. One after the other. As though I had to tear the roots out of my own flesh.

215

"Equal rights obtain between man and woman, including the possibility of seeking divorce. But the man alone enjoys the legal right to punish his wife, notably by cutting off parts of the body: the penalty for adultery is the loss of her nose, for divulging a secret or eavesdropping the loss of both ears. Women who have been mutilated thus are a common sight in Kumasi."

I had to pause here. My eyes raced across my papers, but my heart could no longer endure my own words. The audience was silent, staring at me in bewilderment. I shuddered, and turned over several pages in quick succession.

"No," I said, reading from my notes again, "I do not wish to proceed in this vein, but to stop here after humbly requesting your compassion and forgiveness for your brothers in nature, who in their blind savagery commit such deeds, for these abominations are indeed deemed rightful by them. The people are foolish and deeply superstitious, and from these two deficiencies their priests draw masterful profit, impressing upon the minds of men all manner of alien and unspeakable notions, thus compounding their folly and superstition."

At this point Kwame jumped to his feet. His chair clattered to the marble floor. He took a few tottering steps and seemed about to fall. Lebret made to catch him, but Kwame had recovered his strength. He drew himself up, threw back his head and opened his mouth. He let out a roar like a wounded animal, like an epileptic. It was dreadful, there was no end to it, and when his breath ran out he doubled up as if he had been punched in the stomach, squeezing out the last air in his lungs, groaning, raving. He foamed at the mouth. Linse took his arm to calm him down, but Kwame threw him off. He ran towards the door, but the soles of his military shoes were slippery and he fell flat on the floor, his sprawled body sliding forward. The students on either side of the aisle shrank back, afraid that he would attack them. Jules van der Capellen unsheathed a short hunting knife, and shielded Willem Alexander, who had turned ghostly pale. But Kwame scrambled to his feet and stormed out without a backward glance, as if he could not breathe until he was down in the street again. Linse wanted to run after him, but was restrained by Lebret, who flashed a knowing look in my direction. It took a while for peace to be restored, although the whispering and shuffling did not abate. It was only when I made to take a sip of water that I noticed that I had gripped my glass so firmly that it had broken. There was a small cut in the palm of my hand.

"Now then," I said, dabbing the cut with my handkerchief. Having cleared my throat for the last time, I continued until the end of my exposé without faltering even once: "Let us pause for a few moments to cast an eye into the dwelling of a witch doctor..."

The last guests left the society at first light. I had no desire to go home. I was drunk. Everyone was drunk. After giving my speech I had sent Linse to the van Moocks to enquire after my cousin. He returned half an hour later saying that Kwame had arrived there with a slight case of food poisoning. Mrs. van Moock had given him milk with calcium and had sent him to bed. He was asleep. All was well. Greatly relieved, I called for the champagne to be uncorked. From then on I immersed myself in the festivities and forgot the disarray.

I was woken by a servant clearing the tables. Another domestic was gathering glasses and shards from the floor. I did not wish to stand in their way and struggled to slip my arms into the sleeves of my coat. The insignia of my newly acquired membership of the Five Columns were in my pocket. I drew them out and, weighing them on my hand, staggered to the door. Halfway there, I steadied myself against the wall hung with the portraits of the honourable members. The servants held me in their sights. I made a pretence of studying the row of faces. My air was grave as I contemplated twenty or thirty young Dutchmen of noble birth. There were painted miniatures, several profile portraits, one figure on horseback, another during a hunt.

Earlier in the evening, when I was solemnly presented with my daguerreotype portrait, I had not inspected it so as not to appear vain, but now I could not wait. I slipped it out of its case. The silvered copper plate glittered like a mirror. I narrowed my eyes. Holding it at a certain angle I could distinguish my own likeness, in the pose I had struck in the studio.

Mercury vapour was applied to create a positive image: a proud-looking young man wearing a silken waistcoat and holding his book with the severity of one who has no time for frivolities. His skin is dark, only a shade lighter than his coal-black morning coat. He has the wide cheekbones of the Ashanti and a short beard bordering his full lips.

For a few seconds I was delighted with the likeness. Then I noticed! Behind the shimmering image lay another. I could hardly believe my eyes.

The slightest tremor of the fingers affected the angle of the light, making the surface flash from jet black to silver white and reversing the areas upon which the mercury vapour had condensed into silver—turning black into white and white into black.

I tilted the plate this way and that: one moment the young man paled, the next he darkened. Before my own eyes I switched from black to white and from white to black, again and again, in a spasm of indecision. The process developed by Monsieur Daguerre, the positive–negative action of the reflecting plate, portrayed reality as well as its antithesis. Life and dream.

I narrowed my bad eye. I snuffed the candle in order to lessen the dazzle. But however hard I tried, both figures kept coming back: Kwasi and Aquasi, black, white, black, white, black, white.

Two young men are thus united within the same image: a white man with a black shadow, and a dark man with a white aura. Two men, each fated to become the other, immortalized in a single portrait. I have been both these men.

PART FOUR

WEST AFRICA 1847–50

31 October 1847

How happy I am to have left Holland! Dear friend, happiness is so unpredictable. To be so far away from you, who were my only mainstay for all those years, my better half, from whom I was inseparable—and yet to be happy. You will not hold this against me, for you saw the state I was in. You knew my deepest desires. You shared them once, although you seem to have forgotten that. You have seen how fate trifled with my misfortune for ten long years. Something had to change. So there is no need to blame yourself. It is true that the estrangement between us in the last few months tipped the scales in favour of my departure. After your speech to the Five Columns Club I found I could no longer live among those who had lured you away from me. Rest assured, it has proved to be a blessing. It moved me to do what I had dreamed of doing all those years. Oh, if only you were here to breathe this air.

This evening our ship dropped anchor off the coast. You will remember how heavy the swell is here, and it was too dark to lower a boat for landing. So I shall have to wait until morning. I cannot sleep. I have not set foot on our land and yet I can scent its proximity. I breathe its aroma. The moist warmth, growing more intense with each nautical mile in the past few weeks, has wrapped itself around me. It is as though the pores of my skin are opening to let it in. As though I can relax at last. I am rocked by the waves. Like a newborn babe I lie at the breast, close my eyes and drink. Blindly. There is an inborn trust. I had forgotten its existence and yet, within a few instants, all is as it once was.

There is no moon tonight. Sometimes I fancy I see a flicker in the distance. Is it a lantern, or is it the glitter of stars in the water?

Although I have little news to report at this point, I shall leave this letter with the captain. Tomorrow the ship's company will be replaced by the regiment we have come to relieve. They are to take on cargo at Abidjan, after which they will head back to Holland. Van Moock will forward this letter to you at once. With any luck you will read it in six weeks. To think there was a time when I could just turn round and whisper in your ear. So distant, my friend, and yet so close to my heart.

I try to envisage how you are spending this evening. I cannot. I do not know where you are. How are your lodgings? What do you eat? Write and tell me everything as soon as possible! What sort of people have you met? What are the names of your fellow students, your professors? Are they kind to you? Knowing that, by now, you too have left Holland makes things easier for me. For some reason I would hate to think of you staying in your little room in Delft, in the same old surroundings. Some travelling will do you good, I am sure. Even a brief absence from the flat polderland will remind you that there is more to the world than Holland. Indeed I have no worries on that score. You too are receiving fresh impressions, seeing new panoramas. You will expand your knowledge, meet people and make friends. And I know of one dear friend with whom you will certainly be reunited. I just hope that it will not pain you to see her happy. It is a comforting thought that she will take your welfare to heart. Give my warmest regards to Sophie, and remember to tell me how she is in your next letter.

A bird from the mainland has alighted on deck. The creature is not at all timid, and I have given it some food. It has white feathers and a yellow comb. The gulls tried to steal its meal, but I chased them away. Now it has crept under my chair. It trusts me.

Tomorrow! Tomorrow! My very dear friend, from now on we will keep our gaze fixed on the future. I am certain of that. The present smiles upon us, and we must let bygones be bygones. I have forgiven fate. That is gracious of me, don't you agree? But I mean it. You must believe me when I say I am no longer shackled to the past. I have arrived. My past lies before me. Tomorrow I shall set eyes on my future once more.

1 November 1847

How clear my head is. I see everything in clean, clear perspective. I don't know whether this is thanks to the air or to the light. Or to my soul, which keeps careful stock of everything I observe, albeit with detachment. Like a migrant bird. From a great height I recognize a brittle branch as the blossom of yore. Each rediscovered detail points the way forward, tells me that I *must* go forward.

Governor van der Eb gave me a warm welcome when I came ashore this morning. He had been advised of my forthcoming arrival by the Ministry. He did not address me by my military rank of corporal, but by my noble title. He served the local wine. Palm wine has a sharp tang, did you know that? My tongue curled at the taste, for the memory was of a velvety drink, like liqueur. Do you remember how we broke the seal on one of the casks in the storeroom behind the women's quarters, and drank until we fainted? Surely the taste was sweet? Or not? I cannot recall. Memory sweetens.

After a brief conversation van der Eb insisted that I should not be billeted with the troops. He assured me that I shall receive the promotion that has been promised to me, and offered me a spacious bedroom in the officers' wing. When I demurred, he suggested various alternatives. He was surprised when I chose the smallest cubicle. It is our room, Kwasi! The very same one. I am to sleep in the same cot we shared ten years ago. How could I have explained that to him? It still creaks and wobbles, and it is far too small, but at least I shall be able to dream here. Dear friend, do you remember how frightened we were, how we clung to each other? How sorely I miss you. Just imagine, the chair I am sitting on as I write is the same chair upon which we laid our robes that night, only to find they had been replaced by trousers in the morning. Before long I shall leave my uniform behind on this very chair—at my departure for Kumasi. I wish to return to wearing the *kente* cloth.

I had intended to purchase our traditional clothing here, but there is none to be found. Ashanti culture is taboo in this Fanti settlement. I have been told of a northerner who knows the Ashanti weaving techniques, but I have not been able to trace him.

The absurdity—I was presented this morning with a chest from the ship's cargo, which turned out to contain a turning-lathe. What a gift! According to van der Eb, it was the Ministry of Colonies' idea to give me something practical as a sendoff, since I declined to follow the Wesleyan Society's recommendations as to how to make myself useful. As you can imagine, I would have been infinitely more grateful for some oil paints and an easel, say, or a block of marble and a chisel. I requested van der Eb politely to convey my thanks to the Ministry, and I put the lathe in storage. Then he gave me a handsome hunting rifle, a present from the Dutch government on my departure. Goes to show how glad they are to be rid of me, as well as of the expense of my allowance. I spent the rest of the day wandering in the environs of the fort. I had no plan.

Oh Kwasi, it is amazing how much of what I thought I had forgotten has been stored away in my soul all this time, to return at the slightest provocation. The heavy, aromatic heat. That pungent smell of decaying forest, carried out to sea on a gentle breeze, brings back entire weeks of our life. The red earth. The sinking sun setting the world ablaze. The pride in the eyes of the women. That they can be proud while they possess nothing but the ground beneath their feet. Oh, my dearest cousin, if only I could have persuaded you to come with me.

I have notified the governor of my resolve to return to Kumasi at the earliest opportunity. It was my intention to acquire a horse and some bearers this week. Van der Eb listened attentively to my plan, but was not enthusiastic. He advised me to take some time to *acclimatize*. How about that? As if a man must habituate himself to his native climate!

I have just returned from dinner. I must tell you about something quite extraordinary, something that took my breath away as soon as I entered the dining room. You remember the large room, the hall with the balcony on the outside? You remember where we used to sit at the officers' mess? Well, on the high wall, which used to be quite bare as you know, directly behind the commander's seat . . . I could not believe my eyes . . . I saw you. You and me together, larger than life. I thought I was dreaming, but no, it was your face that I looked upon all through dinner. You were with me. Your beloved face. I could not swallow a morsel. What I was looking at was that huge portrait Raden Saleh painted of us. Verveer in his chair, you on his left, me on the right. The portrait for the Asantehene, which took so many tiresome sittings.

I am told that the canvas was first transported across the jungle, at enormous cost. The package was so unwieldy that the path had to be widened all the way to Kumasi. When the convoy finally reached the capital an official ceremony was mounted for the presentation of the gift to your father. He was horrified, thinking that you and I and the general had been murdered and that our flayed skins had been stretched on a frame. Even after he had been put right he could not abide the painting, so it was taken straight back to the coast.

So here we are then. Virtue having been made of necessity, we now grace the previously bare wall. What a twist of fate. Every meal from now on will give me the opportunity of gazing into those dearly loved eyes.

Not that our condition is anything to write home about. You can imagine what the damp, and especially the briny mist that always gathers around the fort, have done to the varnish and pigments. The canvas is disintegrating. It is being eaten away. Big patches of Verveer have already gone, and some kind of mould is encroaching upon the two of us. The livid bloom on our cheeks makes us both look decidedly ill.

17 November 1847

I am overwhelmed by the world around me. Entranced. I spend many hours each day simply wandering around without purpose. Or rather, my purpose is to be awed. Most people spend their lives in the same place. They are foolish.

People stare at me in the street. I am used to it now. The Fanti are shocked to see an Ashanti wearing the Dutch army uniform. And yet they invite me into their homes and offer me white bread with sugar. A novelty. They got the idea from the regimental baker. This is only one of the many foreign customs the locals are adopting.

When the villagers speak their own tongue I do not understand a word of what they are saying. Was it always like this? I seem to remember being able to understand some words in the Fanti language, but I have evidently lost the ability. Fortunately some of them speak a little Dutch, especially the half-castes. They stop me in the street saying "Good morning master," or "Buy? Buy? Little money!" In the space of ten years the old resentment of the military seems to have faded, making way for eagerness to trade.

Once again everything is different. Customs, gestures, beliefs. The more differences one observes among men, the more obvious it is that all men are fundamentally alike. The particularities are nothing but different expressions of the same emotion. It is as though I have learnt to look through these superficial dissimilarities, as though all I see is the soul. Do you feel the same now that you are a stranger in Weimar?

In Weimar. Weimar. Kwasi, when will my first letter reach you? When will I receive your reply? And God knows when I shall be able to dispatch this letter to you. There is so much to share. So much. The pace is so slow. I write my words as in a dream, where you run as fast as you can without advancing an inch. I can see you clearly in my mind's eye, and I embrace you, but you will not feel my arms until two months from now.

This afternoon I spoke to van der Eb again about my plans to return home. He protested that the path to Kumasi is impassable due to flooding. But I do not wish to postpone my departure any longer. Nature is my friend—how could she not look kindly on me? I asked the governor whether he thought Moses should have been deterred by the Red Sea, but he did not rise to the bait. He has paid one official visit to the kingdom of Ashanti. He did not meet your father, but has an opinion of the Asantehene all the same. He started by saying that much has changed in the ten years since we left. After Verveer's expedition, several other European nations sent delegations to Kumasi. The British, Germans and Portuguese have all established missions and trading posts, it seems, and the surfeit of attention has dampened the Asantehene's interest in anything connected with Europe. My rejoinder was that I myself had had my fill of Europe, so much so that I was glad to leave it behind. My forthrightness made him smile. He softened towards me, but suggested that I would do well to write a letter to your father announcing my arrival. All I need now is a messenger to convey my ardent wish to the Asantehene.

Immediately after our talk I returned to my room—our room—to compose a letter, but had to tear up the first five or six drafts. I kept declaring my love for the land and the people. My tone was exclamatory instead of measured. My scribblings brimmed with emotion, but were lacking in eloquence. How do you tell someone who has forgotten you that you love him? By grabbing him by the shoulders and shaking him. But at the same time you want to be tender and to hold him against your breast. How do I explain that it is possible to yearn for something you no longer know? There is no hurry. It can wait. I shall rest my pen for the day. In an hour it will be dark. (Do you remember how sudden and intense nightfall is in these parts? I was never partial to the twilight—I cannot remember a more depressing hour than tea-time at the van Moocks.) I have taken to running along the beach in the dying light. Far away, as far as possible. Panting, my heart pounding. Once I am past the settlement I shed my clothes and slip naked into the sea. The waves rock me, they know the turmoil in my breast. They draw me out over long distances and cast me back.

30 November 1847

Today the letter announcing my arrival embarked on its journey to Kumasi. Would that I could take its place.

A few days ago a frigate from the East Indies dropped anchor here. On board was a consignment of tea leaves for the Asantehene. The captain recruited a band of Fanti men to transport the goods to Kumasi. I gave the man in charge my letter to deliver to your father, for which I paid him too generously.

I was able to put my wish into words eventually. My wish to return. My letter was emotional, but rang true; it was assertive yet honourable. While writing I imagined how moved the old man would be. I could see your father's face, elderly now, light up at receiving news of you as well as me. So I wrote at some length of you, to which you have no objection, I presume. As for myself, loyalty became the underlying theme; solidarity, a common destiny. Oh my friend, I shall die if I do not return to the Ashanti way of life. I wrote your father as much. And more. From my personal point of view. When I showed van der Eb my missive, he expressed surprise that it was written entirely in Dutch rather than in Twi. I had to explain that we had lost our mother tongue. All I can do now is wait.

At last I have an opportunity to send word to you. I shall give my letters to the captain of the merchant frigate before nightfall. I embrace you and miss you. Write to me if it is within your power.

15 December 1847

It is too soon for news from Kumasi, I am aware of that. Each morning I tell myself so, but my heart will not listen. I am impatient, certainly, and yet confident. I have been separated from my people for too long. I have not yet come home, but here in Elmina I am distant enough from my goal to look forward to reaching it, and near enough not to let impatience spoil my joy. I am in the anteroom, so to speak. I am so sure of my return that my soul permits me to be tranquil.

I spend a lot of time reading. I also go for walks, always armed with pen and paper. I seek out the prettiest places to sit in the shade and address some words to you. I eat the local produce and observe the local craftsmen. I play with their children. Last week I gave them a toy carriage I made out of a cigar box and some corks. This week they are teaching me to fish with live bait. "But are you happy?" you will ask, with your customary insistence. It is a dilemma. How can I be happy when I am deprived of your company? All this waiting, all this time to think and read the classics, has put me in a frame of mind that you, with your preference for rational thinking, would find too mystical. I am more and more convinced that happiness does not exist, only the desire to be happy. It seems to me that happiness is the absence of sadness, of longing. I hope soon to achieve that blissful state. It is an old idea. When I suggested it to you, you were outraged. You were as shocked as a church elder upon being told that the Old Testament is nothing but a collection of picaresque tales after all.

"Every man desires happiness, but in order to achieve it he had better discover what the ingredients are first." Was it not Rousseau who said that? Or is it my own idea? It is quite possible that I merely *think* no one is happy because I have never experienced happiness myself. People who claim to be happy never seem to look it. But who am I to know what happiness looks like?

22 December 1847

I have received your letter! Kwasi my dear, I read it over and over again. The written word is all that binds us now. I must confess, I wept, I cannot help it. I wept because I missed you, thinking of your strolls in the Buchenwald, but especially because I am relieved to hear you are well.

You tell me you are a frequent visitor at Sophie's new residence in Weimar, and that you have found lodgings in Freiberg. I wish I had a map of the area. How far is it from Freiberg to Ettersburg

Castle? Evidently not so far as to prevent you from travelling there regularly.

So your host Lingke is a "Bergmechaniker"—but what does that word mean? Does he work in the mining industry, or is he a lecturer? Tell me everything, but avoid using too many technical terms. They confuse me, as you know.

You say you live in the "Geudtnerschen Hause." What does that mean? Is that the Thüring dialect? You describe Freiberg so clearly: the wide street you look out on to, the "Konditorei Hartmann," the Nicolai Church, the park, your lodgings. I can picture you walking back and forth between your bedroom and the common rooms. How far are your lodgings from the Berg Academy? Please draw me a little map—more than one, if you can. I want to be able to count your footsteps. I am not joking, I long dearly to share your experiences. "At the corner of Rinnengasse and Peterstrasse"—it sounds like a popular tune, and goes round and round in my head all day. "That is where he lives!" I tell myself, "at the corner of Rinnengasse and Peterstrasse."

No, your anecdote did not make me laugh. It reminded me of too many similar incidents. The news that Lingke invited you on your very first day to a dinner with some city councillors and professors naturally pleased me, but that your arrival should have been announced by the shrieks of a startled housemaid who had seen the devil on the doorstep—no, I cannot find that amusing. You yourself don't really think it is funny either, Kwasi—go on, admit it.

Your description of Sophie is so vivid that I can see her before me at this very moment. I can even imagine her being a little more rounded now, a little older. I believe you when you say you are pleased to see her happy. That is in your nature. I never doubted she would receive you with open arms, but that you should refer to Carl Alexander as a friend is quite remarkable. I am grateful to her and to her "Sasha" for the affection they have shown you. I shall write them a note, too. You are, no doubt, enjoying the company of the young dukes of Saxe-Weimar, for you were always fond of Hermann and Gustav. Life at court sounds entertaining and pleasant, but I would not wish to be in your shoes, as you may well imagine. To each his own. I prefer to do my waltzing barefoot in the sand.

No, I was not in the least surprised to hear how charmed you are by little Carl August. Only this afternoon I watched a father with his little girl, also a toddler, taking a bath at the wash-place. Never will I forget how the child clung to her father's neck. The sight of such pure blind trust made me jealous! A child—why should not you and I be blessed with children one day? It is so comforting to think that a new trust is born with each new generation. Although you and I may never be able to trust anyone again, we may still be able to inspire it in others. We are of the age, Kwasi, and I confess that—simply by looking around in the village here—a longing for fatherhood has lodged in my breast. I know what you are thinking, and you are right: I have never in my young life met a woman who inspired true passion in me. I blame that on my displacement. All my longing was concentrated on a single aim. Now I have attained it, I promise you this: as soon as I am in Kumasi, I shall open myself fully to mature love.

I gather that you have not yet received any of my letters, not even the very first one. So once again I must face up to the cruel fact that I am deceiving myself here at my writing table. No matter how many pages I write, my pen cannot bridge the distance between us. Once I am settled in Kumasi, which will be soon, our sluggish correspondence will inevitably dwindle to no more than two or three exchanges a year. The way I feel tonight I cannot imagine surviving on such a meagre ration of news, despite the fullness of my new life. Fortunately you are always in my mind. We have long conversations together. You share every one of my experiences, and believe me—we laugh a lot.

I am expecting a reply from Kumasi any day now, and until then there is little for me to do. I participate in military drill when I can, but it is held less and less often. Now that trade is at such a low ebb the men here are listless and pass the time with card games, palm wine and the women brought to them by the natives for a small fee. There is little else to recount at this point.

24 December 1847

A strange mood prevails at the fort. The locals are well aware that the Dutch set great store by this date. Stalls have been put up around the drawbridge, creating a small market. The troops, too, are affected by the Christmas spirit. These rough fellows turn into little boys thinking of the festivities at home they must forgo. Aside from the officers, all are bachelors, pining for their mothers and sweethearts. Give them a few drinks and their shame vanishes: they sing songs of home and let their tears flow. I have made a few friends among them. Although wary of me at first, they have now grown curious—especially under the influence of drink. They have simple minds, and I approach them accordingly. They are interested in what I tell them about Kumasi, but I have not mentioned that I shall accede to the throne one day. Nor have I referred to my connections with the royal court in The Hague. They confide in me about their sweethearts. When we are gathered together I join in their songs and camaraderie, but all the while I pray that no one will ask after the object of my own love and affection. For I would be at a loss for words. I am so very close to home, after all. Perhaps I shall tell them about you, but how can I explain my feelings? They want to hear of slender waists and round buttocks. It is true that I was with a woman once, and I dream of it sometimes, but still . . . Why did I never fall in love, as they did and you did? Patience. I shall find all I need in Kumasi.

31 December 1847

Far too much time has elapsed since I requested permission to return home. I take many walks, and when I am not walking I read. The commander still has some books he can lend me, and fortunately I came here armed with a fair number of philosophical volumes of my own.

Everyone is celebrating the new year. The troops are permitted to carouse in the courtyard for once. The military band is playing, and a few native women are prancing around, almost naked. I cannot understand their lack of shame. This evening at dinner—no doubt I was staring at your likeness on the wall—the governor suggested I put on a happier face in the new year. One of the officers joked that I was offended by the coarseness of the tableware, as everyone in Kumasi was used to eating from golden plates. That was the least of my concerns. I had clean forgotten what I had told them about my childhood home, but I laughed with the rest and said he had me there.

If only I could be sure that we will meet again one day, then perhaps I would feel in more festive a mood. As it is, I am neither happy nor sad. This evening I am finding it impossible to rejoice at my return to these sorely missed shores. For the second time in my life I have abandoned everything I know.

It is past midnight now, so it is 1 January 1848, and I wish you every happiness and success in the new year.

22 January 1848

Herewith I am sending you my new-year greetings, along with all the letters I have written to you in the past three months. A Dutch brig sailed into the roads this afternoon. She is bound for Flushing. In conclusion I pledge to send further notice as soon as it is in my power to do so. Dear friend, the only preoccupation I have about my return to Kumasi is that it will be virtually impossible to exchange news. What if you fall ill? What if you have something urgent to tell me? I cannot remember a time when we were not in close touch. As it is I have no idea when the next ship will call, so I take this opportunity to assure you of my deepest affection. Also—and this is all the more important, perhaps, now that we are men—to convey my respect for the choices you have made. I think you will understand what I mean. With love, your Kwame.

P.S. It is 23 January and all my hopes have been dashed. A messenger has come from Kumasi with astounding news. Your father refuses to receive me. He has sent me two ounces of gold, that is all. My letter did not find favour. He is said to be deeply shocked that I have forgotten the Twi language. He does not wish to meet me until I have learnt to speak my native tongue. Yet there is no one here who can teach me. The proper place for me to learn the words is in the midst of our people in Kumasi, but I cannot go there. Banishment, that is what it amounts to!

Your father's envoy was attended by two servants, one of whom lacked both lips and ears: they had been cut off for some misdemeanour. It was horrible. For a moment I could not imagine becoming inured once more to the kind of cruelty we witnessed when we were young.

Forgive me my turmoil. My mind is confused, and I must make haste to seal this parcel of letters to you. I will have to run to the quay to be in time for the last dinghy to cross to the *Maria*.

Where are you, oh where?

30 March 1848

The news from Europe is alarming. They say that revolution has broken out in Paris, and that Louis Philippe has been deposed. Van der Eb is sparing with information so as not to cause unrest among the men, but achieves the opposite. There is a wave of dissent in Europe. It is most distressing. Will you be safe in Weimar? Has the world gone mad? Nothing is as I thought it would be.

6 April 1848

What a life you lead nowadays. Your letter of 16 February reached me today in good condition, and your descriptions of balls, receptions and concerts reassure me. The conversations! How stimulating they must be. You will become blasé before you know it. The casual tone in which you mention having heard Franz Liszt conducting Flotau's *Martha* . . . Do you realize that I envy you, if only for the delight of hearing real music. I have a few scores in my possession, which I read when my soul is melancholy. The notes fall into place in my head and I can, with some effort, enjoy a melody and even several instruments at the same time. But instead of abandoning myself to the music, I have to squeeze each note from my imagination. And there you are, enjoying concerts of the very best music on earth twice or three times a month, now that the Hungarian genius has become musical director at court. May you enjoy them on my behalf. When I thirst after beauty, I must drink from a reservoir that is both stagnant and shallow.

8 April 1848

A messenger is about to leave for Holland. I am enclosing a list of books I beg you to send me, for, as you know, reading is one of the few European skills that I consider life-enhancing.

There is little to report at this stage. Try not to worry about me. And continue to write—your letters do me a world of good.

17 April 1848

Thank you for your reply to my letters of late January. Your sympathy is a comfort. What can I tell you about my situation at present?

The news from Kumasi made me ill. I spent February in bed with a high temperature. The army doctor treated me with herbs and compresses against marsh fever. I told him I had respired what he termed *mal aria* for the first ten years of my life without adverse effects, but he insisted that I, like any Dutchman, had been felled by the climate. I lost my temper and told him he was mad, which outburst he took to be ultimate proof of my intolerance of the African air.

Throughout the period that I kept to my bed, Governor van der Eb visited me every evening. He would open the window, against the doctor's explicit orders, and we would sit together listening to the sea. When he thought I was sufficiently recovered he steered the conversation to Kumasi. Hesitantly at first, he spoke of his visit to the capital, casually mentioning someone he had met, a banquet he had attended, just to gauge my sentiment. I listened attentively and wanted to respond to what he was saying, but the words would not come and he did not press for a reaction. Now and then he hummed a tune that had caught his fancy, or drummed his fingers rhythmically on the narrow arm of his chair. One evening I found I could identify the beat. Startled by my sudden intake of breath, he stopped in midair. I grasped his elbow and motioned him to continue. Then he resumed his tattoo, and I joined in. He asked me again why I had written my letter to the Asantehene in Dutch. I replied that I wished to address your father in my own words. Van der Eb said nothing. It was only then, in that long silence, that I realized that I should have waited until I had found a messenger who spoke Twi, and who could therefore translate my missive for me. I was too impetuous, and behaved recklessly.

With the recovery of my health I am gradually regaining hope. I can understand the Asantehene's hesitation now, and have asked van der Eb if there is anyone to be found in Elmina who is fluent in Twi. I must learn the language. He thought there was no such person, but sent out a summons into the surrounding region all the same. Word eventually came from Fort Cape Coast that a suitable interpreter had been found, but that he was away at present on a mission in the interior. There are plenty of people who know a few Twi words or phrases, but never enough to teach me the language. However, I am feeling much better now, and have acquired a notebook from the garrison store in which to write every word of Twi that I hear or remember.

Meanwhile van der Eb is doing everything he can to temper my renewed ardour. Now that he can see that my resolve to return is undiminished, he has come up with an alternative interpretation of the Asantehene's message. The king's refusal to allow me to return, he suggests, was inspired by political motives rather than by any linguistic deficiency. He says the priests are vehemently opposed to fresh foreign influences, and regard me as an unacceptable successor to the throne. Besides, Kwaku Dua is reported to feel threatened by my presence in the region and to fear the superiority of my knowledge. How ironic. For it is he who possesses all the knowledge that I desire, and I would gladly exchange all of mine for his. That is what I shall have to write him. But in what words?

18 April 1848

Van der Eb can say whatever he pleases, but I will not take umbrage. He has won me over for good with the care he lavished on me when I was ill. No doubt he believes he is acting in my best interests. He tells me to face up to reality, to accept that I shall have to stay here in the fort for an indefinite length of time. He suggested that I might make myself useful in the capacity in which I came here: as a soldier. So for the past few weeks I have risen with the troops, exercised with them, and shared guard duties. Once a week I spend an hour telling them about the country, the temperatures, soil conditions and customs, after which we go swimming and carouse in the settlement until sundown. All in good spirits. I do not go into too much detail, and now and then I just invent stories. Firstly because I have already told them most of what I remember, and secondly because it would not be prudent to be too candid. What if a conflict should arise at some time in the future, and I, as the new king of Ashanti, were to find myself at loggerheads with the Dutch? I must say that I enjoy the company of the men. There is a certain appeal to their simple, rough manners. It is only in physical strength that one man can distinguish himself from the rest, or in his ability to impress with tales of ribaldry. I confess that I join in with them from time to time, albeit hesitantly. I borrow their coarse vernacular and paint the kind of picture they expect from me. It is a game. The men listen with enthusiasm and find my fellowship congenial.

My military rank is, of course, too low for someone of my

station. Van der Eb has renewed his promise to promote me to the rank of officer as soon as he receives permission from the Ministry. He has just sent a third letter to The Hague concerning my case. In the meantime he gives me a variety of tasks to perform in a transparent attempt to distract me from the thoughts preoccupying my mind. For example, he gave me the keys of the filing cabinets containing the ancient documents pertaining to Elmina, and suggested I spend the coming weeks writing a history of the fort. Did you know that the great admiral Michiel de Ruyter visited this place, and that Christopher Columbus called at Elmina on his voyage to the Americas? But why should that concern me? I am looking to the future, not the past. The only diversion I desire lies ahead of me.

Did you seriously mean that Sophie supports the liberals? I am not surprised at her sympathy for the lot of the lower classes. After all, she is sympathetic towards *everyone*, but that she should have managed to persuade her father-in-law to accede to their demands is most remarkable . . . Thank God things have turned out well, and that you are no longer in danger yourself. But until the student unrest at Jena has subsided, I think you would do well to be on your guard.

So people in Holland are clamouring for constitutional reform. How does this affect our poor king? Tell me all you know. Dammit, there are times when I hate being so cut off from the rest of the world.

If only I had thought properly about my letter to your father. If only I knew more than a few words of Twi. Today I was seized by the painful truth of the old adage, with which my mother used to caution me: "Words spill out like vomit—you can't take them back."

20 April 1848

I made a new friend today. He is the northerner I had been told about. Joa has been a slave in the Ashanti mines. Now he is a weaver, and supplies the Fanti with material for their famous banners. He is also experimenting with printing textile using a new wax-print method, which originated in Java. This type of oriental cloth, known as *batik*, has recently made its appearance here thanks to the gifts sent home by the Ashanti recruits serving in the Dutch East Indian army. The same men, in fact, who were handed over by your father to Verveer—for which contract you and I served as collateral. The cloths are highly prized by the local population. Joa wants to set up a trade in them.

He learned some Portuguese from the Angolan slaves in the mines. That language is not unlike Latin, so we can understand each other. Unfortunately his knowledge of Twi does not extend further than a string of admonitions. I am able to say "That basket is too light," and, "Be quiet or you shall go hungry," but I hardly think that will get me very far in Kumasi.

Joa has met a Fanti woman here, who cooks for him. His appearance is somewhat forlorn, but his face lights up as soon as she comes near. He is as besotted as a boy. It does me good to witness a little happiness. I intend to visit him regularly. This afternoon alone my memory was sparked several times. Simple Ashanti customs came to mind, such as shaving the armpits, which all our adult men and women do every day. I knew this, and yet I did not know. Little things like that. And Joa uses a brush to clean his teeth after each meal, in the manner of the Ashanti. Why did we stop doing that in Holland? Probably so as not to draw attention to ourselves. I have now removed my body hair and made a brush out of a twig with which I clean my teeth until the gums bleed.

24 April 1848

Two days ago I made a bargain. I took the turning-lathe presented to me by the Dutch government out of storage and gave it to Joa. He said the contraption might be useful for making shuttles and spindles. In exchange he gave me a small hand-loom. I have placed it in my room, on the left wall by the window. I have already learnt how to set it up, but make mistakes with warp and weft. This exercise offers me some satisfaction.

27 April 1848

When I close my eyes I can still see the shuttle flying back and forth. I have made considerable progress in the past few days, and have now acquired a certain ability in weaving. My only objection to the technique is that it is so rectilinear. Weaving a patterned cloth is not like freehand drawing: the configuration of a woven cloth must be fixed beforehand. I have little affinity with such a calculated approach. I do not wish to be hampered by the knowledge that my composition is following a prescribed pattern, that it can be analyzed and reproduced down to the last detail, that there is to be no surprise outcome.

Yet weaving is one of the great arts of our people, and therefore deserves my respect and dedication. I wish to comprehend and master the technique. So I have resolved to weave my own *kente* cloth, and have already designed an ingenious pattern for the clothing I shall wear for my homecoming. I have ordered the yarn from Joa, and it will be ready for me in a few days. I am having it dyed in the colours I remember most vividly. Orange for one. Yellow. And brown.

30 April 1848

Two missives have arrived, in quick succession, both reporting on the turmoil in Europe. The first tells of a plot by Dutch workers against the monarchy. The populace of Amsterdam appears to be calling for a republic, and for the death of Willem II. There have been riots and plundering. Van der Eb has been instructed to deal harshly with any unrest among the troops. The second letter, however, brings news of a reformed constitution, involving the relinquishing of extensive powers by the royal family. There was also a personal letter from the minister of Colonies to van der Eb, which moved him to make the somewhat cynical observation that the king had switched from conservative to liberal within twenty-four hours. Has Sophie managed to win her father over to her ideas, too? Or does he have so little confidence in Crown Prince Willem Alexander that he wishes to save his people from future tyranny? I understand that the king postponed informing his son of the new constitution until the very last—after the event, in fact—and that this greatly offended the crown prince.

What a fuss. It is all so far away. It is hardly my concern. My thoughts here are of other matters.

There has been no change. I have been helping the men with the repairs to the east side of the fort. Since it is no longer used for the slave trade it has been badly neglected. If the outer walls were not whitewashed twice yearly, you would be able to see how seriously they are crumbling.

Interest in Dutch trade is minimal. During the past six months only two transactions have been concluded in Elmina. The forest path to Kumasi is choked with undergrowth, which has slowed down communication to an arduous foot pace.

As soon as we have finished the mortar work, we will start work on the drawbridge. See, the future king of Ashanti is a carpenter! Shades of Peter the Great after all—which would please the Wesleyan Society. I do not mind the hard physical labour, quite the contrary: it makes a welcome change. But the delay in my promotion riles me. That is small-minded of me I know, but none the less irritating for that. I realize I am beginning to set great store by futilities. That is how small my world has become.

Van der Eb tells me that there has been a march on the royal palace in The Hague by disaffected workers, but that King Willem averted a clash by appearing on the balcony and behaving as if the crowd had come to cheer him. The same happened the next day. Poor man. They say he insists that the populace were not calling for his abdication but showing him their respect. His hard-headedness, his proud bluff, was surely inspired by the Russian princess, don't you think? But will the royal family be able to ward off misfortune?

1 May 1848

I beg you to do as follows: when you and Professor Cotta and your fellow students emerge from the mine shaft of the Reiche Seege, and your eyes have accustomed themselves to the bright light, look up at the sky. I see the same sun.

5 May 1848

Again the news from Holland is distressing. I am deeply shocked by the death of Prince Alexander at Madeira. How sad. And only twenty-nine years old. It is true that he was always delicate, but what gross injustice. That young man had a heart of gold. Another cruel blow to the House of Orange. Sophie must be devastated at the loss of her brother. I shall write to her at once. I presume all of you travelled to Delft for the funeral?

1 June 1848

When I accompanied Joa, whose skin is considerably paler than mine, to the local market to purchase a guava and three chicken legs for his beloved, we crossed a Dutch patrol. "Look, there go Light and Dark," the commander called out, to make his men laugh. "Light, dark, light, dark!" they repeated in unison as they marched, as if responding to a prearranged signal. There was no malice in their voices. Van der Eb heard of the incident at supper, and concluded that it was merely a joke on the names of two officials in The Hague whom the king has charged with forming an independent government. He may be right, but I have my doubts. Not that I care. When I told Joa what they were saying, he shrugged his shoulders. "All men are the same colour down the mines," he said, "but I prefer daylight all the same!"

16 July 1848

Our portrait is falling apart. During supper I noticed a fresh tear in the canvas, which is already ragged along the entire lower edge. Van der Eb is apologetic about the neglect. What can he do? The canvas is saturated with damp and the varnish simply dissolves in the salty air. Both the expertise and the means to halt this process are lacking here. Not that the painting is a masterpiece by any standards. Frankly, it makes me smile. Poor Raden Saleh— how upset he would be if he knew! After supper I inspected the damage with the aid of a candle, and when I traced our contours with the tip of my finger the paint simply flaked off. Some sort of mould has crept between the canvas and the oils. Little blisters are appearing. Verveer has already lost several of his medals, I'm afraid. And you and I are turning into lepers.

17 July 1848

This afternoon, when I was weaving, I remembered my mother telling me that in her day people used the silken thread of the spider *okomantan*. For lack of a web, I unravelled some silk handkerchiefs and threaded the strands on to my loom.

26 July 1848

Fancy Hans Andersen showing concern for my predicament. My heart leapt. I met him at that function in The Hague over a year ago, when he was honoured for his work. He is a kind soul, and a gentleman. He carries all the world's sorrow in his eyes, which gives him a compassionate mien. Indeed, such a man's company would be welcome to me here. (Although I would even sooner have you by my side.) I was most touched by his sympathy. I look forward to receiving the translation of his new collection of stories. Could you possibly send me the score of the music Liszt has composed to Andersen's text? I expect it will have been printed by now, as the opera has been so successful.

Tell him that our encounter last year—it was on the eve of my birthday—made a deep impression on me. Indeed, come to think of it, meeting him played a decisive role in my decision to return to Africa. No, do not tell him so. He might feel responsible. Tell him . . .

Did you know that he postponed his onward journey to England, even though Jenny Lind was waiting for him there, and declined an invitation from the author Jacob van Lennep just so that he might visit me? Sophie had pressed him to do so. He did not dare announce his presence until I had read her letter of introduction. Such a gentle man! How privileged we are, Kwasi, to have made his acquaintance. When I picture the two of you together I begin to doubt the wisdom of my decision.

Tell him he was right, regardless of what the scientists maintain: rainbows around the moon are indeed to be seen every night in this place.

I am writing this in the early evening. You may wonder why I did not introduce you to Andersen. I did not even send word to the academy. There seemed little point. He was not concerned with either of us as individuals, his sole aim was to obtain information about our myths and legends. He requested my cooperation in a soft voice, as if he were reluctant to rouse a man who would prefer to remain asleep. I did not think you would wish to be a party to this delving into the past. It was soon after your speech to the Five Columns Club.

I started telling him the story of Anansi, but soon faltered, and had to admit I had forgotten many details. Andersen was unperturbed and did not press me. No, he simply drank his cup of tea as if he were at home, and then told me one of his own stories. At first I thought he was reciting what he had written, as was his custom at public readings. But after a few minutes I saw that he was addressing his words to me personally. I was startled by the emotion in his voice, and made to interrupt him. But he persisted in his narrative, and in this way he soothed my nerves. It was as if he were saying: you and I, we stand before the whole world, let the animals tell our story. After that it was as if the floodgates had opened, and I heard myself recounting an adventure that had befallen Anansi, Tsetse and the tiger. Followed at once by a second, a third and yet more tales, with Hans Andersen taking notes all the while. I was truly amazed at the whirlwind of stories rising in my memory. In retrospect it was like being in a trance, losing sight of the boundaries between memory and invention. I was embarrassed by this, and told him so. He smiled and said it did not matter. "To write," said Andersen, "is to accidentally invent the truth."

We sat together until late into the night. Never since leaving home had I pictured the streets and faces of Kumasi so vividly. Nor has the clarity of my refreshed memories on that occasion ever come back to me, not even now that I am so close to home. Especially not now.

Andersen's ship sailed on the twenty-second. I went to Rotterdam to see him off. I had hoped to exchange a few words with him in private, but he was constantly beset by admirers, and listened politely to one speech after another. I was lucky to get the opportunity to shake his hand.

It is long past midnight now. It was Andersen, you know, who fanned the longing that had smouldered in my breast for so long. I spent my birthday in solitude. You had sent special greetings, and I was relieved by your apology for not coming to see me personally. We were living in separate worlds by then. Nonetheless I walked on air—for the first time in a long while.

4 October 1848

There has been an accident in the Dabokrom gold mines. Fourteen men have lost their lives, including two Dutch mining engineers. Their bodies have been transported from Ahanta to Elmina, where they were buried this morning in Dutch soil. The funeral service in the chapel was solemn, but the air was thick with rumours. The future of the entire mining operation seems most uncertain. Of course I still hope that you will be able to practise your profession here some day, but the risks involved in the current undertaking are so high that I am almost relieved you are not here. Eleven of the thirteen Dutch engineers who founded the company in 1845 have now died. Of the second team of thirteen, who arrived last year, only seven are alive today. No gold has been mined as yet.

5 October 1848

The difference between friendship and love is that friendship is more tolerant of separation. When friends meet again after several years, there is no change in their bond. Love, on the other hand, does not accumulate, but needs constant replenishment. In that sense, Kwasi, I love you. I need you. My reserves are nearly depleted.

18 December 1848

Thank you for sending the book by Goethe. I was under the impression that Sasha's former tutor appealed to young ladies in particular. All I know about Werther is what Sophie told me. There's a touch of the show-off there, wouldn't you say?

You accuse me of not writing often enough. What do you expect? That I have a lot to say?

25 December 1848

A man tormented by the proximity of the woman he loves, whom he sees in happy union with her husband . . . I am beginning to understand why Werther's story appealed to you. Thank goodness you are not a Romantic yourself, for you have both feet firmly on the ground.

26 December 1848

Werther is an observer, he is moved by stage scenery. Nature is a luxury to him. I am a child of nature. Merry Christmas.

1 January 1849

And a happy new year.

2 January 1849

In recent weeks several Europeans have fled Kumasi, seeking refuge in Cape Coast and Accra. There are traders and missionaries among them, and all have bloodcurdling tales to tell about the persecution of Christians. The tide seems to have turned indeed. The Asantehene and the priests have launched an offensive against the European influence. What hope is there for me in the present circumstances?

12 February 1849

Watch out for Raden Saleh. He is a dangerous man, as inscrutable as a snake. A pity he should be so much in evidence, to the extent of receiving a royal welcome in Weimar. Are there no other portrait artists of merit? His personality must clash with the refinement of life at court. The thought of him dining in the company of Andersen repels me. I trust Sophie is sensible enough to see through him. I suppose it is not unreasonable that he should be the guest of her parents-in-law, but Sophie ought to dismiss him firmly but politely. Until she does so, please take care with what you say. That smile of his hides a cunning and spiteful nature.

You were quite right to speak up in your father's defence. Of course! What business is it of his—a sycophant from Java— whether the Asantehene has or has not defaulted on his pledge to Verveer? No doubt it has escaped his notice that it was the English who raised a hue and cry against the trade in recruits, saying it was old-fashioned slavery in disguise.

Tell him, if he ever dares broach the subject again, that the Dutch only desisted from their recruitment activities once international indignation had been sparked. Van der Eb said so himself. It was the Dutch who stopped the supply of men. You can tell our Javanese prince that if he cannot resist poking his nose into other people's business he should look at the treatment we have received. He chose to go to Europe of his own free will—we did not. He went in search of gain, we were abducted to ensure gain for others.

Do not let him provoke you. I am glad to hear that he will soon return to his native land, where he is to paint the portrait of the sultan of Jokyakarta. Good riddance. You can tell him from me—politely if you will—that his work is not very durable in the tropics. My own face, at any rate, is now drained of all expression. I can recognize you by your remaining eye, lower lip and one and a half eyebrows.

There has been another casualty at Dabokrom, although from natural causes this time. The man inadvertently pitched his tent in the path of an army of ants. He was overrun by the termites, and died of his wounds three days later. The first sample of gold dust accompanying the body to the coast was less than one and a half ounces.

10 April 1849

Our entire company is in deep mourning, but none more than I. The dreadful news did not reach us until two days ago. I am sending my most sincere condolences to Sophie and to Prince Hendrik, and of course to the poor, poor queen. Did you ever see a warmer domesticity than theirs? So . . . all things end in anguish. Please write and tell me all, as soon as you can. I gather from what van der Eb told me and from the newspapers that the king was on a visit to the new palace being built in Tilburg, and that he spent the night in the home of a wool-dyer—how typical of his modesty—where he became unwell. Also that sourdough poultices were applied to soothe the intestine, and that Everard was sent for, but it was too late. I understand that Anna Pavlovna came at once from The Hague, but was so agitated when she arrived that she was not deemed fit to see her husband. She was persuaded that he should not be disturbed, and posted by the door to his room, listening. So the king passed away without knowing that his beloved wife was only a few yards away!

Such immense grief puts my own in the shade. There is no limit to adversity, it seems. I am ashamed of my plaintive tone of late, of having regard for no one but myself. I even tried praying, which is something I have never done before of my own free will. In times such as this one can do with all the support one can get.

15 May 1849

Since you have already written to me of the sad events in Holland, most of the questions in my last letter no longer apply. How unfortunate that you should have been away in Switzerland with Professor Cotta at the time, and therefore unable to offer Sophie your moral support. I admire her courage. She is a remarkable woman.

So the new king is Willem III, and Anna Pavlovna has ceded her position to her capricious daughter-in-law. But the dear lady will show her Russian mettle, you mark my words, and will certainly recover from this devastating blow. For the time being the inheritance seems to be giving the main cause for concern. Is it true that the king actually transformed his father's fortune into a debt of four and a half million? In the space of eight years? The glorious Rembrandts lost to St. Petersburg! All the other art treasures, which were such a comfort to me in the old days, sold at auction—furniture, tableware, all gone. It is awful. Even the little covered wagon we used to play with when we pretended to be Red Indians. Time and again one loses all one loves. I have heard that Anna Pavlovna bade the empty rooms of the palace goodbye with the words: "Never more, little father, never more!" I can believe it. A touch of sentimentality there, but what counts for her counts for us.

20 May 1849

I have done as you requested, and have plied Joa with questions about the mining situation in Ashanti. It is no trouble at all. At least this is an opportunity for me to be of some use to you, but I am afraid his information was hardly exhaustive. He is a simple man, and has little knowledge of engineering. His sensitive nature made him unfit for life down the mines, where slaves and horses stay underground for days on end. The tools consist of simple pickaxes, and each team of miners advances no more than a few inches a week. Joa has bad memories of his days as a miner. I have written down everything he could recall in a separate notebook. I am enclosing a diagram of the tunnel in which he worked: it is a cross-section at a depth of forty-five feet. Greater depths are rare. Van der Eb tells me that there are roughly *forty thousand* small-scale mining operations throughout the country.

I told Joa that you, too, frequently descend into the depths of the earth. He found it hard to believe that a king's son would ever do such a thing. I amazed him with your description of the Elisabeth shaft and the Reiche Seege mines. He was familiar with the method of drainage, but was mystified by the endless chain conveyor for lowering and raising the workmen. Here it is customary to lower the men at the end of a rope. He is eager to know more about your methods, and is especially interested in the number of fatal accidents.

I hope the scanty information we are able to offer will be of use to you for your thesis on mining techniques. If you need to know more, please send me specific queries. I could try to visit a mine myself. It would give me an excuse to leave the fort for a while. I have already discussed my plan with van der Eb. He has no objections. He thinks it is good for me to have an aim. (Still no promotion. Complete silence on the part of the ministry, even though van der Eb keeps pressing them to respond. No one seems to care a whit that I was formally promised advancement, and that it is therefore my due. Their demurral is wounding, as you can imagine, but even the rank of major-general would not bring me a step closer to home.)

I am still weaving. After a few bad starts I have now managed to come up with a pattern that is decidedly attractive, if I may say so. My cloth is getting longer by the day. I think it must be big enough for a whole family by now. What shall I do with it when it is finished? Give it away and start afresh? But to whom should I give it? I hardly think you would be thrilled to receive this type of reminder of home. You know, even something trivial can become a problem if you dwell on it long enough. Last night, unable to sleep, I seriously considered unravelling an inch or two, only to delay the moment of completion. Yet like Penelope I have no doubt of a happy end. One must be entitled to some form of reward eventually, if only for having been so trusting. Anyway, if the worst comes to the worst I can always set up a trade in cloths.

21 May 1849

Just one more thing: Joa tells me the miners have a single safety device: a butterfly. Each miner is issued with a butterfly in a small jar. These insects have large silvery-blue wings, which reflect the least ray of light. They are bred specially for service underground. If there is a rock slide, a smell of toxic gases, or the men have any difficulty breathing, the creature is released. It makes straight for the slightest airstream. In this way it points the way to the surface.

One day Joa was underground when a thunderstorm struck. The sudden change in air pressure caused a vacuum in the headway. My friend was the only one of his team to make it to the surface, where he emerged in a cloud of brilliant, fluttering butterflies.

1 June 1849

The regiment is to set sail for Holland today. I shall entrust my mail to their commander. These men, in whose company I came here, have had their fill of eighteen months of life in the tropics. I notice they have been finding the discipline increasingly tiresome of late. Some are sick all the time and nearly everyone is affected by a recurrent intestinal infection. A fresh regiment is to take their place.

Van der Eb will remain here, and of course he has asked me what my intentions are. He has finally admitted that I cannot count on the promotion that was pledged to me. He is sincerely sorry, and can only guess at the reasons for the minister's prevarication. He is no less pessimistic about my chances of finding favour among the powers that be in Kumasi. So you see: I live in the twilight. The governor strongly advises me to return to Holland. He has made it painfully clear that my qualifications will be of little use to me here. I have reflected deeply. In the end I had to concede (also to myself) that my hope has all but died. Yet here I am writing you a letter, instead of rushing back to Europe to embrace you in the flesh. This is my land. Here is my Golden Stool, whether or not I shall ever occupy it. And what have I to look forward to in Holland? I would sooner plunge into the darkness of the night.

29 June 1849

How am I to advise you? Of course my dearest wish is for you to come here. Are you really considering leaving Holland? An annual salary of two thousand and six hundred guilders sounds reasonable. I think you should take the promise of promotion to the rank of chief military engineer with a grain of salt. Elmina is far from The Hague. Promises are sooner given than kept over such a distance.

Oh Kwasi, your question tears me apart. My heart cries out: come here as soon as you can! If only for my sake—for I cannot pretend that the news from the Dabokrom mines is encouraging.

30 June 1849

Today I had a disagreement with my only friend. I had carved a small block of wood to serve as a stamp: the symbol of Anansi the spider. Do you remember? It is a sun with five rays, quite simple, like the spokes of a wheel. I was using my block to print a length of cloth from Joa's stock, when his Fanti sweetheart came in with refreshments. He hurried to meet her and took her hand. They stood still like that, hand in hand, oblivious to the world around them. The trust, the intimacy . . . Not wishing to disturb them I went on pressing my block on the cloth at regular intervals to form the pattern, as he had taught me. He and I took the drink she offered, and as she was leaving he gave her a playful slap on her buttocks. She affected indignation. Then he turned to face me, smiling mischievously. For an instant there was a glint of complicity in his eyes, the kind of understanding that exists only between men. Then the realization that I was excluded from his happiness wiped the smile from his face. He stooped to inspect my work. He pointed out that I had given the sun one ray too many. He was right. The cloth was useless. But I was outraged, and challenged him with a vehemence and passion that took me by surprise. Joa was adamant, and in the end I said that he, not being an Ashanti himself, had no right to teach me about my culture. He threw me a reproachful look and fell silent. I apologised at once and told him I would pay for the material.

. . .

Men and women seem to belong to different races. I cannot understand how they can abide each other. You can bring the two together, but they will never be one. You can use red and yellow yarn to weave a brown cloth, but even then the colours remain distinct; they intertwine but do not merge. And yet, Joa and his beloved seem to have attained true union. He from the north, she a Fanti. Moslem and heathen. Man and woman. This happy bond between dissimilar constituents ought to inspire hope in me, not anguish. Indeed I am glad for them, I really am, but still I fear for myself.

What is it that prevents us from forming lasting attachments? What sort of deficiency is this? I am afraid to look into my heart, Kwasi, for I know I shall find a great emptiness. Being ignorant of the love between man and woman myself, I imagine it to be boundless, reassuring like the affection of my mother, and yet as stimulating as friendship. Ah well, does it matter? You fell in love once, but then you were robbed of your happiness. Nothing can be woven from threads that are cut too close to the spool.

1 July 1849

At times I am perturbed by the shallowness of life here at the fort. The new regiment is made up of fine fellows, I must admit. But they strike me as so immature. They are only four or five years younger than I, and yet I regard their exuberance with the jaded eyes of a middle-aged gentleman. Surely that is not a good thing? My body is drawn to their pranks and debauchery of a Saturday night, but my heart cannot keep the pace.

Once again I have politely replied to a range of questions concerning my position and presence in Elmina. They tut-tutted, shook their heads, and drank to my speedy return to Kumasi. I dare say they were sincere, but their words fell by the wayside. I thanked them kindly, whereupon silence ensued. I can hardly expect from them what I myself do not give.

14 July 1849

There have been two more deaths in Dabokrom—from suffocation this time. That brings the number of Dutch survivors down to four. It is my duty to tell you, even if it means you will not come to these shores. In which case we will never meet again.

21 July 1849

The cloth I had hoped to wear upon my return to Kumasi was completed long ago. I left it on the loom for months, for no particular reason. Today I snipped the connecting threads and hemmed the edges. I washed my cloth and stored it among my possessions. I sent my loom back to Joa. He was speechless with gratitude. His wife has left him for a trader from a nearby settlement. A Fanti, like herself.

26 July 1849

What joy it is to receive your letters! Each time they make my heart race. Even the troops noticed my change of mood. "Aha, fallen in love at last have you?" one of the men joked at the washplace, and when I protested that this was not so, the rascal called out to one of his fellows, "Peter, haven't you noticed the smug look on our prince's face, as if he's hugging a secret." I couldn't help laughing, and went along with their joke. They are good lads, always trying to cheer me up.

Your description of the piano concerts in the Hof Gärtenerei sent me off into a reverie. You will not be surprised that I, unlike you, cannot see anything respectful about calling Liszt and his students "the Pasha and his Moors." No matter. Those pages from the score of *Löhengrin*, which you wheedled the maestro into giving you after the dress rehearsal, are quite amazing, as are the accompanying legends upon which you say the opera is based. (Such a strong streak of animism! All those creatures crawling out of the muddy depths of the Rhine . . .) I'm afraid I cannot appreciate why Liszt is so impressed by the genius of Wagner, but I expect this is because I lack the ability to conjure up the music of such a complex score entirely in my head. Nevertheless I enjoy keeping abreast of new developments. Be so kind as to send me more. You cannot imagine what a wonderful distraction music is.

I spent the evening with Joa. I had not done so for a long while. He noticed my cheerful mood and took it to mean that a letter from you had arrived. He asked how you were, and when I told him about the great depths to which you descend nowadays in the Elisabeth mine, he was most impressed. We drank some wine while he reflected on what I had told him. Then he said he found it hard to imagine you and me being bosom friends.

"Why?" I fumed. He shrugged, as if the answer were perfectly obvious, and said, "One searches in the earth, the other in the clouds."

14 *August 1849*

The time to whitewash the fort has come round again. The salt-laden sea air is so aggressive that no wash can withstand it as long as a year. It is an unpopular chore, and it takes many weeks of hard work. I have volunteered for the task. There are four of us. I have been assigned to the exterior of the south walls, a lonely place at the far end of the fort. I start work early in the morning, take a rest in the afternoon, and then return to benefit from the low sun sliding along the stones and picking out imperfections. At this rate I will be busy for two months. Concentrating my thoughts so intensely on the task before me has made me think in terms of square yards rather than hours or days. I am not in a hurry. The wall is patient.

I work my way from top to bottom, hanging from the end of a rope in a sort of truss, with my feet propped against the wall. I flex my knees to get close enough to brush the paint on the wall, and straighten them again to see how I am progressing. Then I adjust the length of my rope and set to work again further down.

It gives a simple sort of satisfaction. The whole world is reduced to the few square yards directly in front of me. The wall is weatherbeaten and flaky. My task is perfectly clear: continue painting until the whole wall is sparkling white. The result is inescapable. I have rendered service, and the fruits of my labour are there for all to see.

The effect of the sun striking the lime is magical. It clears the mind. It enables me to concentrate on the work in hand and at the same time to let my thoughts wander. Not even the smallest detail of my handiwork escapes attention, and yet I am able to take stock of my situation in a detached, level-headed way. Most agreeable. At the end of the day my body is weary, but my mind is wide awake. I wash the chalk off my skin and fall on to my cot. I have been sleeping well lately, untroubled by wild dreams. I do my dreaming in the dazzling light of day.

2 October 1849

A day runs its course. The position of the sun signals the distance covered since dawn. The moon follows a cycle, making women and farmers alert to periods of fertility. Since sun and moon always move in the same direction, everyone knows life goes on. After the rains come the floods, which in turn are followed by drought. That is as much notion of time as man needs.

Surely it sufficed us when we were boys? True, your father employed astrologers to calculate feast days and the paths described by the celestial bodies, but you and I had no part in such matters. In Delft, therefore, I was overwhelmed by the strict division into days and weeks, months, years and lifetimes.

Van Moock was quite emphatic: he who lives by the waxing and waning moon, by the seasons and by the day, is a prisoner of nature. To him the timelessness that gave us our seemingly carefree outlook signified the shackles of primitive man. Suddenly it was wrong to stretch a random thought to its extreme limits, or to compress an unpleasant afternoon to a mere sigh. Each heartbeat counted, had its exact value.

And so we were placed in time as in a landscape. With each step we took the panorama slipped by. The emptiness was vested with dimension, counting took on meaning. No longer was our existence stationary while the world filed past, we ourselves were set in motion, and overtook the march of time. Our gain was the consciousness of progress, but we were also suddenly aware that all the things we found on our way would have to be left behind, would be irretrievably lost. Even when we were silent and thoughtless we tramped staunchly ahead, leaving a growing wasteland behind us. We were astounded. We had always relied on the lengthening shadows to be our yardstick.

I have been following the shadows again today. They advance across my wall, the few square yards of chalk that constitute my universe. In the morning they tell me discreetly where there is unevenness, in the afternoon they point up the old chisel marks left by the builders long ago, and at sundown they dramatize each protruding grain with long dark streaks.

But now I know what I have been missing. My hours need differentiation. There is nothing to measure them against. There is no scale. There is nothing to mark my time. So nowadays time stands still while I pass by.

12 October 1849

More and more images of the early years are coming back to me. The tedium of my immediate surroundings has made me look inwards. All I have left to cherish is stored within myself.

As I was working on my wall I suddenly remembered the occasion when it dawned on me how life in Europe is subjected to the tyranny of the clock. It was in the autumn. Mr. van Moock and his wife had taken us for a walk in the woods. The headmaster pointed out wild mushrooms and told us their Latin names. He commented on the manner of growth and medicinal value, if any, while his wife held forth on such species as were edible. She went into raptures over the delicious flavour a mushroom sauce gave to roast venison, or something to that effect. What with one thing and another we were feeling quite hungry by then, although it was not long since we had set out. Catching sight of an inn in the distance Mrs. van Moock addressed her husband in a hopeful tone of voice: "Simon my dear, how about it, are you feeling peckish?" At this van Moock extracted his watch from his waistcoat pocket. He raised the lid, which was engraved with a skull as a reminder of his mortality, and declared: "But it is not yet noon, madam!" That every one of us longed for a pancake was immaterial: he was a man for whom nature must be overruled by the clock.

Fortunately the two of us could see the comic side of this obsession with time. The chronological designations soon ceased to confound us, and together we echoed what the Hollanders said. They had certainly come up with an infinite variety of expressions to mark their time. When I said goodbye with the words "So long!," you would ask "How long?"

"As long as it takes to recite the Lord's Prayer thirty-eight times."

"You mean when the cock has crowed thrice?"

"No, not until the cows come home."

"Straight after the overture."

"But during page thirteen I'll be away."

"This century?"

"I don't mean Before Christ."

"At the stroke of two."

"In a second."

"Since my illness."

"Before losing my virginity."

"Well, you can't put the clock back."

After which we collapsed into giggles and hurried to be on time for supper or roll call.

In those days, Kwasi, you were fascinated by everything to do with time. You pored over almanacs, climbed to the top of the church tower to watch the minute hand move to the next slot and plied van Moock with so many questions that he had to obtain a book on the differences between the Gregorian and Babylonian calendars. You practised foretelling the precise moment when the clock would strike, without looking at it. After a few weeks you were accurate not only on the whole hours, but also on the quarter hours. As for me, I went on dating my letters, including the formal ones, in relation to my own age. I would use headings as "in my twelfth year," or, "at Delft, in the fourteenth year after my birth," for I did not see the point of any other specification.

Thank goodness you would cheer me up by poking fun at the Hollanders' absurd notions. Remember those people who claimed that madness could be cured by inscribing the name of the madman on the small hand of the church clock; and put their clocks forward twenty-four hours when it was predicted that a meteorite would fall on a certain day, in a desperate attempt to ward off catastrophe; who thought clock filings alleviated epilepsy, and a drink of the water previously used to wash a bell-clapper a remedy against pain in the gut?

As far as I am concerned, the notion of time flying is just another idle fancy, and consequently a superstition.

Life in Kumasi, when we were young, took its course in silence, sometimes in the mind alone. Birth, fertility, the lunar cycle, death—the occasions that gave rhythm and impulse to our lives were those that affected us personally and were therefore memorable. They were private.

In Holland one is constantly exposed to noisy reminders of the passing of one's life—in public squares, on church towers, mantels and walls. With all those timepieces ticking away in their mechanical, unrelenting way, the Hollanders are merely exorcising their fear of the present and of their own finality. In the land of the Ashanti it is time that kills people. In Holland people kill time.

The fort is as bright as a new pin. My work is done—until nature undoes it again. I have already notified van der Eb that I will volunteer for another stint of whitewashing in six months' time.

12 November 1849

Your letter of 7 October arrived safely. I respect your decision. How this news has affected me is impossible to describe. I do not bear a grudge. I have no doubt that the reports I have been sending you influenced your decision to decline the post of engineer in Dabokrom, and you were quite right to do so. What more can I say? The situation in the mines is as bad as ever. There was another casualty last week. Until now the total yield of the undertaking, in which twenty-one Hollanders and a greater number of natives have lost their lives, does not exceed four ounces of gold, which amounts to one hundred and fifty guilders' worth.

The consternation at your decision is certainly remarkable. But what did you expect? They are stuck. Their hopes of being relieved of you as they were of me have been dashed. And your refusal to return to Holland from Freiberg until you had received official word of your status—no wonder the authorities are nervous! I know you are paying your own tuition fees, but the annual expenses of board and lodging are evidently considered to be excessive. And you tell me that your current allowance of two hundred guilders is not really sufficient for you to conduct yourself properly in Weimar society.

I know what we'll do, some pen-pusher at the ministry must have thought, let's appoint him to the post of mining engineer in Dabokrom. If he shines at his profession he will supply us with gold, and if he's as feeble as the rest he won't survive for very long.

But you turned them down. So they asked Professor Cotta for advice, did they? And he actually told them that you are so fully adjusted to life in Europe that your love of hearth and home has been snuffed out. Well I never. To think that they asked Dominee Molenkamp for his opinion (although why they had to ask I can't imagine—he would have offered it anyhow), and that he blamed your "loss of nerve" on the flattery of the Weimar nobility who "spoiled" you and "undermined your religious sensibility," no less! "Yet another example of a wasted education and dashed hopes" indeed.

The intrigues of metropolitan society hold very little interest for me at present, I am afraid. I need all the concentration I can muster to come to grips with this fresh sorrow.

It is past midnight now, and I have one more thing to say. I may as well tell you, for keeping silent will only add to the anguish in my heart, which is already labouring under the knowledge that I shall never see you again. It grieves me, Kwasi, that you told the minister you had no wish to return to Africa because that would mean "living among men whose morals, customs, ways and religion are not only strange to me, but also repellent." Have you forgotten that I am here? Am I not like them? And are you not like me? Why tell me such things, if you know how they grieve me?

13 November 1849

Upon waking I was filled with thoughts of my father on his deathbed. I do not remember being sad. On the contrary. I loved him with all my heart and yet his passing left me feeling uncommonly elated. Something wonderful had happened.

There was an extraordinary force at work. How shall I put it? Do you remember entering the room where he lay in state? I did not dare at first, for I was gripped with fear at the proximity of death. But no sooner had I crossed the threshold than a great calmness descended. The dead body emanated energy. This was not a fancy—no, it was a veritable storm blowing straight in my direction. I flung out my arms and cupped my hands to catch as much of it as I could. It was like a jet of water splashing against my head and shoulders. When my body was sated I gave thanks to the gods for this gift and bade my father farewell. Upon leaving the room, however, I was overcome with desire to repeat the miraculous experience, and returned to my father's side. The energy flowed as before. By the end of the day I had gone into the room six or seven times. I was in a trance. His love had become fluid.

"Thus I became acquainted with death on the lips of the one who gave me life," René says somewhere. I have never heard anyone else speak in this vein, and yet I believe the experience of death is common to all men.

You must never forget, Kwasi my dear, how closely grief is linked with joy.

One last thing about my father: some time later I felt a sudden urge to visit his grave. I held out my hands flat above the ground and begged him wordlessly to bestow his miraculous strength on me once more. Nothing happened. No, a voice said within me, from now on you will have to marshall your own forces. In this way the dead can fortify the thoughts of the living. Is that the reason for our mortality, do you think? It sounds more practical to me than all those notions Dominee Molenkamp foisted on us. In any case I find it more appealing than the idea of resurrection.

19 November 1849

Will I ever be granted peace of mind? Wherever I turn I see nothing but tragedy. Today was no exception. Oh God, it was dreadful.

Yesterday morning van der Eb came to my room. I absented myself from assembly a week ago, for reasons of ill health. He enquired after the nature of my ailment, and I told him frankly that I lacked the strength to rise from my bed. He sent for some broth, helped me wash and dress, and held my arm as he took me for a stroll round the courtyard. I could see the troops staring at me from the gallery. I went back to bed as soon as I could get away. But in the evening I went down to the dining room, which pleased the governor. This morning he proposed a fresh task to keep me occupied. I was to convey a message to the English commander at Fort Coenraadsburg. Van der Eb is a good man, but *so* transparent.

It was a long time since I had ventured past the drawbridge. When I returned from my mission in the late afternoon I decided to take a walk along the shore as I used to when I first arrived here. The weather was oppressive. The briny air was heavy with mist. Leaving behind the last cluster of dwellings I took the path over the rocks in the hope of being alone. I had hardly sat down when I caught sight of a figure emerging from the misty blur: a man wearing a loin-cloth, covered in grime, stooping as he shuffled along. He was evidently looking for something on the ground, for he stopped in his tracks from time to time, picked up a pebble or a shell, turned it this way and that for inspection, shook his head and threw it away. I did not recognize him as Joa until he was in front of me. I went towards him and laid my hand on his shoulder. He raised his head and smiled.

"I am looking for precious stones," he said, "but I cannot find any." His hair was long and covered in dust.

"You might have to dig a bit deeper to find precious stones," I offered, with a little laugh. I thought he was joking, but the way his eyes bored into mine told me otherwise.

"Sometimes they sparkle. Even in the dark. There are some very pretty ones. The only problem is how to smuggle them past the guards."

"I'm sure you deserve a rest from your labours," I said gently, trying to take his arm, but he shrugged me off and bent over to resume his search.

"I have promised my love a pretty gift."

"I see," I said, reproaching myself bitterly for not having troubled to visit him earlier. "Shall I help you then?" I sank on to my haunches and stirred the pebbles, as he was doing. Suddenly he drew himself to his full height, suspicious that I was mocking him.

"If the burden were the same for everyone, nobody would mind!"

I did not know what to say, and when he trudged off muttering to himself, I did not stop him. And yet, in a rush of selfish emotion, I envied my friend. In his befuddled state he still hoped to find beauty. As for me, I returned to the fort, empty-handed.

6 December 1849

Had we been kept on a leash and openly maltreated we would have put up a fight. We would have summoned our strength. We would undoubtedly have lost, but we have lost anyway. We were tolerated. And that is unforgivable. If you cannot accept a man wholeheartedly, then you should have the fortitude to repudiate him.

Waking up in the night I had a vision of extraordinary clarity . . . suddenly I was staring into the eyes of that poor soldier who jumped off the tower when we were here together as boys, soon after our arrival at the fort. In the limbo between waking and sleeping I saw him spread-eagled on the rocks, exactly as we had found him, but now he was convulsed with laughter.

"Indeed sir," I told him, "they want to press-gang you into life, but you have given them the slip!" I could not conceive of a more radical rebellion against the Christian tradition.

"You are right," he exclaimed. "True liberty lies beyond the gravest of sins!"

Then I swung an axe and cut off his head, which is, as you are aware, the Ashanti punishment for taking one's own life, and I began to realize that it was all a dream. Suddenly I was wide awake, and greatly agitated. I got out of bed, drank some water and shook off the gloom.

Have no fears on my account. These are merely fancies that steal into the night. And it is getting light already. "To advance is to die. To retreat is to die. Better then to advance and die in the jaws of battle!" After all, that is the Ashanti way.

19 December 1849

I have come up with an interesting way of banishing my sombre thoughts. By now I am familiar with every inch of my stone walls, every yard of the fort and every hut in the settlement. The same mist gathers over the sea every day. The only difference from one day to the next is the size of the fishermen's catch, which subject is hotly debated on the beach. I dare say there is more to their conversation than that, but I have lost the desire to engage with their lives. My favourite pastime nowadays is to take a walk along the salt pans in the midday heat and let myself be blinded by the shimmer of the sun reflecting on the crystals. It is a thrilling sensation. First I stare wide-eyed into the glare. Then I fix my eyes on the dark green forest at the far end of the salt flats. The effect is initially of blindness. Then everything resolves into a negative image, so to speak: a fringe of white trees hovering beyond a black plain. After a while the vision fades. In the same way I am able to see patches dancing before my eyes, in which I can make out certain configurations. Geometrical figures. Sometimes there are human shapes, too. I follow them with my eyes as if they were silvery-black butterflies, pointing the way ahead. They flutter this way and that as in a dream. These are nothing but fata morganas, I realize that, but at least they are always different. After twenty minutes or so my eyesight is restored and the figures melt into the trees, after which I start all over again. It is addictive. I often linger there until the flats take on the colour of the evening sky. Then I retrace my steps to Fort Elmina. The solitude of my cubicle is easier to bear when I am reminded that there is life outside.

24 December 1849

Today Joa presented himself at the gate. He asked to see me. He is a little better, it seems, and wishes to return to his native village to recover from his unrequited love. He is free to do so.

There is nothing left for him here. His workshop has closed down. The men who used to work for him have started their own businesses. Joa does not bear any grudges. He has lost all interest in profit-making. He asked me what he should do with my hand-loom. I told him to sell it. The money will stand him in good stead for his travels. I gave him my wages for this month. The journey is hazardous. Both of us smiled as we said goodbye, but his departure saddened me.

This will be my third Christmas in Elmina. The men's spirits are high. They are to return home next week. The new regiment has already reached Accra. So once again I am to witness the changing of the guard. Van der Eb tried to persuade me to go back to Holland with the returning troops. He did not spare my feelings.

"You are intelligent," he said, "well educated, well read, blessed with multiple talents. Why waste your aptitude on a nation that disdains the skills you have mastered? Be a man!"

I replied that I could not imagine anything more manly than hoping for the impossible. He grabbed me by the shoulders.

"You are deluding yourself. Why not face the facts? You are rushing headlong towards the precipice."

I thanked him for his concern. I can see the hopelessness of my situation quite clearly. When he saw the sadness in my eyes he regretted his words and changed the subject. The men were planning a tableau vivant of the nativity; they already had an ox and an ass, and van der Eb suggested I might be interested in taking the role of the black king. An excellent occasion to wear my *kente* cloth, he concluded. I replied that the only role I have is that of Black Peter.

1 January 1850

A fate such as mine, my dear Kwasi, is only to be found in the classics. I am rereading them, and am finding that they contain the last words that still strike a chord in me. Ah well, so many people have known tragedy in their lives.

4 January 1850

What joy! I have seen my mother again. What sorrow . . . Last night, as I was taking my evening stroll along the parapet, I caught sight of a shadowy figure by the gate. I thought—you must forgive me—she was a village girl come to tryst with a soldier. I motioned for her to go away, or she would be noticed. Then she called my name: "Kwame Poku." And again. I could not believe my ears. That voice! "Kwame Poku." I rushed outside barefoot, but there was no one at the gate. For a moment I thought I had taken leave of my senses. Then I found her sitting under a tree. She was weeping at first, but did not wish me to see her tears. She composed herself, dried her cheeks, and only then did she let me embrace her.

Her face looked barely a day older, but she had to study me from head to toe to convince herself that I was truly her child. Her fingertips on my unshaven cheek! She poured her heart out, but I could not understand what she was saying. It did not matter. I understood her meaning. I told her what was uppermost in my mind, and in my agitation the phrases that I had prepared for precisely this occasion came out garbled. She nodded as though she could read my thoughts and smiled at me moist-eyed.

We sat there for an hour, perhaps two, until we were all raw inside. "Have you come to take me home?" I asked, but I had already seen the answer in her eyes. Kwaku Dua is unrelenting. Then she held me against her breast. My God, how I have grown! In this awkward pose she rocked me in her arms. With my cheek against her shawl I suddenly noticed that the pattern was the same as that of the cloth I wove some time ago . . . I jumped up, rejoicing at the resemblance, and made to run inside to fetch my cloth so that I might show her my handiwork, but she would not let me go. We lapsed into silence, without this being painful. Finally she started singing. I recognized the melody. It was our morning prayer of the day of the *Ady.* I understood the words!

Oh spirit of the Earth, you grieve
Oh spirit of the Earth, you suffer

Oh Earth and the dust within you
As long as I am dead
I will be at your mercy
Oh Earth, as long as I live
I will put my trust in you
Oh Earth, which will receive my body
We appeal to you and you will understand
We appeal to you and you will understand

I rested my head on her lap. I am not ashamed of that. I must have drifted off. When I awoke in the morning she was gone. I asked everywhere, but no one had noticed an Ashanti woman. Not in the village, not in the fort and even the night guard maintains that he did not see anyone in my company. No matter. I know what I know.

15 January 1850

I should know better than to hope for another glimpse of her, but I do. I keep my ears and eyes wide open every night. Once I saw someone walking along the surf. I called out, but there was no reply. I know she cannot still be here. Her absence from Kumasi is bound to attract undue attention, so she must have hurried back. I shall try to get some sleep tonight.

4 February 1850

I returned today from an extended walk in the forest, where I spent two nights. I did not go equipped for an expedition. I slept on the ground, ate the fruits of the trees and bathed in the river. It was not my intention to disappear for good. I was roaming the salt flats and was drawn ever closer to that wall of green. Once I reached the edge of the forest it was as though something beckoned me from the deep, shadowy interior.

My absence without leave angered van der Eb. Upon my return he berated me, saying I must not forget that I am still in the service of the Dutch army. I retorted that I had been promised promotion by that same army, and that so long as this advancement was withheld I was under no obligation. His reaction was to strip me of all my privileges for the time being. I am to join the common soldiers in all their duties and exercises. But he is a good man at heart. He must have been worried about me, just as a father would be.

Perhaps I was drawn by the memory of the adventures you and I used to have in the forest. Climbing trees, building shelters with leaves, eating wild berries, hiding out in a secret world of our own where we would survive without any help. This was not easy, as it turned out. I am no longer a boy.

I was carrying my chopping knife, but had great difficulty making headway on the ground. So I climbed up to the next level, above the thick undergrowth, as Kofi taught us, and clambered from branch to branch. In this manner I left the sunlight behind and advanced into the canopied gloom. I made little progress. I stumbled and grazed both my legs. I was bitten by mosquitoes, and my uniform was so scratchy that I had to take it off. I bumped my head and had to bandage the wound against parasites. I attempted to get rid of the leeches clinging to my thighs with a flame, but was unable to strike a spark owing to the moisture. When I picked the swollen bodies off with my knife, they left holes in my skin. Despite discomfort, weariness and frustration at my slow pace I pressed on, until I noticed a suspicious-looking thicket, which I took for a snakes' nest. In order to overcome this obstacle I grabbed a liana and took a flying leap to the other side. My swing creaked ominously under my weight and snapped, dropping me into the very thicket I was trying to avoid. There was not a snake in sight, and as I lay there I imagined that you could see me making a spectacle of myself like the clowns we saw at the circus in The Hague. I could still laugh at my plight, thank goodness. I was too exhausted from my backbreaking tour to go on, and decided to rest during the night. I picked berries, gathered some dry branches to make a fire, and slept through the din of the jungle.

In the middle of the night I was startled out of my sleep by a shrill cry unlike the other animal sounds. I heard something scurrying about quite near. I made a noise to frighten the creature off, but then I heard the distinct sound of whimpering. I took a piece of burning wood from the fire to light my path and soon found a young monkey in the undergrowth. I recoiled, fearing that its parents would not be far off. But the leaves did not stir and the whimpers went unanswered, so I dared to take a better look. The monkey was of the species that is held sacred by the Boabeng and Fiema. He was in a sorry state: one leg dragged behind him and his tail was broken, probably from a fight with rivals or an attack by a predator. His injuries would have made him a liability to his clan, and consequently an outcast.

The poor creature was very thin, but nature had not yet completed her work. The terror in his eyes was so great that I was at a loss as to what action to take. I was afraid his heart might stop if I reached out to pick him up. Yet he did not run away, for he knew: whether I go forwards or backwards, I am lost.

I cleaved a coconut and mashed some fruit on a banana leaf, which I placed on the ground in front of the monkey, away from the fire. I sat down and waited at a short distance. The poor creature cowered in fright, keeping his eyes fixed on me. But his nose twitched at the scent of the food. In the end he gained confidence and ate in my presence. I left him alone for the night, and when I rose in the morning I pretended not to notice him peering at me from the undergrowth.

He trailed after me for the rest of the day, although he was very feeble. I advanced slowly, so as not to let him fall behind. I was beginning to enjoy my outing—it was the first time in a long while that I was not thinking about myself.

Towards afternoon I succeeded in luring the animal to my side with an offer of some food. He sat down to gobble up the fruit. He kept his eyes fixed on me, but the fear had left them. On account of his big eyes and the tufts of hair around his chin I named him Willem Alexander, for his looks reminded me of our new king.

By the end of the day I had won his confidence: he no longer followed behind, but stayed by my side, sometimes even limping ahead. If I lagged behind he would stop and look over his shoulder until I caught up.

The second night I did not get any sleep at all. I was kept awake by my small companion. There were predators about. I discovered large, fresh tracks, but had lost the ability to identify them. I kept the fire going and persuaded Willem to stay close to me. At one point a large beast passed by, which I could not see. I made a lot of noise and brandished a burning stick. That evidently did the trick. When the danger had subsided I noticed that Willem was crouching behind me. Rather than being frightened by my shouting, he had felt protected.

It was time to bring my expedition to a close. I had undertaken it on the spur of the moment, and had persevered out of sheer stubbornness. My muscles, skin and head cried out for a bath, for soothing ointment, clean clothes, soft pillows and cool bed-linen. In the years I was away I idealized nature as the love of my life. But the truth is that I am a stranger to her, a mere pinprick on her skin, a foreign body to be assaulted and repudiated.

I decided to retrace my steps in the morning, but what was I to do with Willem III? As if he could guess my thoughts he crept closer to me than ever. He posted himself at arm's length, a wizened child with his head to one side and an imploring look in his eyes. I imagined him keeping me company in my room. Van der Eb would surely not begrudge me this diversion. The little fellow would be out of danger, he would survive despite his lame leg. But he would never set eyes on his natural environment again, and thus would resemble me. I offered him some food and clapped my hands a few times, after which he kept his distance for the remainder of the night.

I started working my way back at daybreak. After an hour I discovered a salty residue on the leaves and by midmorning I reached the salt flats. In those two days I had probably covered a distance of little more than a few hundred yards. I looked over my shoulder and, seeing my companion close behind, I turned and rushed at him. I gave him a few well-aimed kicks, whereupon he bared his teeth, and when I continued, he bit me viciously. I swung my knife and made to attack him. He cringed and cackled with fear, and still the dumb creature did not flee. I became frenzied, and flung a stone at him which grazed his bad leg. He scrambled up a tree. I took my belt and lashed out at him, striking him on the flank. To my relief he got the message. Screaming piteously, the king vanished among the trees.

I sank to my knees on the salty ground, overcome with exhaustion. My heart ached and yet I was content. These salt pans are replenished with tears.

10 *February* 1850

Osei Tutu's priest Anokye has summoned the Golden Stool, *Sika Dwa*, from the sky. It came down on the knees of the Asantehene in a dark cloud amid rolling thunder, while the air was thick with flying sand. It is the throne to which I am entitled by birth, and it is there that the soul of our people resides. News came from Kumasi today that one of my younger brothers is to inherit your father's title. I sat down at once to write a letter of protest to the Asantehene, and another letter to my mother, begging her to explain how this could have happened. Van der Eb still does not believe that I have seen her in the flesh. However, he appreciates the gravity of the situation, and is willing to send a special envoy to Kumasi at the earliest opportunity.

12 *February* 1850

I have received your cut-out silhouette. It is indeed a deft piece of work. You tell me that these paper mementoes are all the rage in Weimar, and that you have sent them to all your friends and relations who wear them on their person or hang them on their walls as if they were works of art. But what am I to do with such a thing? Of all the manners of portrayal this is surely the most inane. It is flat, featureless and expressionless, and tells me less about you than your footprint.

Forgive me my ingratitude. I have not been myself lately. Setting eyes on your profile distressed me deeply—your cut-out shadow mounted on a white ground, hardly more characteristic than an ink stain. I cannot bear to look at it.

Raden Saleh's painting, too, has been drained of human expression. The salt has won. We have melted away. In many places the canvas is visible through the paint. Your left eye, cheek and shoulder have been spared until now, while all there is left of me is my nose and one of my knees. The colours have gone. You may be doing the rounds as a black silhouette in Weimar, but here your face is deathly pale.

Enough about the young ladies in Weimar, and more young ladies in Freiberg! I am sick and tired of them. All clamouring for a lock of your hair, because they are enchanted by the tight curls. And you allow them to pluck you like a chicken. You tell me they have even named their weekly meetings the "Ashanti Circle" in your honour—my goodness what a tribute—and that you actually grace these gatherings with your presence. You evidently still enjoy being the centre of attention. Attention, Kwasi, is not the same as acceptance. Being tolerated signifies not being equal.

All those balls and hunting parties, the grand personages who pat you on the back, your membership of the rakish Saxon-Bavarian drinking club—they mean nothing to me. Please spare me the details of life at court, the evenings spent in the company of your noble friends and your tête-à-têtes with Liszt. Your message has come across loud and clear—you are finding life at Athens-on-the-Ilm congenial! Enough!

Oh my dearest, most beloved friend, with whom I shared everything. If you do not feel the same as I do, who does? Don't fret. Your friendship is safe with me, and I am only chiding you because I cannot bear the thought of one of those silly young ladies displaying you to her friends and then, after you have taken your leave, gossiping about you at the witches' coven . . . Take no notice of what I have written. Go your own way. I am cursed with a deeply suspicious nature, and whatever you do, do not allow my distrust to divert you from your cause. Thank God you are more sanguine. That does not mean you are safe, but at least you have an open mind.

And remember this: if I were to live my life anew, I would prefer exile with the comfort of having you at my side to a life of ease in Kumasi deprived of your company.

16 February 1850

Since my excursion into the forest my mother has been visiting me in my dreams. She looks real, but I am unable to take her in my arms. She brings images and many words. She sits at my bedside, partially screened by the curtain, and teaches me poems. In Twi. I echo her words. Memorize them. And when I awake I make a note of the words I have learnt. Quite miraculous, don't you agree? I try not to think about the cause or the meaning of this phenomenon. The spirit world is not rational. My notebook already contains one hundred and fifty new words, which I practise during the day in an effort to construct sentences out of them.

I have reached the point in my life where I take more pleasure in reliving past experiences than in living the present. Indeed, memory has more to offer than real life.

20 February 1850

What surprises me above all else is that people can be so blind. The world is so simply construed, but they appear not to see it. There is good and there is evil. That is all. You can tell the difference a mile off. But even the few people in whom I have put my trust over the years have been unable to keep them apart.

To do good is to have a good life. To do evil with intent is to have a bad life. Nature sees to that. I can see wrongs being committed, and I long to warn the wrongdoers of the misfortune they are in fact bringing down upon themselves, but when I open my mouth to speak I see how futile it is. I myself have never wronged anyone, and yet look at me . . .

The truth is this: my little monkey king fell foul of his clan. That is why he had to die. Nature is unequivocal in these matters. I had no desire to be implicated. You and I know better than most what happens when people start meddling with destiny. A king is a king, whether dead or alive, whether here or there. He who is weak must die. I have no regrets. I merely gave nature a hand. One branch withers, the other thrives—as Osei Tutu said.

In three days I have learnt no fewer than forty-five new words of Twi, including the names of a variety of kitchen utensils and several diseases. That bodes well.

21 February 1850

You should have seen their faces. At luncheon today I surprised the officers by addressing them exclusively in Twi. It was quite easy, the words and phrases came tumbling out of my mouth of their own accord. Opening the shutters and letting fly, that is all it takes.

Note in the governor's log book at Fort Elmina:

22 February 1850

Today our small community has suffered a most sad loss. At eight-thirty a.m., in his private room, the Ashanti Prince Quame Poku took his life by shooting himself through the brain. The impact was so great that the poor fellow's face was mutilated beyond recognition.

The four walls of the room, the bed-curtains and the ceiling were splattered with blood and brain tissue. He was dressed in the ceremonial kente *cloth, which was woven by him personally.*

He appears to have put the weapon to his head directly behind the left ear. The weapon, which was found next to the body, is the same hunting rifle that was presented to him by the Ministry of Colonies upon his arrival here. It seems that he used loose gunpowder, as there was no trace of a bullet.

No motive for this desperate deed has been found, other than that his mind seemed strangely confused during the past three days. Yesterday at the commander's mess, for instance, all he did was babble unintelligibly.

PART FIVE

Java 1900

Buitenzorg, 3 August

Mrs. Renselaar burst in on me yesterday morning at an unearthly hour wearing her travelling costume. I was still in my dressing-gown having breakfast—much to her annoyance.

"There is very little time," she snapped, "for we are off to Batavia today!"

"Well then, I wish you a good journey," I said, "and do not hurry back on my account." She stood and watched open-mouthed as I peeled my mangosteen. I divided the fruit carefully into eight equal parts, and proceeded to eat one of them slowly.

"Shouldn't you be getting dressed?"

"Certainly, in good time. But by then you will be halfway there."

"I have no intention of going on my own. You are coming with me."

I choked on a piece of fruit and spat it out into my napkin. "Madam, the last journey I took was to the Salak foothills. From there I had a good view of my house and the plantation, and yet my only desire was to return home as quickly as possible."

"Nonsense, you travelled halfway across the world when you were only a child."

"And you can see what good it did me."

"You have criss-crossed the world all your life, and never complained."

"Those days are over. I have arrived at my destination."

"Don't be absurd. We are going by rail. You can be back by evening."

"Out of the question. I am too old for pleasure-trips."

"Ah," she said, "but it is not pleasure that we seek." She turned away briefly, fumbled in her blouse and produced a small brass key, which she waved at me triumphantly. She seemed to expect me to applaud, and when I did not oblige she dropped her arm, drew up a chair and deposited the key on the table with a flourish.

"Now listen carefully. My husband left the house in the early hours to attend to his business in Batavia. Half an hour ago a courier arrived with a summons for Mr. Renselaar to travel at once to Bandung, where the governor is meeting with a delegation of high officials from The Hague. I told him my husband was already on his way to Batavia. The matter appears to be so urgent that the young man departed at once to go after him."

"Most interesting, I'm sure," I drawled.

"Yes, isn't it?" She beamed.

"How does that concern me?"

"The courier will soon catch up with my husband, who will barely have had time to sit down at his desk when he hears of the governor's summons. He gathers together his necessities at once, notifies his subordinates that he must absent himself, and departs for Bandung post-haste." She mimed the entire scene for my benefit. I interrupted her when she launched into a description of her husband tearing his hair out while consulting his watch.

"Very good," I said, "and what of it?"

"Well, hardly will he have gone when my presence is announced. I will be told that he has been called away on urgent business. This is exceedingly annoying. I fly into a rage. They try to appease me, in vain. I have an appointment to meet him, and have come all this way for nothing."

"So why go there, for heaven's sake?"

"I insist on taking a rest in his office. With you."

"Me?"

"Certainly. You will have made the journey for nothing as well. You just stand there, helplessly. You, a poor old man! They cannot simply turn us away after all our effort. It would be most uncivil. Where would we go? I feel quite faint. I make a scene."

"I do not doubt it."

"Just so as to be left alone for a short while. In his office. At his desk. We sit down."

"At last."

"We ask for some refreshments and tell them we are not to be disturbed. Then I take out this key. It is the key to the drawer of his desk, where he keeps the case containing the dossiers he is currently engaged in. Yours is among them. You will have half an hour to read it." She swept the key off the table and slipped it back into her blouse. "Just half an hour and the mystery will be solved." Feeling she deserved a reward, she pulled my plate towards her and devoured the fruit I had prepared. Meanwhile the implications of her plan began to dawn on me.

"So you purloined your husband's key on my account?"

"Good gracious no, I had a copy made when he was taking his afternoon nap the other day. One never knows when such things will come in handy. Well now," she said, smiling so broadly that the mangosteen juice trickled down her chin, "are you going to get properly dressed or do you intend to parade the streets in dishabille?"

I went to my room in a daze. Ahim came running to help me wash and dress, but I could not bear him touching me and sent him away. I was very agitated, my whole body was shaking. As usual I cursed the woman for making such a fuss, but at the same time I was touched by the trouble she was taking on my behalf. I needed a few moments to compose myself. I pressed my bolster to my mouth to stifle a cry.

The truth is that I have felt no desire to see anyone at all lately. I have been totally immersed in my self-imposed task. Having embarked on my personal memoir—which gave me little pleasure—I started rereading Kwame's letters. I could not bring myself to take out more than one each day. By the time I reached the end I was so sad that my stomach could not tolerate any food. My body rebelled against the torment in my brain. Thoughts can ferment. They are like gin: you keep taking yet another sip in the hope of rinsing your mouth of the taste, but the blood curdles. The older you get, the harder your heart has to work to pump away the toxin.

Last week Ahim ignored all my orders. We had our umpteenth altercation over luncheon. I was unable to eat the food he had prepared. He blamed my lack of appetite on my memoir and on my reclusive ways. I was more inclined to blame his cooking skills, but had the sense not to tell him so. I said he should mind his own business. He lost his temper, and stalked off into the kampung. He searched out my little daughter, whom he took from her mother and brought back to me. He came into my room carrying the child on his back. He pushed aside the papers scattered on the table and sat Quamina down in front of me. All this time he did not say a word. She was lively, and delighted to see me. She stretched out her little arms to hug me. I was non-plussed. I drew her on to my lap, gently, because with children and animals I am always afraid I might harm them. Ahim rolled up the blinds, after which he brought a piece of cardboard and some crayons. He handed me the musical box. I turned the handle and watched the child's fascination at the tinkling notes. After a while we took her to the garden, and for the next few hours my mind was happily free from preoccupying thoughts. When it was time to take Quamina back to her mother, Ahim had to pull us apart. To please him, I ate the food he served me that evening. The next morning I awoke without a headache for the first time in weeks.

Quamina's sudden appearance had moved me much as Mrs. Renselaar's show of concern did now. I hastened to put on the clothes that Ahim had laid out on the bed.

Batavia was thronged with people. Perhaps I am less tolerant of crowds than I used to be, but to me it seemed that everyone was at each other's throats. The close array of stalls encroached on the carriageway, while the vendors vied for attention with a chaos of garish signs and banners. We were jostled by people on all sides, running and shouting. Children played at our feet, and here and there an aged person slept on the ground. The stinking open sewers were choked with filth, and their banks were lined with chickens, rats and stray dogs. It was a madhouse. There was no rest for the eyes. The dust raised by the porters, horses and carts didn't have room to settle, so that it formed a yellow haze which constricted my throat. Besides, the thick evil fumes from the heaps of refuse smouldering on every street corner poisoned each breath I took.

Adeline led the way, swinging her parasol like a scythe, as if she were cutting a swathe through the multitude. We picked our way across the square in front of the railway station and managed to hail a cab. Once we were sitting down I told her how much I disliked the frenzy of the city.

"Well, we are living in a new century now," she retorted. "We cannot turn the clock back. It is only because you knew Java when it was paradise that you are shocked by the hectic pace of today."

"Paradise? Ankle-deep in mud and decaying roots, plagued by monsoons and mosquitoes? No madam, my idea of paradise is on a somewhat higher plane."

"Nonsense. You are devoted to this country. Why else did you stay?"

"Good question, madam."

Our carriage drew up in front of the head office. Adeline alighted first, whereupon she took my arm to help me down. We heard a cry of anguish: an old woman trying to cross the road in front of our carriage had been knocked over by a coolie. The fellow did not stop to see what he had done and no one seemed to be about to help the old woman to her feet. She was even showered with abuse by a rickshaw driver, who had to swerve sharply to avoid running over her legs. I knew this already. All respect for life becomes smothered by the sheer magnitude of the masses. It is each man for himself nowadays in Batavia.

Mrs. Renselaar sprang into action. She tried to help the woman to her feet. The frail figure recoiled. The sight of that enormous white-faced body bending over her shocked her more deeply than her fall. Tenacious as ever, Adeline lost her balance and tumbled on top of the unfortunate old woman. When they were finally on their feet again I saw that both women had streaks of mud in their hair. I took out my handkerchief and offered it to Adeline, but she declined. Her dishevelment, she said, would come in handy. She wiped her hands at length on my lapels, so that I looked bedraggled too, after which she took my arm and drew me towards the gate of the head office.

At first all went according to plan. Mrs. Renselaar overwhelmed the sentry with a torrent of words and strode past him without even slowing her pace. She opened the cast-iron door herself, and crossed the marble hall which gave on to three corridors and a flight of stairs. Without a moment's hesitation she made for the first floor. She thumped up the wooden staircase, with me following quietly behind her.

"Now remember," she said, "you and I are in command today. Keep that in mind and act accordingly, then no one will ask awkward questions." She opened the doors to two or three offices, without knocking and without the clerks raising their heads. We crossed an attendant in the corridor, who gave us a surprised but friendly nod. Adeline enquired where the archive office was. He pointed it out and went on his way. Adeline fumbled with the knob. When the door did not open she threw all her weight against it with her hip. At this point two thoughts were uppermost in my mind: I had to keep my knees from buckling and also to control the ringing in my ears which would prevent me from hearing people coming to restrain us. My eyes darted this way and that in terror, and I was just wondering why I had inflicted all this on myself when the door gave way. She stumbled into the room and found herself staring into the gaunt face of the archivist. He peered at us over his spectacles like a man neither accustomed nor partial to visitors.

"Whom have you come for?"

I could hear her sharp intake of breath. Even she was apprehensive now. She could think of nothing better to say than her name, which came out a little too loud. The archivist went to the door and ran his finger over the lock to inspect it for damage.

"Mr. Renselaar has gone out."

"Oh no," sighed Adeline, "no, he would never do a thing like that, not when I have come such a long way . . ."

From here on she enacted her scene just as she had planned, but the man was not easily swayed. He escorted us to Renselaar's office. Finding it vacant and not wishing to leave us behind alone, he summoned his superior. Adeline whispered reassuringly that she had met her husband's head of department on a previous occasion and that he would be easy to deal with, but when the short, thin man in question stood before her, the only sign of recognition he gave was that he dreaded a conversation with her. He was clearly nervous, and explained that this was an unforeseen circumstance, as the summons had come quite unexpectedly. He appreciated how distressing this must be for us, he said, and offered us a glass of water by way of appeasement. When this did not have the desired effect, he suggested we might join him and his wife in the leafy suburb of Weltevreden for luncheon.

"Alas, my poor nerves," said Adeline. "They are shattered. I simply must take a rest . . . We were involved in a traffic accident only a moment ago. You can see the state we are in. You cannot expect us to go back into that disorderly crowd, it is unthinkable."

"You may have the use of my carriage."

"No sir, all we need is a little time to compose ourselves and recover from the bitter disappointment that the prince, at his advanced age, and myself have journeyed all the way from Buitenzorg to no avail . . ."

"Did you have any particular business to discuss with Mr. Renselaar?" the man enquired, addressing his words to me directly. "Perhaps I can be of assistance?"

I hesitated.

"I hardly think so," Adeline broke in. "No, truly there is no other option than to take a rest here and then to embark on our return journey . . ."

"But madam, may I remind you that these premises are not open to the public."

"And quite right too." She leaned her parasol against the wall, pulled out her hat pin and started peeling off her gloves as if she had all the time in the world. The head of department lost hope. He sighed.

"Surely you are not suggesting that my husband would object to my presence in his office, among his own private possessions?"

"Oh no, it is just that our rules are rather strict."

"There, look at that dear little clock, it was my gift to my husband for his fortieth birthday. And that engraving, and the writing pad—it is hand-tooled. Good heavens, half the accoutrements in this room were provided by me personally, and now I am not to be granted access."

"Please do not take it amiss, madam, of course your husband would have no objection, but as it is I am responsible and my instructions are most stringent."

Adeline affected indignation and threw me a meaningful look. I thought she was about to admit defeat. Then she winked at me. At the same time I watched her physical transformation into a frail old woman. She stooped, crooked her fingers, hunched her shoulders.

"I . . ." she groaned, veering round and collapsing on to the chair behind her husband's desk.

"I wish . . ."

"Madam I beg you." The head of department broke out into a cold sweat. "Do not excite yourself. Please go back to your home. I do not doubt that your husband will hasten to be with you as soon as his affairs are concluded, and that all will be duly explained. He will expect to find you at home when he returns."

She gave him a tearful, imploring look. "He was loath to leave, and it was I who unclenched his fingers from the doorpost with my own hands . . ." She moaned softly. ". . . and I hung his father's rings in his ears—as though preparing him for sacrifice . . ." In the bewildered silence that ensued she planted her elbows on the pile of papers lying on the desk in front of her and buried her face in her hands.

The head of department stepped forward to console her, but his courage failed him. He gave me a questioning, troubled look. I had recognized her words at once as coming from a play. On the way to Batavia she had bored me with her chatter about her role in the play currently being staged by the amateur dramatics society. She told me it was a great success in Holland; it was a fishermen's drama, and she had been given the part of the fisherman's wife. I shrugged, laughed sheepishly and tapped my index finger against my forehead.

"All this is most distressing to Mrs. Renselaar," I said, for good measure.

Upon hearing my words Adeline rose, as if she were about to accept the inevitable. She stared at the head of department as if he had brought tidings of death, and mumbled soulfully: "My husband and our sons . . . now the only hope I have left is my cousin's young son."

At this the head of department stammered a brief apology and fled. Not only were we granted all the time we needed to recover from our exertions, we were also served tea and cake. Then Adeline bolted the door on the inside, unbuttoned her jacket and took out the little brass key to unlock the drawer of her husband's desk.

Among the dossiers in the drawer there was only one with my name on the cover. It comprised some forty documents relating to my first years in Java. The earliest of these dated from September 1850 and contained information on my arrival, employ and temporary accommodation; the most recent (September 1857) was a transcript of my royal certificate of appointment as candidate mining engineer with an annuity of four hundred guilders, and a note to the effect that I was to be kept informed of any changes in the staff of the royal household, in keeping with my status as a prince of an ally of the kingdom of the Netherlands.

It turned out that my own letters, written in the intervening period, were included in the dossier. I recognized most of them at a glance from the handwriting. There were several reports I had submitted on my work and travels, but the majority were appeals to the successive governors-general to assign me to a more responsible position in the Dutch Indies: the early ones to Rochussen were politely and circumspectly phrased, but by the time I was addressing Duymaer van Twist the tone had become terse and strident. I did not spend too much of our precious time poring over these reminders of past ill feeling.

Far more interesting were the confidential reports on my activities submitted by others. Several of these had been drawn up by men I had trusted. They concerned both my performance as a public servant and my private life. As I was moderate in my ways then as I am now, and it was not and is not in my nature to give offence, the facts that were cited were not particularly striking. What did strike me, however, were the names of those who had filed the reports. Among the informers were neighbours and servants, an old friend, the postmaster at the mining department, and even my wine merchant. Now and then there was mention of a fee for providing information, but more often it had been volunteered.

The dossier did not appear to contain items of a more dramatic nature than this. I was beginning to think all our trouble had been for nothing, or that some minor incident had been blown out of all proportion by Adeline and her husband, when I came across a brief note from van Drunen himself. It was a copy, written in his own hand, of an official missive addressed to the minister of Colonies. In it he announced his intention to resign from his post and return to Holland. He explained his motives as follows:

> [. . .] my concern for the fate of the princes of Ashanti, with whose removal to Holland I was charged. Ever since the tragic death of Prince Quame Poku at Elmina I have lived in fear for the well-being of the surviving prince, Mr. Aquasi Boachi. Having overcome considerable personal hardship, the latter is currently residing in Java where, unbeknownst to him, he is denied prospects of promotion. It is my belief that the wilful obstruction of any man's advancement in life is a gross injustice. Moreover, the fact that the authorities have ordained that the mandate regarding the prince's career be treated as strictly confidential is inconsistent with my morals and therefore weighs on my conscience. It is for these reasons that I am requesting you herewith to [. . .]

In 1852 van Drunen, who yearned for tropical climes, had been promoted to a position of rank in Batavia for the remainder of his career by the Ministry of Colonies in The Hague. Although he had taught Kwame and me the principles of the Dutch language and also offered us guidance and support in the subsequent years, a close friendship had not developed between van Drunen and ourselves. He earned our confidence and always showed sincere concern for our welfare, but his loyalty to us was not exclusive. He owed allegiance to the kingdom of the Netherlands too, and thereby equally to the powers that had contrived our removal from our native land.

Indeed, I did not meet van Drunen more than twice in Batavia during the 1850s. On the first occasion our conversation was devoted to Kwame and very little else. On the second I informed him of the problems I was facing in Java. I asked him to speak to the minister on my behalf. He promised to do his utmost for me and even notified me of his initial steps in that direction. Soon afterwards, however, he was relieved of his post, and he repatriated without sending me a word of farewell. I was deeply disappointed by this.

Some fifteen years later he sent me a letter from Samarang in the Indies, telling me that he had taken up residence there as a private citizen. He was living in a settlement inhabited almost exclusively by former "recruits" from the African Gold Coast, whom he astonished with his intimate knowledge of their fatherland and customs. He was making plans to help these "black Hollanders," who found themselves virtually destitute in their old age after serving out their contracted terms. He supported their manufacture of batik cloths, and was able to use his remaining contacts with officialdom to dispatch the occasional consignment to Elmina, where these cloths were in popular demand. He wrote that the profits from these ventures were transferred in full (he underlined the words himself) to the workers. He used his meagre monthly stipend to purchase medicines, and gave the youngest children in that community lessons in the Dutch language. Consequently he often thought of me, he said. He had spoken of me to his African friends and they wished to make my acquaintance.

I did not reply to this letter, nor to the two that followed. I had no desire to make an exhibition of myself. What could I have said to them? There was no further communication from van Drunen. I never saw him again.

Setting eyes on his letter of resignation after so many years made me realize how unfairly I had treated him. Not only had he sought attention for my case, he had even put his own career at risk on my account. Adeline noticed my bemusement. She leaned over my shoulder to read the letter and whispered breathlessly into my ear: "That's it. The secret mandate." It was only then that the significance of van Drunen's letter dawned on me.

The remaining papers consisted of official documents pertaining to my activities in the colonial service, and I divided them between Adeline and myself. We were looking for any further allusions to what van Drunen termed "the mandate regarding the prince's career." We did not come across specific mention of it. However, we did find a note appended to one of my numerous applications for relocation bearing the words, "circumstances do not permit," and another saying, "in vain, alas, given the mandate." Our efforts were not fully rewarded—as usual when hunting for evidence—until the very last document. It was a brief message from Minister of Colonies Pahud to Governor-General Rochussen. With reference to a statement made on 24 July 1850 (a transcript of which was, curiously, missing from the dossier) he made the following comment:

> With reference to your outspoken objections to the appointment of the Prince of Ashanti, you may rest assured that the exceptional measures adopted in confidential consultation with His Royal Highness cover all contingencies. Consequently I see no reason to reconsider the possibility of the Prince being posted to Batavia.

We returned home late to Buitenzorg. Mrs. Renselaar insisted on driving me home first. She had shown consideration for my mood throughout the journey by keeping silent. I thanked her for all her trouble.

"Well, we are not a great deal the wiser, are we," she said, shaking my hand firmly. "Oh, it is intolerable!"

I asked her to wait a moment while I went inside to fetch the manuscript I had been working on. I entrusted the new instalment of my memoir to her. This time she accepted my offer without any histrionics.

"As for your jubilee celebration, if you would rather not . . ."

"Do as you see fit, I do not mind one way or the other."

"In that case we'll call the whole thing off."

"After all the effort you have made?"

"All my effort was for you. I do not wish for your agreement merely as a favour to me."

This was my chance, and I did not take it. In a moment of weakness I was glad to make her happy.

"Excellent," she said with a sigh of relief, "because I have already decided on an appropriate date. The ninth of September, would that suit you?"

"One day is as good as another as far as I am concerned."

"It is the date of your arrival in Java."

"So it is."

"At least, that is what is written in the documents."

"Then it must be true."

When she drove off I went into the house. Ahim made to serve me the food he had kept for me, but I had no patience and did not touch it. The papers I had secreted from the dossier were burning a hole in my pocket.

Although it was far too late to venture out again, I set off for the kampung. The suspense I had gone through in the day had aroused in me the energy of a young man. I longed for release, but when I was halfway there I struck across the fields. There was a full moon, the night was clear. I picked my way through the undergrowth past my gardens, until I reached the pool and sat down at the edge of the silver water. Like a child with a handful of stolen sweets, I did not dare inspect my prize until I was all alone.

There were two sheets, translated and copied by an army clerk. I had only skimmed over the opening lines in Mr. Rense-

laar's office since they had no bearing on the facts we were looking for. But my immediate reaction had been that they should be
in my possession, and not in a dossier. I had stuffed them into my
trouser pocket when Adeline wasn't looking.

To his Excellency Mr. Schomerus,
Governor of Elmina,
dated March second 1854.

I have received your kind letter regarding my son Kwasi Boarchi
[sic], whom I sent to Engeland [sic] for schooling until his return
home. I have been informed and have understood from your letter
that he has declined to come home, and you suggest that I should
not be too saddened by this turn of events; but in truth his
absence is a great sadness to me, and since I long to see his face, I
will be most grateful if you would be so kind as to write to his
master requesting him to give my son leave to travel here to see
my face and then to return to his place of work. I beg you to
comply with my request only so that I may set eyes on him and
his nature once more, in order that he may return to his work
afterward.
    Signed at Kumasi,
    Kwaku Dua, Asantehene of Ashanti

Under these lines my father had not drawn a cross as he used
to do in the old days, but had written his name in a childish scrawl.

No one had ever breathed a word to me about this plea from
my father. I needed desperately to mull over the meaning of his
message, but could not bring myself to reread it. The letters
became blurred in the shimmer of the moonlight. My eyes were
perhaps suffering from fatigue, but my blood remained restless. I
decided to take a bath in the pool. I shed my clothes, which I
folded carefully, hiding the crumpled letter deep among the folds
of my trousers, at a safe distance from the water's edge. The
Asantehene had employed water-based ink, which is intolerant of
moisture.

Dutch East Indies 1850–55

I

– Can what is foreign to us become our Fatherland?
– And the Fatherland has become strange to you.
– That is why my bleeding heart will not heal.

Goethe, *Iphigenie auf Tauris*

Bits of straw, the sweet fragrance of timber and drifts of powdery red earth were carried aloft by the harmattan. I sat on deck in the Gulf of Guinea, two and a-half days' sailing from Dakar. The dry wind blowing out to sea brought us land-birds, white with yellow combs, just as Kwame had described in his first letter from Elmina. Although I had braced myself for this part of my voyage, I was suddenly overcome. I fell silent in mid-conversation. Linse and Lebret, in whose company I was travelling to the Indies, guessed the reason for my melancholy. They replenished my glass of port and left me to my musings.

On that day the *Sarah Lydia* was heading for São Tomé to take on water. At Linse's instigation the ship's captain dropped anchor some distance from the harbour, to ensure that I would not be able to see the African coastline. I enquired after the latitude of our position several times, but no one would tell me when we would sail past Elmina. I did not press for further information.

I felt no desire to visit Kwame's grave. It was the end of May, three months after his death. He had returned to my heart. (Death sometimes brings someone closer than life. You carry with you for ever what was dear to you. Never again can love fail. There is nothing left to lose. Nothing left to ruin. Thus Death secures for ever the very thing he takes from us.)

·   ·   ·

Linse and Lebret had completed their training in London, where they and three other students from Delft were monitored by Cornelius de Groot. It was therefore clear to all concerned why I had chosen to complete my degree in Freiberg rather than in London.

They attempted to distract my thoughts with questions concerning my studies in Germany and my knowledge of the minerals and mines, and the geological research I had undertaken. They were particularly interested to hear about my relations with the famous Professor Cotta, whose theories they had studied in London without ever having met the man. I was able to supply them with some noteworthy information regarding my mentor. But on the whole our experiences were not dissimilar, although the focus of my graduate studies had been more practical and theirs more academic. They conceded that the training I had received would be the more directly applicable in the Indies. For themselves they envisaged working in administrative positions. All three of us had entered the service of the Ministry of Colonies as candidate-engineers before sailing east.

"I have heard," Lebret said, "that you have been given the designation 'extraordinary' following your title. 'Candidate-engineer extraordinary.' "

"Yes, that is what it says in my certificate of appointment."

"And what does it mean?"

"I don't know. I think . . ."

"What did you expect?" Linse interrupted. "That they would treat Aquasi the same way as ourselves? *You* are ordinary, Lebret. Utterly ordinary. I am slightly less so. But Aquasi . . . our Aquasi is extraordinary. Always has been. And always will be." He meant to be kind.

"Nonsense," I said shamefacedly.

"I was just wondering what exactly makes him different."

"Royal blood," Linse said impatiently, as if he had done enough explaining. He was already a little tipsy, but poured himself another drink. Lebret held out his glass, too.

"Or is it something to do with your degree? Aquasi, did you graduate with first class honours?"

"But I got a first too," said Linse. "You aren't going to deny that, are you? My first is as good as anyone else's, make no mistake."

"I was just wondering. The designation. What it means."

"It didn't occur to me to query it," I replied. "I assumed that the same terms applied to us all."

"Never mind." Linse was getting bored with the conversation. "'Extraordinary' sounds pretty grand to my ears. Pretty grand."

"Right you are. It sounds good, damned good."

"And extraordinary service demands extraordinary remuneration. Be sure to remind them of that, Aquasi."

Lebret in particular looked forward to life as a bachelor in colonial service. For the first few months, we fancied, we would have to familiarize ourselves with the civil administration at the colonial capital. Then we would have an opportunity for an extensive tour of the archipelago in connection with our independent field studies. We would be expected to publish our findings in scientific journals devoted to soil conditions and geology. We were eager to put our studies into practice. As we lounged on the deck of the *Sarah Lydia* we made wild plans and fantasized about our careers. Just once I mentioned, in passing, a shared memory of our student days in Delft, our last evening of fun in Kwame's company, but Lebret almost imperceptibly turned the conversation to our future. My friends did their best to divert me for the duration of our passage along the West African coast.

Professor Bernhard Cotta had crowned my studies by inviting me to accompany him on a tour of inspection of several mines in the Tirol, which lasted the whole summer of 1849. After that there was little to occupy me in Freiberg other than my personal friendships. I was always welcome at the homes of Von Beust, Breithaupt, Gätschmann, Reich and all the others. Every Friday and Saturday we went out on the town with our drinking club, of which I was honorary member, and on Tuesdays and Thursdays I was expected to put in an appearance at the young ladies' Ashanti Circle. All these entertainments combined with my visits to Sophie in Weimar made me wish I could stay there for ever. But I could no longer decently defer my departure. Enclosed with my final monthly allowance I received a letter from Minister of Colonies Pahud recalling me to Delft. I lingered in Dresden for a few days, but was eventually obliged to take my leave of Freiberg, which I did with an aching heart. I exchanged silhouettes and locks of hair with my friends, and received many fond notes and declarations of amity, all of which I pasted into the handsome Friends' Album given to me by Sophie and Carl Alexander. Having ordered an engraving of my likeness to be sent to my friends in due course, I started off on a visit to Weimar, to bid farewell to the future grand duke and duchess. They would not let me go and I spent a few final weeks as their guest at Ettersberg Castle.

At Ettersberg, whenever a letter arrived from Kwame it would be brought to my room. I would take it with me to the stone bench on the edge of the forest behind the castle, where the wide view over the valley always gave me a sense of detachment. I had to summon up courage to read my cousin's letters.

"Any news from our dear friend?" Sophie enquired as usual when she saw me sitting there during her daily stroll. At first I told her Kwame was doing reasonably well, despite some setbacks. I did not wish to worry her, as she was still mourning her father's death. But in the end I did read out a few passages. They were somewhat confused, and I had difficulty understanding their meaning. Sophie was shocked and asked if she might see the whole letter. I gave it to her. She read it from beginning to end and then reread it, after which she laid it aside, saying, "Promise me you will never follow him there." She clasped my hand and did not release it until I had given her my word. After that we would read his letters together, trying to make out the state of his emotions at the time of writing. Occasionally Sophie would advise me as to what I should put in my letters to Kwame. She did not think I should try to cheer him up all the time, which seemed to me the most natural and indeed the easiest solution. No, I was to respond to each of his anxieties separately and at length, even if they struck me as unfounded. My show of empathy, she thought, would make him feel less forsaken.

On 1 October I sent a petition, at Sophie's instigation and virtually in her words, to her brother Willem Alexander the new king. In it I stated that I had no desire to return to the Gold Coast. I drew his attention to the impasse in Kwame's prospects and also mentioned the persecution of Christians at Kumasi, the unfavourable forecasts for mining in that region, the high number of casualties and the minimal yields of the Dabokrom undertaking. I wrote that the notion of returning to my native country was distasteful to me, and requested him to secure me a position, of any kind, that would keep me in Holland. When a satisfactory reply did not arrive, Sophie rose up in arms. Only the previous day a most disturbing letter had come from Elmina in which Kwame claimed to have met my aunt, his mother. Sophie thought it wise, in the circumstances, for me to refuse to return to Holland unless I received guarantees for my future as well as the king's personal assurance that I would be permitted to reside there permanently. On 23 January 1850, I did as she had suggested.

One week later I received a missive granting my wishes. I wrote this happy news to Kwame at once, in the hope that it would please him and that it might make him realize that he too could come back to Europe if he chose. That his second fatherland would welcome him with open arms.

I had run out of reasons to postpone my return to Holland. Sophie took my arm, and we took a final walk in the Buchenwald which lasted several hours.

I arrived in Delft at the end of February. The news of Kwame's death reached me earlier than his final letters. It was brought to me by courier on 6 March. I was racked with self-recrimination. I made frantic efforts to discover whether he had lived to read the last letters I had written, and if so whether my tidings had disheartened him. No one knew. None of my letters were found amongst his possessions. One of the sergeants who had been stationed in Elmina at the time gave me the following account. On the day before Kwame died he came across my cousin sitting on the battlement of the left tower in the fort. Next to him lay an open portfolio containing all his private papers, among which the sergeant noted his army commission, some certificates and a batch of personal correspondence. One by one he was throwing the sheets out to sea. When questioned as to his motives he merely said, "I am setting all the words free."

"Why?" I asked the sergeant, an ingenuous young man, little more than a boy, "why was his irrational behaviour not taken as a warning that he needed surveillance and protection against himself?"

All the soldier said, his voice faltering, was, "Indeed, sir, but you see, the prince looked so utterly content."

"The tree has fallen," I wrote to Sophie, aching with regret at having ever left Weimar. The very night that I received the terrible news, my heart turned against Delft. After all the trouble I had taken to secure my permanent domicile in Holland, my soul was lacerated by thoughts of Kwame. I was lying in bed in our old room at the boarding school. Everything around me, even the squeak of the springs when I turned over in the night, reminded me of my dead friend. The mirrors had been draped with cloths. The curtains remained shut. And then there was Mrs. van Moock's grief-stricken look in the morning, the stunned silence of her husband. The headmaster cancelled the lessons and sat by the fire all day, as pale as parchment. Bertha sobbed in the corridor from morning till night. As for me, I found refuge in church.

A memorial service was held in the Old Church, during which I sat alone in the front pew. Mrs. van Moock insisted on sitting further back with her husband, so that she could flee if the emotion became too much for her. Our former classmates were no longer living in Delft. A few pews behind me I glimpsed only the faces of local shopkeepers, whom I suspected of unwholesome curiosity.

I was struck by the grim expression on old Dominee Molenkamp's face as he stepped into the pulpit. He laid his hands on the wooden rail. His grip tightened, and I saw his knuckles whiten. He squared his shoulders and opened his mouth. I was so distracted by the iciness of his attitude that I missed the opening sentences of his eulogy. Then I realized what was missing: there were no smiles. I looked round. All the faces looked equally grim. It was not that I myself had felt even the merest glimmer of relief at Kwame's death, let alone any elation, but the atmosphere of gloom suddenly struck me as utterly heartless. I raised my eyes and glimpsed my friend perching on one of the pediments in the transept. His legs were flung wide and his torso swayed to an inaudible rhythm. This fleeting vision softened my pain. For one happy instant I was elated. Then Molenkamp's words sank into my brain.

There was a note of indignation in his voice. As though he had suffered a personal injustice. The text he had chosen was "The apostles sent forth to spread the Gospel." He reminded his audience sanctimoniously of his intention to send us out into the world as missionaries, "as Christ sent the apostles, two by two." Prince Quame, he said, had refused to take this path. Although he deserved praise for his dedication to his religious studies, it had been proved beyond a doubt that the prince's faith had been too weak, his old mistaken beliefs too stubborn. Alas, hell awaits those who commit suicide, the dominee seemed to be saying, for he shook his head violently and told us to pray as much as we could for the forgiveness of his sin. After which he closed his eyes and fell silent. My gaze was drawn upwards again. There was nothing to be seen, but I winked at the space anyway.

After the service I discovered van Drunen amongst the mourners. He was very perturbed. I told him he need not blame himself. I said the same to the van Moocks, repeatedly. I even requested the delegate from the ministry to convey this message from me to his superior and also to King Willem III, whose absence from the ceremony surprised me. But I did not warm to Dominee Molenkamp. As I was leaving church he grasped my hand, although I had not extended it.

The next day I addressed a forthright appeal to the minister of Colonies to secure me a position in the Dutch East Indies. I thought that would put some distance between me and my grief, another advantage being that I was not a complete stranger to the tropical environment.

I was received by the state councillor. He did not look kindly on my application, for he was still adamant that it was my duty to return to the Gold Coast. He listed the sums of money that I had cost the Dutch State during the past thirteen years, and enquired how I intended to repay the debt. When I replied that I regarded Holland as my fatherland and that I dearly wished to make myself useful as a citizen thereof, he laughed scornfully.

"I have been otherwise informed," he said haughtily, but refused to name sources or facts. Perhaps, had I questioned him further in a tactful manner, I might have discovered what sort of game was being played with me, but I lost my self-control. An argument ensued, which ended in my being shown the door after a stern reprimand. After this nothing happened for some time. I had requested an audience with my old friend, King Willem III, but this was not granted. I then wrote him a letter, telling him of my meeting with the state councillor, and asked whether he knew of any allegations against my person. I concluded with declarations of my deepest loyalty, but there was no reply.

After several weeks I received notice from the ministry of Colonies that I was to be offered a post as public servant extraordinary in the East Indies. I was pleased that my bid had been successful, but then the remuneration caught my eye: seventy guilders monthly. By way of comparison, my monthly allowance in Freiberg had been two hundred guilders, and that was just for board and lodging. Had I accepted the post to the Gold Coast I would have earned five thousand guilders annually. What was there left for me to say? I was desperate to leave.

I embarked on 7 May. It was a happy coincidence that my old friends Linse and Lebret were among the passengers of the *Sarah Lydia*. We were still in the roads when I sent word to the engraver in Freiberg that I approved of my portrait and that he should send copies to all my friends. I instructed him to add the following legend: *Friendship is unrelated to station, distance, nation, religion, morals and customs; it links the cold north to the blazing south; without friendship the world would be a wilderness.*

. . .

Not long after we had sailed from São Tomé, it was announced that Neptune had come on board to baptize those crossing the Equator for the first time—an old tradition. The crew was in excellent spirits and came to fetch us. The mighty sea-god sat on a throne made of kegs. He was swathed in yellow and green, and wore a crown of rope. The youngest sailors were brushed with tar and shaved with a whalebone, after which the poor lads were baptized by being lowered over the port side on the end of a rope. Passengers were less harshly treated. Linse was in good form and volunteered to be the first. His shirt was removed. His hands were tied behind his back. He was forced to kneel in front of a water-butt containing several treacle-covered fruits. When he had finally succeeded in catching one of them in his jaws, the sticky paste was scoured off his face with a brush. After this Lebret demurred. They brushed him so hard that his cheeks almost bled.

When it was my turn I walked towards the water-butt in a daze. I took off my shirt and held out my hands for them to be tied. Then I spotted Kwame among the jeering seamen. He was leaping up and down, jeering with the others. He was actually encouraging them to make me undergo the ritual. When they pushed me down on my knees I found the strength to resist. I demanded in a loud voice to be set free. I declared that I had no desire to participate in customs that were not my own. I was accused of cowardice, but my mind was made up. I bought their silence with bottles of gin, one for every three men. For the rest of the day I was eyed with contempt, but personally I was pleased with my performance.

The *Sarah Lydia*'s passage was slow. After some damage to the ship during a storm off the coast of Angola, we disembarked in Lüderitz, in South-West Africa. The blazing south had turned bitterly cold, but we were given a friendly welcome by the German population. A beer feast was held around a bonfire in the desert, at which a brass band played. I ate with relish the roasted sausages—my favourite food as a student in Germany—and danced to some folk tunes that I had learned from the children in the park at Freiberg. The German colonists were delighted at my knowledge of their simple dances. Everyone wanted to shake my hand as if I were an old friend, for they had heard of me. Only five weeks previously the small farming community had been visited by three explorers. One of them had been presented at court in Weimar, and I knew who they were. The Mayor told me that all three, two men and a woman, had been devoured not far from there. That night I returned to the ship, and did not go ashore again as long as we were detained in Lüderitz.

The southern winter was so cold that it was impossible to spend any length of time on deck. Linse, Lebret and I came together in the dining room for a few hours each evening. We diverted ourselves with port and chess, but the bad weather and general tedium sent each of us to our bunks before ten. I spent long days and nights in the solitude of my small cabin. I tried to read, but had difficulty concentrating. When I was alone I was unable to suppress the doubts that kept rising in my mind.

Once again I had left everything behind. Once again I faced the necessity of conforming to a new culture, of understanding and winning the hearts of a new people. How would people react to my appearance? Once again the life I knew was over, while I had no idea what the future might bring. The first time this happened Kwame and I had run away to hide in a cardboard temple. Now there was no one to run with and nowhere to hide. I huddled under my blankets so as not to see what lay ahead.

I remember a curious experience I had once, in a Tirolean country inn where Professor Cotta and I had taken rooms for the night. While we were having dinner a chambermaid came in and whispered in the professor's ear. Would it be necessary, she asked, to provide clean linen for my bed, seeing as the sheets would turn quite black after I had used them? The professor dismissed the wench with a wave of the hand. We laughed merrily at this incident, but that night I was overcome with disaffection for mankind. I felt as if I had spent my life wading through a morass without making any progress at all. Such sentiments, when I feel utterly defeated, are those that I fear most. As I grow older they become more frequent and also more lasting.

Once we had rounded the Cape and were heading towards Madagascar the weather improved. However, the Indian Ocean is treacherous, and we were hit by two violent storms, which we weathered only thanks to our finding timely refuge in the port of Saint Denis on the French island of Réunion. There I encountered an uncommon paradise, with people of diverse origins living together in perfect harmony. Hindus, Muslims, Buddhists and Catholics celebrated their feast days together. They borrowed each other's saints, and the French bishop even presided over the heathen ceremony in which offerings of fruit, rum and tobacco are made to the spirits of the dead. The slaves, who had been granted their freedom two years earlier, seemed to bear no grudges, nor indeed had there been any bloodshed. They worked their own plots of land alongside Chinese and Creoles. Of the two volcanoes on the island one was permanently active. At regular intervals, and quite innocuously, it erupted to supply the island with a thick layer of fertile soil, like an extra blessing, as though God thought, "Yes, this experiment deserves fostering." The climate was so diverse that all the world's plants could grow there. Vanilla was the mainstay of the economy. I found relief from despondency in the sweetness of this thriving island.

We had been sailing again for two days when—believe it or not—a young deer was caught in the fishing nets. It was still alive, and once it had recovered from its fright it scampered over the deck. There are no deer on Réunion, and we were on the high seas. No one could explain the miracle. I rejoiced inwardly at this example of vitality undaunted by its surroundings.

On 7 September we entered the Sunda Strait at last, sailing past the island of the great Krakatau volcano. As the wind was unfavourable, we dropped anchor at one of the lesser isles. We were approached at once by native canoes laden with goods for sale. The first vendor to climb on board sold bananas. He was accompanied by a parrot and two children, the younger of which went round selling nuts. The man had long hair and wore a wide skirt. His upper body was bare. He spoke with Linse and Lebret, with the ship's captain and all the Dutchmen he could find. But he did not offer me his wares until I had beckoned him expressly. He seemed most surprised that I had a purse of my own and enough money to pay him. He then sent his little boy to me, and I bought a handful of nuts from him.

By morning the wind had risen. Within sight of the roadstead of Batavia, we passed a string of small offshore islands named after Dutch towns: Middelburg, Amsterdam, Haarlem, Rotterdam. As we neared the capital we found ourselves in a forest of masts and multicoloured vessels of diverse provenance, among which we were obliged to drop anchor. Our voyage had lasted four months, but formalities and medical examinations kept us on board yet another day. The harbour made an impression of bleakness and disrepair and the downtown area beyond seemed to consist exclusively of warehouses and office buildings. Farther afield the green hills contrasted darkly with the sky. The air was thick with smoke. The panorama lacked the rosy-streaked azure and the soft contours of the islands of the archipelago we had passed on our way to Java.

Gustav of Saxe-Weimar had kindly made arrangements for me to lodge with his father Duke Bernhard, who was serving as commander of the East Indian Army in Batavia—much to my relief, I may add. I sent him word of my arrival at once. Linse, Lebret and I also announced our presence in the local newspaper. Linse expected our initiative to be rewarded with a stream of invitations from all the families with nubile daughters. We drank to that, not once but again and again.

On 9 September, suffering from splitting headaches, we clambered into the landing vessel, in which we were rowed down a long and evil-smelling waterway, the Ciliwung or Great River. The banks were lined with canal houses in the Dutch style, which stood empty and dilapidated. When we reached the beacon we went ashore. The ground was muddy and we found it difficult to walk. Lebret was overcome with nausea when we came upon a stall selling roasted fish. He threw up behind the stall and asked the vendor for some water, but the man did not respond. Our luggage was inspected by the customs officer, after which we were left to our own devices. There we stood, amid the jostling crowd by the gatehouse. Our aching heads reeled from the blinding sunlight and ear-splitting noise. Fortunately an officer stepped forward to greet us; he said the duke was expecting me in the old town hall, from where he would escort me to his residence in the uptown area. A few coolies went ahead carrying our luggage. I caught a glimpse of my suitcase swinging at the end of a bamboo pole just as it vanished into a throng of Chinese.

The duke gave us a warm welcome. We drank tea in a room on the first floor, which was reserved for his office. He enquired after our voyage and our plans for the immediate future. Lebret and Linse planned to hunt for lodgings, and Bernhard of Saxe gave them the address of a German coffee planter's widow, who would be happy to take them in until they had found something more permanent. He made me promise to look upon his home as my own.

He told us the following anecdote. The previous year, after the battle of Djagaraga, he had organized a thanksgiving feast for his men on the square in front of his residence. They were seated by regiment at long tables in the open air. Among them, he told us proudly, was a company of more than five hundred African soldiers, who had been recruited by my father for the Royal East Indian Army. These men had shown exceptional bravery during the war on Bali. No fewer than forty-one of them had been awarded the Medal for Valour and Loyalty. (This order of merit had been invented expressly for them, as the normal award was for Valour, Initiative and Loyalty. Initiative was not expected of Africans.)

When Duke Bernhard escorted Governor Rochussen past his men to salute them, the "black Hollanders" had stood up as one to raise a toast. One of the African soldiers had cried out: *"Kulit hitam, hati-hati mas!,"* which meant: our skins are black, but our hearts are of gold.

After we had been at the town hall for an hour or so the duke was called away to a meeting. So as not to detain us unnecessarily, he gave orders for a carriage to be provided to take us to the residential neighbourhood of the capital. We bade him farewell and agreed to meet for the evening meal, after which we left him to carry on with his work.

There were a few waiting carriages across the square. We headed towards them, thinking one of them would be for us. I had not gone far when someone grabbed hold of my wrists. I was startled and tried to see who it was, but he was standing with his back to the sun and all I could see was that he was a sturdy fellow with a crown of fair hair. Linse was the first to recognize him: "Cornelius! Good Lord man, you look like a lobster!"

I wrenched myself free and shaded my eyes. De Groot, badly sunburnt and wearing a suit of white linen, took out a handkerchief and mopped his blistered forehead.

"How extraordinary," said Lebret, "that the first person we come across should be you." They shook hands, slapped each other on the shoulders and exchanged brief comments on London and their shared experiences as students there. Linse and Lebret were about to explain what had brought us to the Indies, but he evidently knew already.

"You may find it surprising," said De Groot, "but it is no coincidence that I am here." In his left hand he held a cane, which he flicked restlessly against the heel of his boot. When he noticed that I was watching him, he stopped. "I was aware of your arrival."

"You see," said Lebret. "I told you our announcement in the paper would work wonders." He glanced round to see whether any other people had come to welcome us, preferably young ladies without chaperones. De Groot began to tap his cane gently in the palm of his hand. The gilded handle was shaped like a dragon.

"I'm afraid," he said, "you'll be seeing quite a lot of me." We smiled politely.

"Don't be too sure of that," Linse said.

"Though it would be a pleasure, of course," Lebret hastened to add, and for a moment I wondered whether his deferential tone was sincere. It was not inconceivable that Linse and Lebret had struck up a friendship with their monitor in England. And why shouldn't they? Time changes a man. After all, the course of my own life had changed dramatically over the past few months.

"How does that strike you, Aquasi?"

"What?"

My three companions turned their faces to me, expectantly.

"Cornelius wants to know," Linse blurted, to spare my feelings, "whether you are pleased to be in the tropics again."

How was I to know? I could hardly be expected to give an opinion on such matters, it was too soon. I wanted to get on with what we had set out to do.

"We have been appointed candidate-engineers," I offered. "We are in the service of the new Department of Mines."

"Is that an answer?"

"I mean, you'd better ask how we like it here when we've had a chance to find our bearings. Perhaps, when we've settled in, perhaps then . . ."

"By which time, with any luck, we'll have found ourselves some fine lasses," Lebret continued. "Yes, then we'll be ready to tell you whether we feel at home."

Cornelius tucked his cane under his arm and pulled out his handkerchief again. He mopped his face at length.

"Not too fast, my lads," he said slyly. "You're only candidates as yet."

"Indeed we are," grinned Lebret, whose jocularity knew no bounds when he had a hangover. "While we aspire you perspire, I suppose!"

Cornelius stuffed his handkerchief into his pocket, banged his cane on the ground and took a deep breath. "You see, I have been appointed head of your new Department of Mines."

"Whatever next." Linse's jaw dropped. "I had no idea. My dear Cornelius, how splendid." He shook Cornelius's hand, congratulating him. Lebret followed suit, and so did I.

"So I suggest we go now," said Cornelius. "I shall expect to see you in my office tomorrow morning. You had better do some sightseeing while you can. After today you will need all your time to acquaint yourselves with the terrain. You will no doubt be dispatched out of town shortly, probably as soon as next week. Linse is expected in Sumatra before the end of the month."

"Sumatra, good heavens."

"We have a bauxite undertaking there. The paperwork awaits you." De Groot seemed to be enjoying our consternation. He could barely suppress a smile. "And Lebret, my boy, you are to be posted even further afield. How does Borneo strike you? The government representative there has reported copper deposits outside Balikpapan. Exploratory borings are to be carried out, prior to a full-scale mining operation."

"But seriously, Cornelius, we have been travelling for four months already." The news was having a sobering effect on Lebret.

"According to the information at my disposal I gather that you . . ." De Groot drew a notebook out of his waistcoat pocket and consulted it, "indeed, yes, you received an advance on 1 May. A generous advance, if I may say so. Surely we deserve something in return?"

"Good God, de Groot, I'm not asking for leave of absence or anything like that. Look here, I haven't even recovered my land legs yet." Linse shook his knees to illustrate his point.

"Seems a bit soon to be speeding off to Sumatra, if you see what I mean," Lebret rejoined.

While they were arguing I was hoping for a clue as to what he had in mind for me. At that juncture it made little difference to me where I would be posted. In the faces of the crowd I caught certain glances, to which I was no longer accustomed. I had been spared the curiosity of strangers during the passage to the Indies. Finding myself in the teeming crowd on the main square, the stares irked me. Some public officer in a passing rickshaw had his driver slow down so that he could study my appearance. I noticed a wide-eyed couple peering from behind a parasol as they made their third tour of the square. I could not stop myself: I curled my lips in a pretence of a snarl. They hurried away. A group of Chinese looked repeatedly in my direction, conversing animatedly all the while. A constable, spotting Linse and Lebret waving their arms, came to see whether I was running amok. He realized his error when he saw I was in their company, but lingered nearby, just in case.

Some peace and quiet, I reflected, would suit me quite well. The distraught look on Lebret's face, who saw his chances of meeting well-bred young ladies reduced to nothing, made up my mind for me. On the spur of the moment I suggested going to Balikpapan in his stead. Lebret threw me a grateful look, but de Groot pretended not to hear. When I repeated my offer, he said, without bothering to look me in the eye, "I'm afraid that won't do, my dear prince, for I have something else in mind for you."

"Something else?" I asked, but Cornelius did not pursue the subject.

"You have found lodgings yet?" he asked.

"Aquasi is to be the guest of the duke of Saxe."

Lebret showed him the letter of introduction given to him by the duke. "And we intend to try our luck here."

Cornelius read the address on the envelope dismissively.

"Well, as far as Aquasi's lodgings are concerned"—he was still talking as if I were not present—"I have some advice."

"What sort of advice?" I stood squarely before him, so that he could not avert his eyes. "What sort of advice, Cornelius?"

"The duke of Saxe is a very busy man. He is here on a particular mission, and is to be importuned as little as possible."

"I shall bear it in mind."

"If you are to be of any use to me, I must be able to rely on your availability at any hour of the day or night."

"No problem there."

"Bernhard of Saxe's quarters are not spacious. The disturbance would be considerable. Desk work until late at night. Couriers arriving at ungodly hours. Interrupted meals." He

paused to give his words time to sink in. "I have had a room prepared for you on my premises. Quite private. You will feel at
home there."

"That is generous of you, but I would not wish to disappoint
my dear friend."

"Perhaps I have not made myself clear." He took my arm and
drew me away from the others. "Let me put it this way. You are
under my authority. This is the first day of a very long period in
which you are accountable to me. It is my opinion that it would
be injudicious to impose your presence on that 'good friend' of
yours."

There was venom in his tone. His fingers pressed into my
flesh.

"You do agree with me, I presume?"

I looked round at Linse and Lebret, who were affecting indifference. I overheard the one say to the other, "So that's what
they meant by 'extraordinary'." I decided it would not be a good
thing to antagonize Cornelius from the start. He turned away,
grinning.

"So that's taken care of. Over and done with." He opened the
carriage door with a flourish and motioned Linse and Lebret to
take a seat. He waved to them as they drove off. When the carriage was out of sight he put his arm around my shoulder and
spoke in a more genial tone.

"You see, my friend, the point of having a secretary is to be
assured of assistance at all hours." For a second I actually believed
he was about to tell me who my secretary was to be. Then his
meaning dawned on me.

"I am not trained in office work," I said calmly. "My terrain
lies underground."

"Most unhealthy, all that burrowing into the earth. We regard
you too highly for that line of work."

"But I am an engineer, as you perfectly well know."

"Candidate-engineer. Of course you are. That is why you are
just right for what I have in mind. It will benefit both of us. I will
have a clerk to whom I can dictate my letters without having to
explain every term and technique, and you will have the opportu-

nity to learn the ins and outs of all our undertakings in the Indies. What a responsibility. And so edifying. Every conceivable administrative practice will come to your attention. You will meet the right people. You will have access to confidential reports. Not a single particular will escape you. There will be no one in the colonies with such detailed information of pending construction projects. Of the current state of expertise. Of new techniques. And think of the financial aspects. All the investments. An invaluable apprenticeship." He climbed into his carriage. I followed, and took the seat facing him.

"I have done enough studying, Cornelius."

"I don't think so." He leaned forward to scrutinize my features, and his satisfaction at seeing me again increased visibly. He took my hands in his and shook them warmly. "Here we are again, you and me. Do you recall how we used to lie on the sandy bank of the waterway? All those afternoons. And now we are reunited. Who would have thought it possible?" He leaned back against the cushions, savouring the memory. "Do you know that you were the only boy I ever taught how to fight? I was not going to show the others how they could get the better of me—what did you think? But you were different. You needed some instruction, and you were quick to learn. You weren't bad at all. You could have turned into a good boxer. But there you are, you lost interest."

"Not at all. It was you who lost interest."

"Is that so? I beg to differ."

The driver made to shut the door from the outside. Cornelius restrained him.

"Whatever the case may be," he said, "the lessons are to be resumed. So, if you would be so kind . . ." He motioned me to step down from the carriage. "My secretary will ride on the box."

I smiled because I thought he was joking. But he was serious. He even tapped his cane against my shins to make me hurry. The blood rushed to my face. I would have struck him if I had not been aware of so many eyes fixed on me. In a flash I saw rows of spectators whispering to each other behind their hands. I rose from my seat with as much composure as I could muster, alighted, banged the little door shut behind me and clambered up to the seat beside the coachman. The blood was pounding so hard in my temples that I saw nothing during the drive to Weltevreden.

The room I was shown to was small and simply furnished, but satisfactory. It was located in the grounds of De Groot's residence, and shared a washroom with the adjoining servants' quarters. After my arrival I lay on the bed for some hours. Towards six I had a bath and dressed for dinner. I was very hungry as I had eaten nothing all day since my breakfast of porridge on board ship. I could smell the kitchen, and glancing inside I saw an array of fish, meat, poultry and fruit. The cook was so startled by the sight of me on the threshold that he raised his knife to chase me away, but I held out my hands, open-palmed, to show that I intended no harm. After I had made some complimentary remarks he told me his master was expecting a large company of guests for dinner. I crossed the garden to the veranda, where I encountered Urip. She was the *nyai*, or housekeeper-concubine, and the first native woman I met who dared speak before she was spoken to. She turned out to know all about me, and asked after my health. I was struck by her gentle demeanour, and when I enquired after her occupations she praised Cornelius for his kindness.

Then I noticed the sounds of conversation. I asked whether the dinner guests had already arrived. She hesitated, but I stepped into the house. There were twelve guests. Catching sight of me, de Groot beckoned me to his side. He introduced me jovially as his new assistant and good friend from the old days: the African prince Aquasi Boachi. The company was made up of Auditor-General Dijkstra and his wife, the draughtsman of the Botanical Gardens at Buitenzorg, Mr. Galant, accompanied by his wife and daughter, two army officers and an almoner. There was also a lady wearing a fashionable dress that left her shoulders bare. She introduced herself as a titled member of the van Ketelaar family, but I had never heard the name mentioned before. Finally, there were the deputy head of the civilian medical service, and Mr. van Ophemert, trader in coffee, who had brought along his eldest son.

Drinks were being served. Cornelius offered me a glass of papaya juice mixed with Dutch gin. It dealt a sharp blow to my empty stomach, but animated the exchange of courtesies. When Cornelius revealed my connections with the royal family, which he did with gusto, the guests were all ears. Fortunately I am discreet by nature.

The gong for dinner sounded shortly before seven. The guests rose to take their places at the dining table. I was engaged in a conversation with Miss Galant at the time, and escorted her to her seat. I looked round the table and discovered that all the chairs were taken and that there was no place setting for me. Cornelius motioned for serving to begin, and addressed me across the table in a loud voice: "Cook is counting on you in the kitchen. He is bound to have something to your taste. Bon appetit!"

All I could do was to wish the company a pleasant dinner in return.

It was dark. On the grassy area by the kitchen I saw a circle of domestics squatting around a large pan, laughing and chattering in high-pitched voices. They ate with their fingers. By this time my mouth was watering, and I plucked up courage to join them. When I came near they all fell silent. Urip rose from their midst. She took a bowl which she filled with rice topped by a spoonful of reddish-brown stringy meat. She lowered her eyes in embarrassment as she offered it to me. I thanked her kindly. She sat down again, but did not eat. The others, too, paused in their supper. Some stared, others averted their gaze. I was nonplussed, and considered seeking refuge in my room. But then I hitched up my trousers and squatted down in the circle. The youngest servant moved aside with a friendly smile to make room for me. He showed me how to eat the rice with my fingers. I imitated his gestures, after which he nodded and began to eat. Two of the servants stood up and withdrew, followed soon after by a third. Those who remained resumed their supper in silence. I ate a few mouthfuls. The taste was quite pleasant, but the sauce was so hot that it gave me a runny nose and watery eyes.

2

"Your hand! Give me your hand, Boachi, dammit! And tell that nincompoop I'll chop his head off if we hit those rocks. Is he blind? My God, it's too late, there we go. We're going. Let me go, you fool. Do you want me to drown with you hanging round my neck?"

There were two things Cornelius never mastered: how to open a bottle of drink properly and how to keep his dignity at sea. In both circumstances he relied on me. Whatever the type of stopper or cork, whatever the instrument he was using, he never managed to prise open a bottle of wine or champagne without mishap. Not that Cornelius was all thumbs, but his sheer strength and impatience defeated him. Still, he always insisted on trying, and when he did not succeed he would push bottle and corkscrew into my hands, spluttering as if he had been required to perform an impossible task. When I had removed the remains of the cork or had sieved the wine to get rid of glass splinters, he would growl a word of thanks, despite his annoyance at his own clumsiness. I did not mind helping him out. In these matters he really needed me.

He also needed me on board ship. Even if the sea was as smooth as glass when we sailed out of the harbour, Cornelius would turn deathly pale and rigid with fear. He would scan the horizon for possible tidal waves, and if the sails creaked in a gust of wind he would ask, in a timid voice: "Is anything wrong?" In heavy weather he was the first to panic.

"Are you mad? Boachi, man, steady on, hold me tight, hold me tight! Dear God, this is the end."

When we sailed into the bay of Amboina on 22 June 1852 we were feeling the worse for our rough passage. In sight of the capital our ship had been buffeted by sudden blasts of wind during a dangerous manoeuvre between a cliff and a sandbank. The small vessel that had brought us from Banda was not really suited to sailing in the heavy rains, which reach the Moluccas later than the rest of the archipelago and cause a severe swell. We had endured the stormy monsoon throughout the voyage. Cornelius was in a very bad temper. From the start he had regarded the whole venture as futile. He was convinced that tin mining in the Moluccas, which was the motive for our expedition, would not prove profitable, much less worth risking one's life for.

Once we had arrived in the harbour of Amboina on the north coast of the Ley-Timor peninsula, Cornelius gradually regained his composure. He soon regretted his faint-heartedness and found some excuse to reassert his authority over the crew. I kept a discreet distance on such occasions. In my capacity as secretary I had accompanied him on numerous tours of inspection of the diverse mining districts throughout the islands, where we visited the respective governors and administrators. I knew exactly when he needed me at his side and when it was better to stay out of his way.

The jetty was virtually deserted because of the downpour. We could see knots of people huddling in the shelter of the gateway to Fort van Capellen. There was no one to welcome us except for a few Chinese peddlers and the warehouse inspector making his inventory of cargo and men. Our anchor being useless on the rocky bed of the cove, the ship's ropes were secured to the sturdy bollards. The gangplank was lowered. As I spoke Malay better than Cornelius—thanks largely to my daily meals with the servants—he sent me into the town to discover why we had not had an official welcome. Leaving the fort behind, I found myself in a large square with several straight roads leading from it. I soon sighted Government House, where I presented myself. However, the governor of the Moluccas was absent. No one seemed to know of our arrival, and there was no message awaiting us. I concluded that we would have to apply to the assistant resident, but his whereabouts were unknown. I was told that he lived on the road between Tanah Tinggi and the military hospital, near the bridge over the Wai Tomo. I asked for a carriage, but all I could obtain was a pair of saddled horses.

I was not looking forward to reporting the discouraging news to Cornelius, and lingered on my way back to the harbour. As I walked towards the jetty I noticed a native boy standing in the rain at some distance from the ship. He had no intention of coming any closer, it seemed, so I beckoned him. He took a few steps in my direction, then stopped, pretending he had not seen me. When I went towards him he barely returned my greeting. The lad was drenched. His sarong clung tightly to his legs, and his face and shoulders were plastered with strands of wet hair. He did not look very bright. I could not tell whether he was silent out of shyness or impudence. I had to repeat my question three times before he replied that his master was the assistant resident. He had been charged with guarding our possessions until a carriage was sent to fetch us. At that moment de Groot came ashore. I told him a carriage was on its way, but he refused to wait. He mounted one of the horses and summoned the boy, who was clearly frightened of horses, to approach. I could hear the anger in de Groot's voice, and tried to warn the lad to do as he was told. When he held back, Cornelius dug his spurs into the horse's flanks causing it to rear. De Groot acted in this way for the benefit of the crew watching the scene from the ship's railing. Their laughter egged him on, and he imitated the boy's terrified expression. He pointed at the pile of luggage and ordered him to carry it. The boy turned his eyes on me. When I did not come to his rescue, he said: "The assistant resident told me to guard your suitcases, tuan, until they are collected."

"There are only three cases, and those bags over there," said Cornelius. "You must carry them."

"Please, the carriage will come soon."

"What's the matter with you? Take them and follow me."

The boy looked miserable. He stepped gingerly to the mound of luggage and tried to lift one of the suitcases, which he could barely get off the ground. He glanced at us over his shoulder to see whether we were watching, then tried a large package, which was no less heavy. He gave up and stood with his back to us, his head bowed. Finally he did as his master had ordered and squatted down next to our belongings. He wore an earnest expression, so as to leave no doubt that he would guard them with his life.

This was not good enough for Cornelius. Perhaps he would have softened if the crew had not been watching his every move, but as it was he turned his horse and approached the boy once again, slowly and menacingly. The boy held his head down in fear of the hooves, but did not move away.

"Please, tuan!"

I could bear it no longer, and took hold of the horse's bridle.

"He's only a boy," I said, "just let him be, Cornelius. I can carry the cases with documents myself, then the rest will follow later. What difference does it make?"

There was no reply. Cornelius jerked at the reins to make the horse turn its head, so that I lost my grip on the bridle. Then he kicked the flanks again to make the animal charge ahead over the boy. The horse lifted its forelegs, but refused to jump. For an instant I saw the boy celebrate his small victory with an insolent grin. My heart leaped for him. One of our sailors applauded, which enraged Cornelius all the more. He took his whip and raised it above his head. Without stopping to think I dashed forward and shielded the boy's face with my arm. The leather thong cut into the back of my left hand. The wound was deep, and yet it took a few seconds for me to feel any pain and even longer for the blood to flow. Cornelius did not wait to see the damage he had done. He turned his mount in the direction of the fort, and rode away at a walking pace. I bandaged my wound with my handkerchief, left the boy where he was, and followed my superior.

During my first weeks in Java I had taken a cautious attitude towards Cornelius's erratic behaviour. Bernhard of Saxe had been surprised that I should prefer de Groot's chicken-coop to his own guest room—indeed this had roused his suspicions. When he realized that Cornelius kept making excuses to prevent me from meeting him, he grew indignant at the way I was being treated. He was shortly to return to Holland and offered to speak to the king on my behalf, but I would not have it. Not wishing to arouse his pity I pretended that my secretarial post was to my satisfaction. Somewhat confused by my attitude, Bernhard let the matter rest. However, prior to his departure he arranged for me to lodge with a friendly German family, which was a consolation even though I was too busy with my work to spend much time in my rooms.

Disillusioned by the lack of responsibility of my post, I wrote several letters to the governor-general. At first I requested relocation, then put in applications for research activities, but my bids were unsuccessful. Although I received replies to all my letters, the concern shown for my predicament amounted to little more than prevarication and subtle subterfuge. For example, I would be granted a small extra for my labours: a place of honour in the New Year's parade or a uniform with gold piping on the lapels and cuffs. Each time I wrote back saying that this was not quite what I had in mind.

A few months later I received a note from The Hague informing me that I had been appointed chief of administration in the Department of Mines. My friend the duke had evidently complained to the Ministry of Colonies. The next morning I went to the office in high spirits, eager to hear what my new post entailed. The brief was devastating in its simplicity: the foremost duty of the chief of administration was to assist Cornelius de Groot. As his personal secretary.

This made me realize that nothing is achieved in the East Indies without the right connections. Linse and Lebret were far away. I met few people outside my work, and whenever any public officer took a personal interest in me he would be sure to be posted elsewhere within weeks of making my acquaintance. I was suspicious about this coincidence, but had no proof of deliberate action against me. After a while I took care never to spend too much time in the company of the same person and not to draw attention to myself in public. In order to avoid causing unrest I would refrain from discussing any subjects other than my work, especially if my conversation partner was someone I liked.

Yet there were evenings when Cornelius and I spent hours sitting on the veranda together, in relative harmony. He would smoke and stare into the distance. I preferred reading. If he showed interest in my book I would tell him what it was about and would read out a passage. He would laugh at my sensitive nature when I told him why a certain novel appealed to me, but I did not mind. When we were alone he was not out to impress, but meant what he said.

On such occasions we would get tipsy together as the evening wore on. Drink always loosened his tongue. He would ramble on about women and share his fantasies with me. Now and then he would sing snatches of love songs for my benefit. He had a good voice, which was surprising in a man who was so loud-mouthed in public.

When he felt truly at ease he would talk about his home village on the bank of the river, where his father maintained a ferry service. He would glow with pleasure, picturing the riverside inn where he had played in the stables as a lad and where his passion had been fired by a girl called Frieda. But if the drink made him morose he would speak bitterly of the hardship suffered by his family during severe winters, when the river froze and there were no earnings from the ferry. When that happened the schoolmaster would collect pennies from his classmates during the week, which would be presented to Cornelius on the Saturday afternoon in full view of the children, and he would be obliged to thank each of them in turn, cap in hand.

The day after Cornelius had confided such painful memories to me he would seize every opportunity to demean me in public. But I must admit that I was not always well disposed myself. Our twisted relationship brought out a streak of malice in me that even I found surprising. If he became too hostile in the presence of others, I would seek revenge. I knew him well after so many years, and his confidences had shown me his weaknesses. In his work, too, I knew exactly where his faults lay. So the next time he lost track of his argument and fell silent in mid-sentence during a meeting with his superiors, I would ask him loudly to sum up his statement so I could enter it in the minutes. Or I would embarrass him in a gathering with high officials—preferably in the presence of a native prince—by suddenly inquiring after his father, "Baron Charon," which would make him sweat profusely. When a native family came to us complaining of food shortages in the kampung, I would reassure them that Cornelius himself had known poverty and would find it very difficult to refuse assistance. In the company of Hollanders I could cause him considerable distress by mentioning his place of birth; there would always be someone who took up the subject, so that de Groot would end up floundering in his own web of lies. It was childish of me I know, but for a long time my acts of rebellion kept our relationship, although strained, on an even keel. Indeed, for a whole year and a half we managed to avoid coming to blows.

On the way from the harbour of Amboina to Tanah Tinggi I rode behind my master in silence. The cut on the back of my hand was so painful that I had difficulty holding the reins. At one point de Groot slowed down and glanced at my bloodstained handkerchief. I groaned and cringed quite dramatically, but he had no intention of offering an apology.

After crossing a district of the town where many buildings had suffered serious damage during one of Amboina's frequent earthquakes, we continued along the river until we came upon a house constructed out of solid material except for the roof, which was thatched. The veranda looked out over the road and the grassed area on the other side. Our arrival at the assistant resident's home went unnoticed. We had to call out several times before a shuffling servant appeared. His master was out, he said, and his mistress had left in the carriage to fetch some guests from the harbour. We were shown into the parlour, where we were served glasses of sugar-water. I tipped some of the cool liquid on to my bandage demonstratively. Cornelius pressed his glass against his forehead and shut his eyes, as if to say that after all his travails he was now suffering a bout of migraine.

Half an hour later we heard the clatter of a vehicle crossing the bridge. Next to the driver, under the leather hood of the open landau, we spotted a somewhat bedraggled figure, who waved at us cheerfully. The space behind the lady passenger was filled with our suitcases and packages, on top of which sat the young servant boy from the jetty, dripping wet but triumphant. Catching sight of us as we came out on to the veranda he grinned from ear to ear. He mimicked his mistress and waved cheekily, with both arms, as though unaware that he had been the cause of our dispute. I felt a niggling regret that I had come between him and Cornelius.

The assistant resident's wife alighted briskly. She did not seem to notice the mud and hurried to welcome us, shaking the raindrops from her head. Cornelius whispered that she was Mrs. Douwes Dekker and a baroness to boot—the proximity of aristocracy always excited him—but social niceties were evidently unimportant to her. She unbuttoned her cape and extended her hand warmly.

"Mr. de Groot! What a muddle! We had not expected you today, I must confess, because of the weather. When the rains get as heavy as this the locals tend to avoid going out in their boats."

"You know how it is, madam. For the natives it is of no consequence whether they go fishing today or tomorrow. Each day is the same to them. But for us it is different. We are on an extended tour, and therefore make every effort to adhere to our schedule as closely as possible."

Our hostess inspected the mud on her boots and wiped her heels on the grass. "Actually, my husband and I have always found it rewarding to observe the native customs as much as we can," she said casually. "We benefit from their experience. And besides, it saves us from inadvertently giving offence, and also from peril during stormy weather. But thank goodness you have arrived safely. And who is your friend?"

She turned to face me. I hid my left hand behind my back, thinking it unwise to draw attention to my injury.

Before I had time to say my name, Cornelius broke in with: "This gentleman here, madam, is my secretary. He will not inconvenience you, have no fear."

"Indeed, I see no reason why he should," she said, ignoring Cornelius's imperious tone and keeping her gaze fixed on me. "And how did you fare on your journey, Mr. . . . ?"

"Boachi," Cornelius said gruffly, "Aquasi Boachi."

"I have survived all my travels this far, madam."

"Then you will have plenty of stories to entertain us with this evening. We have been living here for some months now, and are sorely lacking in diversion. I am sorry that my husband is unable to be here to welcome you. He had urgent business to discuss with the governor at Batu Gadja." She indicated a large house on the slope of a hill nearby.

"Not anything serious I hope?"

"I shouldn't think so." She took my arm, saying: "Come, I will show you your rooms."

"Mr. Boachi will sleep with the servants."

"Nonsense." She hesitated, thinking Cornelius might be joking.

"And he will eat with them too. That is our custom," de Groot continued.

"Well sir, if we were to observe all the colonial conventions here, then . . ."

"Surely you do not allow native customs to overrule those of your fellow countrymen?"

"We keep an open mind, Mr. de Groot, so that we may act sensibly." Her smile was so charming that Cornelius let the matter rest for the time being. He glanced at his boots and scraped the mud off his heels.

"All my life," he said with a note of vexation in his voice, "I have known that each man has his rightful place in the world. Maintaining rank is essential in the colonies. It makes life so much easier."

"Our lives maybe, but what about our souls?"

In the meantime our luggage had been dragged to the veranda by the servant-boy. The latter resumed his guard duty by perching cross-legged on top of a suitcase. Cornelius motioned him to get off his property. When the boy did not respond de Groot stepped forward to chase him away.

Our hostess took the opportunity to draw me aside, saying: "Come along, Mr. Boachi, you shall have the room in which François Valentijn stayed. Have you ever met him? A man of great scholarship. My husband will tell you all about him . . . Are you familiar with our seventeenth century at all?"

That evening Mrs. Douwes Dekker herself came to my room to call me for dinner, as though she was afraid I would not dare come. Together we entered the small dining room, where Cornelius was chatting to her husband. The appearance of the hostess obliged Cornelius to rise from his seat. My presence did not please him, I could see that, but he wished me good evening nonetheless. The rain had stopped at last and a welcome breeze came in through the screen door, refreshing us all.

"Does your religion permit you to raise a glass with us?"

"I was baptized a Christian, madam," I replied.

"Indeed," she said, and signalled to a servant to bring me a glass, which her husband filled with cool claret. Cornelius accepted every offer of more wine, which the assistant resident poured generously although he drank little himself.

Douwes Dekker was friendly but taciturn, as if his thoughts were elsewhere. He did not look very strong, and his melancholy air suggested that he was languishing. He mentioned that his health, already undermined by his years in the tropics, had deteriorated further in the short time he had been in office at Amboina. Moreover, in the same period he had been bereaved of his parents, sister and brother and other loved ones. He was homesick and had been trying for some time to obtain a furlough.

"Thirteen years in the tropics," his wife went on, "signifies recurrent bouts of fever. Infections. Sleep disturbances. Constant worries."

On that very day, however, Douwes Dekker had received encouraging news. He revealed that he had just been granted three months' leave to plead his cause in Batavia. His wife was greatly relieved, and sat beside him quietly holding his hand for a long while. It pleased me to see them thus. In those days I had grown unaccustomed to domestic happiness.

Douwes Dekker asked me where I came from. I gave him a brief explanation of the motive for my removal to Holland, which astonished him. He remembered meeting two Africans several years before, when he was serving as commissioner to the resident of Bagelen. They said they had come from West Africa, and seemed quite proud to have served in the Dutch colonial army. However, when their term ended they chose to live out their days as civilians. They had settled at the mouth of the river Progo, where they eked out a living with the production of salt. I agreed that these men must have been among the recruits procured by my father.

Dinner was served. We took our seats at table and as I was obliged to eat with cutlery I could no longer hide my injured hand. I had applied a fresh bandage and tried to cover it with my sleeve, but the wound ached and I had difficulty holding my fork.

"It is nothing serious," I said, but my hostess insisted on inspecting my hand.

"What a dreadful cut, how did that happen?"

"How now, Prince Aquasi," Cornelius slurred. "Been clumsy again?"

"It is nothing, really." To prove my point I grabbed my fork and speared a morsel of food.

"So why make a fuss? Our host was telling us such an interesting story," Cornelius said, after which he dominated the conversation for the next half hour, boring us all with his account of our findings in the wilds of Madura, where the Dutch had long been prospecting for minerals without success.

Mrs. Douwes Dekker turned to address me. "This morning I had no idea that we would be dining with a prince. Cook has done her best, but as you see, we have nothing special on our menu. Come, tell me some more about your people."

I was embarrassed by her attention, and watched Cornelius out of the corner of my eye. He had no intention of ending his monologue, but the table was large and he continued unperturbed. I told her my story and she listened attentively. She straightened her shoulders and interrupted me only once, when her husband ordered another bottle to be opened to replenish Cornelius's glass yet again.

"I must advise you all," she said with a smile, so that no one would take offence, "that drink goes to the head faster here than elsewhere."

The truth of her words was proved almost immediately by Cornelius, whose drunken rambling had unleashed one of his favourite anecdotes about Madura. I had heard him tell the story on several occasions, although never in the presence of a lady.

He recounted the following experience. Impressed by the interest Cornelius had shown in his lands, the chief of Bunbungan had sought to draw the Dutchman's attention to his eldest daughter, in the hope of marrying her off in exchange for certain privileges pertaining to the administration of the region. Cornelius had not broken off negotiations forthwith, but played for time so that the young lady would be sent to his rooms for approval. As usual, he paused at this point, in order to whet his listeners' appetite. I felt the blood rush to my cheeks and did not dare meet the eyes of our hostess.

"Next morning," Cornelius went on, throwing a meaningful look at Douwes Dekker, as though they were alone and united in spirit, "I sent her back to her father with the message that I could not see why the Madura maiden was so highly esteemed. That I had received a better love massage in the slums of Batavia, and that a Dutchman does not exchange his integrity for a few spasms."

He was so pleased with himself that it took a while for him to notice that no one was laughing. Douwes Dekker rang for the servant.

"May I remind you," he said, "that you are our guest. We are not accustomed to barrack-room talk."

When it finally dawned on Cornelius that he had committed a grave social offence he looked so crestfallen that our hostess tried to rescue him by broaching another subject, but she soon ran out of things to say.

"I only mentioned the incident," Cornelius floundered on, "by way of illustration—how to nip corruption in the bud, what?" No one spoke.

"Hardly respectful," I hissed. Cornelius turned his eyes on me.

"Not respectful?" he echoed, in a low menacing voice. "If anyone lacks respect it is you." He jumped to his feet, spoiling for a fight. I did the same, whereupon our hostess came into action. She rose from the table as if dinner were over and took my arm.

"My dear Prince," she said, "we must do something about your poor hand. Come along, we'll get the house-boy to give you a fresh bandage."

She drew back my chair and swept me out of the room. "One cannot be too careful. The climate is most inflammatory."

Her house-boy turned out to be the lad who had been the cause of our altercation on the jetty. He brought clean water and a small chest containing assorted herbs. I eyed him suspiciously. He squatted on the ground before me and resolutely pulled the handkerchief off the wound.

"Ouch!"

"Forgive me. Such a deep cut."

He rolled up my sleeve and poured the water liberally over the back of my hand. With deep concentration, the tip of his tongue between his lips, he disinfected the wound with a dried leaf and then sprinkled on some powder. It stung painfully, and I shrank back while he blew on my hand.

"Pain, tuan?" he enquired gently.

"No pain."

He raised his eyes to see whether I meant it, whereupon he stopped blowing on the wound and proceeded to prepare an ointment of palm butter, to which he added a variety of ingredients. He looked at me again, deliberating whether he dared speak his mind.

"So bad, the wound," he said eventually, and resumed stirring the ointment, rapidly at first and then dragging the spatula this way and that.

"When the farmer beats his buffalo it refuses to budge," he said finally, smearing the ointment thickly on the back of my hand. He looked hard at me to see whether I understood his meaning.

"The buffalo has a thick skin," I said gruffly, "and a short memory."

"A man is not the same as a buffalo."

"No, a man can try to understand motives."

"The buffalo is strong, but stupid. That's why he puts up with it."

Not wishing to get drawn into an awkward conversation I broke in with, "Are you always so talkative?"

"Always, tuan!"

"Then I expect you often get yourself into trouble."

"Always, tuan!"

Cornelius and I had once been received by the susuhunan of Surakarta, where several tigers had been caught in recent weeks. The cages were overcrowded and there was a shortage of food for the wild beasts. They had been fed all the poultry, monkeys and dogs that could be found, and were growing alarmingly thin. One tiger had already perished, and its death was considered to have brought shame on the court. Now it was time for the largest specimen to be disposed of without loss of face.

All the public officials arrived in full dress, the officers and princes wore uniform. We joined the grand procession and were admitted to the second forecourt of the palace, where the susuhunan awaited us on his throne.

A circular enclosure made of wooden poles and bamboo stakes had been erected on the grassed area. A buffalo wreathed in flowers was led into the pen. Then a cart bearing a large Javan tiger pacing to and fro in a cage was drawn up to the palisade. The spectators held their breath. The only sound was the gamelan orchestra. The air was filled with reverent suspense.

Cornelius, who was sitting next to me, drew himself up. I noticed him clenching and unclenching his left hand, as he always did when mentally preparing himself for a fight. His agitation was beginning to attract attention, so I nudged him with my elbow. He took no notice and cracked his knuckles with a single flick of the wrist.

The trap door in the cage was opened, after which there was no barrier between the lithe, muscular tiger and the mountain of flesh. Nothing happened. Instead of pouncing, the tiger sank on to his haunches and lay down, then settled his head on his front paws, keeping his eyes fixed on the buffalo. Sensing danger, the buffalo raised his heavy head and glared with bulging eyes. He turned to face the tiger, and advanced at a slow, steady pace.

"Look at that," exclaimed Cornelius. "So majestic. So fearless."

The buffalo lowered his head, pointing the horns at his adversary, and stood there, quite still. There was some whispering and shuffling about in the audience. Only Cornelius did not lose his concentration. His breathing was fast and shallow and he was sweating. The combat had already started in his mind. He thrilled to the ominous silence. His mouth was open, his lips were parched. He had difficulty swallowing because he was so focused on the beasts. A muscle twitched in his jaw. I followed his eyes and saw a ripple of tension on the buffalo's flanks. No one else seemed to notice, but I knew that the threat always holds more violence than the attack.

At a sign from the susuhunan five attendants climbed on to the roof of the cage. From that vantage point they dropped handfuls of burning straw on to the tiger's back. Although visibly roused by the pain, he did not attack. Next, boiling water was poured over the buffalo, which bellowed and retreated a few steps. The tiger did not rise. At last a powdered herb was sprinkled on to both animals, which stung so badly that they were galvanized into action. The tiger emerged from his corner and lunged at the buffalo. I could hear a sharp intake of breath at my side. The buffalo, undaunted, watched the wild beast slinking around him in circles, keeping his horns lowered menacingly. Finally, the tiger marshalled all his forces to pounce. He leaped in a great arc over his adversary's head and sank his teeth into the neck. The buffalo was momentarily stunned, and did not make a sound. Then he rolled his eyes in rage and heaved his head from side to side with great force, slinging his attacker against the sides of the cage. But the tiger did not let go.

The buffalo paused to brace himself for a renewed attempt to shake off the wild beast. He dashed the tiger against the ground repeatedly and with such violence that the creature was forced to give way. At this point the buffalo took the offensive: he lowered his head and butted the tiger again and again with his horns, pushing him towards the palisade. Eventually the tiger sprang away, and lurked at the opposite end of the enclosure. He seemed confused by his failure to gain immediate victory over his lumbering foe.

"That'll teach him," rejoiced Cornelius. And then he turned serious: "Finish him! Finish him! Show him the stuff you're made of!" He slapped his thighs. This gesture was not a sign of contentment, it served to sharpen his senses for the finale.

The royal tiger attacked again, frontally this time, and again he was gored. He leaped on top of his cage, making the attendants flee in all directions, paced the roof a few times and then took a flying leap, claws outstretched, on to the buffalo. The buffalo caught the great cat on his horns, mortally wounding him. The tiger did not charge again, but slunk round in circles, cowering and hissing and lashing out feebly. Finally he sank to the ground, exhausted, whereupon he was impaled to death by the buffalo.

The crowd cheered. All around us people were commenting on the fight. I too expressed admiration, but my neighbour did not speak. I turned to look at Cornelius. He had thrown his head back, as if in supplication to the heavens, and heaved a deep sigh of relief. His eyes were moist and he was shivering with elation. When he came to his senses, a grin spread slowly across his face and he took a long hard look at the dead beast as it was being dragged away. He wiped the sweat off his chin with his fist and stuffed his fingers into his mouth to suppress his glee. He seemed deranged. I saw a trickle of blood oozing from the corner of his mouth, and glanced around anxiously to see whether his behaviour was attracting attention. Grabbing his arms I shook him fiercely. Pleasure unleashed in him a passion no less violent than rage. It took a while for him to calm down. He glanced at me as if surprised to see me sitting next to him. There were tooth marks across his fingers. He stared at them blankly.

"Splendid, Boachi, what?" he said finally, "to see how stolid resolve conquers innate strength."

"They seemed an equal match to me."

"But the tiger lost. He underestimated the buffalo's power because he believed he was superior by nature. Splendid. Splendid."

"Nonsense. Neither of them wanted to fight."

"But circumstances brought them together."

"Even so, they would have left each other unharmed if they had not been driven to it. They had to be goaded into action no less than three times." I was shouting now. "Three times. Don't you see that both creatures had one common enemy?"

"Tuan Douwes Dekker does not beat his buffaloes," said the house-boy. The dull ache in my hand was soothed by his ointment. He pressed the sides of the wound together and held them in position by clenching my hand between his bare knees while he started wrapping the bandage crosswise.

"And what next? He is to return to Holland. What will become of me then?"

"People can adapt to change, you know."

"Some people can, tuan. Not me. I am not like you. I love myself too much."

He held the end of the bandage between his teeth to make a lengthwise tear, then tied the strips in a bow and asked me to flex my fingers. The bandage was in place. He was satisfied, took the hand again and held it a while, for no apparent reason.

"I look at you and your friend and I can tell." I withdrew my hand from his. "You should not put up with it," he said urgently.

"It is no concern of yours. I warn you."

I rose and made to leave. He replaced the herbs in his little chest and smiled as if he had said nothing.

"The bandage, is it not too tight? Remember: change it every other day, yes? Will you return to the dining room now? Cook has prepared a delicious dessert."

"How would you know?" I asked with mock gravity, to show I had no ill feelings.

"I know because I stole a taste."

I thanked him and asked his name.

"Ahim," he said. "That is my name. You will not forget."

JAVA, DELFT, WEIMAR, JAVA
1856–62

Java

I have never been daunted by the hostility that has been directed at my person. Quite the contrary. Pain strengthens the awareness of self. I have seldom been more conscious of my own worth than when subjected to humiliation. Such anguish gives rise to spiritual insight, a lucidity of mind. The bond arising from the exertion of power by one man over another may not be edifying, but it is certainly unequivocal. Hostage and hostage-taker need each other in equal measure. They determine each other's position. The least token of goodwill is gratefully seized upon by either side.

Indeed, during the years I spent in Cornelius's service there were days when we got on together quite amicably. Not only did we compare notes on the lands that we visited, we sometimes formed very similar opinions and expressed them in virtually the same words. After a while we even shared jokes. While on our travels we would discuss new extraction methods or plan more efficient means of distribution. We even devised a labour-saving machine to bring ore to the surface. Together we admired the ornamentation and architecture of the temples we encountered on our way. We developed a similar liking for the landscape and a preference for *deng deng ubi*, a sauce of dried meat and sweet potato, although we never took our meals together: he dined at table, I ate elsewhere, even when he did not have company. On our day-length excursions we would surprise each other with offers of *kwee kwee* or *gulali*; the cakes were Cornelius's favourite snack, the sweets were mine.

Such a degree of sympathy between master and slave tends to be met with incredulity. But the truth is that neither of us hesitated to take the other's arm when crossing a fast-flowing river.

No, what daunted me in the end was the colonial government. I was promoted to the rank of engineer, third class, but that did not improve my position. The designation "extraordinary" was retained. To my demand for an explanation the Ministry replied: "Since you are a political ward of the Dutch State and maintain an uncommon, or extraordinary, relationship with our nation, that designation was chosen deliberately and in your best interests, notably to entitle the colonial government to offer you a more challenging post and a range of activity that is more sympathetic to you, and even a rise in remuneration or allowance without undue comparisons being drawn with your peers . . ."

But I never received a reply to my repeated applications for a position in keeping with my skills.

In 1853 the East Indies Life Insurance and Annuity Company was established for the benefit of civil servants in the Indies. Since I was and still am thrifty and prudent by nature, I sent in an application. A letter of rejection came by return post. The motive given was the unlikelihood of my pursuing a prolonged career in the colonial service in view of my reduced chances of promotion. I wrote back saying I had no knowledge of this. I requested them to substantiate their claim or else to reconsider my application, but all I received in reply was a non-committal note accompanied by a brochure from an investment company.

Time and again I received vague signals of this kind. I could feel something was seriously wrong, but found no tangible evidence. There was a sense of injustice, but it was impossible to put a name to its cause. How can a man take a stand against what is nameless? He feels demeaned, and consequently loses faith in himself. Without faith there is no future.

I was not yet twenty-seven years old. I had turned my back on my past. I had no choice but to fight for my future.

·   ·   ·

When I entered my sixth year in the Indies without having secured any guarantees for my career, I put in a request for a furlough so that I might put my case before the authorities in Holland. On 24 May 1856 I embarked from Batavia. I was alone, without regrets, and without expectations.

The dockside was alive with nervous activity. I recognized several government officials in the crowd. For a moment I thought they had come for me, but when I greeted them they said little. I stowed my belongings in my cabin, took the midday meal on deck, and was idly watching the busy traffic in the harbour when I noticed the arrival of a closed carriage, from which a gentleman alighted and hurried on board. He did not appear at the dinner table, but it was soon rumoured that we counted among our passengers former Governor-General Duymaer van Twist, who had handed his resignation in to Minister of Colonies Pahud two days earlier.

Duymaer van Twist, a man of gentle disposition, had shown himself to be an enlightened governor-general by taking such measures as curtailing statute labour, improving popular education and lowering the leases for the bazaar. Unfortunately, a kind nature does not always spell strength of character. So it came to pass in the final months of his term that a shadow was cast over his merits by his attitude in a case involving Douwes Dekker versus a number of chiefs and the Council of the Indies, in which he had failed to support the former in his campaign against unfair treatment of the natives. This betrayal had wounded Duymaer van Twist himself as much as Douwes Dekker, who went on to write a controversial novel dealing at length with the debacle. I am in two minds about the affair. Of course I admire Douwes Dekker's humanitarian ideas, but I cannot see the worth of propagating them so loudly that one is discharged from the very post in which, with a little more diplomacy, one might have dealt with abuse and injustice from the inside. However, I cannot claim to have been more successful with my attitude of patience and discretion.

I had hoped for an opportunity to bring my own case to Duymaer van Twist's attention during the voyage to Europe, but he did not appear on deck until we reached Madagascar, and only rarely afterwards. Now and then I would catch sight of him at night, when we were both unable to sleep. If he noticed my presence he would greet me cordially, but usually he was sunk in thought. I did not disturb him, but found myself a quiet corner and put out my lamp, after which each of us regarded our private ghosts in the shimmer of the moonlit waves.

It was on one of these nights, before we had rounded the Cape, that I found him on deck leaning back against the railing, resting his elbows loosely on either side. Before him stood a young sailor, who was explaining the position of the Southern Cross in relation to the Pleiades. My interest was aroused, and I sat down on a coil of rope to listen. Then the boy was called away, and for a long while we gazed in silence at the swathe of the southern milky way. When he at last spoke his question startled me.

"Do you long for the fatherland, Boachi?"

"The fatherland?"

"You have been disappointed."

"I think I have one fatherland too many."

"Which one is that?"

"I cannot say."

"No, I suppose not," he said, and lit a fresh cigarette.

"I have changed sides too often."

"And I not often enough."

The governor-general had proved to be a friend to me several times without any prompting on my part. The first of these occasions had been soon after our visit to Amboina. Duymaer van Twist and Douwes Dekker were still on good terms at the time. They shared a hatred of injustice and Douwes Dekker was able to arrange for Cornelius to be summoned for an official interview. What was said on that occasion I do not know, but—as I might have expected—the show of concern for my lot turned against me. The ill treatment I was subjected to only became more cunning, the malice went underground so to speak, where it was more difficult than ever to keep track of.

For a while, Cornelius had managed to control his hot temper. It was not until the following year, in Celebes, that things got really out of hand. In the course of an arduous journey across rough countryside, during which we had to forgo an escort party owing to a cut in our budget, he injured me more gravely than he had intended. I suffered a broken rib. Shocked by my cries and by the sight of blood oozing from my side, he abandoned me at the side of the road. A group of children found me and guided me across a mountain pass to the hamlet of Tembamba. My black skin caused a sensation there, but the villagers nursed me so lovingly that I was soon well enough to make my way back to Batavia, where I arrived only four weeks after Cornelius. It transpired that he had reported me "missing, probably lost." This incident was investigated at the instigation of Duymaer van Twist. As I myself felt somewhat uneasy about having quarrelled with my superior and also ashamed of my own weakness, I had not mentioned the cause of my injury to anyone, but the affair earned de Groot a reprimand and his career suffered as a result. After this I resumed my position, albeit reluctantly, and for a while my nemesis lay low.

"You know, we seem doomed to get in each other's hair, Boachi," he said in a jocular tone. Then he told me to open a bottle of his best claret and offered me a glass. "It's not as if we have any friends. It's a matter of each man for himself. That's what I've been trying to get across—it's time you took charge of your life."

We drank far too much that night and sang soldiers' ditties together, arm in arm. He never reproached me for the loss of face he had suffered as a result of our clash in Celebes, and for some time life was not unpleasant. He demonstrated how wrong it is to fortify one's opponent by a show of weakness. I was still Cornelius's pupil.

A direct consequence of this affair was that Duymaer van Twist set about improving my situation. In April 1854 he ruled that I should be released from my secretarial duties for seven months of the year, during which time I was granted a provisional licence to conduct research.

During the first weeks of my—temporary—release from de Groot's service I felt quite lost. I barely ventured out in public, and now that I was in a position to take the initiative I had no idea in which direction to turn.

I spent much of my seven months writing, as I had done previously, but from now on my words were my own. Not only did I begin to keep a diary, I was also inspired to revive my correspondence with Sophie, who had recently become grand duchess of Weimar. I initiated several research schemes, and reported on my findings in various publications. (My article "Coal samples from the shores of Seagull Bay, Bantam Residency" was published in the *Scientific Journal for the Netherlands Indies*, and "Notes on the Chinese in Java" in a German periodical devoted to oriental studies.) The factual terseness of these texts made me thirst after a more imaginative undertaking. I cast around for a source and found a small wellspring from which I drew several poems and three short stories, which I sent to Sophie. I also started writing a play, which I did not complete. Then I composed some essays, after which I attempted to write a memoir of my youth. However, the feelings were still too raw.

I re-entered Cornelius's service in November 1854 with far more confidence than before. De Groot made various attempts to break my will, but I was determined not to give up the few privileges I had secured. Within two months I felt obliged to appeal to Duymaer van Twist, who had already been so helpful of his own accord. I wrote him a letter requesting relocation to Holland. But although I sent him reminders of my request, a reply never came.

"There was so much at stake. With all respect, sir, you cannot imagine how much was at stake."

"Indeed I can," I said.

Duymaer van Twist had sent for two chairs to be brought on deck, as well as sugar-water and some bread. A few clouds in the east were set ablaze by the first rays of sunshine, making them look like ships with flaming sails chasing across the horizon. A few seconds later it was light.

"I am aware of the stakes involved," I said. "I owe my removal from Africa to them. But it wasn't the fault of one particular person. The forces that come into play in such cases are impossible to contain, much less to control. They defy all comprehension, all legality. In the past people would have attributed them to fate."

"I made a point of completing the arrangements for your furlough before Pahud took over from me. I hope you will find a more ready ear in Holland for your pleas than in the Indies. Decisions made in Europe cannot be unmade in Batavia. I advise you to appeal directly to the king, and not to leave the country until you have received formal confirmation that your demands have been met. I'm afraid you cannot expect much from Pahud as governor-general."

"Why not?"

"Trust me."

"It is my fate, I suppose. A comforting thought. No one is to blame for fate."

"And you are prepared to accept that?"

The belly of the ship awakened. A hatch opened and a party of sailors poured across the deck, each setting to his appointed task.

"I am tired," I said. "It is hard to know what to think. Political motives are incompatible with justice, it seems. What I do know is that the wishes of the group always take precedence over those of the solitary individual."

"That is why we choose to follow the Greek model. In a democracy every man has an equal say."

"That does not mean he will be heard."

"But at least he has a voice."

"Just one. And who will hear it when everyone else is shouting in chorus? Most people tend to align their opinions with those of their friends and neighbours. It is a natural propensity. To deviate from the norm is always seen as a greater risk. First they establish the norms, and then they are frightened they will be unable to observe them. That is why they huddle together. They find their identity by joining forces against anything deviant. They can't help reinforcing each other's prejudices. No, there will always be groups. Democracy merely legitimizes the dictatorship of the majority."

"Are you saying that you would prefer the tyranny of an old-fashioned despot?"

"At least tyranny is forthright. You are either in favour or out. If you are out of favour you must keep silent. You can seek refuge or flee, but at least you know your enemy. There is no cause for suspicion of your fellows. To me at any rate such a state of affairs is less irksome than the tolerance of the masses, for tolerance is capricious, imponderable, no more than a mask."

"But don't you believe in the righteousness of majority rule in all things?"

"Quite the contrary, for it means that the minority must always bend to the will of the majority. There is no benefit in this for the few."

"Does that mean you believe that the rights of the group necessarily curtail the rights of the individual?"

"I am sure of it," I said. "I do not belong in any group, big or small. And yet my presence is seized upon, for people find it easy to judge a man who is different in every respect, a man who stands alone. No sir, for the likes of me democracy is surely the least favourable of systems."

Duymaer van Twist leaned back in his chair so as not to miss a moment of the sunrise, which was now flooding the crests of the waves with orange. When he spoke it was in a low voice: "Do you realize how much better I would feel if I could feel certainty?"

"Certainty?"

"As you have. As Douwes Dekker has. The certainty of being right."

"You do not understand," I said, rising to my feet in order to return to my cabin. "Douwes Dekker stands alone because he made a choice. I stand alone because I lacked the courage to do so."

Delft

The streets of Delft were veiled in a light mist. The August sunshine was steaming the cobbles dry after a shower. I had my hired carriage draw up in front of my old boarding school. As I alighted I was struck at once by the paint flaking off the woodwork, then by the deep silence in the hall. I found Mrs. van Moock in the parlour, where the curtains were drawn. Her eyesight was poor.

"But do come here, my dear Prince. Come close to the window, closer, closer." She opened the curtains a little way and drew me into the shaft of light. Placing her hands on my shoulders she rocked me gently at arm's length, peering at me through her eyelashes.

"No, a dark smudge. That's all I can make out." She pressed me to her bosom. I had forgotten how small she was.

"He is deceased, did you know?" she whispered in my ear. I had already heard the sad news and offered her my condolences.

"Ah well, the end came as he would have wanted. He was standing among the ruins of Troy. He had taken Anchises on his shoulders. Father and son wept to be leaving their city. Mr. van Moock turned round for a parting look, and the emotion was simply too great. He died there and then, on his feet. When he was lying in his coffin I said: 'My dear van Moock, at least you gave one of your classes an unforgettable impression of the anguish of exile.'"

After this she called for some refreshments and demanded to hear all my news. She persuaded me to lodge with her for the coming weeks, but I insisted on paying for my board. I ordered my luggage to be taken upstairs and settled into my old room. I sat down at once to write King Willem III a note, brief though affectionate, asking him to receive me as soon as convenient. I enclosed a copy of my latest publication entitled "Coal in the Region of Cilacak Bay, Preanger Regency" with a fond dedication on the flyleaf, sealed the parcel and arranged for a messenger to take it to the royal palace. Then I dispatched the maid to buy meat and fresh vegetables, and instructed her to make a strong broth for the old lady every day from now on.

At supper Mrs. van Moock did not speak much. She brought her face close to each of the dishes, sniffing at it and screwing up her eyes to inspect the contents. She ate hungrily, pausing only once with her spoon in midair to say: "Pray tell me—you did come by carriage this morning, did you not?"

"Certainly madam."

"Good. Yes indeed, in a carriage, quite right too."

A few days after sending my first letter I wrote a second, after which I presented myself at the king's council-chamber in The Hague. There was a large anteroom with chairs along the walls, several of which were occupied by waiting citizens. They raised their heads when I came in, their expressions turning rapidly from hope to disappointment, after which they followed my footsteps across the parquet with their eyes. There was a small desk at the far end. Behind it sat a court official, who did not look up when I approached. He went on shuffling the papers on his desk, unperturbed. I cleared my throat, and still he did not raise his eyes. Then I noticed a table bell, which I rang. I introduced myself and said that His Majesty was expecting me.

"Then you will be the fourteenth today. And it is only half past ten."

"I sent advance notice of my visit."

"Did you now?"

"I have come a very long way."

"Really?"

"The king is my friend."

"Indeed."

"I am sure he wishes to receive me."

"No doubt." Sighing deeply, he put on his spectacles, opened a large ledger, took up his pen and asked for my name and place of residence. "All I can do," he said, "is put in a request for an audience. Presuming you have proper identification, of course."

"Very well. I have important business to discuss, you understand."

"I know," he said. "I know."

"You know about me?"

"Not really, but all His Majesty's affairs are important."

"At what time do you think he will receive me?"

"It will be a few weeks . . ."

"Weeks?"

". . . before you are notified whether your request has been granted."

"And if it is not granted?"

"Then I fear you will come here again. Most of them do. Good morning."

I spent the next year fighting a losing battle. I presented myself no fewer than fourteen times at the king's council chamber. I wrote a total of twenty-two letters to His Majesty, in the course of which my tone progressed from affectionate to imploring and finally to indignant. Not one of them received a personal reply. Thanks to Gustav of Saxe I was invited to a falcon hunt at the Loo palace, but the king did not attend. I tried to reach him through the Ministry of Colonies and through director Simons of the Royal Academy of Sciences at Delft, all to no avail.

Eventually, as a last resort, I found the courage—or swallowed enough pride—to appeal privately to the king's relatives. I called at the queen mother's new country estate, which had already earned the nickname the "Palace of Loneliness." I was informed that she was away visiting her sister and daughter in Weimar. I wrote her a letter there. While I was waiting for a reply I was granted an interview with the queen. The king's estranged wife remembered me primarily as an acquaintance of her mother-in-law, but nonetheless received me quite civilly. She showed sympathy for my cause, but as she was no longer living with the king she had no influence over him whatsoever. She spoke bitterly of her husband, adding that I would stand a good chance of finding him in one of the "houses" he patronized. (Ever since Willem had made her wait in the carriage while he paid a quick visit to a brothel, she seized every opportunity to deprecate his behaviour. Everyone in The Hague knew about the time she had blown the king's cover by sending the royal coach drawn by six plumed horses to fetch him from such a house.) After a while I realized that her disdain for Kwame and me in the old days had been nothing but an expression of her contempt for all men. A week later I received a note from her advising me to attend a gala performance

343

in the royal theatre. I took her advice, but was not admitted to Willem's box.

Weimar

In September 1857 I travelled to Weimar in response to an invitation from Sophie to attend the unveiling of a monument to Goethe and Schiller. "Zum Elefanten," the best lodging house in town, was fully booked for the duration of the festivities, and I was lucky to find a modest room in a lodging house nearby. Although weary from the journey, I set out at once for a walk along the Ilm. As I crossed the Frauenplan I caught sight of the head librarian of the Anna Amalia Library, who doffed his hat when he recognized me. The serving girl at the "Konditorei am Horn" ran outside to welcome me with a platter of butter-cake. Setting eyes on this place again was far more gratifying to me than revisiting Holland, where I was constantly reminded of Kwame. Here, where I had experienced something akin to happiness, I walked on air.

My spirits rose further when I returned to my hotel to find a message. The lilac notepaper told me it was from Sophie, who had evidently received prompt notice of my arrival. She apologized for being unable to welcome me in person that evening— she had to attend the reception at the castle for King Frederick of Prussia and King Maximilian of Bavaria—and told me that my old room in Ettersberg Castle overlooking the hunting grounds had been prepared for my accommodation. As this was the very room in which Goethe had composed his *Iphigenie* it was in great demand among her honourable guests, but she had rejected all their pleas for my sake. A carriage was waiting to take me there.

Upon my arrival at the castle I was offered supper, but was so overcome with emotion that I could not eat. I asked for a lantern and hurried outside. I sought out the round bench that had been named after me, and sat down. Although the night was cloudy and I could see nothing of the panorama I loved so dearly, I sat there for a long while. I extinguished my lamp and gazed into the black void while I ran my fingertips over the cold slab. And so help me God, I swear I perceived a force emanating from that cold stone. I can give no rational explanation. There was a sense of communion with the divine, a current passing through my body. Perhaps that was all it was—a current of hope. Fortified by the proximity of friends and by the familiarity of this beloved place, my hopes burgeoned. I felt that my future would soon be decided. Again I braced myself for change, unsure of what it would bring.

I stood up and wandered into the deep shadows of the Buchenwald. I had once known every path and lane in the hills, the location of the ditches and where the slope fell away into the valley. I was consumed with desire to express my joy physically. I shut my eyes and started running, wildly, crying out, happy as a child. I dashed blindly through the forest. I jumped and skipped. I ran headlong, and yet I was not afraid. I had never felt more confident.

Before joining the company in the smoking lounge I was at pains to suppress the laughter welling up in my chest. At the foot of the stairs I regained my composure, but when I glanced in the hall mirror to adjust my cravat as my presence was announced, I could still see a broad grin. I bit my lip and went inside.

The company was not large. Of those present I knew only Hans Christian Andersen. A circle of gentlemen had formed around him. As soon as the author caught sight of me he greeted me warmly and asked how I was. I replied evasively. He understood my reluctance at once, did not press me further and introduced me to his audience.

I could feel that my presence was not appreciated. I had become accustomed to reactions of this kind: no more than a supercilious curl of the lip, a muttered comment that I could not quite catch, a smile, a tone of voice, a curt acknowledgment, a reluctance to make room for me in the midst of others. To dwell on these experiences, of which I have had many, is a waste of time. On that occasion, however, I did not withdraw under some pretext, such as a sudden urge to gaze at all the paintings gracing the walls. I had no intention of effacing myself in this place which was so dear to me.

"You will not find our conversation very interesting, I fear," one of the guests said in French. "Our topic is typically German."

When I replied in French that I was quite familiar with the Teutonic legends they were discussing, they could not very well exclude me from the conversation. The speaker turned out to be Captain Friedrich von Schiller, an Austrian and the famous author's grandson. He was accompanied by his son-in-law Freiherr von Gleichen Russwurm and his son Leopold.

It transpired that this threesome had visited Eisenach that day, where the restoration of the castle was nearing completion. They were brimming with enthusiasm for the legends attached to the ancient keep. I was aware of the Germans' fondness for Teutonic mythology, but these gentlemen got so carried away that they revered Tannhäuser and his men not as heroes but as saints. The captain spoke of them as emblems of a uniquely German nobility of the soul. His son-in-law referred to an underlying force that had been suppressed for too long, notably by the Church, but which was now, thanks to Grand Duke Carl Alexander, being restored to former glory. Their tone was passionate and strident. I remarked that they sounded like soldiers on the eve of battle, and that their belligerence could hardly be congenial to the gentle-natured grand duke, whose commitment to the Teutonic heritage arose only from love of history and art. Had Carl Alexander been present he would not have tolerated their braggadocio, I had no doubt. The men outdid each other with quotations from the works of the great authors whose monument would be unveiled in the morning. Champagne did the rest. After the umpteenth bottle the captain demanded to hear Andersen's opinion.

"I know about folk tales, gentlemen, not myths," Andersen replied diplomatically. "I try to reduce everlasting truths to the level of a good story, so that they may be enjoyed by simple folk. In the legends you are discussing, simple human emotions are exaggerated to a point where they become everlasting truths. There lies the difference."

A silence ensued. Andersen kept aloof behind a screen of civility. Then von Gleichen Russwurm remarked that Richard Wagner was expected to come from Zurich and that he would have a seat on the grandstand. The conversation turned to the myths and legends that had inspired the operas composed by the newly appointed musical director at court. Someone disparaged the music, someone else hummed a few bars. Finally the captain, rather the worse for drink, observed that this was the music of the goddess Holda calling out from her mountaintop at Eisenach, invoking the fertility of the Teutonic tribes in order that they might outnumber all other peoples, and he clutched the front of his trousers as though about to answer her summons.

"I am reluctant to temper your enthusiasm," I said. "But I cannot see that your German legends are essentially different from those of other peoples. One finds the same symbols and heroic exploits depicted on the walls of Buddhist and Hindu temples as well as in the tombs of Egypt. They are also to be found in the tales of African storytellers. However, whereas in Africa such tales are cherished, not as truth, but as a hoard of shared history, here in Europe I was brought up to believe that tales about women living in rivers and dwarves converting mud into gold arose from ignorance and a lack of Christian teaching."

At this Leopold, the youngest of the group, took a step towards me. His cheek bore the German student's ritual scar or Mensur. The blade had probably severed a nerve, for there was no expression on his face.

"You'll see," he growled, "things have changed since your last visit to Weimar. We have rediscovered our past."

"Surely you have no objection to that?" Captain von Schiller said.

"On the contrary," I replied, "there are wise lessons to be drawn from your history."

"Our history is so rich that we have no need of others to remind us of its greatness." Leopold sounded so menacing that I glanced at his father, expecting him to silence his son.

"You are quite right, Prince," the father said with a smile. "Sometimes it is vital to remember one's origins," he added, stepping aside to reveal a small glass-fronted cabinet with tortoise-shell inlay standing against the wall. All eyes were drawn to the finely carved ebony base: a kneeling figure of an African youth supporting the cabinet on his bowed head. The jest broke the tension. Everyone was highly amused. I received a jovial slap on my shoulder and before I had time to react, the conversation continued as animatedly as before.

Hans Andersen took my arm and drew me to the terrace, where he was waylaid by a pair of ladies: Goethe's daughter-in-law Ottilie, who had travelled from Dresden, and her sister Ulrike von Pogwisch. They wished to hear about his visit to England, and were especially curious about certain peculiarities his host, Charles Dickens, was rumoured to have. I lingered nearby, but paid little attention to their exchange.

I was given a generous reception the next day. Two grandstands had been erected on the square. I was directed to a place of honour in the same row as the king of Prussia, who had donated the granite base for the monument, and the king of Bavaria, who had donated the bronze for the statues on condition that the poets be portrayed in modern garb and not in the usual Greek robes. The two kings, each believing his contribution to be the better one, exchanged pleasantries. I ventured to remark that the division was particularly apt, what with Prussia being represented by solid rock and Bavaria by splendid metal. This pleased them greatly.

Soon Anna and Maria Pavlovna arrived. They came in sedan chairs of the Sänfte type which was still popular in Weimar, but Sophie and Carl Alexander came on foot, cheered by the throng. I was greeted with much ado by all the members of the family, at which the Schillers farther down the row looked somewhat crest-fallen.

The ceremony opened with the new national anthem of Saxe-Weimar-Eisenach composed by Liszt: *"Von der Wartburg Zinnen nieder . . ."* Leopold von Gleichen Russwurm's voice could be heard above the others. The patriotic words seemed to confirm his claims of the previous evening. Then the headmaster of the boys' college gave a speech in the same exalted vein. I soon realized that the object of the event was not merely to commemorate Goethe and Schiller but that we were gathered together, as Professor Heiland put it, "to celebrate Weimar as the heartland of a spiritual movement such as has not been seen since the days of Pericles in any place on earth that is blessed by the gods." I sat straight-backed and still, so as not to give the people in the rows behind me cause to speak ill of me.

Although Sophie was much in demand at the grand ball that evening, we managed to escape to the park for a while. I had longed so dearly for this occasion that now it was upon us I could barely find the words I had been saving to tell her. She was as radiant as ever, and I filled the lapses in our conversation by observing her closely and revelling in our reunion. She wore her blonde hair drawn back into a snood on the nape of her neck. The skin under her eyes was plumper than before, and when my stares made her laugh I saw two charming tiny wrinkles. At the same time, however, I discovered around her mouth a slight tremor, which did not make it easier for me to speak. It was as though we were waiting for the old familiarity to return and were both somewhat startled that it did not do so at once. Sophie was the first to regain her composure, displaying a charm and tactfulness that she had no doubt mastered during her frequent diplomatic functions. She guessed what I was thinking and assured me that all a friendship as old as ours needed was to listen together to the whispering of the Ilm. We strolled to the Roman villa and from there along Goethe's parkland back past his country house. When we arrived at the Grotto of the Sphinx we sat down on a bench facing the stone statue. This fabled creature did not have the arrogant pose of its counterpart at Giza, but seemed slightly ill at ease with its ambiguous body as it lay crouched to one side of the cavern, its gaze averted from the small stream and the elderberry bushes alive with birdsong. I was fond of that spot, as of so many others in Weimar, and was prompted to reminisce, but Sophie soon interrupted me.

"I have read your letters carefully," she said, "and have already written to Willem that he must do something to improve your situation."

"I am afraid he will not listen."

"In that case he will compromise me. Because the root of your troubles lies here."

"In Weimar?"

"Yes. You need look no further. Do you remember your encounter with Raden Saleh when both of you attended a function hosted by us?"

"All too well."

"You had some difference of opinion."

"Yes we did. He mentioned the contract which sealed my fate, and also accused my father of failing to keep his end of the bargain."

"Then you complained about the Ministry of Colonies and the treatment you received."

"That may be so. I was provoked. I spoke in defence of my father, that was all."

"What you and I did not know, was that in those days Raden Saleh was an informer for the Dutch government. As an artist he had access to all the royal courts of Europe without rousing suspicion. Being an ambitious man he seized this opportunity to ingratiate himself with those in power."

"He spied on me?"

"He submitted negative reports. He accused you of ingratitude, and cast doubt on your loyalty to the State, after which the Ministry . . ."

She hesitated and glanced round to make sure we were alone.

"I don't know when we will be able to talk again in private. So . . ."

She fumbled in the pleats of her dress and drew out a minutely folded note.

"I want to give you this," she said, showing me a copy of a report dated 1849, which someone in The Hague whose identity she declined to reveal had secreted on her behalf. I had to pledge secrecy before she let me read Raden Saleh's words.

What surprises me about Boachi is that he alleges that his father, the king of Ashanti, was misled or tricked by the Dutch govern-

*ment in the matter of the <u>recruits</u> and that General <u>Verveer</u>
obtained <u>diverse goods</u> under false pretences. I told his friends
at Weimar and Dresden that this was false, and advised
Boachi himself to guard his speech, as he would be dispatched
to his homeland forthwith if word of his allegations reached
the authorities in Holland.*

"But why did no one ever ask me to explain myself?"

"I rose to your defence, of course," Sophie replied, "and so did
Professor Cotta—quite vehemently—but the seeds of doubt had
been sown. When I heard of the way you were being treated in
Java I wrote to the king at once in no uncertain terms that I would
not allow this silly incident to ruin your career. I feel responsible
for what happens under my own roof. He is my brother after all,
and will not refuse my plea for your rehabilitation."

"But do you really believe," I asked, "that such a petty offence
could be the cause of all the opposition I have encountered?"

"Isn't it enough? I am telling you that this is the crux of the
matter and that your problems will be solved in due course.
What more do you want? For goodness sake stop tormenting
yourself."

At that point we were spotted by a few guests, among whom
was Captain von Schiller. He came forward to claim Sophie for
the quadrille she had promised him. Noticing my disappointment she sent him ahead saying she would follow presently.

"I am told that you have now had a disagreement with the
Schillers."

"They take a different view of certain truths from you and I."

"That may be so, but you must understand that they are the
custodians of a literary heritage that is of paramount importance
to Weimar. Believe me, the works and ideas of Goethe and
Schiller are the heart and soul of our people." I said nothing,
which made her uneasy. "Anyway, I promised him this dance."

"I dare say they take excellent care of their ancestor's intellectual heritage in the material sense, but I hardly think their behaviour is in keeping with his spirit."

"There is a serious risk that the captain plans to remove the manuscripts, indeed Schiller's entire library, to Austria. I want to prevent that, whatever the cost."

"Very well," I said curtly. "Yes, do take Schiller's heritage to heart. Paper ideas strike me as a sight more attractive at this juncture than the ideas that are being propagated here."

She rose, took two steps and paused for me to take her arm. As we walked back to the ballroom she held me close and squeezed my arm now and then as if to make sure I was still there.

"I'm sure you'll understand, since you're my friend. It's not worth making enemies over a mere lapse of decorum, is it?"

"I am warning you, no more melancholy! I have had more than enough gloom and doom as it is." Anna Pavlovna rapped her fan across my fingers, but the look in her eyes was grateful. She dismissed her lady-in-waiting with a wave of the hand so that I could take the seat beside her.

"What's got into you—did you think to do a poor widow a favour by harking back to happier days?"

"If my presence distresses you I am deeply sorry, but there is nothing I can do about the way I look."

"Just as well, too. Whatever next! Right now I can think of no face that is dearer to me than yours. A beacon in a sea of new faces! Young and new, as far as the eye can reach. But who are they all and what are they doing here? That is what I should like to know!"

Sophie whirled past in the arms of the captain.

"Never mind, at least this is a festive affair, so I shall not complain. Nowadays I seldom go into society. I stay at home, alone with my thoughts. When you reach my age you will feel the same, I have no doubt. In old age there are two sides to remembering the past: one takes comfort in fond memories and yet it is infuriating that there is nothing new to be discovered among them."

When the quadrille came to an end the orchestra struck up a gavotte. Sophie did not change partners.

"You must visit me in Holland soon. I insist! There is a picture by Pieneman that I want to show you. It is not a masterpiece by any means. I myself am barely recognizable in the painting, but it shows my husband's coronation in the New Church in Amsterdam. Such a splendid event, don't you think? Everyone who attended is in the picture. Row upon row. You are in it too, next to Prince Quame. Those days are gone forever. All gone, as you well know from personal experience. And now, each time I look at that scene afresh I have to strike off those who have passed away. That combined with the shoddiness of the composition make it resemble one of those advent calendars with all those little windows, except that they are shut instead of opened. One becomes impatient to know who will be next, in spite of oneself. It is only a matter of time before the shutter on my own portrait will be closed . . ." Her voice trailed off and she pondered these thoughts for a few moments. Then she drew herself up and exclaimed with renewed vigour: "Look what you are doing! You are talking me straight into a *crise de nerfs!*"

I offered her my apologies, but could not keep my eyes off the dancing couple. They were evidently enjoying themselves. Anna Pavlovna followed the direction of my gaze.

"Will you not dance?"

"I have not danced in years."

"All the more reason to do so now. I can recommend it. Go on then, ask someone to dance!"

"I have learned not to embarrass ladies with such requests."

"Embarrass them? Whatever do you mean?"

"Not everyone sees me as you do."

"I do believe you are determined to depress me. And the look on your face! While I commanded gaiety and fun! Am I no longer to be obeyed? Do as I say and enjoy the evening, sir, for I am too old to settle for anything less."

"So you wish me to dance?"

"Dear me, have you grown hard of hearing too?"

"In that case," I said boldly, "you and I shall dance together." And before her amazement could turn to indignation I added: "In our imagination. No one will notice. We'll dance in our heads."

She glanced at me, then, lowering her head to hide a coquettish smile, she peered at me girlishly through her eyelashes.

"There is nothing to stop us," she replied, straightening her back. She was delighted. "By God, woe betide anyone who gets in our way!"

The next dance was a waltz, which we sat out side by side. After a few measures I heard the old lady humming the tune under her breath and on every third beat her skirt gave a little bounce.

The next morning I left Weimar feeling a lot more sanguine than when I had arrived.

Each link that is severed brings a man closer to his goal—I am convinced of that. Even as a child I strove after solitude. In light of this, the difficulties I have faced in my life can be said to have served a purpose. Could that be the reason why each loss I suffered left me with such mixed feelings? Alienation from others has always been both wounding and arousing to me.

Kwame's death triggered a similar experience. You lapse into a trance-like state in which all is crystal clear. Life shows its true features for once, it looks you straight in the eye. Suddenly you find yourself face to face with a force that is overwhelming and yet utterly predictable. But this is not a depressing insight, it is a relief. You become light. Literally so—you become *en*lightened. Yes, you think, at this very minute I have a clear perception of existence. I write these words reservedly. If they strike a chord my meaning will be understood, and if they do not may they be forgotten at once.

At all events I felt so confident upon my return from Weimar that I wrote to the minister of Colonies the following day, stating in no uncertain terms that I demanded compensation in the form of the lease of an estate in Java, for the injustices I had suffered.

Java

Early in 1858 I returned to Batavia. My demand for land had been passed on to Governor-General Pahud and his Council of the Indies, who delayed their concession for several more years. All that time I had to survive on my monthly allowance of four hundred guilders.

I had one last encounter with Cornelius de Groot. He wished to consult me about the Billiton mining company, which had been founded some years earlier by Prince Hendrik partly at my instigation. The tin yields were proving so low that the whole undertaking was at risk. At the time I had charted the whole area, I was familiar with the terrain and had conducted soil research on various sites.

De Groot now owned a handsome residence at Batavia, which he invited me to visit, not out of hospitality, but to show me how well he had done for himself. He was quite amiable on that occasion and asked after my welfare, which was not like him. I told him bluntly that I was living in a boarding-house and that my financial situation was dire. Although I had dreaded this meeting, I found that I no longer cared what he thought of me.

He had suffered misfortune too during the last six years, he said. He had married twice, and both his wives had died within six months of the wedding. He told me these things trying to look unmoved while he focused his attention on a bottle of expensive burgundy which, because of its age, he insisted upon opening himself. He had difficulty removing the lead cap, and when he succeeded at last he cut his finger. He swore and sucked the blood from the wound, then set about uncorking the bottle.

He told me how he had hoped to have a family; now that he was in a position to offer his children a better start in life than his own, he longed for sons to whom he might pass on his knowledge.

The cork would not budge and Cornelius needed a firmer

grip. He sat on the edge of his chair and clamped the bottle between his knees, and although he held his head down I noticed a flicker in his eyes. I asked him whether he was in love again by any chance. Startled by my correct guess he looked up and then broke into a grin. At that point the cork broke, and he sat there looking so crestfallen and clumsy that I acted as I would have done in the old days—I relieved him of the paraphernalia, blew away the crumbled pieces of cork and proceeded to open the bottle. We drank two glasses while he explained the problems at the tin mine. I promised to think about a solution.

After some time a servant came in to announce the arrival of guests for dinner. Cornelius told him to show them into the other room while he took his leave of me. He said there was no need to hurry and I could finish my glass at leisure in his absence. We wished each other good luck and he made for the door. With his hand on the doorknob he turned to look at me. I thought he was going to invite me to join the company for dinner after all.

"One piece of advice, Boachi: find yourself a wife. It can make all the difference. She needn't be pretty. Not clever either. I have had both, and believe me, neither beauty nor brains are important. Even a sweet nature can be dispensed with, so long as she is your match. Someone who knows you so thoroughly that there is nothing to hide or to be ashamed of, someone whose company is congenial to you regardless of time and circumstances. Yes indeed, to be without shame is worth a darn sight more than all that love."

"Do such women exist?"

"Let's hope so, Boachi. Let's hope so."

I investigated the Billiton affair and recommended mining in the vicinity of Tanjong Pandan. Cornelius promptly ordered a shaft to be dug, after which yields improved steadily on that island. Some time later I heard that he had found a third wife, but she did not survive him either.

It was not until late 1862 that I received word from the authorities offering me the lease of a tract of land in southeastern Java, to wit one thousand *bouw* (seven hundred and ten hectares) for the cultivation of coffee. The latter concession was presented as a privilege, as the government had a monopoly on coffee production. I packed up my belongings and departed as soon as possible. The only delay I encountered was at the sultanate of Yogya, where an over-zealous functionary insisted I should visit the palace. He showed me a gallery hung with portraits of the sultan and his relatives, all painted by Raden Saleh. I made as much haste as propriety would allow and proceeded to Madiun.

Upon my arrival in that mountainous region I was directed to a steep valley with rocky outcrops; a wilderness upon which the surrounding forest was rapidly encroaching. There was a small wooden house that had evidently been abandoned long ago. Parts of it had been dismantled by natives in need of planking or firewood. The door had vanished, and the vegetation was coming in through the floorboards. In my search for a bed or a bench or somewhere to lie down, I startled a civet. The creature responded by raising its tail and emitting its stench, making me almost thankful for the holes in the roof.

For several hours while I struggled to make my way through the thick undergrowth I believed that some mistake must have been made, but upon reaching the poppy fields of Dungus I was assured by the foreman at the opium store that I had come to the right place. I returned with a heavy heart, made a fire to chase away the vermin and slept in a borrowed hammock on the veranda.

In the next few days I was able to lay bare some of the old plantation bushes among the tangled weeds. The old stock had exhausted the soil, and in spite of my ignorance of farming I knew that my land would have to be cleared throughout, ploughed, equalized and manured before an entirely new crop could be planted. But that was not all: the watercourses were all silted up and the footpaths were virtually impassable, even with a chopping knife.

I did not gain an overall view of the estate until I had managed to clear a path leading up one of the steep slopes. From the top I could see a sprawl of muddy banks like gigantic, dark red fingers grasping the land. The mud had slid farther down the mountain-side with each heavy rainfall, dragging rocks and debris with it and effacing the boundaries of the old plantation. These vast accumulations of mud would all have to be removed in turn; one avalanche had already reached the back of my house, making the rear wall buckle. The house would have to be taken down and constructed anew. I also discovered three ravines on the property, with three or four reasonably open fields in between, which how-ever would be useless unless bridges were built to connect them with the surrounding area. I was standing there contemplating all the work that had to be done, and wondering how I could possibly finance these operations on my modest salary, when a column of smoke alerted me to the presence of a hamlet in the distance.

All the inhabitants saw me approach their huts, but none of them showed respect by sinking to their haunches. Once they got over the shock of my appearance they laughed loudly and gave me a friendly welcome, although the youngest cowered in fright and the eldest kept a wary distance. There were six families, all of whom worked in the opium fields. Some villagers responded to my queries, but all eyes were fixed on me. I bought a chicken and engaged one of the older men as a foreman.

This man, by the name of Budi, had known the plantation in his boyhood, before it was struck off the list of government plan-tations. He claimed that the site was unsuitable for the cultivation of the Robusta coffee bush. In summer the dry stifling heat was trapped in the valley by the surrounding mountains, while in the rainy season every passing cloud caught on the peaks, causing downpours that were disastrous for this type of crop. He pointed out other problems, such as the lack of storage space, the lack of manpower in this remote region, and the difficulty of the access route, which would hamper transportation of produce from the estate. Nevertheless I instructed him to recruit men for the recla-mation work, telling him to go as far as Solo if necessary to find them. He took the money I gave him and left without a farewell greeting. I could not bring myself to slaughter the chicken for supper.

.   .   .

For several months I had about eight men in my employ. Their number varied. They would come and go without telling me, and when I complained of their unreliability Budi merely shrugged. The work progressed too slowly. At first they grumbled at my orders; as time went on their dissatisfaction gave way to indifference. They nodded to everything I said, the way one placates a child, after which they proceeded to do as they pleased. The more I pressed them the more blatantly they ignored me. If I was overly strict they simply left; if I was too lenient they walked all over me. On one occasion I became so enraged that I grabbed the nearest worker's axe and hacked wildly at the underwood to show them what it means to work like a man. This was met with gales of laughter, whereupon the others tried to needle me into taking over their work as well.

Initially I blamed their recalcitrant behaviour on the fact that I was not accustomed to giving orders. I thought they claimed privileges because I could not pay them a better wage and because they knew there were no other workers to be had.

The situation got so out of hand that I decided to appeal directly to Budi, as a last resort. I ordered a meal to be served for us both in my room, which was the only part of the house that was habitable at the time. I softened him with small gifts for his family and told him candidly what I was up against. I explained that my funds were limited and that my survival as a planter depended on a speedy harvest. I had already placed an order for seedlings of the Arabica Bourbon with a nursery at Buitenzorg which specialized in varieties suitable for land such as mine, where coffee seeds were slow to germinate. My batch of seedlings would soon be ready for transportation to the estate. I begged Budi to tell me how to go about persuading the men to prepare the ground for planting before it was too late. I made no attempt to hide my anxiety, but he did not seem to appreciate the seriousness of my predicament.

"They work as hard as they can, tuan."

"That is not true, Budi, and you know it." He did not react. "Come on now, I need your help. I am asking you as a friend."

"But what can I do? This is the way they are. This is how they work."

"I'm sure they aren't so slow when they work at Dungus?" I asked.

Budi gave me a condescending look. He did not even bother to beat about the bush. "The master of Dungus is a Hollander."

"But I am a Hollander too."

"Surely not, tuan." A smile spread across his face in the typically Javanese manner, with a hint of contempt under a veneer of deference.

From then on I became stricter with them, I threatened them with wage cuts or even dismissal, although I could not afford to miss a single man. I myself worked from dawn till dusk, although my body protested at such hard labour. The attitude of the men did not improve.

Despite the unwillingness of the workers we succeeded in clearing the terrain extending from the house to the ravine, and by the time the seedlings arrived the earth had also been tilled. It was a miracle, for which I impulsively rewarded all the men with a bonus. I painted a sign and hammered it on to a post at the side of the road: *Suka Radya*, or Prince's Pleasure.

The day the cartloads of seedlings arrived from Buitenzorg my men stood at the ready by the gateposts, and did not hesitate to help unload the vehicles when the road into the estate proved impassable. Some jumped up on to the carts while others formed a human chain. I was among them of course, and was gratified that my persistent efforts to rouse their enthusiasm had apparently had effect. Soon there were hundreds of crates stacked by the side of the road. I sent my workers and the party of drivers and porters, who numbered about ten, to my house, where an elaborate meal had been prepared by the women of Dungus to celebrate this milestone.

As for me, I stayed behind with the crates, which I inspected lovingly one by one. The seedlings were smaller than I had expected, but the stems were sturdy, with vigorous budding leaves. They were still securely rooted in their rich compost, and I offered up a quick prayer that they might find sufficient nourishment in my soil.

I weighed a couple of plantlets in my hand and tried to envis-

age the fully grown bushes that would constitute my surroundings for years to come. My heart rejoiced at the promise of this
new life, this fresh start. Never again would I have to adapt myself
to a situation that was not of my making. For the first time in my
life I was about to create my own environment!

I was so absorbed in my happy thoughts that I do not know
how long it was before I noticed Budi at my side. My workers had
gathered not far off.

"Have you finished already?"

"Yes, we have eaten," he said. He was flustered, and I was not
accustomed to seeing him in that state. He threw a look at his
men over his shoulder, as if in need of reassurance. Two of the
men stepped forward hesitantly.

"Good. Did you enjoy your meal?"

"The men and I," he began, "have had a conference."

"A conference?" I had no idea what he was referring to, and
was secretly amused by the formal expression, which I assumed
he had picked up at Dungus. "So tell me, what was the conference about?"

"There is much work to be done, yes?"

"Indeed yes, a lot of work. We must start at once, don't you
think?"

"I don't think so, tuan."

"But we must, Budi. All the seedlings have to be planted out
within the next few days."

"That is why . . ."—he glanced back at the men to make sure
they were still with him—". . . we think, we must speak with you
now."

"Speak? What about?"

"Conditions, tuan, you understand. A lot of work. Hard
work. All quickly quickly."

At last it dawned on me why they had been so energetic earlier on: they were merely hastening the moment when I would be
utterly dependent on their cooperation. I listened to what he had
to say. Not only did they want more money, they even demanded
a portion of the land to cultivate for their own needs.

"No question," I said, as coolly as I could. "But I can assure you that I will raise the men's wages as soon as the first harvest has been reaped. This is normal procedure; indeed it is followed on the other plantations too."

"Well, tuan, we like working at the other plantations."

"More than at mine?"

"Every man prefers to be his own master, tuan. But we have grown accustomed to working for foreign masters. For Hollanders. Now these men, who must work for you—how do you think their families receive them when they return from the fields?"

"I don't know."

"They are mocked, of course! Their wives no longer respect them. People laugh at them. And so, tuan, they are ashamed."

"What of?" I asked testily. "Tell me, Budi, what they are ashamed of."

"You must understand: they have their pride. Think of it: men like them having to obey a master like you."

"Like me?"

"Black, yes?"

Perhaps it was the smirk on his face that inflamed me, perhaps it was just that I could not bear having my dreams shattered again. At all events I lunged at the little fellow, making him tumble backwards. I pressed my knee on his chest and struck his face. He flailed his arms to ward me off.

The workers made to intervene, but thought better of it when they saw the look in my eyes. Budi and I rolled over the ground, but in the swirl of dust I imagined I had the whole band of men to contend with. In that instant, I swear I felt a surge of opponents. Among all those bodies I glimpsed my father's hand waving at me, also Kwame swimming in the waves and Sophie whirling past, and all the while I was throttling Cornelius, who was beaming with pride because I was finally putting his lessons into practice.

Budi soon gave up. I panted as I scrambled to my feet and dragged him up by his hair. I took off my belt and lashed him harder and harder, deaf to his pleas. And he was an old man.

The noise attracted the women who had prepared the meal in my house. They came running with the porters from Buitenzorg trailing behind and formed a circle around me. No one spoke.

Their silence brought me back to my senses. Suddenly I had the sensation of standing with them and looking at myself, from afar so to speak, with my belt poised in midair to strike again. Feeling the sting of the lash on my own skin, I recoiled. I was horrified, almost panic-stricken, and helped the poor fellow to his feet.

"Forgive me," I cried. "Forgive me!" I called out to the others, but no one responded. One of the women came forward, took Budi's arm and led him away in the direction of the village. The others turned round and followed, in silence. The porters from Buitenzorg climbed on to their carts and drove off. I stood there, transfixed. Eventually I dropped to my knees and buried my face in my hands, and as I crouched on the ground I inhaled the fragrance of freshly tilled earth.

I felt a hand on my shoulder. For a moment I thought the workers had come back seeking revenge. I looked up. Stooping over me with his back to the sun was one of the Buitenzorg nursery-men, who had stayed behind.

"Well now, tuan besar, hardly a thriving plantation, is it?" It was not so much the voice that sounded familiar as the impertinent tone.

"You see!" he laughed. "You remember me. I knew you would." Instead of reaching out to help me to my feet he squatted down beside me as if we were old friends. I shielded my eyes against the sun and recognized the houseboy from Amboina, older maybe but not wiser. "It's Ahim! Ahim! You could not forget him!"

He seemed to feel utterly at ease, as if he and I were in the habit of sitting on our haunches, side by side in the open air. Over his chest and shoulders he wore a cloth into which he had knotted some belongings. He drew out a betel box, which he opened. He crushed some leaves in the palm of his hand with a leisurely gesture, sniffed them and held up his hand for me to test the sharp, acrid aroma. Then he busied himself with areca nut, a pinch of lime, tobacco and *gambir* extract. He did not look at me once during the ritual, as though wishing to grant me time to accustom myself to his presence. His impassiveness helped me to regain my composure. Finally he offered me a plug, which I declined with a frown, after which he popped it into his own mouth. He shut his eyes and chewed blissfully until the scarlet juice seeped out between the stumps of his filed teeth.

Ahim had remained in the employ of the assistant resident Douwes Dekker until the family sailed for their furlough in Holland. After that he had worked in dozens of places, but never for long. That did not surprise me. When Douwes Dekker returned to the Indies in late 1855 expecting relocation, Ahim had found him, first in Batavia and later in Buitenzorg. On both occasions he was sent away; he would not be re-engaged until Douwes Dekker had been appointed to a new post. Ahim had looked for temporary work to pass the time in the vicinity of his former master, and had found it at the nursery of Buitenzorg. When Douwes Dekker left for Lebak in January 1856 Ahim was not free to join him, and by the time he reached the end of his term of employment Douwes Dekker had already left his position, so that Ahim had stayed on at the nursery. When my name cropped up on the order list he was very pleased—especially as I was now the owner of a coffee plantation—and resolved to offer his services to me.

"What good will that do me?" I said. "Or you. You put your money on the wrong horse, my friend. This undertaking is doomed. You have seen it with your own eyes."

"I have seen everything." His level gaze made me uneasy.

"Right," I said. "You can go now." I waited for him to rise, but he pretended not to have heard. Ahim is like a stray dog: stroke him and he will snarl, chase him away and he will not go.

"It's unfortunate, isn't it," he said, "that the Javanese can be so proud. They will not obey you."

"Quite so," I snapped.

"But if you had a middleman . . . not black. Not white either. Someone who is not above them, but who is their equal and yet capable of predicting their behaviour. Such a man might palaver with them. He would have to be modest, and very clever . . ." He grinned so broadly that the betel juice dribbled out of the corner of his mouth.

"How unfortunate," I said with deliberation, "that I do not happen to know anyone in the least clever."

Ahim rose to his feet.

"Tomorrow I shall find new workers for you. Time is running out, Prince. You have little choice." He went to the stacked crates, took out an armful of seedlings, wandered off into the field and began to plant them.

"You'll damage the roots, you fool!" I cried. I jumped up and rushed towards him. "And don't plant them so far apart either!"

In short, everything he did I had to do all over again, but before nightfall we had managed to put out twelve rows in the first field.

Java 1900

Buitenzorg, 9 September

"Do not have the heart to surprise me with some memento. I will not have it. I am too old to be indulged."

"I know that, tuan, better than anyone else."

"I mean it," I said. "If you dare to give me a surprise I shall drop dead, out of sheer spite, just to teach you a lesson."

Indeed, such was my awakening this morning! Opening my eyes I saw Ahim standing over me, dressed for travel.

"I'm asking for the morning off, that is all."

"Today of all days?"

"When have I ever asked for leave?"

"Never. That's the trouble. It's too late to start now."

"I shall go anyway."

"Of course you shall. Just like you to leave me in the lurch."

"There's a cold meal waiting for you in the kitchen, and I've put some fruit and water in your study."

"You don't care a whit about my jubilee, do you?"

"Well, you made it quite plain you disliked the idea from the start."

"I did, but such things are imposed on one by others. Not that you would stop for a moment to think that an old man having a fuss made of him against his will would be glad of some distraction from his sentiments—you think of no one but yourself."

"So I do. I'll be back in the afternoon. Goodbye."

The villain shut my bedroom door softly behind him. How could I go back to sleep now? The festivities are off to a good start, I reflected, what with Ahim disturbing his benefactor so rudely first thing in the morning. Is there no end to the man's ingratitude?

First I resolved to stay in bed all day, but as time wore on I felt increasingly anxious about the celebration that evening. I pictured myself at the centre of attention, with all eyes fixed on me while there was no one I trusted sufficiently to turn to for moral support.

I rose and dressed myself—sorely missing Ahim's helpful hands—and walked to the kampung. Wayeng was already at work in the fields, but Lasmi was at the wash-place with Quamina. I told her about the festivities and asked her and Wayeng to be my guests of honour. She lowered her gaze and said she would certainly be with me in her thoughts. When I urged her to explain she said she was a simple woman and could hardly seek the company of dignified Hollanders. I gave her some money, enough for them both to purchase suitable clothing, and told her I would refuse to attend the party myself unless they were beside me. She smiled uneasily. I lifted her chin and still she averted her gaze. She handed the money back to me, and when she finally raised her eyes and saw the frown on my face a chuckle of delight escaped her. She told me Adeline had been to see them weeks ago, to invite them as well as the children to the fête. This first visit had been followed by a second and a third during which food and other details were discussed, and finally they had been told to fit themselves out in new clothes at her expense. All this was done in the strictest confidence, so as to surprise me with their presence at the festivities. There you go, I told myself, goodness knows what other shocks Adeline has in store for me. The deviousness! This is exactly what I have been so afraid of.

When Lasmi noticed how upset I was she regretted having given their secret away. I reassured her by promising not to let on that I knew, and gave her a little demonstration of the faces I shall pull this evening—ooh! and ah!—when I set eyes on her in her finery. She and Quamina held their sides laughing. When Lasmi withdrew to continue her work, my little girl was beside herself with excitement, and insisted we play hide and seek. When I grew tired I sat her on my knee. She sang me a song that she had only just learnt, about the deer that leaped on to a rock in the middle of a fast-running stream. That single leap had used up all its courage, leaving it too timid to jump from the rock to the far side.

I felt a great surge of love for her and for my other children, and was filled with regret at having banned such feelings from my heart for so long. When she came to the end of her song she asked me if I knew any songs too. I told her I never sang. She asked whether this was because no one had taught me songs when I was a boy. I pressed her tightly, so tightly, to my bosom although she could not have known why. I said I had learned many songs from her grandmother in Africa, but that I had forgotten nearly all of them except perhaps one that was special. She wanted me to teach her that song. I began by tapping the rhythm. Although this was quite different from the monotonous beat of the gamelan, with which instrument she is familiar, Quamina soon picked it up. Hearing the old cadence tapped by her little hands filled me with pride and love, but when I opened my mouth to sing I could not find the right tone. I tried again, with hardly more success. I stopped beating the rhythm, and set about teaching her the words first: "We are the children of Spider Anansi and the whole world is our web . . ." But I found that at this precious moment I could not recall the rest. This distressed me, and I gave up.

"Well, my father the prince," said Quamina, "it's very nice, your Ashanti song, but it's not very long, is it?"

Before the sun grew too hot I was back at ease, and I spent the rest of the morning trying to remember the song. I kept hearing the tune in my head exactly the way it was supposed to sound, but when I opened my mouth the words refused to come. I had to force myself to think of other things.

I got another shock towards noon, when Adeline suddenly turned up with a pan of soup.

"A little of this will do you good," she said, lifting the lid so that the sour smell of peas wafted on to my fresh shirt. "You must not go hungry now that Ahim has absented himself."

"I might have guessed this was all of your doing! Since when do you give orders to other people's servants?"

"Just today, my dear Prince, and in a good cause." She handed me a spoon and sat down opposite me while I made a polite effort to taste her offensive soup. She did not make things any better by adding: "Not too greedy now! You don't want to spoil your appetite for tonight's dinner with the governor."

"It's time you told me exactly what I've let myself in for."

"A banquet. And I will say no more."

"Who will be there, who will be giving a speech, what am I to expect?"

"Relax! You'll be the life of the party, you'll see—all you have to do is sit back and enjoy the surprises we have prepared for you. You are very dear to us all and everyone has done their bit."

"I insist on knowing what is going to happen. In detail, so you can tell me right now. Or else I'll refuse to go."

"All right then"—she could see that I meant what I said—"I'll let you in on the secret, shall I? The ladies of my eurhythmics group and I have rehearsed a little performance. We will take the floor during the second sorbet, the one we have planned between the fish and meat courses, and we have called it 'The Princes of Ashanti.' There, I've told you now, are you satisfied?"

"Satisfied is hardly the word," I said, trying not to show my revulsion.

Adeline pushed her chair back and stood squarely before me. "It starts with the children's grief at being taken away from their African home." She raised her arms and sashayed across the room. "And then their fear for the unknown when they arrive in Delft. Fear! Fear!" She recoiled. "But in the end they find themselves in the bosom of the royal House of Orange, which makes them so very, very happy. And as our finale we enact the triumphant moment—Hosanna!—when, having reached manhood, you embrace the Lion of the Netherlands." At this she clawed the air and growled like a wild beast. Panting heavily she collapsed into my armchair, swung her legs on to my footstool and beamed at me as if she expected a compliment.

"And is that all?" I asked.

"Yes. Come on now, how does it strike you?"

"It is, how shall I put it . . . quite remarkable. But what has this got to do with Ahim? God forbid that he should skip along behind the ladies too."

Adeline did not react. She held her tongue and gave no indication of rising from her seat. I grew impatient, and said: "At my age a banquet is a rather daunting prospect, and to be honest I had planned to spend the day quietly, on my own, so as to prepare myself mentally."

She went outside, but soon returned with a large jug of orangeade and two glasses.

"You and I are always alone," she said. "This is our great occasion. Today we are together."

Less than half an hour later it dawned on me that Adeline had ulterior motives for lingering at my house. As soon as Ahim arrived—in a carriage, no less—she hurried to meet him at the garden gate. They were evidently plotting something. When I stepped on to the porch Ahim fled into the kitchen, supposedly to fetch me a cold lunch. I called out to him that my stomach could not take another morsel of food, and demanded to know where he had been. Adeline, who had posted herself by the carriage, saved him from having to reply.

"Do sit down," she cried, "there's someone to see you."

Adeline came forward with a frail old man shuffling at her side. His shirt was stained. If he had not grasped my hand so firmly and given me such a long searching look I would never have recognized him as van Drunen. His cheeks were unshaven and he was dressed like a workman. He was emaciated, his eyes sunken, and he seemed mortally ill. I made to help him into a chair, but he insisted that I remain seated. He took two steps back and bowed his bald head to me, and also inclined his body as far as he was able. He had obviously planned this beforehand. Then he bestowed on me the same honour as when we first met: he addressed me with my full Ashanti title. This only moved me because he was so manifestly emotional himself.

Adeline drew up a chair for him and Ahim brought us a tray with refreshments. I was under the impression that they had conspired together to arrange for an old forgotten friend to attend my jubilee celebration, and forgave them their interference. They withdrew discreetly.

Van Drunen spoke in a weak voice. His lungs rasped. He stopped now and then in mid-sentence to get his breath back. His thoughts evidently wandered during these pauses, because the gist of his words was unclear. I leaned forward to concentrate on what he was saying. His face was weathered like that of a peasant, and there were dry brown stains on his nose and forehead. His blue gaze had turned grey, and his pupils looked ragged along the edges. Eighty-seven! I reached out and took his hand to ease him back from his musings to reality. The look he gave me seemed to say that it was only now that he realized fully who I was.

"The little prince . . ." he said, as if he were face-to-face with the child I once was, ". . . out in the wide world."

I asked after his current situation.

The modest batik-printing industry at Semarang that van Drunen had set up four decades ago with the "black Hollanders" resulted for a while in a lively trade with their tribal relatives on the Gold Coast. The Javanese designs were complemented with African patterns, and in many places the new style supplanted the traditional West African dress.

Around 1875, however, news of the popularity of wax prints in the African coastland reached the Dutch cotton manufacturers. As they had been facing diminishing sales of their batik in Java they were eager to expand their activities to West Africa, which they did with a vengeance. The African market was flooded with Dutch cloths, thereby ousting the import of wax-print textiles manufactured by the *blanda hitams*. The black community in Java had been living in poverty for the past twenty years.

Van Drunen himself is still living in their kampung, despite his failing health. He is regarded as an eccentric by the Dutch colonials, whose contact with him is limited to his occasional appeals for assistance in finding work for the half-caste offspring of African fathers and Javanese mothers.

"Like my own children," I said, at which van Drunen's eyes lit up. He was noticeably pleased at my fatherhood, but somewhat taken aback that it had come at my advanced age. I sent Ahim to fetch my little ones.

"In our kampung . . ." said van Drunen, "the next generation is already growing up. It has all gone so quickly. The very men that I recruited in Africa—grandfathers already. Last month a boy-child was born with skin so very pale . . ." His thoughts drifted off, then he regained his composure, adding triumphantly: "John!"

I stared at him uncomprehendingly.

"They have called the child John." He was radiant.

"Is that your name too?" I asked.

His fingers trembled as he traced the outline of the infant's head.

"Like John the Baptist!" He puffed up his wrinkled cheeks until they were as round as a child's.

"I never knew your Christian name."

"Didn't you?"

"We were children. You were *Mijnheer* to us."

His face fell. He nodded briefly.

371

"Children." This time his thoughts strayed so far away that I was afraid he would forget to breathe.

"I try to help them," he said finally, sighing. "These children were born of my shame." He fixed my eyes with his, as if he expected something from me. I began to feel that he had not come here to attend the festivities. I glanced round, but Adeline was nowhere to be seen.

"I have read a letter you wrote long ago," I began, "in which you requested to be relieved from your government post." Van Drunen nodded. "I did not get the impression you abandoned your career to devote yourself to charitable works."

"No indeed. That came later."

"Yet it was your own choice to live so modestly." My no-nonsense tone made him sit up. He struggled to regulate his breathing as best he could. It was as though he had been saving his energy to give me a full, uninterrupted account of what had transpired.

"In that letter you saw I surrendered my position and all that went with it. My superior began by delaying my missive, then tried to dissuade me. My fellow colonial officers were amazed: no man in his right mind would freely give up the influence he had accumulated during so many long years of service. I was even taken to a doctor, who examined me for symptoms of malaria, homesickness and tropical fever, but I was adamant.

"My salary was discontinued and I lost my credit with the bank. I forfeited my pension rights as well as my rank and my government residence, which meant that I was no longer invited to social functions. As I had not explained my motives to my friends they were perturbed, and consequently I caused them some embarrassment. In order not to compromise them further I stopped making social calls. I broke off the engagement with the fiancée I had found in Holland after much soul-searching. Even the clothing for which I had received an allowance from the government was confiscated, so that I was left with only a couple of old suits, which I sent out to be mended in turns. My carriage went, too, after which all I had to my name were some savings. Those I spent on a strong horse, because in my penurious state I longed only to be free to travel.

"So I did not hunt for a lodging house, and sold off my belongings and any effects connected with my former post. I was able to survive on the proceeds from that sale for eighteen months, during which time I crossed the archipelago from end to end, sleeping under the stars and eating with the natives. In no way did I rise above them, nor did I make the old mistake of believing I could become their equal. I was different, and was tolerated as such in their midst."

Here he paused for a moment to take a sip of water. Then he mopped his neck and head, folded his handkerchief and tucked it into his breast pocket again.

"You, Prince Aquasi," he continued, "you can see into my heart more clearly than any other man. When I returned to Batavia from my travels, eighteen months later, I found every door closed to me. I wrote to my relations at home asking them for money, and in my attempts to exculpate myself it was tempting to give a noble twist to my self-chosen fall from grace; when a cousin of mine suggested that I had no doubt been moved to resign because I shared the great writer Douwes Dekker's hatred of injustice, I did not contradict him. But it was not the truth, of course. Although I was driven by indignation at the injustice I had seen, my motives were purely selfish."

"In what way?"

"In the sense that Douwes Dekker, too, served his own interests. No man sacrifices his future unless he believes he can save his soul by so doing."

"So what *was* your motive?"

"My true motive? It was you."

He met my gaze at last. A smile spread across his face, but there was a faraway look in his eyes. I tried to revive the old affection I had had for the man, but found I could not.

"Yes," he said, "it was all because of you."

"Did you feel guilty by any chance?" I asked bluntly. He became rather agitated, and although he spoke evenly I noticed a tremor in his nostrils.

"Whatever sins I may have committed will be revealed to me soon enough when I meet my maker. If the Lord asks me why I took you and your cousin away from your homeland my answer will be that I was not merely obeying orders, but believed in the righteousness of my action. Do not think I have come all the way here to ask for forgiveness. When I was in Africa I was a young man. It was my first expedition. I knew nothing about the world, and less about its peoples. When I first saw you, you were half naked, illiterate. I had no doubt that you would benefit from a sojourn in Holland, indeed that it would be your salvation from a life in a land so brutal that I tripped over a heap of human heads during an evening stroll. When I took you boys under my wing it was because I believed I had the Lord's blessing."

"Hardly an act of unselfishness," I said. His tone was beginning to chafe me. I had never reproached him for his deeds, but now I felt bitter. I had no wish to appear unfriendly, so I stood up as if the subject were of no particular interest to me, and fixed my gaze on the garden path. I wished Ahim were with me—Ahim, who always managed to deflect me from my gloomy reminiscences with his impudence. For a moment I thought I saw the old buffoon in the shadows and I beckoned him without van Drunen noticing, but it was only the sun shining on a banana leaf at the bottom of the garden.

"What I have been saying to you does not mean," the monologue continued behind my back, "that I did not feel responsible. The day I left Kumasi with you and your cousin changed the course of my own life, too."

"Do you expect me to sympathize?" I asked.

"Not a day goes by without my thinking of you. Not a night, not an hour." His voice faltered. "Prince Kwame's death grieved me as if he were my own son. You do not believe me? That is your right. You are hearing the story of a man who lost less than yourself, a man, moreover, who contributed to your loss, albeit unknowingly. Even if you are sceptical, please let me finish.

"Your cousin's death opened my eyes, but I could not yet face the truth. I decided to leave Holland in the hope of resting my soul. I requested relocation to the East Indies. I hoped to recover the vigour and commitment I had known when I first travelled to the tropics. It was not until I arrived in this colony, where social

374

hierarchies are magnified out of all proportion, that I discovered the workings of the machine in which I myself was a cog.

"I had not been in Batavia for a full year when you paid me your first visit. I was so happy to see you—a grown man now, a university graduate, and a colonial officer to boot! You stood alone, but you were strong and full of energy. I was relieved to see that our adventure had produced such a positive result, and was most gratified by the way you and I shared memories of your dear cousin, that we were able to laugh together and also to weep over incidents I had never dared countenance until then. The effect of your visit was like that of the folk medicines the Bantamese use for colic: the cause of the ailment is not taken away, but all the internal organs are cleaned and oiled for a new lease of life. You made me think.

"By the time you came to see me I was beginning to feel at home in my new surroundings. Once I had settled down I had plenty of time for the thoughts I had banished for so long. Our conversation brought Kwame back to me in a way I had not believed possible. It was no longer his death that I pondered, but his life. I could not understand why you were able to succeed in life and not he. And if it was true that I had in some way contributed to your success, had I not equally contributed to your cousin's tragic fate? Sometimes, on sleepless nights of inner turmoil, I would ask him outright whether I was to blame. I could feel his presence in my room—although my nature is rational and down-to-earth. One night he appeared in a dream. He sat on the edge of my bed and consoled me, saying I had been merely a pawn in the game."

"And that made you feel better, no doubt."

"After that the visions stopped. I thought I had found peace at last. Two years later you visited me again. As soon as you crossed the threshold I knew you had suffered misfortune. Grave misfortune. And I thought to myself: dear God, may he be spared!

"You told me of your lonely struggle. I promised to look into your situation and said goodbye without undue emotion, as was my custom. But a new zeal stirred in my heart, as if God Himself had roused me. You may find it hard to understand, but the sadness I felt at your suffering was mitigated by a sense of challenge, of a calling. Indeed I was glad of the opportunity, thanks to you, to do a good deed. I resolved to do everything in my power to help you. However, my loyalty to the government was still intact. My God, if I had known then what I would soon discover . . ."

Van Drunen's voice broke, as if he dreaded telling the story up to the end. He shook his head and drank some water, fumbled in his pockets for a piece of paper, which he laid on the table between us, and mopped the perspiration from his neck. The handwriting was his.

At that very moment Ahim, who is never there when you want him and always when you don't, turned up with my children skipping along behind him. They greeted the old gentleman politely the way I had taught them, and I truly believe that van Drunen was moved by the likeness between them and me. However, I was eager for him to continue his discourse which, I feared, was in danger of being ousted from his mind in the stir caused by my children. I told Ahim that I was otherwise engaged and ordered him to entertain the children until we had concluded our conversation. Despite the severity of my tone the fool insisted on fetching fresh fruit for us first, but eventually he took my little ones by the hand and went off into the garden, where they squatted down to make a small fire with twigs and dead leaves.

The note had been lying on the table all that time. At last van Drunen picked it up. He unfolded the sheet, folded it again and then held it up briefly between his fingers, where it shook like a leaf. I was impatient and about to take it from him when he broke the silence.

"The first step was simple. I requested a meeting with Governor-General Duymaer van Twist. He was aware of your case, and had already received several complaints about de Groot's treatment of you. Those complaints had, he assured me, resulted in an official reprimand. I retorted that in my estimation you were too highly placed regarding both training and social rank to serve under de Groot. I proposed that you should be released from his employ and granted licence to work independently as you had been promised. When I pressed him for further details of the arrangement he changed the subject tactfully but firmly.

"Later that day I asked to see your dossier at the head office, as I still had the authority to do. I expected to find a handful of reports, but to my surprise I was presented with a bulky portfolio which, although the contents referred to a period of less than four years, was so heavy that it took two men to carry.

"In addition to the usual conduct records, salary lists and quarterly reports I came across memoranda giving detailed accounts of your day-to-day activities. De Groot, for instance, not only reported on all the expeditions you undertook together, but also included a record of each and every private engagement, complete with dates, times and durations. Appended to these papers were notes submitted by others, often with suggestions of such an intimate nature that I felt obliged, contrary to my code of honour as a civil servant, to remove the offending items from your dossier before returning it to the records officer.

"The seriousness of your situation became fully apparent when I attempted to discover the reason for collecting such a mass of information. I broached the subject with the governor and his close associates, but met with only prevarication. After a while I realized that the gentlemen concerned had agreed among themselves not to reveal any further details to me.

"Towards the end of January 1855, after I had spent several weeks delving into your case, something remarkable happened. One night a native boy came to my door saying I was urgently needed by one of my colleagues. I hurried to his house, which was in one of the more disreputable parts of the city, only to find him in bed and quite content. We laughed at the misunderstanding, and I returned to the main road to call a rickshaw. At that point some beggars emerged from the gloom. They bore down on me and robbed me of my small change, pocket watch and meerschaum pipe. I pretended to be knocked out and cursed myself for being so heedless in a neighbourhood where such attacks were frequent, when suddenly I heard one of the men mention my name to his cronies—how could he possibly have known who I was?

"The very next morning my department received a visit from your superior, Cornelius de Groot himself. He had come for a drilling licence, he said. Hearing of my accident he made a show of concern for my injuries. He advised me in a genial tone to be more careful about where I went at night. He sat down as if we were old friends and assured me that he remembered me well from a visit I had paid to the boarding school when you were young. He told me he was your friend and protector and that he had great plans for you, despite your occasional disagreements. He was sorry to say that you had applied for relocation to Holland, presumably because you were homesick.

"I suggested that your request for relocation might have been inspired by the inequality that had arisen between him and his 'old friend.' Cornelius said it was regrettable but impossible to avoid 'given the mandate.' He refused to expand on this, saying the matter was confidential. I did not press him further and we turned our attention to administrative affairs. No more than two days later I received orders to join a military expedition to Borneo, where I was to stay for nine months.

"I received assurances that your relocation was being taken care of, and as there were no official grounds for refusal I left for Borneo confident that all would be well. When I returned in October 1856, I learned that your situation was unchanged and that you had put in a request for a furlough so that you might put your case before the authorities in Holland."

While van Drunen was holding forth, I watched my children out of the corner of my eye. The flames of Ahim's bonfire leaped up now and then in the wind, which frightened my youngest and made him cry. Ahim soothed him, and set about folding scraps of old paper into butterflies and birds, at which he was remarkably adroit. He let the children throw them up to be wafted away by the hot air, but most of them caught fire and fell to the ground blazing. When it was Aquasi's turn he looked round to make sure I would see the flight of his bird. I waved at him.

"At that time," van Drunen continued, "my department was in disarray due to complications arising from the Lebak affair. The situation became chaotic in April of 1855 when the governor-general was about to be replaced. His rooms were cleared and refurbished for his successor. In the ensuing commotion the civil servants performed their respective tasks without supervision. I took an enormous risk: I contrived to forge a special licence permitting me access to the classified dossiers, in which I came across several statements and some correspondence dating from 1850 between Governor-General Rochussen and Minister of Colonies Pahud, who was eventually to take over from Duymaer van Twist. Those letters sealed your fate, and I hastily copied out the most important passages." Van Drunen indicated the note lying on the table.

"The investiture of the new governor-general took place on the 22nd. I sent a message saying I was unwell, for I was plagued by a guilty conscience. I was to escort Duymaer van Twist to the docks two days later, and as you were travelling on the same ship to Holland I could have revealed my discovery to you on that occasion without our meeting raising any suspicions, but I did not dare."

I took the note and unfolded it. Van Drunen spoke rapidly now, as though afraid that I was not yet sufficiently prepared for what I was about to read in black and white.

"I was afraid," he said, "that this knowledge would discourage you at the very time that you were about to sail to Holland to take matters into your own hands. You needed all the strength you could muster. What good would it have done to know how the odds were stacked against you? Most important of all, however, was the deep anxiety I felt about the similarity between the situation you were in and that of your deceased cousin prior to his final act of desperation. Like him, you were at the mercy of the powers that be. I was fearful that, should you notice the similarity, you might even be moved to follow Kwame's example. That would have been more than I could bear." He fell silent. Then he turned his gaze on me, adding: "You see, once again my actions were not unselfish."

Since the matter was evidently of the utmost importance to him I ran my eyes down the page. My attention was caught by a few lines from a statement drawn up by Pahud on 24 July 1850.

"The principle of *'noblesse de peau,'* of the pre-eminence of a white skin over black and of the moral and intellectual supremacy of the white race over all others, upon which our domination in the Indies rests, would be seriously undermined if Aquasi Boachi were appointed to any post of authority which is the preserve of white men . . ."

"Noblesse de peau!" I spluttered.

"Yes, nobility of the skin!" van Drunen echoed weakly, and I could sense that he was keeping a watchful eye on my reaction. I laid the letter on the table in front of me, and folded the paper lengthwise.

"Once I had seen the evidence I could not countenance serving under Pahud, who had after all been the cause of my misfortune. So I handed in my resignation. In later years I had the opportunity to make up for my past ineptitude by standing up for the *blanda hitams,* my black Hollanders." He leaned forward. "Long ago, when I took you and Kwame away from your parents, I told you that the Dutch realm would be your new mother. Little did I know that she would cherish only her own sons and make foundling orphans of all others."

I made two diagonal creases at the top of the sheet.

"Your news, sir," I said, "is stale after fifty years." I folded the paper to make two wings and a tail, took aim carefully, and to my intense satisfaction my missile struck Ahim on the back of the head. Stung, he turned round but when he saw my amusement he joined me in my laughter. I put out my tongue and waved at him with both hands. The children were delighted that I was willing to play with them at last, and pounced on the paper bird. Quamina sent it sailing through the air to catch the warm current. The note fluttered upwards, circled and as it spiralled downwards it was singed by the flames, then shot up again to be suspended for some time in the smoke.

I excused myself and left van Drunen behind with my children, because I wanted to make some additions to my journal. Then I took a brief nap, after which I set about preparing for the fête. I stood in front of the large mirror in my room and rehearsed my valedictory speech. It was not an expression of thanks, for I did not feel grateful and besides, I am too old for pretence. Just a few sentences so as not to disappoint the assembled guests. I had merely planned—and Adeline thought it was an excellent idea—to entertain my guests with a personal recollection of Africa: some snatches of that nursery song which I had never totally forgotten. I began by tapping out the rhythm and then tried to hum the tune. I opened my mouth to sing, but had to give up after three words and just stood there, rocking from side to side.

That is how Ahim found me a few moments ago: in front of the mirror, swaying on my feet. He came to tell me that Mrs. Renselaar has come for me in an open landau. She has brought a photographer with her, to take a picture of me with my children, and has ruled that Aquasi is to wear his velvet breeches and Quamina her new collar. What a fuss and commotion. Am I to have no say in anything at all?

Ahim undressed me, helped me to wash and shaved my cheeks. He cut my nails and trimmed my beard. He laid out my best suit of clothing, helped me into my trousers, shirt and starched front, laced up my shoes and knotted my bow tie. He handed me my gloves and spat on my top hat, once for luck and a second time to make it shine. I felt uncomfortable in my tight, scratchy clothes, but Ahim ignored my grumbling and drew me to the mirror again, beaming at my reflection over my shoulder.

"Perhaps the song wasn't such a good idea after all," he whispered in my ear in a conciliatory tone. I cannot abide him fawning on me! When he even had the cheek to suggest an alternative conclusion for my little speech I snapped that I would dock him a week's wages for impertinence.

"Nothing take away nothing leaves nothing," he chuckled, and before I could give him a kick in the seat he had gone. Still, his suggestion was not bad at all. I might even follow it up. Why not? Tonight I'll tell them how two twigs were taken from the kuma tree.

Afterword

After the bankruptcy of the Suka Sari plantation, Prince Kwasi Boachi settled in the village of Bantar Peteh. He died after a long illness in the Military Hospital at Buitenzorg on 9 July 1904.

A memoir entitled *Notes on the Black with the White Heart* appeared in the *Freiberger Anzeiger*, in which several citizens of Weimar described how the Prince of Ashanti let them sit on his lap and allowed them to "feel his woolly hair and his fine, velvety skin."

Kwasi Boachi's personal possessions were confiscated by the authorities prior to his funeral. His eldest son Quamin spent four years in Delft at the same boarding school as his father, but upon his return to Java was able to find employment only as a foreman at a tea estate in the Preanger district. Aquasi junior and Quamina Aquasina lived modestly. After the Indonesian proclamation of Independence in 1948 their children moved to the Netherlands.

The Two Hearts of Kwasi Boachi is a novel, but the main characters are based on historical figures. I have reconstructed their lives around the facts I encountered in official and private documents.

Most of Kwasi's personal effects are kept in the municipal archives of Delft, including his "Book of Friends," the daguerreotype, photographs and silhouette portraits, his notes and sketches, numerous letters and the speech he delivered at the Five Columns student club. The Algemeen Rijksarchief in The Hague constitutes the chief source of official documents, the majority being kept in the archives pertaining to the Ministry of Colonies, the King's council-chamber and the Dutch territories on the coast of Guinea.

My research also took me to the Anna Amalia Library in Weimar, the Sächsiches Bergarchiv in Freiberg, the Sächsiches Hauptstaatarchiv in Dresden, the Hochschularchiv of the Freiberg Bergakademie, the National Museum of Ethnology in Leiden, the Royal Tropical Institute of Amsterdam and the Asante National Archives in Kumasi, Ghana.

Two eyewitness accounts of Verveer's expedition to Kumasi survive: by van Drunen and J. Doorman respectively. All the facts about that expedition, even the most improbable, are mentioned therein. My understanding of the Ashanti history and culture owes much to *Ancient Ashanti Chieftancy* by E. Obeng, *The Akan of Ghana* by D. Warren, *The Akans of Ghana* by N. Kyeremateng, *The Fall of the Asante Empire* by R. Edgerton, *De oorsprong van de was-druktextiel op de kust van West-Afrika* by W. Kroese and *The Language of Adinkra Symbols* by A. Wuarcoo. René Baesjou of Leiden University kindly shared his notes with me and answered my questions. Thanks are also due to Professor Larry Yarak of George Williams College, Texas, whose monograph *Kwasi Boakye and Kwame Poku: Dutch-educated Asante Princes* offered a valuable framework.

Among the many people who have helped me in the course of the ten years of research and writing, I would like specially to thank Mrs. van Heumen and Mrs. de Gruyter, Kwasi Boachi's granddaughters.

Kwasi Boachi as an old man

A NOTE ABOUT THE AUTHOR

Arthur Japin is an actor, opera singer and writer who
lives in Amsterdam. This is his first novel.

A NOTE ON THE TYPE

This book was set in Monotype Dante, a typeface
designed by Giovanni Mardersteig (1892–1977).

Composed by North Market Street Graphics,
Lancaster, Pennsylvania
Printed and bound by Quebecor Printing,
Fairfield, Pennsylvania
Designed by Virginia Tan